Ryan Love was born and raised in the island town of Enniskillen in Northern Ireland. An NCTJ-qualified journalist, Ryan was the first Showbiz Editor at Digital Spy and has written for publications including the *Independent*, the *Telegraph*, *Attitude*, *Radio Times* and Yahoo. After moving into music PR, Ryan worked on campaigns for global superstars including Britney Spears, Shakira, Usher, John Legend and OneRepublic. Ryan is passionate about mental health and enjoys speaking and writing about his own experiences. When he isn't writing, Ryan can be found tweeting, watching – and playing – Countdown or enjoying cuddles with his two golden retrievers. *Arthur and Teddy Are Coming Out* is his debut novel.

Arthur and Teddy are COMING OUT

RYAN LOVE

ONE PLACE. MANY STORIES

This novel is entirely a work of fiction. The names, characters and incidents portrayed in it are the work of the author's imagination. Any resemblance to actual persons, living or dead, events or localities is entirely coincidental.

HQ
An imprint of HarperCollins*Publishers* Ltd
1 London Bridge Street
London SE1 9GF

www.harpercollins.co.uk

HarperCollins*Publishers*
Macken House, 39/40 Mayor Street Upper,
Dublin 1, D01 C9W8, Ireland

This edition 2024

23 24 25 26 27 LBC 5 4 3 2 1
First published in Great Britain by
HQ, an imprint of HarperCollins*Publishers* Ltd 2023

ISBN: 9780008647636

This book is produced from independently certified FSC™ pape
to ensure responsible forest management.

For more information visit: www.harpercollins.co.uk/green

This book is set in 10.7/15.5 pt. Sabon by Type-it AS, Norway

Printed and bound in the United States of America by
Lakeside Book Company

Mum, put simply, this wouldn't exist without you. Thank you for never ever doubting I could do this, for keeping my dreams alive when I had given up and for being the first person I send every chapter to. I hope I, Arthur and Teddy do you proud xx

CHAPTER ONE
Arthur

EVERYTHING LOOKED AS perfect as it could for what might be their final family meal together. They hadn't all been together since Arthur and his wife Madeleine had celebrated their fiftieth wedding anniversary last month. The 'happiest, most perfect couple' had been toasted and spoiled by friends and family at a lavish party thrown by their two children, Elizabeth and Patrick.

Today, Arthur had been up since 6 a.m. pacing the house. It had been another long night of broken sleep. Every time he managed to close his eyes, a new scenario entered his head, jolting him from his light doze with no mercy. He had eventually given up on finding any comfort in the single bed he now occupied. It had been two weeks but he wasn't going to complain to Madeleine. His new double bed was ordered; it wouldn't be much longer until it arrived. He spent much of the day in a bit of a daze, frequently glancing at the clock as he counted down the hours until dinner.

Madeleine smiled softly as she appeared in the doorway between the kitchen and the dining room. She was every bit as beautiful as when Arthur had first met her. His father, then mayor of Northbridge, had been particularly excited to present his son to Madeleine and her father, William Montgomery. The Montgomery family were practically royalty to the people of Northbridge. Arthur could still hear his mother clearly; 'Money follows money, and the Montgomerys are money.' Arthur imagined what his now deceased father and father-in-law would make of what he was about to do. After all these years the thought still made his stomach churn.

'Everything's almost ready,' Madeleine said. She walked over and stood beside her husband. 'It all looks perfect.'

Arthur smiled. 'I can't thank you enough. I wouldn't be doing this without you.'

'Don't worry, once tonight is over it's a whole new beginning.'

She grabbed his hand and gave it a tight squeeze before returning to the kitchen. He knew she was right; he had told himself the exact same thing. This was the moment he had been waiting for, there was no turning back now. He pulled out the chair closest to him and sat down. He could feel his heart beating faster now. Arthur closed his eyes and concentrated on his breathing.

In.

Out.

In.

Out.

The bright headlights lit up the dining room as the clock chimed the quarter hour. Arthur heard a car door slam shut. Elizabeth's heels confirmed her arrival on the other side of the dining-room door before she pushed it open. It was impossible not to smile when Elizabeth entered a room. Arthur had always known she was destined for greatness. Even as a child she captivated people with her confidence and outgoing personality. That confidence had served her well as she had gone on to a successful career as a journalist; she was now well known for her opinion columns. Once she was old enough to realize that her mum was the editor of the local newspaper, she had been determined to follow in her footsteps. Arthur and Madeleine didn't always agree with her opinions, but they knew that they had raised someone to stand firm behind what she believed in – even if this did occasionally lead to some tense discussions over the dinner table.

'Hello, Daddy,' she said, striding across the room to embrace Arthur. She kissed him on the cheek before sitting down on the chair next to him. 'Where's Mum?'

'She's in the kitchen putting the finishing touches to dinner.'

'It all smells amazing. So, what's all this in aid of?'

Arthur felt his chest tighten as he forced his mouth into a small smile.

'Nothing to worry about, it's just nice to spend some quality time together. Anyway, how is everything at home?'

'You know what the girls are like,' she sighed, happily latching onto Arthur's change of subject. 'It was Teddy's first day at *The Post* today. He still wasn't home when I left, but I'll take that as a good sign.'

'How do you think he'll get on? He's such a talented writer, just like his mum and grandmother.'

'I know it and you know it, Dad. I hope this helps him realize it and gives him some direction in life again. Calling in a favour like this isn't easy, especially when he's refused it so many times.'

'Don't push him too hard, Lizzie. He said yes eventually. Let him find his own way, like we let you.'

Arthur poured himself a glass of water from the jug in the middle of the table.

'How is Ralph doing?'

'Good thanks, busy as always. He was a little disappointed not to be invited tonight, actually.'

'I just wanted some time with you and your brother.'

'I presume Patrick won't be bringing Scarlett then?'

'No, like I told you, it's just the four of us tonight.'

'Hello, Mum,' Elizabeth said, turning around as Madeleine returned to the room carrying a bottle of wine.

'Hello, darling, you're looking lovely,' Madeleine said, kissing her daughter on the cheek.

'How was the town planning meeting today?'

'Don't get me started, I've a good mind to run for the council next year if they don't start paying more attention to the local community. As for that MP of ours, nowhere to be seen.'

Arthur laughed, but he knew nothing would stop Madeleine once she had set her mind on it. After retiring, she had been approached to join every possible organization and committee. He was still in awe of how she found the time to juggle all her commitments.

'This town would be bloody lucky to have you,' Elizabeth said, as a second car pulled into the driveway. 'Here's Patrick. Only twenty-five minutes late, he's making progress.'

It was almost time. He'd wait until after dessert. That's what he and Madeleine had discussed and agreed upon. Perhaps they'd react better on full stomachs.

4

'Evening all,' Patrick said striding into the dining room. He threw his jacket over the back of the chair closest to him. 'Before you say anything, Lizzie, I got caught up in traffic.'

'You're here and that's the most important thing,' Madeleine said as she gave her son a kiss on the cheek. 'Lizzie, could you please come and give me a hand in the kitchen?'

Patrick sat himself down on the vacated seat beside his father. Arthur couldn't help but notice how tired he looked, but he wasn't going to bring it up. After the breakdown of a previous relationship and the death of his best friend, his son had turned to alcohol. It was only when Madeleine had reached breaking point and begged him that he had agreed to go to a rehab facility. With his life now back on track, Patrick had thrown himself into work following Arthur's retirement.

'So, what's going on? I figured it must be bad when you said I couldn't bring Scarlett.'

'How are things with you two?'

'You know what, things are great. I really think she could be the one, Dad.'

Arthur smiled. Seeing Patrick happy after the last few years meant the world to him.

'Well, you know what you need to do then, son. She's a special lady, don't let a day go by where you don't make her feel that.'

Elizabeth reappeared carrying bowls of food.

'If you've got two working legs, you could actually come and help, Patrick.'

'I'm on my way, no need for the sarcasm,' Patrick said, before turning back to his father. 'I'll never understand how she got two men to propose to her.'

Arthur tried to join in the chat and laughter as much as he could throughout dinner. Every so often he felt Madeleine's bright green eyes on him from across the table. They were still filled with the same energy they had been when he first looked into them over fifty years earlier. Her freshly layered, snowy white hair framed her delicate features.

'You're on another planet tonight, Daddy. Do you want a top-up?'

'Go on then, why not?'

Elizabeth stretched across and filled his glass. 'There's so much depth to the flavour of this one.'

Madeleine gave her glass a little shake. 'It's a little rich for me.'

'She says after almost half a bottle.'

Arthur laughed loudly. It felt good to momentarily forget, even if it was fleeting. Patrick was slouched in his chair, one hand resting on his stomach. He had put on a little weight over the summer, which he was quick to put down to Scarlett's good home cooking.

'Mum, dinner was amazing. We have to do this more often if you're going to spoil us like this.'

'Forget more often, I want to know what's going on and why we're here tonight,' Elizabeth said, before taking another sip from her almost empty glass. 'I know you pair, there's something. I've seen those glances at each other.'

'You're right,' Arthur said, prompting all three heads to turn in his direction. 'There is a reason we asked you to come here tonight.'

Madeleine reached across and held her hand out. Arthur took it, and their fingers knitted together. He squeezed it tightly.

'Is something wrong?' Elizabeth said. The mood in the room had shifted. Arthur hated hearing the sudden sense of panic in his daughter's voice. He felt Madeleine's wedding ring press into his finger as she gripped his hand even tighter.

'Is Davina McCall about to arrive with our long-lost brother?'

'Shut up, Patrick,' Elizabeth hissed. 'Daddy, please, what's going on?'

Arthur took a deep breath.

'Your mother and I will always love each other very much, but we are not together anymore and it's not because we don't still love each other very much.'

Arthur paused. His next few words would change everything. There was no stopping now as his two children stared back at him, their eyes wide with anticipation. He closed his eyes and allowed the words to finally leave his mouth.

'The truth is, I'm gay.'

CHAPTER TWO
Teddy

'EDWARD MARSH?'

'Hi, just Teddy is fine.' He lurched forward awkwardly to shake the man's hand. 'Thanks for this opportunity, Mr Stone. It's great to be here.'

'Not at all. We're delighted to have you join us. When Elizabeth Marsh says her son wants to be a journalist . . . well, she's a persuasive woman, your mother.'

There it was. Teddy knew it wouldn't take long; it would be the first of many mentions of his mum, Elizabeth Marsh, their cherished, award-winning columnist. It would no doubt be common knowledge already that she had had a private word and secured her only son a trainee reporter role. He was genuinely grateful for the chance to prove himself, even if it meant accepting that he needed a helping hand. That hadn't been easy to stomach, but he knew he had no other choice. He needed to get his life back on track.

It felt strange to be sitting in a shirt and tie. The summer sunshine was beating through the large glass windows into the open-plan office. He had been directed to the desk belonging to

Dylan Wicks. After a ten-minute wait, an out-of-breath Dylan had arrived carrying a steaming mug of coffee.

'Forgot you were starting today,' he said before taking a sip of his drink. 'Right, so long story short, I'll be your mentor over the next few months. Your mum was mine when I first started, so I'm sure you've a fair idea of what to expect here anyway. We don't see her slumming it in the office much these days of course.'

Teddy knew all of this already, of course. Elizabeth had been quick to tell him all about how she had helped shape Dylan into the senior journalist he was now. She had made it very clear that he had big shoes to fill. She might have given him a foot in the door, but she still had high expectations.

'Sit yourself down here.' Dylan gestured to the desk next to him. 'You might need a few phone calls with IT to get logged in, but we'll get you sorted before the end of the day. Any questions?'

Teddy wracked his brain for something, anything to ask. He didn't want Dylan to think he thought he knew everything.

'Um, well, I was wondering—'

'Sorry, are you Dylan by any chance?'

Both Dylan and Teddy looked up at the person who had interrupted them. He pushed his floppy brown hair back off his forehead. His cheeks looked slightly flushed, as if he had just completed a light workout.

'Who's asking?'

'I'm Benjamin King, I'm starting training with you today.'

Dylan's head spun towards Teddy as if he expected him to know what was going on.

'That can't be right. No one mentioned you to me. Let me just give upstairs a call.'

Teddy sat quietly, feeling increasingly awkward. It seemed that a communication failure had resulted in Dylan not being told that he was getting two trainees. He looked far from pleased at the discovery.

'I'm just surprised,' Dylan said, once Ben was sitting down on the other side of Teddy. 'I presumed once your mum sorted it out for you that they wouldn't bother with anyone else, I mean, after all why bother telling me . . .?'

Teddy felt his cheeks burn. Great, that was all he needed. A fellow trainee who had been forgotten about because his mum had pulled some strings.

'Well, that was a bit of a waste of a morning,' Dylan said after confirming that both Teddy and Ben would be working together under his guidance. 'Two trainees; it's like they don't want me to do my own job.'

Teddy felt Ben lean across towards him. 'That wasn't exactly the warmest welcome, was it? I feel like a bit of a spare part now.'

'Yeah, sorry, I didn't know me being here would cause any hassle,' Teddy said. He shifted uncomfortably in his seat.

'Why would you?' Ben said. 'If my mum could click her fingers and make things happen, I wouldn't worry about it either.'

Teddy stared at him, taken aback by the insinuation that he would happily trample over someone else for his own gain. Just as he was about to defend himself, Ben swung round in his chair to face him.

'You can call me Ben by the way,' he whispered, holding his hand out. He gripped Teddy's tightly as he shook it, oblivious to the offence he had just caused. 'So, Teddy Marsh, what's your deal?'

'Nothing much to tell. I'm just here to learn.'

Teddy wasn't going to give much away to the newcomer.

Ben's neat eyebrows were raised as he observed Teddy's reaction to his questioning.

'Keeping your cards close to your chest, eh? You're a bit of a dark horse already.'

'I'm not a dark horse. I just want to keep my head down and get on with things.'

'Don't let me get in the way.' He smiled at him. Teddy couldn't help but notice the deep dimples which formed on his cheeks as he did. His eyes drifted across Ben's handsome face. A light stubble accentuated his perfectly chiselled jawline. Irritated, Teddy turned his eyes back towards his own screen.

Almost an hour later, Teddy felt his stomach rumble as he finished the task Dylan had set. He glanced at the clock on his screen; thankfully it was almost time for lunch. He thought of the sandwich he had packed into his bag that morning and wished he had remembered to ask Dylan if there was a fridge he could store it in. He didn't want to take it out in front of Dylan and Ben now. It would be less awkward to slip off and eat it in private where no one would notice.

'I've got a lunch meeting, so you two can . . .' Dylan didn't bother finishing the sentence before grabbing his phone and leaving the office.

'Do you have any plans?' Ben asked.

'I'm meeting my friend.' Teddy didn't know why he said it. The words had escaped him before he had even had a chance to think it through.

'Cool. Well, I'm going to go and introduce myself to people. Get to know a few names, you know?'

'You are?' Teddy said, surprised by Ben's plan to ingratiate himself.

'Yeah, can't do any harm to say hello and let people know I'm here to learn and help as much as I can.'

Teddy stood up and grabbed his bag. He felt ridiculous at having caught himself in an awkward lie while Ben planned to get to know their new colleagues. He should really have thought ahead like that. 'I probably won't be that long, so I'll see you when I get back.'

He quickly made his way to the toilets. If he ate his food quickly he could be back within a few minutes and claim his friend had to cancel at the very last minute. Teddy slipped into an empty cubicle and locked the door. He pulled out the small lunch box and unwrapped the ham and cheese sandwich he had made himself. After a number of hours trapped in his bag it wasn't in the freshest of states. He imagined his mum scowling at him for hiding away instead of making as much effort as Ben to integrate. He washed down the tasteless, moist sandwich with a gulp of warm water from the bottle at the bottom of his bag. This was not the way he imagined his first day going, but there was still time to turn it around. He left the cubicle and stood in front of the mirror. His jet black hair was messy, but in a way that looked intentional. He checked his teeth for any bits of food.

'I think you got it all.'

Teddy jumped as Ben came into view behind him in the mirror.

'Oh, yeah, just checking.'

Teddy could feel his ears burn as he watched Ben disappear into a cubicle without another word. '*I think you got it all,*' he muttered to himself, frowning. He hurried back from the toilet to his desk, hoping to compose himself before Ben returned. It was a couple of minutes later when he realized that Ben was now talking to someone else halfway down the office. It was impossible to hear the conversation, but he was sure that they had both looked in his direction at least twice.

'Sorry about that,' Ben said as he sat back down in his chair a few minutes later. 'I was just chatting to Manoj, do you know him?'

'No, what does he—'

Teddy stopped talking as he realized Ben was grinning broadly at him.

'Is something wrong?' Teddy braced himself for questions about why he had decided to eat lunch alone in the toilets.

'Not at all. I was just wondering how long you were going to keep it a secret that your mum is Elizabeth Marsh?'

Teddy felt an immediate tightness in his chest.

'Oh, erm, it's just not something I like to bring up.'

'I should've known when Dylan mentioned your mum sorting your place here. You're practically guaranteed a job.'

'You can think that all you want. I'm here because I want to work and learn, same as you.'

Ben rolled his eyes. 'Come on, they already forgot I was coming. I bet it didn't happen to you. Did they forget to roll out the red carpet?'

'You've got a lot to say for yourself.'

'Hey, I'm just saying what other people are thinking. And yeah, I worked my ass off to get this chance and then find out they forgot about me on my first day. It's not a great feeling.'

'That's not my fault,' Teddy said. 'You and the rest of them can think it all you want. As I said, I'm here to learn.'

'As long as you know I'm here to get the job I want. At least I know I'm going into the competition as the underdog now.'

'What? This isn't a competition,' Teddy said, but suddenly feeling less confident in his response, quickly added, 'Is it?'

'Unofficially, I guess. After the traineeship there's usually a job. If there's two of us, it's likely one of us will be heading home unemployed. And I can't let that happen.'

As far as Teddy had been concerned, this was nothing more than a chance to learn the ropes and experience life in the newsroom. Now here he was, in competition with someone he had just met, for a job he wasn't even sure he wanted. It took every ounce of restraint not to leave his desk and phone his mum. He realized she hadn't told him so that he would finally accept the offer.

Dylan seemed oblivious to any tension between the pair as he returned from his lunch meeting. At one point Teddy was sure he had almost forgotten that they were there altogether, only remembering to set them a task when one of his colleagues stopped by to introduce herself. Teddy was even more sure that he had heard a noise come from Ben's direction when he had responded to her request to say hello to his mum for her. She had, at least, highlighted that she knew who he was in a more subtle manner. He could tolerate that if he had to. It was something of a relief when Dylan finally said that they both could call it a day.

'Any plans for tonight?' Ben asked, breaking the silence as they both stood waiting for the lift.

'I'm just going to meet a couple of friends now. They work close by. What about you?'

'That sounds nice. I'm just heading ho . . . back to my flat first and then going to a gig.'

'Do you live alone?'

'I just moved into a little studio. Nothing fancy. Are you planning to move into the city?'

'No, I'll stay at home in Northbridge and get the train in.'

The doors opened allowing a large group of people to push their way into the lift. They stood in silence until it reached the ground floor. As they made their way through the foyer Teddy spotted his best friends Shakeel and Lexie standing outside, deep in conversation.

'Well, I'm heading this way. Bye,' he said, turning to head in the opposite direction as quickly as possible without waiting for a response.

'Come on, I need a drink,' he said to the pair, glancing over his shoulder to confirm that Ben was still watching him.

CHAPTER THREE
Arthur

THE ROOM WAS silent. It was as if nobody dared breathe in the seconds which followed.

It was done; he had said the words out loud, there was no taking them back now. He looked intently at his two children. Patrick stood up, shaking his head slowly.

'Is there a punchline to this? I don't get it.'

'It's true. Please can you sit, Patrick.' Madeleine was soft-spoken, but they knew when she was serious. Anyone who had ever worked for her knew when Madeleine was not to be argued with. As she had requested, Patrick sat back down. Neither he nor Elizabeth looked in Arthur's direction, instead directing their attention to Madeleine.

'You knew about this?' Elizabeth said.

'I've known for a while, yes. That is not what is important here, though, this is about your father telling you something very personal.'

'I think we have a right to know what the hell is going on and why you are tolerating this.'

'No, Elizabeth, you don't. All you need to know is that

I am here beside your father and asking you to listen to and love him because he is still the same man. He is still your dad.'

Elizabeth put her head in her hands.

'I cannot believe what I'm hearing. You've been married fifty years and you're sitting there like he's just told you that he forgot to buy milk.'

'That's enough,' Arthur said. 'Don't start on your mother. She doesn't deserve your anger.'

'This isn't anger. This is confusion,' she said, before turning back to Madeleine. 'You can come and stay at my house, Mum. Stay as long as you need to.'

'I won't be leaving my home, Elizabeth. And neither will your father.'

Patrick was silent, taking in every word, his hazel eyes darting between the two women like he was watching an intense Wimbledon final.

'Can you say something? Why are you just sitting there mute as per usual? Talk some sense into her!' Elizabeth shouted at her brother.

'What am I supposed to do? We can't force Mum to do anything she doesn't want to do.'

Arthur could see his daughter was growing more and more frustrated. Her neck and the top of her chest were breaking out in a blotchy red rash.

'Lizzie, please. Let me explain,' he said, reaching out his right hand to touch her.

'Don't you dare *Lizzie* me. Don't even touch me. I can't believe this. Everything is just one big lie.'

'I need you to understand that I never wanted to hurt any of you, especially your mum.'

'Why now? What reason is possibly good enough to destroy the life you had? All of our lives.'

Arthur hesitated. There it was; the question he had been dreading the most. The answer he needed to get right more than any other he would give.

'I couldn't live another day not being who I am. I know . . . I know that will sound too simplistic and ridiculous to you, but I had to do this now.'

'Had to? You didn't have to do anything. Are you saying you've spent fifty years lying to yourself? To Mum?'

'I wasn't lying. I love your mum more than I can ever explain. She's the best friend I've ever had. We've had an incredible life together and been blessed with both of you, but that doesn't change who I am, who I have been my whole life.'

His voice was beginning to crack. He took a sip from the glass of water in front of him.

'Is there someone else? Are you cheating on Mum? I swear to God, if—'

'I'm not, I promise you that. I would never do that.'

'So why? Why now? It doesn't make any sense.'

'I know it's hard to get your head around, but I'm seventy-nine, you're all grown-up and living your lives and I . . . well, I just couldn't go on another day not being true to myself. To all of you.'

'Bullshit. This is all for you. How could you do this to all of us? What am I supposed to tell the kids? Did you even stop to think about your grandchildren?'

'Don't speak for me or them, Elizabeth,' Madeleine interjected. 'I know what I'm doing. I understand you're shocked and angry, but don't be on my behalf. We grew up in different times. Your father did what he had to do and gave me the best life. You don't get to stand in our house and judge him.'

'None of this makes any sense. You've both lost your minds. I have to get out of here.'

'Please, Elizabeth—'

'No! I feel sick. I need to go. I feel like I can't breathe.'

'Don't leave like this. I'm still your dad.'

'Dad?!' she repeated incredulously. 'No, you're not. Not anymore. I'd rather you were dead. You're dead to me.'

'Stop it, Lizzie,' Patrick said, reaching out to her. She slapped away his hand.

'I mean it. Stay away from me and stay away from my family.'

Without another word, Elizabeth pulled her jacket off the back of the chair and stormed from the room. Nobody spoke as they heard the front door bang shut, quickly followed by the sound of her car pulling out of the driveway.

'Are you okay, Patrick?' Arthur asked. 'Is there anything you need to say or even ask?'

'I've a lot of questions, but to be honest, I don't really know where to start.'

'That's perfectly understandable. I'm here whenever you're ready.'

'Are you really both going to live here?'

'Your mum has been very kind and said I can stay. We're in separate rooms, but we're getting used to the new arrangement.'

'This is a lot to take in. I can't believe this has all been going on and you're both just sitting here with each other.'

'We still love each other, Patrick,' Madeleine said. 'It's

a different kind of love, but hopefully one day you and Elizabeth will learn to understand that.'

Patrick stood up from his chair.

'Maybe. Look, I'm sorry, I have to go. I . . . I just can't do this right now.'

Madeleine squeezed Arthur's hand as their son left the room. The night had gone as badly as he had feared.

CHAPTER FOUR
Teddy

TEDDY, SHAKEEL AND Lexie found themselves in a cute little pub near the office called the Mayflower. Once they had drinks, Teddy brought them up to speed on his first day. By the time he was finished, Lexie was smirking at him.

'Come on, Teddy. I've only known you a few years and even I know this is classic you,' she said.

'What's that supposed to mean?'

'You assume someone is going to judge you for who you are and you make them the enemy before they even have a chance to show you who they are. You did the same thing when you met me, even though I'd no idea who your mother was!'

'Not this time. This guy is so full of himself, making little remarks . . . you should have heard him. It's not my fault they forgot to tell Dylan he was coming, is it?'

Teddy understood what Lexie was saying, but more often than not, he was right about people judging him. They didn't need to remind him who his mum was or take the opportunity to grill him on his life choices just because she chose to write about hers.

'Can you find this guy on Instagram?' Lexie said, interrupting them. 'I want to see if he's hot.'

'Not as hot as he probably thinks he is,' Teddy said as he took the phone and typed in Ben's name, instantly recognizing him in his profile picture. He clicked on it and scrolled through the few images he had shared.

'Gimme a look then' Lexie said, grabbing the phone back and beginning to browse through the profile.

'Hmm. Lots of selfies. No family. No pets. Most importantly no boyfriend or girlfriend. I can only see one problem, I'm afraid.'

'What?'

'He's obviously way out of your league.'

'Excuse me, I thought I was going for a drink with my friends. Have you seen them?'

'Look at him, Shak!' Lexie said, thrusting the phone towards him.

Shakeel stared at the screen for just a couple of seconds before half-heartedly shrugging his shoulders. Teddy couldn't help but grin at Shakeel having his back. If there was one person he could always rely on, it was Shakeel. Their friendship had only grown stronger as they entered their teenage years and both came to realize that they were gay. Confiding in each other had made those years tolerable, and when Shakeel left for university Teddy struggled as he found himself without his best friend. When Teddy's dad passed away suddenly, Shakeel had made several serious offers to drop out of his first year and come back to support him. Teddy had shut down the very notion of him doing something so drastic, but it had meant the world to him, even if he didn't know how to show it.

'I think Teddy can do better,' Shakeel said, as Teddy beamed back at him.

'Oh come on, you don't think he's hot either?' Lexie sighed. 'There goes your opportunity for an office romance, Teddy.'

'No chance. This guy is going to be a bloody nightmare to deal with, I can feel it.'

Teddy's phone was vibrating. It was his mum. He wasn't in the mood to talk to her right now so he stuffed it into his pocket.

'Honestly, you pair, I want to bang your heads together. You're twenty-one, get out there and start having some bloody fun!'

'We've been through this, Lex.'

'Yeah, yeah,' Lexie teased. 'I know. But why? Why couldn't you just go home tonight, rip the Band-Aid off and just tell everyone you like guys?'

If only things could be that simple. He'd come close to having the coming-out conversation with his mum several times, but had always talked himself out of it. No one else could understand his justification for delaying it and God knows they had tried to on numerous occasions. But whether she intended to or not, Elizabeth put enormous pressure on her family to live up to her high expectations. She had frequently talked about longing for Teddy to bring home 'a nice girl' and even written multiple columns on her excitement about the thought of having grandchildren. Bringing home a boy he liked would only give her something else to write about.

Shakeel, on the other hand, had still only been on a handful of dates, much to Lexie's disappointment. Despite all of his fears surrounding coming out, Shakeel's family had been nothing but supportive, with both his mum and dad joining a local group to meet other LGBTQIA+ parents. The only time he heard Shakeel complain about them – much to Lexie's amusement – was when his mum was pressuring him to meet a 'nice, clever boy'. Shakeel and Lexie had met at university. Trusting Shakeel's judgement of her as a friend, Teddy had also grown close to her during his frequent visits, so he was thrilled when she decided to move to the city for work. Despite encouragement from them both, though, Teddy still wasn't ready to tell his mum he was gay, even if Shakeel's experience had given him fresh hope.

'Sorry, guys, I have to go. I've a few things to pick up before I go home,' Shakeel said suddenly, jumping up from his seat. 'I should be able to do something at the weekend if you still wanna see that movie?'

'You're on,' Teddy said.

'Great, it's a date.'

'It's a *what*?' Lexie laughed as the colour rose in Shakeel's cheeks.

'I didn't mean . . . I just . . .'

'I'm only messing, Shak. Does this mean I can tag along?'

'Of course you can, right, Shak?' Teddy said.

'Uhm yeah . . . of course . . . just an expression,' Shakeel stammered.

Lexie waited until Shakeel was out the door before turning to Teddy.

'That guy needs to get laid. I know you both do, but it's been nearly a year since Marcus.'

'We don't all have our own flat to do as we please, Lex.'

'Yeah, because that's what he's waiting for.'

'What's that supposed to mean? What's he waiting for?'

'Nothing, I don't know, I just think he needs to have some

fun. Let loose. Both of you need to. Anyway, like I was saying, you're going to go straight home to tell your Mum you're gay and get this over and done with for all our sakes.'

It was just after 9 p.m. when Teddy climbed out of his taxi, still laughing at the prospect of following Lexie's order of announcing his sexuality the minute he got home. There was no denying that it would be a quick and easy way of getting it over and done with. He could just walk in, blurt it out and head straight for the stairs. He gripped the door handle. 'You can do this,' he said to himself. 'It's only a few words.'

He pushed the handle down and stepped into the brightly lit hallway. The moment he walked in he knew that the words would never leave his mouth in such a situation. Lexie was just going to have to wait a little longer.

'Hello, I'm home.' He hung his jacket on the coat rack inside the entrance hall.

'I'm in here,' Eleanor shouted from the living room. The TV was on, but she was glued to her phone. She was three years older than him and the eldest of the three siblings.

'Still nothing from Mum?' Teddy asked as he stood in the doorway. He had expected her to be back from his grandparents' house by now.

'Not a word. I thought she might text to put us out of our misery. The longer she's there, the more worried I am.'

'I know, I was really trying not to dwell on it today. I didn't want to overthink it and then find out it's nothing.'

'We'll just have to wait and deal with whatever it is when we know more,' Eleanor said. 'Anyway, how was day one at Elizabeth Marsh HQ?'

'Don't even joke! Everyone knew who I was as soon as

I walked in the door. And I'm stuck working with this know-it-all who hates me already.'

'Just be on your best behaviour. You know mum has eyes and ears all over that place. She'll know what you're doing before you've even done it.'

The thought of it made his stomach churn. This was exactly what Lexie didn't truly understand. As much as he loved his mum, he now felt like he had walked into a perfectly set trap. This was exactly why he had turned down the offer of help several times. He'd only caved and accepted it after another day of applying for jobs he knew he didn't really want. With Shakeel and Lexie both enjoying their new careers, he didn't want to be left behind any longer.

'She's home!' Evangelina shouted from the upstairs landing, making both him and Eleanor jump. Their younger sister came bounding down the stairs, pulling on her fluffy pink dressing gown as she did.

'Has she texted either of you?'

'No, we've heard nothing at all.'

The three of them stood waiting in the entrance hall, exchanging concerned glances as they heard the car door slam shut.

The front door swung open as their mother walked in and spotted her welcoming committee.

The streaks of mascara down her face failed to hide her red and blotchy cheeks.

'Mummy? Are you okay? Come on, sit down,' Eleanor said, rushing forward. 'Teddy, grab a chair.' Teddy didn't move. His mum was shaking her head.

'It's fine, it's fine. I don't need to sit down.'

'What's going on? Is something wrong with Nan or Grandad?'

She gave a small, hoarse laugh, her throat struggling to produce any kind of sound.

'After all these years. You think you know someone.'

'Mum, please, you're not making any sense. What's wrong? Is it Grandad Arthur?'

'I never want to hear that man's name in this house again. You won't talk to him. You won't see him.'

'Why? What's he done?' Teddy asked.

'Your grandfather has decided that after fifty years of marriage he's just had enough.'

'What? That doesn't make any sense. Why would he do that?'

'Well, that's the best bit,' she said, her eyes widening. 'He's decided to tell us that he's . . . that he's gay.'

Teddy stood frozen to the spot. He felt completely numb. All connection between his brain and body had been lost. In every potential coming-out scenario he had run through in his head over the last few years, the one thing he had not accounted for was the possibility of being beaten to it by his grandad.

CHAPTER FIVE
Arthur

ARTHUR WOKE WITH a start. Luna stared at him; her blue eyes closing again as he reached out and stroked her. She purred softly, snuggling down so that her head rested on his knee. He'd dozed off in the large armchair at some point, he couldn't be sure when. Time seemed to have become meaningless since Elizabeth had stormed from the house hours earlier. Madeleine, once she had stopped crying, had stayed with him in the lounge for a while, but had since gone upstairs to bed. She had insisted that he should do the same thing, but he knew there was no point. He'd be fine here, especially now that Luna had come to join him.

Every so often he drifted off, Luna's soft purring helping to ease him into the lightest of sleeps. They didn't last long. Images of Elizabeth's disgusted face would cause him to sit up with a jolt. Her angry words echoed in his ears. The still silence of the darkness only served to make each one sound louder as he replayed them over and over again. He had known it was going to be difficult, but no amount of running through the moment in his head had prepared him for her reaction.

*

Madeleine made every effort to try and coax Arthur out of the house in the days after the dinner.

'Why don't you come with me and help out?' she suggested hopefully. She had been volunteering at the local food bank for the last ten years. But Arthur wasn't going to leave the house. If he did, it was guaranteed to be the moment the phone rang. He sat in the same armchair closest to the landline telephone. His mobile sat on the small table beside it. He only reluctantly left the chair to go to the bathroom or to the kitchen to eat.

'I've got something for you,' Madeleine said, setting a bag down on the table beside him.

Intrigued, Arthur opened it up and pulled out the magazine inside. It was a copy of a magazine called *Gay Life*. He had seen it in the newsagent's before when browsing the magazines. He felt his cheeks burn as he opened it to a page featuring an attractive male model wearing only a pair of tight briefs.

'Don't worry, there are articles in there for you to read, not just pictures of men in their pants.' Madeleine grinned.

'You didn't have to do this,' Arthur said, setting the magazine down. 'Thank you. I don't think I'd ever be brave enough to buy this for myself.'

'You won't have to. I've bought you a subscription.'

Arthur could feel his eyes begin to fill with tears. He had never allowed himself to imagine the most perfect scenario of having Madeleine's support while he navigated living as an out gay man.

'I don't know what I did to deserve you, Madeleine Edwards. You've been there at two of the hardest moments of my life and here you are still standing by me. You know I have no regrets about our incredible life together, don't you?'

29

'I know, Arthur. It doesn't matter what anyone else says or thinks. I know that you saved me from a life I didn't want and I'll be forever grateful.'

With tears in their eyes, Arthur took Madeleine by the hand and brought her to her feet. She rested her head on his shoulder and he held her tight.

Later that afternoon, the telephone finally did ring. In his rush to answer it, Arthur knocked over his glass of water. He had drifted off in the armchair with the magazine open on his lap.

'Hello, hello, Arthur Edwards speaking,' he said, grabbing the receiver.

'Grandad. It's Teddy.'

The crushing disappointment that it was neither Patrick nor Elizabeth on the other end of the line was quickly replaced by delight at hearing from his grandson.

'Teddy, it's so good to hear from you.'

'I'm sorry it's taken me all week to get in touch. Are you okay?'

'I've had better weeks. Does your mum know you're calling?'

'No, not that it matters. Look, I just wanted to check you'll be at home tomorrow. I'm going to come round.'

'Are you sure that's a good idea? Your mum won't be happy.'

'Don't be silly, Grandad. Just don't mention it to anyone and I'll see you and Nan tomorrow.'

Teddy's call was short, but it meant the world to Arthur. His grandson had made contact and was planning to visit. He wouldn't do that if he was angry, would he? Arthur shook his head. No. He'd sounded concerned about him. Elizabeth would be furious if she found out. He might be twenty-one, but Teddy did still live under her roof. There were twenty-four hours before Teddy would be there though; a lot could happen between now and then.

'Maybe Elizabeth will come with Teddy,' Arthur said to Madeleine as they discussed the impending visit. She nodded along in silence, clearly not wanting to commit to the theory.

'I have to go into town, would you come with me?'

Madeleine had taken the opportunity of good news to spring the idea of having him join her as she ran several errands. He knew it was intentional, but it didn't matter.

'Let me just put on the call divert in case Lizzie calls the landline.'

Arthur and Madeleine had lived in Northbridge their whole lives. They had considered leaving in the early days of their marriage, but the death of Madeleine's younger sister in a car accident had put an end to that conversation. Her parents, William and Alice, were never quite the same after Gracie's death. The birth of their granddaughter, Elizabeth, had helped, but as the years went by, Arthur and Madeleine's dream of escaping the clutches of the town faded away. That wasn't to say they hadn't had a happy life in Northbridge; they would both greatly dispute that. Arthur kept his distance from his own parents, but they were still a part of Elizabeth and Patrick's lives until they both passed away in the early 1980s. It was only over the last month that Arthur had been thinking about his parents more frequently.

Arthur sighed as they drove past the old town hall. 'You are nothing like your father,' Madeleine reassured him. 'For a start, you would accept Elizabeth and Patrick no matter who they loved.'

Arthur knew in his heart that this was true, but the older he got the more he considered the position he had put his father in almost sixty years ago. Madeleine knew what was going on his head without him needing to say a word.

'Stop dwelling on it, Arthur. You know, even back then, that you would never have done what that man did. It was beyond cruel.'

Even now, Madeleine was still thinking the best of him.

He watched out the window as they drove through town. Friday afternoons had always been busy in Northbridge. The weekly farmer's market wasn't as big as it used to be, but it still brought crowds to town. They pulled into a parking space outside the butcher's. Every Friday, Madeleine would visit and collect her order of meat for the weekend. The great-grandson of the man who had served their parents owned it now. Northbridge was built on businesses handed down over the generations. Arthur was guilty of it himself, having retired and handed the reins of the company he had inherited and expanded to Patrick. Arthur watched from the car as several people stopped Madeleine in the street to say hello. Every so often he was convinced that someone would walk past the car and stare at him for longer than they should have. Madeleine emerged just a couple of minutes later carrying two large bags of meat.

'I got young Henry to give me some pork chops. We could see if Teddy wants to stay for tea,' she explained, setting the bags carefully on the back seat.

They drove to the other end of town, parking as close to the newsagent's as possible.

Arthur hesitated when Madeleine asked him to come in with

her, but before he could talk himself out of it, he had unbuckled his seat belt and stepped out of the car. He didn't even know why he felt nervous. It wasn't like he was front page news or suddenly had a flashing rainbow sign above his head. He was just Arthur; the same person people had always known. He followed Madeleine as they entered the large shop. She left him browsing the shelves of brightly coloured books as she went to use the post office at the back of the shop. He hadn't ever been much of a reader. He had found himself listening to one of Madeleine's audiobooks one night and discovered how much he enjoyed the experience. Now he relied upon her recommendations and help to add new books to his mobile. Arthur moved on to the large display of magazines.

Photos of celebrities he didn't recognize lined the shelves. In the past he had found himself learning names he would see on the covers just to repeat them back to a bewildered Elizabeth.

'How on earth did you hear about that?' she would exclaim when he mentioned a scandal that he knew absolutely nothing more about. It was always worth it to see her kick off a fifteen-minute monologue about the celebrity and the chain of events which had led to the latest dramatic headlines. She would typically end by insisting that she was only casually following whatever was going on, just in case she needed to reference it in her latest column. The same issue of *Gay Life* which now sat in his living room was staring back at him. He still couldn't believe Madeleine had come in and bought it for him. His eyes widened as he saw another magazine with the words THE SEX ISSUE emblazoned across the cover, protecting the modesty of three seemingly naked men.

'Anything else you'd like to get while we're here?'

'Oh no, no, nothing at all,' Arthur said, spinning round to see Madeleine beside him. 'Did you get everything sorted?'

'All taken care of. It was Cicely's granddaughter who served me – you know, the one who lives in that new development – she was asking after you.'

'Really? Why? Did she know something?' Arthur felt a sudden flutter in his stomach.

'No, nothing, she was just being friendly. Nobody knows anything, Arthur.'

Just as they were about to leave the shop, the door swung open. Elizabeth stepped inside and let it close behind her before she noticed that her parents were standing right in front of her. Without as much as a word, she turned in her high black heels and reached for the handle again.

'Lizzie, please!' Arthur called after her. 'Don't walk out on us.'

'I'm walking out on *you*, not Mum.'

'Then talk to her. You're hurting your mother for no reason.'

Elizabeth looked directly at him. She pulled off her large black sunglasses; her eyes wide and filled with fury.

'*I'm* hurting Mum? You've got some nerve to stand there and say that to me. I don't know why she is walking around with you like everything is totally normal, but I won't be joining in this charade.'

'Please don't do this here, Lizzie,' Madeleine whispered, glancing around the shop to make sure no one was paying attention.

'Why not? If Dad wants to rip this family apart to be who-ever he thinks he is, shouldn't he be proud of that?'

She threw her hands in the air and raised her voice. 'Hi,

everybody, have you all met my father, stalwart of the community, Mr Arthur Edwards, newly out of the closet and ready to live his own life!'

She stormed from the shop, slamming the door behind her. Arthur and Madeleine stood in shocked silence. Arthur heard a small cough behind him and looked round to see Cicely's granddaughter, her perfectly manicured eyebrows raised so high that they threatened to leave her forehead. There was nothing he could say or do; they both knew his secret would be town gossip within the hour.

CHAPTER SIX
Teddy

TEDDY TOOK TWO paracetamol as he stood alone in the lift waiting to reach the 13th floor. He'd made it to the end of the week. He felt physically and emotionally drained, but he only needed to get to 6 p.m. and then he could go for a drink with Shakeel.

'You'd better have a pint waiting for me,' he had warned Shak. 'Maybe two.'

The initial shock of what his mum had announced to him and his sisters on Monday night had given way to a mixture of confusion and sadness. How the hell could Grandad Arthur be gay? Teddy had barely slept that night. He was reliving every moment he could remember spending at his grandparents' home. There had been absolutely nothing to give it away. Wouldn't he have noticed *something*? They had a close relationship, especially following the death of his dad, Harry, when Arthur had become something of a father figure throughout Teddy's struggle. In the weeks and months after his dad died, Teddy had lived mainly with his grandparents, desperate to escape the house that was now filled with painful memories.

His grandfather was hugely important to him, but all the

same, his revelation had left him shocked, and for a few hours he had briefly understood his mum's shock and anger as he processed the news. The following morning, Teddy had attempted to speak to his mother as they stood alone in the kitchen.

'Are you going to talk to Grandad today?'

'I've got nothing to say to him, Edward,' Elizabeth said, carrying on tapping on her phone screen. 'And I'd rather you had no contact with him either.'

'What? You can't expect—'

'This isn't up for discussion, Edward. You might want to be the man of the house, but while you're under my roof, you will respect my wishes.'

Teddy continued making his breakfast. It was too early for a row.

It was almost a relief to escape the confines of the house and spend time in the office. At least no one there knew anything. His mum had made sure to warn all three of them not to breathe a word of the news outside the family. For now, he had to carry on as he was and do everything he could to make sure his own sexuality remained a secret.

Teddy had thrown himself into every task he had been set by Dylan, determined to enjoy the distractions while he could. Anything that took his mind off events at home was welcome; everything, that was, except the person he was being paired up with for most of the work.

'Thanks for sending over that piece last night, Teddy, it was exactly what I wanted,' Dylan said. 'I'm going to send you over another one later.'

'Thanks, Dylan,' Teddy said, pleased with the feedback. 'I can do it now if you want?'

'No rush. I've got something else for you both this morning. Sarah on the online desk is looking for a round-up of the reactions to the Royal documentary that was on last night.'

'I watched that,' Ben said.

'I want both of you to have a go at writing it,' Dylan explained. 'Sarah will check both pieces and she's going to publish the best version. It'll be your first online byline. She wants them by midday, so off you go, get cracking.'

'I've written a few of these kinds of articles before, this shouldn't be too difficult,' Ben said. Teddy was growing used to Ben being the louder and more aggressive of the two of them. While he hadn't written this sort of feature before, he had read plenty of them. The stories usually comprised a selection of social media reactions about the biggest talking points of the programme. He wished he had joined his sisters in watching it now so that he knew immediately what to search for. He'd originally planned to have an early night, but had ended up lying awake staring at his phone until after midnight. The sound of Ben loudly tapping on his keyboard was pushing every thought out of his head.

'I've sent mine over to Sarah,' Ben said to Dylan, with twenty minutes left to spare. 'Is there anything else I can get on with in the meantime?'

'I'll email you over a press release I just got. You can write it up while we're waiting for Teddy.'

Teddy rolled his eyes. He hadn't meant to make the noise with his mouth, but it was loud enough to get Ben's attention.

'Something wrong?'

'Just something in my throat. I'm almost finished,' Teddy said, avoiding eye contact with him.

With just two minutes to spare, Teddy sent his report over to Sarah. He knew it wasn't his best work; he needed to up his game if he was going to stand a chance against his new rival.

'Why don't we go up and grab lunch now,' Dylan said after checking his watch. 'It'll be easier for one of you to take the bad news on a full stomach.'

The staff canteen was on the 17th floor. After his error on Monday, Teddy had eaten there for the rest of the week. Once Dylan had informed them of a trainee discount, Teddy was truthfully more than happy not to go searching for a meal deal in the nearest supermarket. So far he had avoided eating with Ben, but now that Dylan was accompanying them up to the canteen it was impossible to sneak off to one of the few empty tables.

'How do you think your first week has gone?' Ben asked. They had eaten most of their lunch in silence after Dylan had left them to talk to another colleague.

'Not too badly. You?'

'Better than I expected, given how Monday started.'

There he goes again, Teddy thought, bringing it up as if he was responsible for someone forgetting to tell Dylan about Ben.

'You've made your point about that, Ben. I get it, you think I'm only here because of my mum pulling a few strings.'

'I never said that,' Ben said, his eyes widening. 'You're clearly paranoid, that's not my problem.'

'A journalism expert and a psychologist. Anything else I need to know about you?'

'Come on, you clearly resent the association. Every time her name pops up you get defensive. You're walking round with a massive chip on your shoulder.'

'I don't need a therapy session from someone I don't know. Why are you so bothered about me and who I am? Just focus on yourself, Ben.'

Ben stared at Teddy, his eyes narrowing as he weighed up his response.

'I am, Teddy. This is what you don't get. People like me, we work hard every damn day and occasionally we manage to land an opportunity like this. It's life-changing for me. Then I come here and find someone like you, naturally talented, connections in all the right places. It's just a bit of a kick in the teeth to know that I have to fight for everything continuously when for you it's as simple as someone pulling a few strings.'

Before Teddy could even contemplate replying to Ben's accusation, Dylan returned to the table: 'Sarah's going to come down and give you both some feedback. If you're ready, we can head back now.'

Back at their desks, Sarah pulled over a spare chair and sat down between them.

Teddy recognized her from around the office floor. After some quick formal introductions, she went through both versions of the article.

'This one had a slightly better variety of opinions, which is something we really strive to do with these pieces. We like to find the biggest talking point, work out the most newsworthy angle and then provide a balanced selection of the comments,' she explained. Teddy knew immediately that he hadn't done that as well as he could have. Ben was nodding along with every word Sarah said.

'Ben, you had an excellent selection of comments from viewers and picked some great celebrity opinions to include too. Nice touch including Elizabeth. He pipped you to that one.'

It took Teddy a second to realize the comment was directed at him.

'My mum? She commented on it?'

'Yeah, she tweeted about it,' Sarah explained, looking at him like he had suddenly grown a second head.

'Oh. I didn't know that. I never thought to look.'

Teddy zoned out of the remainder of the conversation, only realizing that Sarah had chosen Ben's article to publish when he gave a small cheer. Sarah left them alone and started talking to Dylan.

'No hard feelings, right?' Ben said, holding out his hand for Teddy to shake.

'None at all. Well done.' Teddy met his hand and gripped it tight.

'Ironic, isn't it. You do nothing but complain about her, but your mum ended up helping me win.'

Teddy felt the colour rise in his cheeks. He'd only himself to blame.

'Any plans for the weekend?' Ben asked him after they left their desks a few hours later. Teddy couldn't believe he was even attempting to make conversation with him. However, deciding to try to be the bigger person, he answered, 'Nothing much. I'm just going to meet my friend Shakeel. What about you?'

'I've a date later,' Ben said with a grin on his face. 'It's my first since I split with my boyfriend last year.'

Teddy made a noise that was something between a grunt and a laugh. So Ben was gay. A wave of panic washed over him. What if Ben discovered he was gay too? It wouldn't take long before that piece of gossip travelled to Dylan and then back to . . . Teddy's insides squirmed.

'Listen, I can see my friend,' Teddy said quickly, pointing towards Shakeel who was waiting outside the glass doors. 'Have a good date . . . weekend, I mean, have a nice weekend.'

He felt his cheeks burn once again as he hurried towards the exit.

'Get that down you,' Shakeel said a few minutes later, setting a pint down on the table in front of Teddy. 'You look absolutely shattered. Are you sleeping at all?'

'Not this week,' Teddy said taking a sip from the glass. 'You have no idea. I'm knackered.'

'I'm all ears. Gimme the gossip.'

Teddy told him everything about his first week of training. Shakeel was furious in all the right places, eye-rolling at Ben's article-winning inclusion of tweets from Teddy's mum.

'What the fuck? He knew exactly what he was doing, and the fact he didn't tell you just shows that he was being sneaky about it. That's a red flag right there.'

'I mean, it was quite clever when you think about it. It embarrassed me and made me look stupid all at the same time. Even if his was better, he knew what he was doing including my mum's tweets.'

'This one gives off bad vibes, I'm telling you,' Shakeel said. 'You owe him nothing. Pull your finger out and show him how Teddy Marsh gets things done.'

'Thanks, mate, you're right. I need to remember that this is what I want. I'm good at this too!'

'There you go,' Shakeel said, beaming at him. 'He'll be a distant memory in a few months.'

Once they had exhausted the subject of Ben, Teddy listened as Shakeel told him about his own office drama.

'I'm impressed at you standing up for yourself, Shak,' Teddy said.

'Took myself by surprise to be honest. I'm not going to be walked over by someone when I know I did what was right.'

'Yes mate! I'm bloody proud of you.'

Shakeel grinned at him. 'Thanks, Teddy. Right, I'll grab us another drink.'

While he was away, it suddenly dawned on Teddy that he hadn't told Shakeel about what had been happening at home that week. Once he had returned with their drinks, Shakeel sat in stunned silence listening as Teddy told him about his grandad's shock announcement.

'So, she hasn't spoken to him in days and at home she's acting like everything is totally normal.'

'Holy shit, I knew your family was . . . well, you know. But your grandad? Wow. I would never have guessed it.'

'Right? So yeah, it's been a totally normal, quiet week.'

Shakeel sat quietly for a moment before downing the end of his pint.

'It's really sad when you think about it,' he said. 'Arthur kept this secret for all these years, and we've no idea why, but here we are trying to figure out how we didn't spot a clue.'

'I'm going over tomorrow. I've been debating whether or not I should tell him about myself, but I don't want to add to the whole drama.'

'Do you think he knows you're gay?' Shakeel said suddenly.

'I hadn't actually thought about that. I've been so focused on me not noticing anything about him.'

'He'd have said something, wouldn't he?'

'Do you think he would, though? Am I that obvious?'

'I've seen you pissed and dancing to Lady Gaga at 3 a.m., I can't answer that objectively.'

Teddy threw his hands over his face. 'Mate, don't remind me.'

'Hey, don't be embarrassed. You've got some nice moves.' Shakeel laughed.

The bar had been getting steadily busier throughout the night, filling up with young professionals all eager to put off returning to their overpriced box rooms for as long as they possibly could. Teddy had kept an eye on one particularly loud group which had been getting rowdier as the rounds kept coming. Large groups of men had always made him anxious, like he was waiting for someone to identify him as being different and launch an unprovoked attack.

'I'm going to the toilet, then we can get out of here,' Shakeel said.

He pushed his way through the crowds which filled the small amount of floorspace with relative ease. At six foot three, Shakeel had always been the tallest of any group Teddy had been part of. Teddy watched his friend as he reached the noisy group. Even with the racket they were making, the angry roar was heard clearly throughout the pub.

'Watch where you're going, faggot!'

Before Teddy had a chance to reach him, Shakeel was already pushing his way back, ready to grab him by the shoulders and drag him from the pub.

They burst through the doors. 'Why did you do that?' he shouted at him as the cold air hit them. 'You heard what he called you!'

'Of course I did. Everyone did. So what? It's not an excuse for you to go charging in.'

'But he—'

'But nothing, Teddy! I don't need you to fight my battles.'

'He insulted you!'

'Exactly; me, not you. I'm the one wearing the rainbow badge that he saw. I'm the one who's out. If I don't want to throw a punch, that's my choice.'

'You should stand up for yourself for once, Shak. Stop letting people walk all over you.'

'You can talk, Teddy,' Shakeel spat back at him. 'And why give people like that the satisfaction? They're ignorant morons.'

Teddy knew deep down that Shakeel had a point. It was an argument they had had numerous times before. He had always been hot-headed when it came to defending himself and his friends, struggling to understand how Shakeel could tolerate the verbal abuse regularly directed at him.

'I love that you've always got my back, Teddy, but sometimes it can do more harm than good.'

Teddy hoped that ordering Shak a taxi home would go some way towards an apology. According to the app he had just opened, there was already one on the street; he watched it turn the corner and slowly pull up beside them.

'This is for you,' he said, opening the door.

Shakeel climbed in without saying anything else.

'Night,' Teddy said, shutting the car door.

With Shakeel on his way home, Teddy ordered himself

a taxi. On the journey back he thought about Shakeel's words. Maybe he was right. Things could have escalated quickly; Shakeel had done the right thing dragging him out of the pub. There were too many stories of situations turning nasty. Every day seemed to bring more horrible news that made him feel sick to his stomach. He needed to learn to know when to step back and protect not just himself, but those around him.

Teddy didn't know when he drifted off, but he was woken by the driver tapping him on the leg. 'Mate, we're here. Come on, out you get. You don't want the vomiting fine.'

After clambering out of the back seat, slightly dazed after banging his head on the door, Teddy walked up and down the driveway to get some fresh air. The gravel under his feet crunched loudly as he paced and stared up at the clear night sky. The light in the porch went on, distracting him from the stars.

Eleanor opened the front door. 'Someone looks like they had a good night.'

'Ha, I wish, it could have been better,' Teddy said.

'Yeah, well at least you weren't here.'

'Why, what the hell's wrong now?'

'Everyone knows. Grandad's the talk of Northbridge.'

Teddy groaned. This was the last thing they needed.

CHAPTER SEVEN
Arthur

MADELEINE WAS ROLLING out dough on the large granite work-top. She sprinkled more flour over it as Arthur sat across from her, watching her work. He had always told her that she could be a professional baker. Her breads and cakes were better than any he had ever tasted across the country. Too modest to accept the praise, she had insisted it was better to keep something she enjoyed so much as a hobby. Her only annoyance was that her children had never taken any interest in learning from her.

'How much are you going to tell Teddy?' she asked, looking up at her husband.

'Enough of what he needs to know. He'll have the same questions Elizabeth had, except he might actually listen.'

'He's a good boy. Kids these days are so much more under-standing of the world around them.'

'Did we do something wrong with Elizabeth?' He hadn't intended to bring it up, but he had found himself wondering if he was somehow to blame for Elizabeth's attitude.

'You know the answer to that, Arthur. This isn't about you being homosexual, don't even think that for a second. She's hurt and confused, but she'll come round.'

Arthur glanced up on the clock on the wall. Two hours to go. He couldn't wait to hug his grandson.

The doorbell rang, echoing throughout the whole downstairs. Madeleine and Arthur stopped what they were doing and stared at each other. It was too early for Teddy.

'I'll go,' Madeleine said, wiping her hands on the nearby tea towel. She scuttled out of the kitchen and down into the entrance hall. Arthur listened carefully as he heard the front door opening and a familiar voice greeting Madeleine.

'I'm so sorry to land unannounced.' Harriet Parker's shrill voice filled the hallway. 'I couldn't wait until tomorrow's meeting to see you, I just had to come and check and make sure you're okay.'

'That's very kind of you, Harriet. Everything is absolutely fine, why wouldn't it be?'

'Awful how that kind of gossip spreads. I thought I'd misheard it when Alice and Iris were talking, but then Agnes asked about you both and I just had to come straight over to make sure.'

Arthur moved off his chair to stand closer to the door. He could see Madeleine standing in the entryway, blocking their visitor from his view. He had never been keen on the Parkers. Harriet and her husband lived several minutes up the road. They were the kind of neighbours you enjoyed having for the first six months, but then you found yourself pretending not to be in when they arrived at your door unexpectedly yet again.

'You'll have to bring me up to speed on whatever it is you're trying to say, Harriet.'

Arthur knew that tone. It was still friendly, but now laced with a less than subtle impatience; an early warning that

Madeleine was not going to tolerate the cat and mouse game Harriet was engaging in much longer.

'About your lovely Arthur.'

She whispered the words so quietly that Arthur was only just able to make them out. His stomach flipped. If Harriet Parker was already on their doorstep, it was guaranteed that gossip was already making its second, possibly even third, round of Northbridge. Arthur took a deep breath and stepped out from behind the doorway.

'Madeleine, your mobile is vibrating,' he said, attempting to look surprised as he realized that they had a guest at the front door. 'Ah, Harriet, how lovely to see you.'

'Oh, Arthur! You're here. I wasn't sure if you would be.'

'Why's that now?'

The question took Harriet by surprise, her mouth hanging open dangerously wide as she clearly struggled to think of a response. He couldn't help but enjoy watching her scramble for something to say.

'Not to rush you along, but we have our Teddy coming round soon,' Arthur continued.

'Is there anything else we can help you with? A bowl of sugar perhaps?'

She attempted to force a small laugh. 'No, not at all. Just wanted to say hello and . . .'

Her voice trailed off before they could discover what else she had possibly wanted to say.

Looking confused and disappointed by her unsuccessful visit, she gave them a small smile before slowly walking back down the driveway. She was already tapping at her mobile phone before Arthur and Madeleine had closed the door.

'Well, that might hold off the gossips for another few hours,' Arthur said.

'She'll be back, don't you worry. You know what Northbridge is like. She's probably already called a town meeting to alert them that you're still living here.'

'How are you so calm?'

'I told you, you made your sacrifices. I'm not letting you do this on your own.'

'They're judging you. They'll say you should take me to the cleaners, they'll want to know why you aren't burning my clothes on the front lawn.'

Madeleine laughed. 'Let them! As long as we've got our family, we'll get through this and you will . . . well, you'll be who you are meant to be. You deserve that.'

'I just want you to know that I am sorry. No matter what else is said, I never wanted to hurt you or for you to endure any of this.'

'We've been over this, Arthur. We did what we had to do and nothing will ever make me regret that.'

She went straight to the oven to check on her batch of scones. The smell filled the kitchen as Madeleine lifted each golden-crusted scone from the tray and carefully placed it on a cooling rack.

'Remember, I've counted them,' she said, flashing a warning smile at Arthur.

Arthur was ready and waiting at the door when Teddy arrived. He couldn't help but beam at his grandson as he traipsed up the driveway. He remembered the day Teddy had been born like it was yesterday; his first and only grandson. He was so proud of the handsome young man he had grown into.

'You look like you had a late night,' Arthur said, wrapping his arms around Teddy. 'It's really good of you to come over.'

'Don't be daft, of course I had to come. I'm just sorry I had to wait all week.'

'Work is far more important, young man, I hope all of this wasn't too much of a distraction.'

'No, don't worry. I'll tell you all about it later on, I promise.'

Madeleine was waiting in the lounge as they walked in. 'Hello, love, it's so good to see you.' Teddy kissed her on the cheek.

'Hi Nan. I could smell the scones when I was coming up the driveway.'

'They're just fresh from the oven, so I hope you're hungry.'

She left the room as Arthur and Teddy sat down on the large sofa.

'Where does your mum think you are?'

'I just said I was going to meet Shak and Lexie for the afternoon.'

'How are your sisters?'

'They're good. Both send their love.'

'That's good,' Arthur said. 'And your mum?'

'You know what she's like. I heard about the newsagent's yesterday.'

'I've never seen her so angry. Everyone must know by now of course. There's nothing this town loves more than some fresh gossip.'

'I wouldn't worry about them, Grandad. Let them talk.'

Arthur had tried not to dwell on the repercussions of his coming out. Harriet's visit had been an early indication that it was not all going to be smooth sailing when it came to finding acceptance within their circle of friends and neighbours.

'I can't really worry about everyone else until I know that Elizabeth, Patrick and you lot are all right. Nobody else matters right now.'

'Well, I hope you know that you being gay changes nothing. You're still my grandad and I love you very much.'

Arthur didn't have a chance to compose himself. A week's worth of emotion hit him. He pulled a tissue out of the box on the table beside the sofa. Madeleine, as intuitive as always, had placed it there just before Teddy had arrived.

'Sorry, I didn't want to upset you.'

'No, don't be silly lad, it's just me being daft. It's been a long week . . . a long life.'

'I don't know if you want to talk too much about all of it. We can another time if you'd rather.'

'I don't mind if you have questions, which I'm sure you must. I'll do my best to answer them.'

Arthur knew it was best to at least give Teddy the chance to ask whatever he wanted to so that he and his sisters could begin to understand. It felt like the very least he owed them.

'I guess, how long have you known?' Teddy said quickly. Arthur knew the question must have been on the tip of his tongue.

'Would you believe me if I said forever?'

'Really?' Teddy asked, his eyebrows raised.

'I believe so. It was a different time. Even in a town so close to the bright lights of the city, it wasn't possible to live like that.'

'You stayed here, though. You could have escaped and lived your own life somewhere else.'

'It wasn't that simple, Teddy. I couldn't just run, I had responsibilities within the family. The business. You gave up going to university and stayed here for your mum and the girls when your father died. We make choices and have to live with them.'

'But you gave up being who you are.'

'It's hard to comprehend, I know. I can't regret the sacrifices I made. How could I when I'm sitting here with you? Life is full of sacrifices, Teddy. We'll make good and bad choices, but we shouldn't let regrets define us. I'm not perfect, but I hope when I'm not here that the people I love will remember me for the good things and know I did my best for them.'

'I'm really proud of you,' Teddy said.

The statement took Arthur aback. It was one thing to find acceptance from those around him, but to have his only grandson say that he was proud of him meant the world.

'Are you really?'

'Of course I am. You deserve to be happy, no matter what age. When Dad died, I thought I would never be happy again, but you showed me that I could be. If Nan can understand that, you don't need to worry about anyone else.'

'I wish that was true.'

'It's Mum, isn't it?'

'I'd give anything for her to walk in that door now and just hug me.'

'I think she's being selfish.'

Arthur shook his head, his forehead furrowed. 'I know she can be tough, but your mum is an incredibly loving person. When she's ready, she'll talk to me and hopefully I can help her understand.

'I'm going to do everything I can to help her see sense.'

'Don't push her too much. Let her get there in her own time.'

'But that's not fair on you.'

'Teddy, I've been waiting all these years. I can give your mother as long as she needs.'

'Well, I can't,' Teddy said, jumping from the chair so fast he shocked Arthur. He watched as his grandson paced around the room, his head in his hands, mumbling something he couldn't quite make out. He had never seen him like this before.

'What's wrong, Teddy?'

'All of this. I just want everything to be normal again. I want my family together.'

'It will be. Your mum will come round and everything will get back to normal.'

'You don't understand what I'm saying. It won't be. I've seen how she feels now.'

Arthur shook his head. Teddy was right. He didn't understand what he meant. He watched as his grandson stopped pacing and took a deep breath.

'It's not just you, Grandad. It's me too.'

'You've upset your mum?'

'She doesn't even know. She'll probably cut me out too when she does.'

'Teddy, are you saying—'

'I'm gay! I'm gay too.'

For a brief second Arthur thought Teddy was going to topple over as it looked like his shaking legs were about to give way.

'Sit yourself down,' he said, helping Teddy into the chair. 'Better?'

Teddy looked up at him, his eyes filled with tears.

'I can't believe I just said that out loud. I'm sorry, I didn't mean to just blurt it out like that. I wasn't going to say it today, but listening to you talk about regrets and making the right choices . . . I can't sit here and lie to you, not when you've been so brave.'

Arthur couldn't quite believe what he had heard. He was almost tempted to ask Teddy to confirm it, but the smile on his grandson's face seemed to do that by itself. He'd always known Teddy was a little different to many of the other boys of his age, but they had always put that down to his shyness. Everything suddenly made more sense to Arthur as he smiled back at Teddy.

'You really didn't know I was gay?'

'About as much as you did me.'

They both laughed loudly. Arthur couldn't remember the last time he had felt his stomach ache from laughing so hard. The noise was loud enough to attract Madeleine's attention, and she came rushing into the room, her face filled with concern.

'Is everything all right?' she asked, looking at them both.

'Sorry, Nan, everything's fine. We were just reminiscing.'

'Oh good, the noise took me by surprise. Are you both ready for tea?'

'We'll be right out,' Arthur said, pushing himself up from the sofa with a soft groan.

'Does anyone else know, Teddy?' he asked once they were alone again.

'Not yet. I don't know what I'm supposed to do. How can I possibly tell Mum when she's reacted so badly to you?'

'She's still your mum.'

'And you're still her dad. I know what you mean, but I'm just not ready to deal with any of this. Not yet.'

'I understand, just remember that every day you aren't being true to who you are is a day wasted. I know I am very blessed to have had a good life, but you deserve to have the best life, the one you really want, not the one other people think you should have. Learn from my mistakes, Teddy, that's the most important advice I can give you. Now come on, your nan wouldn't let me touch those scones until you were here.'

CHAPTER EIGHT
Teddy

TEDDY DIDN'T STOP smiling for the rest of the afternoon. It reminded him of days spent there with Shakeel when he visited during his holidays from university. They would happily spend hours listening to his grandad's stories while his nan kept them well fed and watered.

When Teddy got home he pulled a bottle of water from the fridge and escaped upstairs to his bedroom without bumping into anybody else. His room was his safe space. The shelves his dad had put up for him were still filled with various academic awards from his school days. He'd always been proud of his achievements, even when winning 'Excellence in English' for the fourth year in a row meant being teased by his classmates.

And then his dad had died. Clashes with his mum had followed when Teddy decided that he was planning to stay in Northbridge instead of taking up his place at university. Teddy couldn't bring himself to leave the place where he felt closest to his dad. With Shakeel gone, he shut himself off from family life. It was only after regular sessions with a grief counsellor – his nan's suggestion – that Teddy began to see a way forward again. He had to step up for his mum and sisters and it was impossible to do that by leaving them behind. He also had to think of his own future; his dad would want that.

Teddy threw himself down on his bed and tucked two pillows under his chest. Opening up his laptop, he hit Call on Shakeel's name. He wasn't going to let the previous night at the pub turn into anything more than a disagreement. It rang for almost a minute before Shakeel finally answered.

'Hello,' he said, his face popping up on the screen. It was bright red and glistening with sweat.

'Sorry, mate, were you having a private moment?'

'Behave yourself.' Shakeel grinned. 'Bloody spin class wrecked me, but I needed it after last night.'

'You and me both.' Teddy laughed. 'Listen, about last night, I just wanted to apologize again.'

'It's forgotten, but for what it's worth, I'm sorry too. I know you mean well and only tried to get involved because you care. Anyway, how did today with Arthur go?'

Shakeel adjusted his camera, hiding his unmade bed from view. Teddy hadn't yet had the chance to visit his new studio flat. Shakeel had explained that it was ridiculously small, but that the location had made it impossible to turn down. He only had to walk five minutes to work and it was surrounded by bars and cafés.

'Honestly? Better than I expected,' Teddy said. 'It was a bit weird being there with him and Nan at first, but after a while it was like nothing had changed.'

'Did he say why he decided to come out now?'

'Nah, just that he was getting old and knew he had to take the opportunity.'

'I still can't get my head round it all. I could never have waited that long.'

'Only 'cause you were desperate to beat me to it,' Teddy teased. 'And about that. I do have some good news for you.'

'Oh yeah?' Shakeel said, shifting in his chair so that his head almost left the screen.

'I told Grandad that I'm gay.'

The seconds between Shakeel hearing the words and processing what they meant felt like they lasted forever. Teddy burst out laughing as he watched his best friend's confused expression turn into a beaming smile.

'Holy shit! That's incredible, Teddy! I'm so proud of you. Tell me everything.'

'It was totally unplanned. We were just talking and suddenly I said it.'

'What did he say?'

'Typical Grandad.' Teddy laughed, feeling a wave of giddiness spread over him as he remembered how good it had felt. 'Just took it in his stride. He didn't have a clue, though, so that made two of us I guess.'

'Does this mean you're gonna tell the rest of them?'

'Not yet. I just can't do it while Mum's still not talking to Grandad. Listen, Shak, I can hear someone calling, I better go down. We'll catch up tomorrow?'

'No worries. Text me if you come out to anyone else.'

Teddy grinned and waved at the camera before closing the laptop.

After making his way downstairs, Teddy sat down beside Eleanor, opposite his mum and younger sister. They had already filled their plates with the Chinese food which their mum had brought home. Teddy didn't realize how hungry he was until he started piling the food onto his plate.

'Nice of you to join us, Edward. I wasn't sure if you would have eaten in town or not.'

'No, I just grabbed a snack.'

'Good, it's nice for us to eat together. We've hardly seen you all week.'

'Sorry, work has been quite full-on.'

His mum's eyes lit up at the mention of work. He immediately regretted having said it. 'How are you finding it? Isn't it such a thrill being on the newsroom floor?'

'Yeah, it's been good. I think I'm learning a lot.'

'That's excellent. I knew Dylan would be a great mentor for you.'

'How did you know I was working with Dylan? Actually, don't even answer that, I don't think I want to know.' He took a bite of a spring roll.

'Excuse me, Edward, don't take that tone with me.'

'I wasn't taking a tone. I just forgot that you have to oversee every single detail.'

'I think I have every right to check in on how my son is doing, especially when I've tried so hard to get you this opportunity.'

'You do, Mum. You have every right. But you can ask me. I'm right here and can tell you anything you need to know.'

'Don't overreact, Edward. I thought it might be a good idea to check in with Dylan now and again to make sure everything is going well. You're not always as communicative as you could be, you know.'

'I would tell you if you asked.' Teddy could feel the colour rising in his cheeks as he tried to stay calm. This was exactly the kind of thing they always ended up arguing about. 'And maybe I'd talk to you about this stuff more if you didn't automatically assume you know what is best for me. I'm not twelve anymore.'

Eleanor slapped her hand down on the table with a bang, making them both jump. 'That's enough!' she snapped, glaring at them. 'Can we just have one dinner where we pretend to be kind of normal?'

'Sorry, El, I didn't mean—'

'No, Teddy, you never do, but it always ends the same way. Just talk to each other instead of whatever this is.'

They ate in silence for several minutes after Eleanor's telling-off. Teddy glanced in his mum's direction several times. He hated these silences. They were frequently deployed when her children disappointed her. She kept her gaze focused on the food she was aimlessly moving about her plate with her fork and didn't wait much longer before excusing herself and leaving the kitchen.

'Nice one, Edward,' Evangelina said once the kitchen door had closed behind her.

'Don't do that,' Eleanor said. 'I just about tolerate it from Teddy and Mum without you joining in to start another argument.'

'You need to give her a break,' Evangelina said. 'We gave you time and space when you needed it, Teddy, even when your behaviour hurt all of us. She's obviously having a hard enough week dealing with everything going on. Try to give her the chance to focus on something, even if it is you.'

'Easier said than done.'

'You could be less of a dick about things, Teddy.'

Teddy didn't want to get into an argument with his sisters over it. They had had their own difficulties with their mum, especially in the wake of their dad's death, but they had always been sympathetic to the pressure she had put on him in particular.

'Keep this between us, but I went to visit Grandad and Nan today,' Teddy said, grabbing the opportunity to change the subject. Eleanor and Evangelina spun toward him, their eyes round with surprise.

'How was it?'

'It was lovely. I just needed to make sure Grandad was doing okay.'

'Is he?'

'I think so, he was asking after you both too.'

'And Nan?' Eleanor asked.

'Baking. Everything was weirdly normal. I think she's just making the most of this time before it becomes common knowledge.'

'That might be sooner than she thinks,' Evangelina said. 'I've already had a few texts today. People in town are talking and it's not all good.'

'Seriously? What are they saying?'

'It's mostly about how he could hurt Nan and why now. We'd probably say those things too if it was happening to another family.'

'We still don't know though, do we?'

'Know what?'

'Why now? People are going to keep asking how he could do this to Nan and why she's being so calm about it. I don't know what to say because I don't understand either.'

'I know, but we can't focus on that. We have to accept that they both have their reasons and need our support. They'll get through all of this if they know that they have us and Mum by their side.'

'She'll get there,' Eleanor said. 'It might take a little longer than we'd like, but she will. She loves him.' Eleanor had always been an optimist. She smiled as she carefully stacked the empty dinner plates on top of each other.

'I hope you're right,' Teddy said. 'I don't know how much longer any of us can carry on like this.'

For some reason, Teddy's mind drifted to Ben as he sorted out his outfit for work the following morning. He wondered how his date had gone. Could he find out without having to ask? The last thing Teddy needed was to make Ben think he cared what he was getting up to. He opened up Instagram and went to Ben's account. Teddy scanned the posts. He opened one showing Ben with his arm round another guy. It had been posted four months ago. Even just seeing them both smiling irked Teddy. Why was he even bothered? He slammed the laptop closed and set it on the cabinet beside his bed. He thought back to Shakeel's warning about Ben on Friday evening. He needed to tread carefully, especially at work.

Dylan seemed to be enjoying finding new ways to pit Teddy and Ben against each other. Every task was so quickly turned into a competition that Teddy almost suspected his mum was behind it. It was exactly the kind of thing she would do. Even the simplest of household chores completed by Teddy and his sisters had been a contest. She would, of course, serve as the only judge, deciding who had performed the task to her standards. Teddy couldn't help being competitive; it had been instilled in him from a young age. His mum didn't believe in just taking part or, heaven forbid, coming second. No matter how many teachers pointed it out, he had found himself unable to keep it under control. Competition was in his blood.

But that was *before*. After his father had died, none of that stuff seemed to matter. No amount of competitiveness could win him his dad back. He stopped competing at home and at school. Teddy knew his mum's efforts to engage him in what she called silly games were done with the best intentions, but he simply didn't have it in him anymore.

Or so he'd thought. But now, with Dylan egging him on, he was starting to feel that urge to win again. It didn't hurt that he was finally competing against someone he actually wanted to beat.

'Right, bit of a task for you both,' Dylan said. 'I want 600 words on a topic of your choice. Get it up on the website by midday and we'll see whose article has the most views by the end of the day.'

'Don't be texting your mates getting them to click on your story,' Ben said as Dylan returned to his desk.

'Afraid of some actual competition?'

'It would be nice to have some at some point,' Ben said with a laugh, leaving Teddy seething.

CHAPTER NINE
Arthur

CORA'S CAFÉ FELL silent as Arthur entered, only the voice on the radio carrying on. The tea rooms had always been one of his and Madeleine's favourite places to go in Northbridge. Cora Woods, who was around the same age as Elizabeth, was one of the rare outsiders who had found success there. Normally, the locals would save their custom for the businesses run by someone with connections to the town, or a surname that stirred memories of days gone by. After selling Cora a car and hearing her plans for the café, Arthur had insisted that they show their support. And almost fifteen years later, the little shop had been extended into the neighbouring property and was busier than ever.

'Hello, Arthur.' Cora popped up from behind the fridge, her round face flushed from rushing around. She ignored the sudden change in atmosphere as customers shifted in their chairs, craning their necks to watch the man who had just entered the premises. Arthur's heartbeat quickened as he stumbled towards the counter.

'Morning Cora, could I get the usual for myself and Madeleine please?'

'No problem, my love. Go ahead and take a seat and I'll be right over.'

Arthur found a table at the back; the furthest possible from the entrance and the large window overlooking the main street. Several customers were still staring at him as he took his seat and waited for Madeleine to arrive. Arthur wished he had brought a newspaper with him. Even if he hadn't been able to focus on the words, it would have been something to hide behind.

'There she is, that's her,' he heard one customer attempt to whisper before the door of the café had even opened. He watched as they craned their necks, their eyes following Madeleine as she made her way to the table.

'Everything okay?' she asked, sitting down and setting her handbag on the empty chair beside her.

'The circus is in town and we're the main attraction,' Arthur said grimly.

'Has somebody said something?'

'No, it'd be less awkward if they did.'

Madeleine turned and looked across at the nearby tables. Several people shifted in their chairs, averting their eyes from her stern gaze. Cora arrived carrying a tray, interrupting the silent exchange.

'Hello, Madeleine, it's lovely to see you,' she said. 'An Americano for you and flat white for Arthur. Can I get you a bite to eat?'

'No thank you, Cora. This is perfect,' Madeleine said, taking a sip from the steaming cup.

'I just want you both to know that you're always welcome here. If anyone gives you any grief, you just send them to me and I'll sort them out. There'll be none of that awfulness under my roof.'

'That's very nice of you to say, Cora. We both really appreciate that,' Arthur said, feeling his heart glow with warmth. Thank heavens she was still their friend at least.

Cora had just left the table when the door to the café opened again. Madeleine groaned as she saw who was leading the group of three women. It was too late to avoid being seen. Harriet Parker was already striding across the room towards them.

'Good morning!' she said, arriving beside them. 'Madeleine, you were missed at the spring festival planning meeting yesterday. I hope we won't be without our chairwoman for too long.'

'Don't worry, Harriet, you won't be.'

'We totally understand if you need to step away for a bit. I wouldn't want to fuel the gossip either.'

'Am I fuelling the gossip now, Harriet?'

'You know I'm not one for tittle-tattle, Madeleine, but things do get said.'

'Anything in particular you'd like to repeat?'

'I just hope you're okay and know what you're doing.'

Arthur had heard enough.

'What is it Madeleine is doing, Harriet? Do you mean being seen out with me?' he said, aware of the growing anger in his voice.

'Now, Arthur. You know how people talk. They're just shocked and concerned, that's all.'

'They have absolutely no need to be concerned, thank you. I'm gay, not a serial killer.'

The small gasp from the table beside them almost made Arthur smile. Harriet pursed her lips.

'Now don't be like that, Arthur. We've known each other a long time. I didn't want a scene. Like you, I'm just looking out for my dear friend.'

'If you are my friend, Harriet, you will stop what you're doing and give us some privacy,' Madeleine said. 'We simply wanted to have a quiet coffee, not sit here like animals in a zoo. You should remember what that feels like.'

'And what is that supposed to mean?'

'We all remember the gossip about Brian and his assistant a few years ago, Harriet. You would do well to remember how it feels to be the headline news in this godforsaken town.'

Harriet gasped, but before she could say anything, Cora reappeared.

'Is everything all right here?' she asked.

'Everything is fine, thank you, Cora. Harriet was just leaving.'

Harriet raised her left eyebrow and sighed dramatically. 'I was trying to be a good neighbour. I'm afraid I don't think we'll be stopping this morning after all, Cora.'

They watched as Harriet ushered her little group back out onto the street.

'I'm sorry, Cora,' Arthur said. 'I've a feeling she won't be the last.'

'Bah,' Cora said. 'Who needs them anyway? Nosy do-gooders, the lot of 'em. You were missed at the meeting. Don't let people like that keep you away.'

Madeleine waited until Cora had left them alone again before leaning across the table.

'Are you worried about tonight?' Her voice was grave.

'Not so much worried, I have a feeling that was just the warm-up. I'm only glad you won't be there to have to deal with it.'

Madeleine reached across the table and gave his hand a gentle squeeze.

Arthur was due to attend the meeting of the Northbridge Foundation, a charitable organization his father had co-founded almost seventy-five years ago. The group raised money throughout the year and distributed it to various community organizations in the area. It would be Arthur's first meeting since coming out; the first time he would see some of the locals he had grown up with. He'd been dreading it.

The fifteen members of the committee met once a month to discuss new ideas and approve any requests for donations. Arthur had previously served as chairman, but the role was now held by Eric Brown, the managing director of a haulage company which had opened when Arthur was seven. He remembered his dad meeting Eric's father; the two had been good friends which in turn led to Arthur and Eric becoming inseparable as boys. They had remained friendly over the years, and Eric was Patrick's godfather.

'How do you think Eric will be?' Madeleine asked him just before he left the house.

'It could go either way. He's as conservative as they come, but I haven't ever heard him say anything that makes me worry.' But Arthur was worried, more worried than he wanted Madeleine to know. Eric was a good friend, but he wasn't always very understanding.

Arthur pulled up outside the community centre. Eric's car was the only one there. It was empty; he must already be inside setting up. Arthur took a deep breath before going in to see if he needed any help.

The main door was locked. Arthur hit the buzzer and waited. The plaque on the wall beside the entrance caught his eye.

THE CHARLES EDWARDS COMMUNITY CENTRE
OFFICIALLY OPENED
17TH JUNE 1958

Arthur remembered attending the event alongside his parents and siblings. He had never seen his dad look as proud as he did that day, standing beside the mayor and unveiling the plaque. Arthur knew the donation which had secured him the honour had all been part of a wider, more-calculated strategy, one that would come to fruition several years later when Charles became mayor himself. That was how his father always operated. Nothing was ever done by accident. Everything was planned out in advance. It was the very reason Arthur and Madeleine had decided to pursue their relationship in the first place.

'Arthur, I didn't know if you'd make it.'

Eric's gruff voice startled him.

'Sorry, I know I'm a few minutes early, I thought I'd check if you needed any help setting up.'

'Oh, well, erm, I doubt we'll have many here tonight. I very nearly rescheduled.'

'We're here now, we may as well see who else comes along and do what we can.'

Arthur followed Eric into the hall. The large table had been pulled into the centre of the floor, with two stacks of old plastic chairs waiting to be set out around it.

'Before everyone else gets here, I thought we might talk,' Arthur said, as Eric lifted two chairs down for them. 'I presume you have heard some things over the past few days,' he added. His sweaty hands were shaking.

Eric nodded.

'I'm sorry I didn't get to talk to you before you heard from someone else.'

'I can't deny it, Arthur, hearing news like that as a bit of gossip was not what I expected. I thought you thought more of me than that.'

'I'm sorry, I hope you know it was never intended to come across like that. Things happened fast and I had to deal with my family first.'

'How is Madeleine?'

'She's been incredible. I know there are some people who would rather see me run out of town, but you know what she is like.'

Eric shifted, looking uncomfortable. 'Why did you marry her, though? Why put her through all of this?'

'It wasn't as simple as that, Eric. You know what it was like in those days; what my father was like.'

'You could have had anyone. All those girls, you knew you could have had the pick of them, but you went after her.'

'That's not true and you know it. I can't believe we're still having this argument.'

'I stood by and supported you when you knew it was breaking my heart.'

Arthur hadn't expected Eric to dredge their history up again in the wake of his own news. Yes, Eric had been in love with Madeleine in the old days – but that was over fifty years ago. Surely he couldn't still be bitter about it? Their friendship had withstood that test.

'Eric, you were there. You know we did what we had to do. My father—'

'Your father this, your father that. You had a voice, Arthur. You let him push you into living a life you now want to call a lie.'

'That's not fair. Madeleine and I made our choice. You couldn't possibly understand.'

'Maybe I don't want to, Arthur. I'm embarrassed to call you my friend.'

Arthur's stomach lurched as if it had just been on the receiving end of a punch.

The sound of voices carried into the hall and the door opened to reveal a group of people arriving for the meeting. Eric got up out of his chair and walked towards them.

None of them acknowledged that Arthur was sitting just a few feet away.

The chair next to Arthur remained vacant once those who had turned up had sat down. He had to fight the urge to get up and leave. The group fell silent as Eric raised his hand to get their attention.

'Before we begin this evening, Arthur has let me know that he will be stepping down from the committee for the foreseeable future.'

Arthur felt his face burn as heads turned in his direction. He sat there, frozen.

'While his private life is in disarray, he doesn't want that to become a distraction and get in the way of our important work here.'

'What . . . what are you doing?' Arthur barely managed to get the words out.

'It's for the best, Arthur. You know how this will look.' Eric wasn't even looking at him.

'That's absolute rubbish and you know it.'

Eric finally turned to stare at Arthur. Arthur was shocked by the anger in his friend's eyes.

'You should leave now, or we will vote on your membership remaining in place at all.'

Arthur stood up and looked around the table, at the faces of the people he'd thought of as friends. Not one of them could look him directly in the eye.

'I'll go,' he said. 'But I hope you all take a good long, hard look at yourselves. You're free to judge me for the decisions I've made, but don't judge me for who I am. What if it was your son or daughter, or your grandchild? Would you kick them out of a meeting? Would you kick them out of their home? Northbridge is *my* home. It's supposed to be a safe and happy place. We all know this town has only ever been that for the right people, the people with money or the right surname. I've led a very privileged life, but before I die, I'll make sure that this town helps more than just the people sitting around this table.'

Without waiting for a response, Arthur turned and left the hall. By the time he was back in the car he was breathing heavily. That was not how he had expected the evening to go. His blood was boiling. How could he have let Eric speak to him like that and dismiss him from the meeting? And nobody had spoken up for him. They must all feel the same way as Eric.

He couldn't go home yet. That would mean telling Madeleine what had happened and she didn't need to know. Not yet anyway.

A sudden knock on the passenger side window made Arthur jump. Patrick's face was staring in at him. He unlocked the door, allowing Patrick to open it and climb into the front seat.

'How did you know I'd be here?' Arthur asked.

'Mum. I went round to the house and she said you had come to the meeting.'

'I shouldn't have bothered coming.'

'What happened? Did you not go in?'

'I almost wish I hadn't now. Eric's thrown me off the committee. None of them tried to stop him. They all just sat there, too scared to make eye contact.'

'I know he's an old friend of yours, but I never liked that guy,' Patrick said through gritted teeth. 'And his son's not much better. All out for themselves that lot, slimy gits. Are you all right?'

'I'm fine, son, don't worry. I knew the people closest to me were going to be hurt. You just can't prepare yourself for how it feels to see that hurt turn into such visceral anger.'

'I'm sorry I added to all of that by not being there for you since you told us,' Patrick said softly.

'You don't owe me any apologies. You didn't ask for any of this.'

'It doesn't matter. At a time when you and Mum needed support the most, I put myself first and left you both alone to deal with these kinds of people and their gossiping.'

Arthur reached out and took his son's hand.

'You're here now. That's the most important thing to me. I had a father who expected his children to forget their own lives and live by his rules. As did your mother. I don't ever want to make you feel that way. It doesn't matter whether you're happy, sad or angry, I'll still be your dad and I'll always be here for you.'

'I'm happy as long as you and Mum are happy,' Patrick said, wiping his eyes with the sleeve of his jacket. 'You've both got me through my own bad times and you still trust me to look after the business you built.'

'I couldn't be any prouder of the man you are, Patrick. You and Elizabeth make everything about this silly old fool's life worthwhile.'

'Are you happy though, Dad? Does telling us help?'

'It's impossible to explain, but it really does. I'm not hiding anymore. I'm just me, and I get to be me for however long I have left.'

'You've got years left in you. You'll outlive us all, wait and see.'

Arthur stared at the window. His mouth was dry.

'What about dating or meeting someone?' Patrick said. 'Is that something you've even thought about?'

Arthur hesitated. He couldn't deny that he had considered it. He knew people would assume that his decision to come out must be related to a desire to be with someone else, but it wasn't his priority.

'I don't think that's going to be happening any time soon.'

'Well, you have my support if you do. Go out there and live, Dad. You deserve this. Don't not do something because of how others might react; isn't that what you've always taught us?'

'I'm not sure your sister would feel the same way.'

'Don't worry about Lizzie, Dad. She just needs to process all of this in her own way. Anyway, I better go and let you get home.'

Patrick opened his arms and reached across to hug Arthur, who wrapped both of his arms around his son.

'Right,' Patrick said, pulling away after a long moment. 'I'm going now. Scarlett will be wondering where I am. Love you, Dad.' Patrick got out of the car and gave him a small wave as he walked back to his own.

Arthur smiled the whole way home. It was progress. If Patrick could forgive him, it was worth clinging on to the hope that Elizabeth might too.

CHAPTER TEN
Teddy

SOMEWHAT RELUCTANTLY, TEDDY had arranged to meet Ben outside the Riverside Hotel at 9 a.m. Dylan had only told them at the end of the previous day that they were both going to interview reality TV star Neena Anderson.

'You'll do the interview together, so you need to get your heads together and talk about questions,' Dylan explained. 'I want 800 words, and this time, whoever delivers the best story will get it in the paper. I think they will anyway, I should probably double check that.'

Teddy had been slightly surprised by Ben's giddiness about the job as they left the office. 'I loved her on *The Dating Game*. She's actually had a really tough few months since the show ended, but I'm not sure if we should really focus on that.'

'Yeah, probably not the best place to start.' Teddy sighed. He didn't want to admit it to Ben, but he had had no idea who Neena Anderson was until he had looked her up online. As soon as he had done that, he'd alerted Shakeel and Lexie to the news in their group chat. As reality TV aficionados both had been extremely excited and wasted no time in helping

Teddy come up with questions about some of Neena's most memorable moments.

'Ask her about being arrested,' Lexie suggested while they FaceTimed later that night. 'It was front page news!'

'Oh yeah, I'm sure her publicist would love that, Lex.'

Teddy was used to listening to his mum complain about celebrity interviews and 'busybody' publicists who would shut down questions that they didn't like. He didn't want to piss off either the celebrity or her publicist on his first ever interview.

He looked up at the hotel. It was a typical boutique city hotel, usually filled with men and women in business suits heading off to important meetings. He hated these places and the stuffy people who looked down on those they didn't believe belonged there. As he waited outside, he looked at himself in the glass door. He had reluctantly worn a tie for the first time in several years, only finally deciding to put it on when he got off the train.

In the reflection, he spotted Ben walking up behind him. He was wearing a navy blue shirt that clung to his torso.

'Something wrong?' Teddy said as he saw Ben's eyes scan him.

'Not at all, I didn't know it was an occasion for a tie, that's all.'

Teddy groaned.

'I'm sure Neena will appreciate the effort,' Ben said with a grin.

'You never know. Maybe you can charm her with your dazzling personality.'

Ben playfully threw both hands over his chest.

'You've got such a way with words, you know, you should consider that as a career.'

'Someone woke up in a good mood today,' Teddy said as a man whose face he vaguely recognized from his research walked past them. 'Isn't that Neena's boyfriend Joey?'

Ben glanced round and nodded. 'You mean *ex-boyfriend*, but that's him. I wonder why he's lurking around.'

'Oh right, yeah, maybe they're back together,' Teddy said. He was sure Lexie had said that they had been photographed out together at the weekend. He needed to double-check before they went in. The showbiz desk would love to get an exclusive quote on their reunion. He could already imagine Ben watching on as he told Dylan the news.

'Come on then, we better get in there,' Ben said. 'Her publicist Stuart is meeting us in reception.'

Stuart, who barely glanced up from his phone, was ten minutes late in coming to get them, but they were soon sitting at a large rectangular table in the restaurant waiting for Neena to arrive.

'You're the first interview of the day,' Stuart said, all business. 'So, let's keep it nice and light. She's here to promote her make-up range, but obviously you can talk about the show and her other projects. No silly stuff please; she's not going to talk about Joey or their relationship, so don't even waste time going there.'

With his warning issued, Stuart disappeared back off to the foyer to meet his client, who had somehow got lost while making her way down from her room.

Teddy scanned the questions he had written down in his notepad. He wasn't sure what Ben planned to ask, but he had included several potentially tougher questions to consider towards the end of the interview. If he was going to stand out, he knew that he needed to take a risk and not be afraid of asking what could get him a story. His mum's proud face flashed before his eyes as he read the final question. Shaking it off, he looked up just in time to see Stuart walk back into the empty restaurant with Neena by his side. She was dressed casually in jeans and an off-the-shoulder top. Teddy was struck by how attractive she was in person.

'Neena, this is Teddy and Ben from *The Post*,' Stuart said, as she sat down opposite them.

'Hi, guys, lovely to meet you both. Was it one of you who wrote that story about me and Joey the other day?' Her voice was soft and sweet, but her piercing blue eyes narrowed as she watched for their immediate reactions.

Teddy and Ben both shook their heads. Teddy knew from Ben's expression that he wasn't alone in not knowing which article she was referring to.

'It wasn't us, but don't worry, we're going to focus on the make-up range today,' Teddy said quickly, hoping that she wasn't already put off chatting to them.

'Sure,' she said, sounding much more cheerful. 'Well, let's go. I'm ready to talk!'

Teddy made sure to check his watch regularly, determined to ensure that they covered all of their questions in the allotted time. They had five minutes left when he passed back to Ben, who was talking about the people Neena had kept in touch with after her time on *The Dating Game*.

'If you're back together with Joey; does that mean you've forgiven him for cheating on you?'

Teddy looked up in time to see the smile on Neena's face

fade. He had assumed Ben wouldn't risk asking about their relationship after her publicist's warning.

'Excuse me?' she said curtly. 'Who said we were back together?'

'No, I didn't mean—'

'Just because your paper prints some photographs doesn't mean you know everything going on in my life. How dare you sit there and just assume.'

Ben's mouth was hanging open, his eyes wide with alarm. He clearly hadn't anticipated such a shift in atmosphere. Watching him struggle to find the words to explain himself almost made Teddy feel sorry for him. It would have been tempting to leave him to it, but then he realized that Ben's eyes had filled with tears. Alarmed at how quickly the uncomfortable situation had escalated, he cleared his throat.

'Neena,' Teddy interrupted. 'Sorry, we didn't mean to assume, we just know that your fans have been asking and of course care deeply about you. They just want to make sure that you are doing the best for yourself.'

'Well, I am. I haven't forgiven Joey. He knows he royally fucked up. He's got a lot more grovelling to do before I even consider forgiving him. It doesn't mean we can't be friends, but that's all we are right now.'

The final few minutes of the chat were more than a little tense despite Teddy scrapping his own planned questions in favour of easier ones about the various products she had been promoting. To his relief, Neena was smiling again by the time they lifted their Dictaphones off the table and said goodbye.

'Sorry about that, I didn't mean to offend,' Ben said to Stuart as they walked out.

'Good luck to anyone else who tries that today,' Stuart snorted, still tapping away on his phone. 'She's not normally so forgiving.'

'I owe you big time,' Ben said once Stuart was out of earshot. 'I knew time was running out and really thought it was worth the risk to ask.'

Teddy nodded. After Ben's fluffed attempt they hadn't been able to get anything particularly exciting out of Neena. As bad as he felt for him, if Dylan wanted to know why they didn't have better content than they did, he'd have no bother telling him exactly who was to blame.

'We got some good lines in there, didn't we?' Ben asked. Teddy knew he was trying to sound as hopeful as possible about the stories they could get out of their interview. Unsure himself, he spent most of the journey thinking about which of Neena's quotes he would be able to use as a headline and how he could spin it.

They had only been back at their desks fifteen minutes when a shaken-looking Ben tapped Teddy on the shoulder and asked him to come with him to the kitchen. His eyes were wide with worry as he stood in front of Teddy, waiting until they were alone before speaking.

'I've messed up. I don't have any audio.' His voice was filled with panic.

'What? Your Dictaphone was on, I saw the light.'

'I don't know what went wrong. It's just a load of noise, I've got nothing!'

The same helpless face that had been staring back at Neena earlier that morning was now in front of him. Teddy hadn't noticed just how dark Ben's eyes were until he stood there, staring into them directly. It was in that moment that he fully appreciated just how much all of this really meant to Ben, who now feared that his two consecutive mistakes could cost him the opportunity he valued so dearly.

'Teddy, I'm really screwed. What am I supposed to tell Dylan?'

'Calm down. Mine is working fine, I'll just send you the file.'

'Are you serious? You'd . . . you'd actually do that for me?'

'You would have had the exact same audio as me, it's really not that big a deal.'

'I don't know what to say. You could tell me to piss off and I'd probably get the sack.'

Before Teddy had a chance to react, Ben threw both of his arms around him and hugged him. He couldn't believe what was happening as he stood there, his arms hanging loosely by his side. This wasn't meant to be happening. He was distracted from his discomfort by the rich floral scent of Ben's aftershave. For the briefest of seconds he could close his eyes and imagine they were alone in a vast meadow filled with flowers of every colour. Ben stepped back awkwardly, surprised by his own actions. Without saying anything, he hurried from the kitchen leaving Teddy standing alone, confused by the moment they had just shared.

Once their features were written and submitted to Dylan, they sat at their desks and anxiously awaited his feedback. They watched in silence as he scanned their documents, scribbling illegible notes on the pages in front of him.

'Before we begin,' Dylan said as he wheeled himself over

to sit between the pair, 'I spoke with Stuart a little while ago to get his feedback too.'

Teddy heard Ben groan. Neither of them had anticipated feedback from Stuart.

'He was very complimentary about you both. Arrived on time, mostly stuck to the approved topics, and when you didn't, you acted quickly to rectify the situation and keep the interviewee happy and engaged.'

'Really? That's great, I thought we might . . . well, I didn't know it had gone so well.'

'Oh, don't worry, when you piss off a publicist, you'll know all about it,' Dylan said with a grin. 'He did single you out, Teddy. Said he was really impressed with how quickly you reacted and brought the question round to something she could answer positively.'

'It's true,' Ben said, taking Teddy by surprise. 'You saved my ass and Stuart knew it.'

'Don't make a habit of it, Ben,' Dylan said. 'But there will always be days like today. Wait until you've a politician ring your mobile to call you a . . . well, I'll let you guess what.'

Dylan had highlighted various things he would have done differently in both of their submissions. Teddy could see plenty of red pen scrawled across the two pieces.

'You've both done things well here,' he concluded. 'It's pretty neck and neck, so I think ultimately it's better if you combine them into one article. Can you work together to do that?'

'So, we'd both get a byline in the actual paper?' Ben asked, sounding incredulous at the outcome. 'If it actually goes in of course.'

'It won't if you don't meet the 4 p.m. deadline,' Dylan warned, pushing himself back over to his desk.

'I can't believe it,' Ben said. 'But I don't really deserve this at all.'

'Of course you do. You heard Dylan, you obviously wrote a good piece.'

'I didn't even record it!'

'That could have happened to either of us. You know for next time to double-check.'

'An actual story in the paper, I can't believe it,' Ben repeated. He sounded giddy.

Teddy smiled at Ben's excitement. He was suddenly forced to appreciate just how much he had taken the opportunity at *The Post* for granted, not understanding just how much it would mean to him to see his name in print. Years of reading his mum's pieces and seeing her name had made it feel almost ordinary to him. It didn't matter that it would appear alongside Ben's name. In fact, seeing how much it meant to Ben made the experience even more momentous.

'Sorry about the hug earlier on,' Ben said sheepishly a short while later. 'I don't know why I did that. I'm a bit embarrassed to be honest.'

'Don't be at all,' Teddy reassured him. He couldn't help but think about the moment Ben had thrown both of his arms around his body, the smell of his aftershave. It had been nice to feel that closeness with someone.

'Listen, I'm meeting my friends Shakeel and Lexie after work. You're coming with me to celebrate. I'm not taking no for an answer.'

He didn't know what had prompted him to say it, but the

words had left his mouth before he even had a chance to talk himself out of the idea.

Lexie was practically grinning from ear to ear as she introduced herself to Ben. She didn't waste a second of their short walk to the pub and peppered him with questions about what it was like to work with Teddy. Ben smiled broadly as he explained how both he and Teddy were going to have a story in the print version of the paper.

'I can't believe you shared it,' Shakeel said, as Ben and Lexie walked ahead.

'What?' Teddy was taken aback at the tone of Shakeel's voice.

'The audio. You had the perfect chance to get ahead when he messed up. You're too nice for your own good, mate.'

'I couldn't do that, Shak. He knew I had the exact same audio anyway.'

'Just ask yourself: do you think he'd have done the same for you? I think we both know the answer to that one.'

At that moment, Ben turned around and smiled at him. Teddy felt a momentary flutter in his stomach but tried to ignore it, Shakeel's words ringing in his ears.

'I love this one!' he said, gesturing at an oblivious Lexie who was still chatting away.

Lexie was quite happy to continue her interrogation of Ben once they had got their drinks and sat down. Teddy could tell that Shakeel was trying his best to contribute, laughing and nodding along throughout the conversation. Every so often he caught Shak's eye and gave him a small smile. Lexie and Shakeel only stayed for two drinks before announcing that they had to leave. Teddy sensed that they had conspired to leave him alone with Ben. Shakeel glanced back at them as they made their way towards the exit and for a brief second, Teddy was sure he was about to stop and come back to the table.

'You feeling a bit more relaxed after today?' Teddy asked as Ben swapped chairs to sit in the one next to him.

'Much better, all thanks to you. I know we got off to a bad start with the whole competition and everything, but I just want you to know I really appreciate what you did for me today.'

Teddy felt the tingling in his stomach again as the corners of Ben's mouth rose, highlighting the deep dimples on his cheeks. What the hell was happening? This was the last thing he expected – or wanted. He shook his head. He didn't need a distraction from focusing on the job at hand. What if Shakeel was right? Would Ben really have done the same for him today? After all, Teddy was all that stood between him and the job he so desperately wanted.

'I presume you're not out to your family then,' Ben said, leaning in so close to talk that Teddy could feel his breath on his neck.

Teddy felt his chest tighten. 'Um, no. How . . . how did you know?'

'Just a guess. You remind me of when I wasn't out. I suspected you were gay too, but the fact you never mentioned it or gave anything away helped. Are you worried about someone finding out and it getting back to your mum?'

'Pretty much. I can't risk that, not yet.'

Ben listened intently as Teddy explained his relationship with his mum and why he was still hesitant about coming out.

Teddy knew that the day was approaching when he would have to deal with the situation. He couldn't put it off forever.

'I've not been easy to live with since Dad died, I know that,' Teddy said, playing with the damp beer mat on the table. 'I took a lot of my anger at the world out on Mum, especially when she started dating Dad's business partner, Ralph. It felt like everyone was moving on and I didn't really know how to. Recently, another relative came out and she hasn't exactly handled it well, so I'm not really in a rush to go through that myself.' Teddy momentarily contemplated telling Ben about his grandad, but it felt too soon to be sharing something so personal with him.

'Anyway, I didn't have too much going on when Mum told me about this opportunity, so I agreed to it to keep the peace.'

'You didn't go to uni then?'

'No, I just didn't want to leave Northbridge after my dad died.'

'That makes sense,' Ben said. 'You wanted to be there for your family. I'm sure they appreciate that.'

Teddy rolled his eyes.

'Maybe a couple of years ago. Until I said yes to doing this job, I was just there at home, watching everyone else get on with life. Sorry, a couple of drinks and I'm blabbering all of this at you.'

'It's fine, mate. It's good to get to know the real you,' Ben said. 'You're so much more than your surname or some journalist's son. You're clearly a good writer and you're a good guy, so stop putting yourself down.'

'Give over. Stop being so bloody nice or I'll think you're just buttering me up for something.'

Ben grinned back at him before taking another sip of his drink.

They left the pub a short while later. Teddy tightened the scarf around his neck as they pushed their way through the blustering autumn wind. He watched as Ben shoved both of his hands into his jacket pockets to protect them from the cold. There was something about this guy. Sure, he was his rival, Teddy thought to himself, but they had a lot in common too. They couldn't be anything more than friendly colleagues though, right? But even as he thought it, he felt his stomach flutter again. Damn. This was definitely not meant to be happening.

CHAPTER ELEVEN
Arthur

'WHY EXACTLY ARE we getting rid of all this stuff now, Grandad?'

'No time like the present,' Arthur said, panting as he finally reached the top of the narrow ladder and stepped into the large attic.

Teddy had gone straight to his grandparents' house after arriving back in Northbridge from work. Arthur wasted no time in beginning to rummage through the cardboard boxes, carefully examining various objects, most of which he no longer recognized.

'Your Nan would know what to do with all of this much better than I do,' he grumbled. 'I have no idea why we kept half of this stuff in the first place, but here we are.'

Madeleine called them downstairs for lunch a short while later, eager to find out what they had discovered. She was particularly intrigued by a tall, narrow vase Teddy described, convinced it was one which had belonged to her late mother. Arthur also delighted her by pulling a gold brooch out of his pocket.

'Arthur!' Madeleine said, her eyes immediately filling with tears. 'Where did you find it?'

'At the bottom of a big bloody box. It was just lying there. Only caught a little glint in the corner of my eye and went digging and there she was, beautiful as the first day I saw her.'

'What's this?' Teddy asked.

'Years ago, your grandfather, being the romantic he is, took me to a car boot sale. I was furious with him for dragging me along to look at all kinds of junk. Then he spotted this. We both knew it was worth more than it was on sale for, but this one still couldn't resist haggling with the pair selling it.' She looked over at Arthur, her eyes sparkling.

'Knew as soon as I laid my eyes on it that it was special,' Arthur said proudly. 'Just look at it still – 18-carat gold, William at the jeweller's told me.'

'I forgot how much you loved car boot sales, Grandad,' Teddy said. He remembered going to several when he was younger with his dad. They were usually selling, but Teddy had enjoyed being able to walk around and see the things other people were getting rid of.

'It's been years since I was at one, I don't even know if they still do the one in the big car park near the hospital.'

'Oh!' Madeleine said. 'That reminds me, they phoned about your next review. Doctor Thomas is back from holiday next week.'

'That's great, I'll call back and confirm. I actually wanted to have a quick word with him,' Arthur said, before turning his attention back to Teddy. 'Could you find out about the car boot sale for me please, Teddy?'

'Sure, you want to see if you still have an eye for a bargain?'

'Better, I think we could go and make a few quid ourselves.'

The thought of being able to offload some of the finds in

the attic gave Arthur a new energy as he dug through the stuffed boxes that afternoon. Now their objective was to separate the items worth selling into a pile for Madeleine to give her approval to. Teddy was going through a box of old clothes. One worn leather jacket in particular caught his eye.

'Was this yours?' he asked, holding it up.

Arthur nearly gasped.

'For the love of God, I can't believe that thing's been sitting up here all this time. That takes me right back.'

'This is a really cool jacket, Grandad.'

'I remember buying it with my first pay cheque. I thought I was the bee's knees with that thing on.' Arthur smiled fondly.

'You just needed the bike.' Teddy laughed.

'I had it!'

'*You did not!*'

'As I live and breathe, the Norton Commando my uncle Frank gave to me. Your grandmother hated that thing. She was sure I was going to come off it. I sold it just after your mum was born. Broke my heart seeing it go.'

'Whoa, you've had such a cool life. Well, I mean—' Teddy stopped, embarrassed.

'It's okay. I have been very lucky, you're right. It's a good reminder of just how lucky I've been.'

They fell silent for a moment.

'Do you want to add this to the sell pile, Grandad?' Teddy asked gently.

Arthur stared at it, his eyes widening in delight as an idea popped into his head.

'Why don't you try it on? Go on, see how it looks.'

Teddy pulled the jacket on over his T-shirt, grinning as he looked down at it, impressed.

'Would you look at that, it fits like a glove. I think that jacket has chosen its new owner.' It filled Arthur with warmth to see Teddy in his beloved old jacket.

'Are you sure, Grandad?'

'If you want it, of course. Don't feel obliged to for my sake.'

'No! I absolutely *love* it. Thank you so much.'

'That's that sorted then. We'll call it twenty-five quid with family discount.'

Teddy laughed.

The sell pile grew into two large bundles. There weren't that many boxes left now, only a few battered ones tucked away under a beam.

Several spiders scuttled away at speed as Arthur pulled open the box on top, wiping away the dust and cobwebs. It had clearly been a number of decades since these boxes had last been opened. His hands stilled. Arthur knew instantly what was inside.

'Are you okay, Grandad?'

Arthur looked up to see Teddy staring back at him.

'Just memories. You forget about the things you store away sometimes.'

'What is it?'

'Nothing valuable. Old stuff.'

'Grandad, you can talk to me. You don't have to keep things hidden anymore, remember?'

Arthur reached into the box and lifted out a photo album. The bottle-green cover was faded and battered. He couldn't bring himself to open it.

'You can have a look, if you'd like,' he said, handing it across to Teddy.

While Teddy opened up the album, Arthur reached back into the box and lifted out a small bundle of white envelopes. His heart pounded as he stared at the neat handwriting on the top one. His own name stared back at him. Every letter of it had been written with great care. He could picture the very fountain pen that had been used.

'What are those?' Teddy asked, looking up from the album.

'Just some old letters.'

'From Nan?'

'Yes, nothing that you need to be reading.'

Arthur stuffed the bundle into his back pocket. He didn't want to focus on the letters right now.

'Grandad, I don't know who half these people are,' Teddy said, turning the album round to show Arthur the photographs.

'That's your great-great-uncle Gregory and his wife Margaret. They moved to the United States not long after this was taken,' Arthur said, pointing.

'And this is Frank with the bike?'

'It is indeed. He was great fun. Poor man, just dropped dead one afternoon. It was the first time I remember seeing my dad cry.'

'Your dad's in here, too,' Teddy said, skipping back several pages to find the photograph he had seen. 'Here he is.'

Arthur looked down and saw the younger version of his father smiling back at him.

'He looks happy,' Teddy said.

'He does. It's not a memory of him I really have.'

'Really? That's sad.'

'Different times. He had so much going on.'

'Do you miss him, Grandad?'

'I do. He wasn't perfect and I've felt a lot of anger towards him over the years, but he was still my father. He gave me the chance to build the life I have.'

Arthur stared at the picture. He recognized the suit his father was wearing. It had been one of his favourites, usually saved for only the most important meetings or events. Arthur knew he must only have been a toddler when the image was taken, so he had no idea what the event might have been.

'Did your dad know you were gay?'

Teddy's question took Arthur by surprise. He closed the album and held it against his chest. He could feel his heart thumping as he allowed himself to focus on the memories of his youth.

'He did. We didn't really talk about it like that. It wasn't about who I might have loved. He called it a sickness, a disease.'

'Grandad, that's awful. I don't understand how or why you stayed here.'

'Fear, Teddy. I had nothing except what he allowed me to have. And then . . .' His voice trailed off. Arthur hadn't spoken about this to anyone for over fifty years.

'You don't have to tell me if it's too difficult.'

Arthur waved his hand to reassure Teddy that he was fine with the conversation. Just knowing that Teddy was gay too seemed to make it easier for him to open up and revisit the painful memories.

'It was 1963 when Jack Johnson arrived in Northbridge. My father had hired him to work in the garage with me and old Derek Brady, a lovely fella who had worked for him for twenty years. Jack was a hell of a mechanic. He walked in there looking like someone from the silver screen, like a young Brando. I hated everything about him.'

'You did?' Teddy asked, leaning forward. 'I know that feeling.'

'He was everything I wanted to be, or so I thought. He had my father's respect, the confidence to tell him when he was wrong about something.'

'So what changed?'

'I did,' Arthur said quietly. 'I understood why I was forcing myself to fight Jack on everything. He knew it too. One night, well, we had a few drinks and we . . . well, it's all ancient history now, isn't it?'

'How long did you keep it secret?'

'It was nearly three years. He waited and waited for me. I kept telling him I would do it and that we would finally be free of this place.'

'Why didn't you?'

'I couldn't bring myself to do it in the end, to tell either of my parents. I thought we were safe and we'd eventually have our time. It was foolish of me to think that could ever happen.'

Teddy frowned and shook his head slowly. 'Jack left Northbridge?'

'Derek Brady caught us. He wasn't due to come back to the garage. He went straight to my father. I'd never seen Dad so angry. He'd never been physically violent towards me until that night.'

'I'm so sorry, Grandad. That's awful.'

Arthur paused. He hadn't let himself think about what had happened for so long that it was hard to find the words.

'I thought there might be a chance things would improve once it was out in the open,' he finally said. 'But it didn't. The next day some thugs attacked Jack and left him for dead.'

'Are you serious? You're not saying your dad—'

'He made sure it happened. Then he warned me that Jack wouldn't survive the next time. He told me I'd be next if I didn't *fix* myself.'

Teddy sat in total silence.

'I let Jack leave so he could go and live the life he deserved.'

'But you deserved that life too!'

'I thought I had missed my chance. I almost got Jack killed for it. I married your grandmother and did everything I could to make sure we were happy.'

'What about Jack?'

'He wrote a couple of times. He avoided saying where he went immediately after leaving here. I told him he had to stop sending letters. It wasn't fair to either of us, we both needed to move on.'

'And?'

'I presume he did. I haven't heard from him since 1967.'

Teddy was silent. Arthur waited patiently.

'How much of this does Nan know?' he finally asked.

'Everything. She was the one who found Jack after the attack. I was in a complete mess, but she was there for me. She knew what it was like to have a father like mine. William Montgomery was a brute of a man. He was already trying to marry your nan off to the son of one of his business associates.'

'What?' Teddy said, shocked to learn about the life his nan had escaped. 'How did she get out of it?'

'I proposed. We planned it for weeks. At first, I thought our relationship might just be enough to save us both from our families, but over time, we found our kind of happiness. One year turned into ten.'

'Did you love Nan?'

Arthur closed his eyes as if he was taking himself back over fifty years.

'We fell in love over time. It was a very real love, I can't explain it. I'll always love your nan, but it was never the same love I had for Jack.'

'Do you ever wonder what he's doing now?'

Arthur's hands felt clammy. It had been many years since he'd spoken about Jack out loud to another person.

'Sometimes,' he said softly. 'I just hope he had a good life, whatever he's doing, wherever he is.'

'You know we could probably find him if you wanted to, right?'

'No,' Arthur said sternly, sitting up straight on the stool. 'You mustn't do that. Please promise me that. I'd rather have the memories.'

'I understand. I promise I won't.'

'Thank you. I don't want to disrupt his life. I didn't do any of this for that.'

Teddy's phone started to ring. Arthur watched as he glanced at the screen and put it back in his pocket.

'Avoiding someone?' he asked.

'Mum. I'll probably need to get home soon.'

'How is she?' He felt a twinge of guilt at sharing so much with Teddy and expecting him to keep it all private, especially when he was keeping his own secret from Elizabeth.

'She's fine. Between work and wedding planning, she's too busy to follow my every move.'

'Be nice, young man.' Arthur laughed. 'You've got a mum who loves and cares for you.'

'I suppose. I don't think she'd run the boy I think I like out of town, at least.'

Arthur's ears pricked up.

'The boy you *think* you like? When did this happen?'

He listened as Teddy told him all about Ben, from the tension between them as the competition got underway to how they were now texting outside of work. Arthur clapped his hands together as Teddy finished talking.

'That butterflies in your stomach feeling takes me back. You're smiling even talking about him. I think you know exactly how you feel; you just need to *talk to him*. What's the worst that could happen?'

Teddy gave a small hollow laugh.

'The thing is, I can't do anything about it, so why bother telling him?'

'Did you just listen to what I told you, young man?' Arthur said, throwing his arms up in the air. 'Don't waste these years trying to please other people. This boy might not last forever, but give yourself that chance to find out. Your mum has found happiness twice. Don't pass up your own chance.'

'Thanks, Grandad. I'll try to find the right moment.'

It was only a few minutes later, as they carried on sorting through more old belongings, that Teddy said that he had an idea he wanted to run by him.

'Go on,' Arthur said, excited.

'If we're going to the car boot sale, do you mind if I invite Ben to come along?'

'Of course not! I can make myself scarce,' Arthur said, delighted.

'Don't be daft, we'll need you to stop those hagglers taking advantage of us!'

Their laughter was interrupted by the abrupt sound of someone calling up the ladder.

'Edward Marsh!'

Arthur felt his blood run cold at the sound of Elizabeth's voice.

Teddy staggered forwards towards the ladder and looked down onto the landing. Arthur saw the colour drain from his grandson's cheeks.

'I should have known,' she said, and Arthur could hear the sneering tone in her voice. 'Of course you would sneak round here when I specifically told you not to.'

'You can't stop me from seeing my own grandad.'

'I've told you before; while you're under my roof, you will respect my wishes, Now get down, we're going.'

Arthur nodded at him. 'Go on, do as she says now, good lad.'

He watched as Teddy reluctantly stepped onto the ladder and began his descent. Arthur hesitated but decided to go after them. They were already back downstairs.

'Elizabeth,' he called out to her as he made his way down the stairs towards them. 'Please, don't be too hard on him. He was just helping us clear the attic.'

She stopped, her hand still gripping the door handle.

'Because he's a good boy. He idolises you, but that doesn't

mean you get to encourage him to go against my wishes. You could do that much for me at the very least.'

'I miss you all,' Arthur blurted out as Elizabeth pulled the door open.

'You know what, Daddy? I woke up this morning and it was the first morning I thought I missed you too. Then I find out you're both here, hanging out like I just don't matter, like what I want isn't worth paying attention to. Do you both just complain about what a terrible person I am? A horrible daughter and mother?'

'Nobody has ever thought or said that, Lizzie. Your mum and I mean it when we say that we want you to take all the time you need, and we'll be here when you're ready.'

'Good! If you really mean that, you'll tell Teddy to stay away.' She left without looking back. Teddy mouthed goodbye and followed behind her.

Madeleine came out of the kitchen, wiping her flour-covered hands on her apron.

'Why are you smiling, Arthur?'

He turned to her, taking both of her warm hands in his. 'You heard her, she missed me. It might not be much, but it's a start. That's all I needed to hear.'

Madeleine pulled her hands free of his and wrapped her arms around him, leaving two small white handprints on his back.

CHAPTER TWELVE
Teddy

HIS MUM AND Ralph had spent most of the week organizing the guest list for their wedding. Despite her initial insistence that it would be a low-key affair, Teddy knew that Ralph knew better than to argue as the plans began to develop.

'If we aim for 150 at the ceremony, I can keep the reception to around 250.'

'Dare I ask how many of those are from my side?' Ralph asked, playfully rolling his eyes in Teddy's direction.

'You know I'm still going to be upsetting people, even with that number of guests.'

'I know, darling. They'll have to wait for the photographs.'

'You're including Stace and Oliver in that figure, Mum?' Eleanor piped up.

'Of course, of course, all taken care of.'

'Hang on,' Teddy said, suddenly paying more attention. 'You're bringing your best mate and your boyfriend to Mum's wedding?'

'Stacey is like family,' his mum said. 'And we need to see how good Oliver looks in his tux.'

'Mum, stop! He hasn't even hinted at proposing yet,' Eleanor said, blushing.

'Sorry, before we start marrying off Eleanor and Oliver, can I bring Shak and Lexie?'

His mum bit her lip. 'I have you down for a plus one. I thought you might like to try and find someone to bring along in a slightly different capacity.'

Teddy felt Eleanor's eyes on him.

'I hadn't really given it much thought. It would just be fun to have the guys there too, you know. You've known Shakeel as long as Stacey.'

'That's fine, I can squeeze them both in. It's just a shame you won't have anyone special there, like your sisters. It would be lovely to see you happy.'

For the tiniest of moments Teddy felt the urge to grab the opportunity with both hands, but before he could even begin to contemplate it, Eleanor changed the subject. He zoned out as she started talking about her day at the veterinary surgery.

'I hear work is going well,' Ralph said, leaning in to talk to him.

'Yeah, it's not bad at all. I'm enjoying it much more than I thought I would.'

'I figured.'

'Oh? What makes you say that?'

Ralph paused for a brief second, his eyes darting across towards Elizabeth.

'Well, we couldn't help but notice that you've had a bit more of a spring in your step the last couple of days. You've been, dare I say it, smiling a little more around the house, especially when you're on that thing.' He pointed at the phone in Teddy's hand.

Had he really been that obvious? It had been much simpler when Ben was just the annoying know-it-all he could complain about. Now he had to remind himself not to walk around with a permanent grin on his face both at home and work.

'Is that why Mum was talking about a plus one for the wedding?'

'Let's just say it has been discussed.'

'Oh God, that's mortifying!'

'You know she only wants to see you kids happy, especially after everything you've been through over the last few years.'

'Thanks, Ralph, I'll bear that in mind.'

Teddy thought long and hard about what Ralph had said that evening. Everything was telling him to finally do it, to take control and be brave. He was proud of who he was after all, wasn't he? There had been a period in his early teenage years when he had tried to convince himself that he wasn't gay, but that had been short-lived. He'd avoided it for too long. All he wanted to do was finally tell the people closest to him the truth.

His phone vibrated.

'Hey, Shak,' Teddy said, as his friend's face appeared on the screen.

'Hello. Thought I'd check in and see how everything's going.'

'Not bad, you know how it goes. It was a bit awkward when Mum caught me up at Grandad's house, but she seems to have let it go. It helps that she and Ralph are living and breathing the wedding. By the way, you're going to need a tux for the big day.'

'I'm coming?' Shakeel sounded surprised.

'Of course, you are!' Teddy grinned. 'You're like the closest thing to a brother I've ever had.'

Teddy was too busy talking to notice the corners of Shakeel's mouth drop suddenly.

'I couldn't not have you and Lex there. I don't think I could get through it without you, honestly. Eleanor's already practising catching the bouquet.'

'Don't get any ideas about beating her to it,' Shak teased, quickly recomposing himself. 'But if you ask me nicely, I'll consider marrying you.'

'You're far too good for me. I wouldn't stand a chance.'

'I could slum it for a while.'

'I'll save you the hassle,' Teddy said with a laugh. 'Anyway, I don't want to scare Ben off, but do you think he'd come with me?'

'You . . . you actually think you want to ask him out still?'

'Honestly, Shak, ever since that day interviewing Neena, something has changed. He's really quite sweet. I know we got off on the wrong foot, but a lot of that was down to me misjudging him. He's not like—'

'I'm actually going on a second date with someone tonight,' Shakeel blurted out. 'I don't want to jinx it, but he's really lovely.'

'Shak!' Teddy exclaimed, forgetting what he had been saying about Ben. 'That's great news. Tell me everything.'

'I will, but not yet. It's early days.'

'Pleeeeeeease, come on, give me his name.'

'No chance! I'll tell you more at the weekend if you're free, okay?' he said, eventually cracking under pressure from Teddy's best puppy-dog eyes. 'I know Lex is away, but it'd be great to see you.'

'Ah sorry, mate, not this weekend. I really need to catch up on some work on Saturday and I'm going to a car boot sale with Grandad on Sunday.'

If Shak was disappointed, he hid it well. 'I could come to the car boot sale and give you both a hand, if you like? I've not seen Arthur in so long.'

'Well actually . . .' Teddy hesitated. 'I'm thinking of inviting Ben.'

'Oh, right, that's okay.'

'It's a stupid idea, isn't it? What the hell am I thinking? Why would he want to hang out with me and my grandad in his free time?'

'Hey, I'd drop everything to spend the day with your grandad, even if you weren't there.'

'Piss off!' Teddy laughed. 'But listen, if you do want to pop along, it'd be great to see you.'

'Sorry, I just remembered Sunday isn't a good day. I forgot I'd made plans already. Listen, I better go, my dinner's almost ready.'

'All right, Shak, chat you—'

Click. The screen went black.

Teddy stared back at his own reflection. That had been so . . . abrupt. Shakeel must have been in a rush to go; perhaps he was already running late for his mysterious date. Teddy made a mental note to press Lexie for more details. Perhaps she would have more luck in getting information out of Shakeel about this mystery new man.

*

Teddy waited until Friday afternoon to pluck up the courage to invite Ben to Northbridge. He wasn't sure how Ben would react to the offer, but they'd been getting along much better recently. He couldn't deny that it was nice to have someone to have lunch with every day. Over the course of their conversations he found out that Ben was still single and going on dates to keep himself occupied in the evenings.

'I was wondering if you might like to spend Sunday in Northbridge with me?' Teddy said, after swallowing a mouthful of his lunch. He watched as Ben processed the invite while chewing on his own sandwich.

'I'm intrigued,' he said. 'What have you got planned?'

'It's nothing major, I'm just helping my grandad out at a car boot sale and thought it might be fun to hang out together.'

'I've never been to a car boot sale for a date, Teddy.' Ben grinned.

'I . . . who said anything about a date?'

'Your face did. You've been far too nosy about my dating life all week. I just can't believe it took you until this afternoon to finally pluck up the courage to ask me. Were you afraid I'd say no?'

'Don't make me regret this,' Teddy said, knowing full well he couldn't possibly regret it if he tried to. 'It's fine though, don't worry if you have plans.'

'I don't,' Ben said quickly. 'And if I did, I'd already be cancelling them.'

Teddy couldn't help but smile as he felt his cheeks flush. Ben had said yes, he was finally able to breathe. Now all he had to do was keep the date a secret, right under the nose of his entire family.

*

'Have a lovely time, you two,' Teddy said as he stood at the front door to wave off his mum and Ralph. Ralph had surprised Elizabeth with an overnight stay at a spa hotel. Teddy couldn't believe his luck when he found out over dinner the previous night. He wouldn't need to be looking over his shoulder, worried his mum might see him in town with Ben and his grandad. Lying in bed, he wondered what the hell he had been thinking suggesting that Ben come to Northbridge. This wasn't a risk he would normally take at all. Even with his mum away, there were eyes and ears all over the place. It would only take one nosy neighbour to say something in passing.

'No parties,' Ralph said with a wink.

'He's joking, but you know what your sisters are like,' his mum added. 'Don't give me any reason to ask your grandfather to come down and check on you.'

The words had left her mouth before she could stop them. Her eyes widened as she realized what she had said. 'Don't say anything,' she said, pointing her finger at Teddy. 'Just . . . best behaviour please.' Teddy was convinced he saw her eyes fill with tears before she climbed into the car.

Teddy had arranged to meet Ben at the town's train station first thing on Sunday morning. He had already been up at his grandparents' and helped pack the car. Arthur was going to drive out to the site early, and he and Ben were going to meet him there at 10 a.m. to start setting up.

'Fancy meeting you here,' Ben said.

Ben threw both arms around him and hugged him. Unlike his first experience of hugging Ben, this time he replicated the gesture and put his own arms around him in return. The smell of Ben's freshly applied aftershave hit Teddy and his heart leapt as it filled his nostrils.

'You, erm, smell really good,' he said, stepping back and almost bumping into someone walking past.

'Especially for you. First time I've got to wear this one actually.'

'I'm honoured. Are you hungry?'

'I am if you're buying.'

'Well seeing as you've ventured out of the city for me, I think I can spring for a sausage sandwich.'

'Sausage on a first date? I knew you were a dark horse.'

Cora's café wasn't too far from the station. Teddy was surprised to find that there were only a handful of empty tables when they arrived.

'Busy today, Cora,' Teddy said as they took the small table closest to the counter. Cora followed them so that she could move the empty plates which had been left behind by the previous customers.

'The car boot sale always draws the crowd, lovely,' she said. 'They come from far and wide to get rid of their junk. It's not my idea of a fun day out, I'll tell you that for free.'

He didn't bother explaining that they were going to be among those doing just that as she tottered off back to the kitchen. Distracted by his plan to invite Ben along, Teddy realized that he hadn't given much thought to actually trying to sell some of what he and his grandad had saved for today.

'Have you ever done this before, Ben?' he asked.

'Had breakfast with someone?'

'No,' Teddy sighed, rolling his eyes. 'Have you ever sold stuff at a car boot sale before?'

'No, but it can't be that difficult, can it?'

'I hope not. The locals will all know Grandad so that might make it a bit easier.'

'You'll have to give me the official tour of Northbridge. I'm intrigued from everything you've told me about it,' Ben said, leaning forward in his chair.

'It's really not that exciting, but we can walk through town when we're finished here.'

Cora arrived back carrying two full fry-ups and two mugs of tea. The smell of the crispy bacon and fried tomatoes made Teddy's mouth water. He hadn't noticed just how hungry he was until he began piling the hot food onto his fork.

'So far though, I'm pretty impressed by what Northbridge has to offer,' Ben said as he tucked into his breakfast. He looked up at Teddy, and Teddy suddenly wondered if Ben was talking about the town or about Teddy.

After leaving Cora's, Teddy took Ben along the high street as they made their way towards the car park beside the hospital.

'It's not so bad here,' Ben said, looking around at the shops. Teddy really couldn't argue with him. The town always looked welcoming, especially on a sunny autumnal day like today. The perfect displays of every shop front along the high street were ready and waiting to draw in shoppers who suddenly found themselves eager to spend their money.

'Do you like living here?' Ben asked as they crossed the quiet street.

'I guess. I always imagined getting out of here, but now I don't know anymore.'

'Did you want to leave because you were gay?'

'Pretty much,' Teddy said, glancing around to make sure

no one had heard Ben. 'I know it's a cliché, but haven't we all had the dreams of living in the big city where no one really cares who you are?'

'I get you. I was the same, but there's still a part of me that wants that whole life in the suburbs thing I grew up knowing.'

'Really?' Teddy said, his voice filled with surprise at Ben's admission.

'One day, maybe. I could imagine myself somewhere like this.'

'And you had the cheek to call me a dark horse! Let's see if you still feel the same way after chatting with my grandad for a few hours.'

Arthur had pulled up and secured himself a prime spot in the large car park when Teddy and Ben arrived. More cars were arriving, with small groups of eager people already milling around the tables.

'Watch that lot, they'll stand over you when you're unpacking just to make sure they're first to spot a bargain,' Arthur said, indicating the early patrons.

'Grandad, this is Ben King,' Teddy said, ignoring the couple who were already standing on the other side of the table.

'Pleasure to meet you, Benjamin. Thank you for coming along today to help.'

'Lovely to meet you too, Arthur. Let me know what I can do to help.'

'Eager to get his hands dirty,' Arthur said, laying his hand on Ben's shoulder affectionately before turning to Teddy. 'I like this one already.'

'Not just my hands,' Ben whispered to Teddy as Arthur

began unloading the boot. Teddy suppressed a gasp and rushed forward to take a heavy box from his grandad.

People were making offers for their items before the three had even had time to finish unpacking the car. Arthur took charge of sales while Teddy and Ben added items to the table to replace those which had been sold.

'He's a born salesman,' Ben said, watching as Arthur somehow offloaded an old belt for more than he had originally asked for.

'They don't stand a chance against that charm.' Teddy laughed. 'Who's going to argue with someone who's almost eighty over a few quid?'

The crowds kept coming throughout the morning and into the early afternoon. Teddy recognized a few faces, but on the whole he didn't know many of the people who rummaged through the contents of their table. He remembered what Cora had said about the event always attracting people from far and wide to the town. He was glad they were all strangers. It was nice not to feel like he was under observation or worrying about who could report back to his mum about seeing him with his grandad.

Teddy felt Ben's elbow gently poke into his side, disturbing him from watching an elderly couple who were enthusiastically discussing items on the table.

'What's up?' Teddy asked.

'That guy, do you know him?' Ben nodded towards a middle-aged bald man who was staring across at them. He was engaged in conversation with another man of a similar age, but seemed distracted by their presence. Teddy didn't recognize either of them. The bigger of the two was scowling in their direction, but it wasn't until he started walking towards their set-up that Teddy could see that his attention was focused on Arthur.

'Do you really think you should be here at a family event?'

The man's voice boomed from behind several people who were directly in front of the table. Arthur looked up, his eyes wide and suddenly filled with fear. The man towered over those who had now turned around to see who had caused the sudden disturbance.

'Why don't you and your friends pack up and leave. No one wants your kind round here,' the bald man said, his voice carrying. 'There's families having a nice day out.'

Those caught between Arthur and the man were now watching for Arthur's response as if they were special guests in the Royal Box at Wimbledon's Centre Court.

'Sorry, who do you think you're speaking for?' Teddy asked. He could feel his heart thudding in his chest. Shakeel's words of warning advising him not to escalate a situation filled his head.

'Everyone who is too afraid to say what they're really thinking,' the bald man yelled. 'Disgusting that anyone would even touch, never mind buy this old pervert's junk.'

Teddy clenched his fist but felt Arthur's hand grip his shoulder before he responded to the man himself.

'I'm very sorry to hear you have a problem with me being here to sell some bits and pieces,' Arthur said mildly. 'I don't think I know you, but I assume you have a problem with me being a gay man?'

'Bloody disgusting. Pack up and go home,' the man spat back.

'You certainly don't have to buy anything from me, but we won't be going anywhere.'

The man stormed off shaking his head. Several people who had stopped to watch the altercation began to move on without saying a word. Others kept their heads down as they began to filter out to various other sellers.

'Are you okay?' Teddy asked. His own heart was still pounding, and his hands were shaking.

'You have to promise me you won't get caught up in fights, Teddy,' Arthur said, looking up at him. 'If you ever face men like that, don't rise to it and give them the satisfaction. I couldn't bear to see anything happen to you.'

'I won't, Grandad. But I'm sorry you had to experience that.'

'He isn't the first and he won't be the last. Things have changed a lot since I was a young man, Teddy, but there are still plenty of people out there who will think who you love is a good enough reason to hate you. They shout loudest to make themselves heard.'

Teddy shook his head. 'So we just have to keep ignoring them? I'm really trying to get my head round that.'

Once he felt calmer, and was sure his grandad was okay, Teddy returned to the table.

After a while Arthur rejoined them and was quickly back in the flow of selling. It wasn't long before they had nothing left in the back of the car and only a handful of items remained on the table to be picked at by the stragglers.

'Fancy a little walk around?' Teddy asked Ben as a woman tried to haggle the price of a cup and saucer down.

'Sure, I want to see what that car over there has left.'

'You've been keeping an eye on the competition?'

'Damn right, they've been even busier than we have!'

They walked in the direction of the black BMW estate. Several people were huddled around a corner of the table, seemingly deep in conversation with the man who owned the vehicle. Teddy scanned the table. Nothing particularly interesting had been left behind by the bargain hunters. He was almost ready to walk away when Ben gasped.

'I haven't had a Rubik's cube in years!' he said, lifting the toy out from under an old edition of the *Radio Times*. 'I was able to solve this in forty-five seconds when I was younger.'

'I've never been more attracted to you.' Teddy laughed.

'You joke, but people at school actually paid to see me do this.'

'Buy it then! How much is it?'

'Excuse me,' Ben called out to the man. 'How much for the cube?'

'Two quid, mate.'

'I'll give you one. Come on, every little helps clear the table.'

'Or . . .' Teddy interrupted. 'If he can complete it in less than a minute, you just let him have it.'

The man folded his arms and considered the offer, his eyes narrowing. 'Fifty seconds or less and you can have it.'

'Deal!' Teddy said, so excited he forgot to even check with Ben that he could take on the challenge.

'What are you doing? I haven't done this in years,' Ben whispered, suddenly looking slightly nervous.

'I know you can do it.'

The other browsers had stopped to listen to the exchange and were now eagerly watching Ben. One of them called out to a friend to come over, and before long a small group had assembled around the table. Ben shook his head at Teddy, who couldn't help but laugh at the situation they had suddenly found themselves in.

'Fifty seconds,' the man reiterated. 'Starting in three . . . two . . . one.'

The crowd gave a cheer of encouragement as Ben began twisting the cube. His fingers were moving so fast Teddy couldn't even begin to figure out what he was doing. Whatever it was seemed to be working, as the coloured sides began to take shape.

'Go on, Ben!' Teddy called.

'Ten seconds.'

'Five seconds.' The group of watching people began to join in with the countdown.

'Four . . .'

'Three . . .'

'Done! I'm done!' Ben shouted, his face now bright red, holding the completed cube up in the air.

A round of applause broke out among the crowd.

'It's all yours,' the man behind the table said, joining in with the clapping. 'That thing has been lying around our house for years and nobody has even come close to doing what you just did.'

'I knew you could do it,' Teddy said, reaching out to grab Ben's hand. 'That was bloody brilliant!'

'It really was,' a familiar voice said, interrupting them.

Eleanor was walking alongside Teddy, smiling like she had just cracked an unsolved mystery.

Teddy felt his heart sink as his arm dropped to his side again.

'Hey,' she said, giving a little wave in Ben's direction. 'I'm Eleanor, the older sister.'

'What are you doing here?' Teddy hissed.

'Chill, Teddy. I just thought I'd take a little walk down and have a look around.'

'Yeah right, because you love a car boot sale.'

'Fine. Daisy got a text from Cassie who mentioned seeing Grandad here with you. Then she mentioned the cute boy you were with. So . . .'

'This is exactly what I meant about escaping here,' Teddy muttered to Ben who had stuffed the cube into his jacket pocket. 'You came down here just for a nosy, Eleanor?'

'I couldn't turn down the chance to come and see the boy who has been making my brother grin like a lovesick puppy!'

Teddy felt the colour drain from his face.

'Wh . . . what?'

'Oh, come on, Teddy!' Eleanor laughed. 'Do you think I live on another planet?'

Ben attempted to step away. 'I should let you guys talk in private.'

'No!' Teddy and Eleanor said in unison.

'You sure?'

'Absolutely. What the hell, Eleanor?'

'I thought you'd be happy that I know.' Her eyebrows edged closer together.

'I am, don't get me wrong, I just didn't expect to be ambushed.'

'Don't exaggerate, Teddy. It's not like Mum's here.'

Teddy's blood ran cold. 'Wait, does she know?'

'Oh, not a clue. I'm pretty sure she's totally oblivious. She probably still thinks you're madly in love with Lexi.'

Teddy's heart sank. It wasn't the answer he wanted. Deep down, part of him had hoped that his mum would pull a similar stunt and admit that she had known all along.

'Do you think she'll react like she did with Grandad?'

'She'll be fine,' Eleanor said breezily. 'It's not like it is with Grandad. No matter what you think of her sometimes, you'll always be her baby boy.'

Eleanor stopped to bend down and tie her shoe lace.

Teddy felt Ben nudge him as they continued to walk on slowly. 'I didn't know you liked me that much.'

'That could change if your head gets any bigger.'

'You know what?' Ben laughed, practically skipping as they made their way back to Arthur's car. 'I'm starting to really love it here in Northbridge.'

CHAPTER THIRTEEN
Arthur

'WHAT'S WRONG? YOU'VE been quiet ever since you got back from the boot sale yesterday,' Madeleine said, settling down to catch up on their latest recording of the *Antiques Roadshow*. 'I thought you all had a nice time?'

Arthur gave a non-committal shrug. He had tried not to dwell on it, but the bald man's words kept playing in his mind.

'What happened?' Madeleine asked, pausing the programme.

'Just some idiot. I didn't even recognize him, but somehow he knew me.'

'Oh, Arthur. Don't let them get you down.' She watched him closely, her face filled with concern at the despondency in his voice.

'I normally wouldn't, but it was just the last thing I expected and it happened in front of Teddy. What about that man's children? Are they growing up listening to those same views?'

'Did Teddy or his friend not say anything?' Madeleine asked him.

'They did. I don't want him worrying about me, but it's such a stark reminder that no matter how much changes around us, some things never do. Those words take me right back to that time all those years ago . . . and I'm that coward who almost let a man die again.'

'Arthur Edwards, don't you dare. You are not responsible for men like your father.'

He didn't want to dwell on the subject any longer, so decided to change the subject.

'Teddy's young friend was very nice,' he said. 'It's a shame he couldn't come back for dinner.'

'I'm sure there will be plenty of opportunities for that. It's lovely for Teddy to have another friend to spend some time with.'

Arthur nodded. Madeleine still didn't know about Teddy, and Arthur would continue to honour his grandson's request to keep it to himself. Madeleine hit Play on the programme and became engrossed in the valuation of a pair of old paintings. She had always loved art, and had been responsible for starting an art class in Northbridge for senior citizens which was still going strong. Having had his fill of trying to put a price on old junk for the weekend, Arthur excused himself and went out to the back garden.

He strolled down the narrow garden path towards an old metal table and chair which were tucked away out of view under the shade of a large willow tree. Once upon a time this had been his 'thinking place', or as Madeleine had correctly named it, his 'secret smoking spot'. He hadn't smoked in over twenty years, but the urge to have a cigarette had been building in him all week. It didn't matter though; he would never smoke again. He had just celebrated his fifty-eighth birthday when he had collapsed in the showroom. Having a stent inserted had been a wake-up call, so with Madeleine's encouragement he had given up smoking and never looked back. His father had died of a heart attack in his seventies, something that had hung over Arthur as he celebrated his most recent birthdays. Now, as he approached his eightieth birthday, he knew he should feel excited about having a second chance. Instead, he felt torn.

He hadn't given much thought to what would follow coming out to his family. Life had simply moved on and seemed to expect him to do the same. There was no guidebook for this, no one to advise a seventy-nine-year-old on how to suddenly live the life he had only ever imagined in his head. He had to figure everything out for himself now. He thought of Teddy and Ben, potentially embarking on something new and exciting and with their whole lives to look forward to.

But Arthur felt the weight of his years keenly. He had taken to scanning the daily newspapers for anything that might inspire him to the old passions and excitement of youth. His searches had proved fruitless; he'd tried most of it before.

Bowls made him feel older than he was.

Fishing required a level of patience he had never had.

Scrabble had been fun until he was beaten by Maureen Green's granddaughter, who still took great pleasure in reminding him every time they bumped into each other.

It had become impossible to talk to Madeleine about his thoughts. She didn't need to hear about these worries after being so supportive of him. Despite her insistence that she was there for him, he knew that she must be experiencing something similar as she tried to work out what was next for her.

'Can we talk?' Arthur asked Madeleine that night, once the evening news had finished.

'What's wrong?'

He immediately felt bad when he heard the concern in her voice.

'That's what I wanted to ask you.'

'You did? Why?'

'I've been thinking . . .'

'Oh dear.'

'. . . and I don't want you to feel like you have to stop living just because of me and the choices I've made.'

'We've been over this, Arthur.' She unfolded her arms.

'I know we have, but I can't do this for ever.'

'Do what?'

'Just sit here, day and night, both of us just existing under the same roof.'

'I'm trying my best, Arthur.'

'I know and I'm so thankful.'

'So, what are you saying? You want to move out? Because you know we discussed that and I really don't think it's a good idea.'

'No, no, I understand. I just want you to know that you aren't stuck here, tied to the house, for me. I can't live with myself knowing that you are giving up your life for me.'

'I told you, it doesn't matter how long we have left, I'm not letting you do any of this on your own. Don't let the words of people who don't know us make you doubt that.'

'But I don't know what to do, that's the problem. I don't know what I'm meant to do now that I've taken the first step. I never stopped to picture a life where this was a reality.'

Madeleine got up from the chair and sat down beside Arthur on the sofa with a soft sigh.

'You have to do what feels right. Whether that's just being here or going out for dinner with friends, you can do any of it. Don't waste any more time wondering.'

She took his hand and stared directly into his eyes. He could see his doubt reflected in hers.

'I don't think anyone is rushing to invite me out for dinner,' Arthur said sadly.

'Arthur,' Madeleine said sternly, 'what do you tell Elizabeth and Patrick to do when they feel like this?'

'What?'

'Get out there. Be brave. Make new friends.'

'I'm almost eighty, Madeleine! I'm not signing up for those silly dating programmes on the television.'

'You don't have to go on national television, but there's nothing stopping you meeting new people, even if it is just for friendship.'

Arthur sat quietly, trying to imagine what it would be like to sit across from a total stranger while sharing a meal. Just the thought of being surrounded by Northbridge residents in a crowded restaurant made his palms sweat.

'I don't know, Madeleine.'

'New people in your life might be exactly what you need. You can't give up before you've even started. Failure is not defeat until you have stopped trying.'

'What about you? Me going on a date doesn't stop me worrying about you.'

'I don't want you to worry about me. What am I meant to do to convince you?'

'I've got it,' Arthur said, clapping his hands together. 'We should *both* go on dates!'

'You've lost your mind.' She giggled. 'The kids will definitely disown us if we start double dating.'

'Not *together*!' He laughed. 'But we should both do this. That way, we both know we are out there and making the most of what we have.'

'I can't believe I'm agreeing to this. Fine.' She smiled, her eyes shining. 'Let's give it a go.'

Arthur jumped from the sofa. He leaned down and kissed Madeleine's forehead.

'I'll need to make sure he's good enough for you, of course.'

'You saved me from dating Eric Brown, remember?' Madeleine said, frowning as she recalled how Eric had asked her out multiple times over that long-ago summer. 'I trust you.'

Patrick and Scarlett visited the following afternoon to bring Madeleine a birthday present. She had been insistent that nobody was to organize anything or go to absolutely any fuss whatsoever. That hadn't stopped Arthur surprising her with a delivery of her favourite flowers, followed by their traditional breakfast at Cora's café.

'I didn't know you were coming!' Madeleine exclaimed, opening the door to her smiling son and his girlfriend.

'Dad invited us to surprise you.'

'We've brought afternoon tea to you!' Scarlett said, proudly gesturing to the hamper Patrick was carrying.

'Come in, come in, go straight through.'

Arthur was waiting at the kitchen door. Patrick hugged him before they both made their way over to the island.

'It's good to see you, Dad,' he said, setting the hamper down on the island before they both sat down opposite each other.

'How's everything at work?'

'Good. Sales are up again this month. It shouldn't take long to put the summer behind us. Do you remember Thomas Breen? He was asking after you.'

'They're talking about business already.' Scarlett sighed as she and Madeleine perched themselves on the stools beside them.

'Nothing changes,' Madeleine said. 'This one is itching to get back down to the showroom and sell. I told him, though, he should have joined some groups to keep himself busy. The local Men's Shed would love him to come along.'

'I am not *itching* to get back to work,' Arthur said, looking across to reassure Patrick. 'I'm perfectly happy knowing it's in safe hands. You're the future of the business.'

'Thanks, Dad. You're always welcome to pop in, you know that.'

'I do, and the day you see me coming is the day you know I've finally lost my mind.'

Scarlett and Patrick both laughed.

'This looks lovely,' Madeleine said opening up the hamper and beginning to lift out various packages. 'Some of my favourites.'

As they ate, conversation turned to the family plans for Christmas.

'I still think you should all come here again,' Madeleine said. 'The last few years have been so lovely having everyone get together.'

'What about she-who-must-not-be-named?' Patrick whispered.

'Behave, Patrick!' Scarlett slapped him on the arm.

'I'm serious, what's the chances of her agreeing to Christmas dinner here? I'm sure Teddy will insist on coming,' Patrick said. 'She could never stop that lad from spending time with you two.'

'I want to spend as much time as I can with everybody. We're wasting too many days as it is.'

'That's such a lovely thing to say, Arthur,' Scarlett said, dabbing her eye with her napkin.

'Don't set her off, Dad. That mascara makes a horrible mess.'

He yelped as he received another slap on the wrist.

'You should listen to your dad more!'

'While we're here, why don't you tell Dad what you were saying about setting up a dating profile?'

Scarlett's eyes narrowed as she glared at Patrick.

'I can't believe you would bring that up now,' she muttered. 'We're here for your mum's birthday.'

'Don't be fretting. In fact it's funny you should mention that,' Madeleine said quietly, prompting both Patrick and Scarlett to turn and stare at her.

'*You* want a dating profile, Mum?'

'We both do!' she said with a short nervous laugh.

Scarlett shrieked so loudly Arthur was surprised she didn't set off the car alarms. 'This is *amazing* news! You both want to get back out there?'

'I'm not sure you could say either of us were ever really out there, Scarlett,' Madeleine said.

'Don't pull that one, Madeleine.' Scarlett laughed. 'I bet you broke a few hearts back in the day.'

'Back in the day,' Madeleine repeated with a laugh. 'Oh gosh, you're making me regret this already.'

'Nonsense! We are going to get this done *today*. Where's your laptop?'

Arthur was relieved to take to his armchair as Scarlett fussed over the laptop with Madeleine. He was already dreading having to go through the various questions he could hear Madeleine answering now. He didn't even have a suitable picture they could use. Dating was starting to sound like a very silly idea. It was going to be pointless anyway. Surely people their age weren't going online to find dates?

'It's not just about dates though, Arthur,' Scarlett said after he admitted his doubts. 'You'll find all kinds of people on there who are looking for different things. Some might want dates, some might just want to be friends and to meet new and interesting people.'

'Really?'

'Absolutely. Just you wait and see. Come on, let's get a nice photo of you.'

Madeleine finger-combed Arthur's hair as he stood in front of the fireplace. He was finding it impossible to feel natural while staring at the tiny mobile phone camera.

'Do I need to smile?'

'You could a little, just whatever's comfortable.'

'*None* of this is comfortable.'

'And we're done!' Scarlett said, turning the screen to show Madeleine.

'You've taken one? You didn't count me in.'

'Look, I took a few while you were moving about. This one's really cute.'

Arthur examined the image on the screen. He didn't hate it, that was a start.

'It'll do, it'll do,' he said, anything to avoid having to repeat the performance.

Just as he was finishing his profile with Scarlett, Patrick burst back in to announce Elizabeth's arrival. Arthur followed Patrick towards the sound of voices in the kitchen.

'Hello,' Elizabeth said as he walked into the room. Her voice was guarded.

'Hi, love.'

'I just stopped by to drop off a gift for Mum.'

Madeleine was holding a wrapped present and card in her hands.

'That's lovely, it's good to see you.'

'Well, I don't want to gatecrash and get in the way.'

'Don't be silly, you're never in the way,' Madeleine said. 'Patrick and Scarlett just brought this lovely hamper round and we were having a chat. In fact, we were talking about our Christmas plans. Are you . . .?' Madeleine left the question open so that Elizabeth wouldn't feel pressured to make a decision, Arthur knew.

'Sorry, Mum, I've been so busy with the wedding, I just haven't even had time to worry about Christmas. I'll have to get back to you on that.'

'Not to worry. It's just lovely of you to come round. You've made my day.'

'And mine,' Arthur said brightly.

The corner of Elizabeth's mouth twitched slightly.

'Arthur!' Scarlett shouted, rushing into the kitchen, holding the laptop. 'You'll never guess what.'

'What's wrong?'

'You've already got two messages!'

'What?'

'Two different people have sent messages! Your profile has only been on for a few minutes.'

'What's going on?' Elizabeth asked. 'Messages from who?'

'We set up dating profiles for your mum and dad!'

Arthur stared at Madeleine. He wanted the ground to swallow him up immediately. His mouth was dry. This wasn't the conversation he wanted to be having when Elizabeth had made the effort to come over, even if it was only to bring a present for Madeleine.

'Look, this man seems really lovely! He's got such a caring face, do you know what I mean? You can just tell these things, can't you?' Scarlett continued excitedly, turning the laptop round to show him the profile of one of the men who had made contact so fast.

The kitchen fell silent. Arthur knew Madeleine and Patrick were waiting to hear what Elizabeth would say. Arthur was too. Elizabeth's response would tell them everything – where she was with it all, what she was feeling. Would she storm out? Arthur dreaded the idea.

After a long moment, Elizabeth spoke. Her voice was carefully neutral. 'Well, I'm going to head off. I have to go and get the dinner started. Happy birthday, Mum.'

Elizabeth nodded curtly in Arthur and Scarlett's direction, her gaze falling on the profile of the man currently on the laptop screen. Without another word she hurried out of the kitchen.

CHAPTER FOURTEEN
Teddy

THEIR CORNER OF the newsroom had emptied out early. A handful of people were still at their desks, staying behind to keep the website updated. Teddy and Ben hadn't been given much to do all afternoon, and had spent most of it chatting.

Despite his promise to his grandfather, Teddy had told Ben about Arthur and Jack's secret relationship. He hadn't been able to stop thinking about the possibility of finding out more about the mysterious Jack Johnson. So far, his initial searches hadn't produced any results. It didn't help that he knew so little about the man his grandad had once loved, but it was almost impossible to know where he might have ended up after leaving Northbridge. He couldn't ask too many questions without raising his grandad's suspicions and that was the last thing he wanted to do.

'I'll help you,' Ben said. 'I'm a member of an ancestry website. I spent summer helping my uncle build a family tree. We even got one of those DNA test kits.'

'Do you really think we can find him with so little information? I can't ask Grandad for anything else. I promised I wouldn't look into this.'

'Leave it with me. I love this stuff. I'll check all the different registers and maybe find out if he had any family. That could help us narrow down the search.'

'Thanks, Ben,' Teddy said. 'Don't spend too much time searching, I don't know if I'll ever be able to tell Grandad what we find out anyway.'

Teddy knew that he was only satisfying his own curiosity by trying to find out more about Jack. He hadn't given much thought to the prospect of discovering bad news, and whether – or how – to share that with Arthur.

'What are you going to do if you find him, though? What if he's died?'

'I dunno, let's just see what we do actually find out first. There's no point in worrying about it until then.'

Teddy browsed through another electoral register from the 1970s, but this latest Jack Johnson turned out to be a man who had been in his sixties at the time. Frustrated, he gave up and began packing his backpack.

'Did Dylan say goodbye to you?' Ben asked Teddy.

'Now you mention it, no. I don't know where he was going.' Dylan had left hours earlier after appearing more distracted than usual.

'How strange,' Ben said, sounding annoyed.

'Why, what's wrong?'

'Oh, well, I had asked him if I could tag along with him to that media conference he mentioned the other day. He said there was a spare ticket, but he'd have to confirm I could have it. You don't mind, do you?'

'Not at all,' Teddy lied. As soon as he had heard Dylan talk about the conference he had been tempted to ask if he could go, but after hearing that there was only one spare slot, had decided not to, as it would mean Ben missing out. 'It sounded really interesting, you'll have to tell me all about it.'

'Of course, maybe I'll manage to turn on my Dictaphone this time and record it for you.'

Teddy forced a laugh, still angry at himself for missing out on the opportunity. He was going to put it behind him for now, especially when they were about to meet Shakeel and Lexie. During a video chat the night before, Teddy had suggested to them that they should meet him and Ben at the pub. He half expected them to decline, but was pleasantly surprised when both enthusiastically agreed to the plan.

'Is Shak bringing the mystery man?' Teddy had asked Lexie in a post-video chat debrief.

'Behave yourself. I think he's still worried we'll embarrass him.'

'As if we would do that.' Teddy wanted to feel as light as his words sounded, but it made him sad to think Shak might be a little ashamed of them.

'I know, it's not like you would tell that story about him getting locked out and having to go back to his hook-up's flat,' she said, laughing.

'Exactly. I learned my lesson after the, erm, third or fourth time,' Teddy said, thinking back to the telling-off they had received from Shakeel before he made them promise to never bring up the story again.

Ben had returned from the toilet where he had changed into a new shirt.

'You forgot to take the tag off,' Teddy said, as he stood behind him and pulled the back of the collar to find where the string was tied. He felt Ben slightly shudder as his fingers touched his neck.

'You could have warmed your hands up,' Ben teased as Teddy attempted to undo the stubborn knot.

'Got it,' Teddy said as he pulled the tag off the shirt. He straightened the collar and ran his hands along Ben's firm shoulders, not daring to breathe as he did.

'Thanks. The shirt was a little birthday present to myself. Do you approve?' Ben said as he turned around to face him.

'You're a great fit. I mean, it's a great fit.' Teddy stumbled over his words. '*The shirt*. The shirt is a great fit.'

'You don't look too bad yourself.' Ben laughed, taking Teddy's shaking hand in his.

The office light above them flickered. It was unusually quiet in their corner of the floor. Teddy's heart raced as they stared at each other; Ben's soft lips seemed to be calling at him to take just one more step forward.

'You know they won't pay you overtime.' The voice startled them both. Dylan had walked back into the office, staring at the newspaper in his hand. He threw it down on the table as Ben dropped Teddy's hand and stepped away from him.

'We're just about to leave,' Ben said quickly. 'We're going for a drink if you fancy one?'

Teddy frowned, confused as to why Ben was suggesting he join them.

'Not tonight,' Dylan said, almost sounding bemused at the invite. 'I've got plans with my better half.'

'Why did you invite him? What if he'd said yes?' Teddy asked as they walked towards the lift. Dylan was following behind them, tapping on his phone screen.

'Obviously I wanted to find out if he, you know, saw anything. I don't care if he did, but for you . . . I know you don't want people to know about . . . *you*.'

Teddy tried not to think about the moment Dylan had interrupted them. His annoyance at Ben for grabbing the final place at the conference felt like a distant memory. They had been about to kiss. Their first kiss. Teddy had kissed several guys before, but no single moment had made him feel like he had while standing in front of Ben in anticipation of their lips finally meeting.

Shakeel and Lexie met them outside the building. Teddy let Ben go ahead alongside Dylan, who was heading towards the station, so that he could walk with his two friends.

'Is that the aftershave I bought you?' Shakeel said, sniffing.

'It is! Good spot, Shak.'

'It smells even better on you than it did in the shop.'

For a crazy moment, Teddy thought he saw Shakeel frown.

'What's the plan tonight, Teddy?' Lexie asked. 'You're not staying out late, are you?'

'No, I told Ben it was going to be an early one.' There was only one reason Teddy was going to consider staying late, and it certainly wasn't one he was going to share with his two friends.

Teddy and Ben carried the first round of drinks over to the table Shakeel and Lexie had found towards the back of the pub.

'Cheers, mate,' Shakeel said, taking his drink from Ben. 'So, you want any dirt on this one?'

'Every little bit.'

'We're going to be here for a while.' Lexie laughed, opening up a bag of crisps.

'Can I at least finish one drink before you guys start?'

'Don't worry, Teddy. I'm not going to judge you based on your ex-boyfriends.'

'He'd actually have to have one for you to do that,' Shakeel said. Teddy's mouth fell open as he glared at his best friend. 'Shit, sorry, I didn't—'

'Fucking hell, Shak. Thanks for that.'

'Hey, don't worry, it's all good,' Ben said, resting his hand on Teddy's knee. 'I couldn't care less if you've had ten boyfriends or none. I've only had one proper relationship, so it's not like I'm judging you.'

'I'm really sorry, Teddy. I was just messing about.'

Teddy found it impossible to stay mad at Shakeel. He knew it hadn't been said with any malice. If anything, Shakeel dropping that particular piece of information saved him from having to do it himself.

'How's the fella, Shak?' Lexie grabbed the opportunity when she could to try and change the subject. 'We were all hoping to meet him tonight.'

'I told you both already, when the time's right. Anyway, he couldn't come tonight even if I'd wanted him to.'

'Why's that?' Teddy said.

'He's working. He's a fifth-year medical student, so you know, he's busy.'

'You've bagged yourself a doctor?' Lexie said, raising her hand for a high five. 'I am so proud of you!'

Shak met her hand and laughed.

'I just want things to be right and you'll be the first people he meets, I promise.'

'Oh God,' Lexie said dramatically, setting down her empty

glass. 'I can't believe I'm the only single one here now. I'm going to need another drink.'

The table in front of them began to fill with empty glasses as two hours turned into three.

'You guys don't need to hang around if you don't want to,' Teddy said to Lexie and Shak, hoping that they might take the hint that he wanted to be alone with Ben. But Shakeel insisted that he didn't need to leave just yet, while Lexie was more than happy to hang around if Ben was still getting the next round.

Teddy noticed that Ben was frowning at his mobile.

'What's up?' Teddy asked. 'You look stressed.'

'Yeah, all good. Just a friend I haven't seen in a while wanting to meet up.'

'Oooh, is this a cute friend?' Lexie shouted across the table. 'More importantly, is it a straight one?'

'He's not, sorry, Lex!' Ben laughed. 'I don't think he's going to come—'

'Tell him to come,' Lexie insisted. 'They can buy the next round after you!'

'I'm going to give him a ring, I'll be back in a second.'

'Is anyone else hungry?' Lexie asked, jumping up from her chair. 'I want crisps. Or nuts. Or maybe both.'

Shakeel was fidgeting with the buttons on his shirt.

'Got any plans for the weekend?' Teddy asked him.

'Nothing much, I think we might be going to the cinema, but it'll depend on schedules.'

'Ah yeah, the hospital.'

'What about you?'

'Nothing much. But you'll never guess what. Grandad has only gone and got himself a date.'

Shakeel turned eyes wide with disbelief onto Teddy who told him about his grandad's plans.

'I can't believe it's happening. I thought it was a joke when I found out.'

'He's putting the rest of us to shame at his age,' Shakeel said with a sigh.

'Me maybe, not you!'

'I just mean overall. Being brave, coming out and admitting what he wants.'

'Why, what is it you wish you were brave enough to do?'

'What? Nothing, I'm just talking generally, Teddy; stop taking everything so literally.'

'I'm just pulling your leg, mate. You're one of the bravest people I know.'

Shakeel downed what was left in his glass with a loud gulp instead of answering.

'I'm going to the toilet, back in a minute,' he said, jumping to his feet so fast he almost lost his balance.

Teddy waited alone for several minutes until Lexie and Ben arrived back at the table carrying bags of crisps and nuts. 'Ben came to help when he was finished on the phone and we got both!' she squealed, throwing a bag of ready salted in Shakeel's direction. 'Shak's favourite. Where is he?'

'Toilet. I thought he'd be back by now. Maybe I should go and check on him.'

'He'll be fine, Teddy,' Ben said, 'Here, cheese and onion or prawn cocktail?' He dangled the two options in front of him.

'Either. I'm easy.'

Ben raised his eyebrows playfully. 'Fine, we'll share. Half and half, deal?'

Teddy was relieved when Shakeel rejoined them just seconds later.

'Everything good?' he asked.

'Yeah, I'm fine. Hungry, that's all.'

Teddy watched as he opened the crisps Lexie had bought him and began eating. He knew it wasn't his imagination that he caught Shakeel glowering in Ben's direction on several occasions.

'Benny!' an excited voice shouted over the noise a short while later. Teddy looked around. A familiar face was coming towards them, but he couldn't figure out how he recognized the man who had now locked Ben into a tight bear hug.

'It's really good to see you,' he said, slapping him on the back.

Once Ben had broken free and steadied himself again, he introduced the newcomer to the three people staring back at him.

'Everyone, this is Connor. Connor, this is Teddy, Shakeel and Lexie.'

'Nice to meet you all, can I get anyone a drink?'

Lexie disappeared to the bar again, this time accompanying Connor. Teddy was wracking his brain to try and figure out how he knew Connor's face. He was confident that he had stared into those bright green eyes before.

'Teddy? Earth to Teddy.' Ben was shaking the open bag of crisps at him.

'Yeah, oh right, no thanks. Not hungry.'

The volume of the music had increased in the last fifteen minutes. Several people had turned the small amount of floor space into a makeshift dance floor. Lexi went to join them after unsuccessfully attempting to drag Shakeel with her.

'So, Ted, is it?' Connor asked.

'Teddy actually.'

'How do you know Benny boy here?'

'We work together.'

'Oh, do I need to make sure I say everything is, what is it again, off the record?'

Ben laughed. Teddy knew it was the polite laugh he used in the office and tried not to smirk at hearing it.

'You're good. Unless you've got any dirt on this one.' He indicated Ben with a jerk of his head.

'I'm not one to kiss and tell, but buy me and a drink and I'll tell you everything you need to know about this lad here.' Connor laughed.

Teddy felt his insides tighten as Connor reached out and squeezed Ben's shoulder.

'None of which anyone wants or needs to hear, thank you very much,' Ben said primly, swiping his hand off. 'I told you to behave yourself.'

'You know I love you really.'

Teddy was staring at the pair when it suddenly clicked. It had been a photograph on Ben's social media profile. Connor had been standing with his arm round him.

'Are you two together?'

He felt Shakeel sit up in the chair beside him as Ben's mouth fell open at his abruptness.

'No!' Ben blurted out.

'Not anymore,' Connor added, pretending to look outraged at Ben's quick dismissal. 'We dated for a while. But we're just mates now, that's all, no matter how hard I try.'

'I can't shake him off,' Ben said. He was gazing at Teddy

directly, as though making sure he was being clear that there was nothing going on between them. At least, that's what Teddy hoped he was doing.

Ben broke his gaze and turned round to Connor: 'Will you go and get yourself a drink or something please?'

'What's the matter? We're just having a laugh.'

'It's fine,' Teddy said, his throat finally clearing enough to get the words out. 'It's nice that you stayed friends. More people should do that.'

'See! Ted gets it. Let's get some shots in.' Connor was gone before he had even finished the sentence, heading straight through the crowd to the bar.

'Sorry about him,' Ben said, moving closer to Teddy so that he didn't need to shout.

'It's cool. It's not often you get to meet an ex before a proper date.'

'Are you asking me out?'

'Maybe,' Teddy said. 'It'd be nice to go out properly, you know, somewhere that isn't the office canteen.'

'You're right. Let's talk about it tomorrow. We'll give this another few minutes and then make an escape. Right, I've got to go to the toilet before he comes back.'

This wasn't exactly the evening Teddy had been expecting. Being alone with Ben in the office just before Dylan had interrupted them felt like a lifetime ago now. All he wanted to do now was go back there. Just them. No interruptions. No Connor. Just him and Ben.

'Where's Ben?' Lexie said, arriving back at the table.

'Toilet. Connor?'

'He's gone to the bar.'

Shakeel's mouth opened.

'Something wrong?' Lexie asked, staring at him. He shook his head without saying anything and sunk down into the chair.

'I'm going to the toilet too,' Teddy said suddenly, rising from his chair before he could stop himself. He was going to find Ben. It didn't matter where it was. They had to finish that moment.

Teddy shouldered his way through the tightly packed groups towards the loo. He stopped as he finally made it to the bathroom door. There was no turning back now. He put both hands on the door and pushed it open.

Teddy immediately recognized Connor's voice when he entered the small bathroom. It helped distract him from the unpleasant smell that hit him. The middle cubicle door was open. Teddy realized that Connor was standing in front of Ben, having pushed the unlocked door open.

'It's not happening again, Connor,' Ben was saying. 'Last time was . . .'

Teddy held his breath.

'Don't you dare say it was a mistake, we both know it wasn't. Why did you agree to me even coming here?'

'I thought we agreed to be friends, Con? You've had too much to drink.'

Teddy's feet were glued to the spot as he saw Connor throw himself forward and kiss Ben on the lips.

'Ben!' Teddy called out before he could stop himself. Connor spun round in shock, while Ben's eyes were filled with relief at the interruption.

'Do you make a habit of spying on guys in toilets, Ted?'

Connor stepped out of the cubicle to move closer to Teddy. It was only as he did that Teddy observed how well-built the other man was.

'It sounds like Ben wants you to go, Connor. I'm beginning to think you're not wanted here.'

'Why do you care?' Connor said, before the realization spread across his face and he began to smirk. 'You? You and Ben? Mate. That's cute, but I wouldn't waste your time trying.'

The tips of Teddy's ears burned as the weight of Connor's words hit him squarely in the chest.

Connor moved even closer to him, so that Teddy could practically feel his beery breath on his face as he spoke.

'Run along now, Ted. Ben and I are talking and it's none of your business. Isn't that right, Ben?'

Before Connor could say anything else, Ben had pushed past him and was pulling Teddy out of the toilets.

Teddy didn't stop to ask any questions as they made their way back to the table where Shakeel and Lexie were chatting.

'Ignore him, Teddy,' Ben said once they were finally seated. He tapped his foot against the side of the table as he stared in the direction of the toilets.

Teddy had never seen him look so agitated.

'Ben,' he said. 'If you want to go with him, you can.'

'Why on earth would you say that?' Ben said, as bewilderment spread across his face. 'Is that what you actually think I want?'

'No, I'm just saying . . .'

Teddy stared at the floor. He felt stupid for even suggesting that Ben would want to leave with Connor.

'I know you've not done this before, Teddy, but I think there could be something between us. I'm happy to wait for you, but I need to know that you're not just stringing me along.'

'Stringing you along? I didn't know you felt like that, Ben.' Teddy could sense that Shakeel and Lexie's conversation was no longer as loud as it had been.

'I'm not saying I think that's what you're doing, I just want to be sure that you have some intention of actually coming out. You don't expect me to wait around indefinitely, do you?'

Teddy didn't know what to say as Ben stared at him. He thought Ben had understood his situation better than that. Why was he now putting pressure on him to come out?

'Maybe we should forget about this,' Teddy said. He felt his stomach churn as the words left his dry mouth. They echoed in his ears as if he was hearing someone else speaking them for the first time.

'Are you serious, Teddy? What the hell?' Ben's nostrils flared as he processed what he had just heard. 'You'd rather hide in the closet forever?'

'I'm not saying it will be forever, but I don't need you putting pressure on me, Ben.'

'It's not pressure. I want to take you out. I want our second date, a third date. I just don't want to feel like I'm wasting my time.'

'That's what I'm saying,' Teddy said, his voice cracking. 'You might be.'

'You know what, Teddy. If that's what you think, maybe you're right. If you don't value yourself enough to come out and live your life, why should I expect you to show me the same courtesy?'

Ben said goodnight to both Shakeel and Lexie and without

as much as another word to Teddy, left the pub. Lexie was first to wrap her arms around Teddy, squeezing him tightly.

'That was really stupid of me, wasn't it?' he said miserably.

'No! You can't make promises,' Lexie said. 'If he doesn't want to wait for you, that's his loss.'

As much as he appreciated the sentiment, Teddy knew that the feeling in his stomach was telling him the opposite. He didn't want to push Ben away before they had even had a chance to try. Shakeel remained uncharacteristically quiet as he finished the drink in his hand. It was a silence that usually meant he was debating whether or not to offer his opinion.

'Come on, Shak. I know you're dying to say something,' Teddy said, unable to wait any longer.

'I don't like or trust the guy,' Shakeel said, not looking up from the table as he spoke. 'But . . . I get his point. Maybe this is your moment to finally do it. Why not now, when there's someone you obviously like?'

Teddy didn't remember Lexie going to the bar to get them another round of drinks, but before he knew it, he was on his way back to her flat to stay the night.

'Sorry, Lex, I hope you don't mind me staying over,' he said, throwing himself down on the sofa with the pillow and duvet she had retrieved for him.

'Don't worry about it. You and Ben can chat over the weekend and sort this out. I think you might already know what you need to do though.'

Teddy buried his head in the pillow and groaned. It might not be tomorrow or next week, but he finally had to accept that he needed to come out sooner rather than later.

CHAPTER FIFTEEN

Arthur

ARTHUR FROWNED AT his reflection. He had never felt so old. Two nights of broken sleep hadn't helped the bags under his eyes. He pulled at his skin. It could be worse, he thought. He'd always taken good care of himself thanks to Madeleine and her habit of buying him new skincare products. Gels and creams, sprays and moisturisers; there wasn't a product on the market that he had not tried over the years. Of course, there was only so much that even the most over-priced products could do, and it was impossible to hide any blemishes when the person using them was tossing and turning all night.

He'd not actually believed that having a profile would result in being asked out, never mind ending up with two dates on one day. If he was a betting man, he would have been confident that Madeleine would be asked out before he was. As it turned out, he had only beaten her by two hours. Now, both he and Madeleine were preparing themselves to meet total strangers. Scarlett had excitedly reeled off information about the two men who had so promptly messaged him.

'Walter is seventy-nine and lives in the city, but he's happy to travel. And then there's Oscar. He's eighty-two and he lives only a few miles away, outside Little Birchwood.'

Before she had left that evening, the plans were made. He was going to meet Walter on Saturday afternoon in Cora's and later that evening he would meet Oscar in a restaurant on the high street.

He tried to relax and not dwell on spending time with two strangers; at worst it would be a couple of hours with people he would never see again. Teddy had attempted to reassure him when he had admitted his concerns during their latest telephone conversation.

'I don't know anything about dating. What if I make a fool of myself?'

'You'll be fine, Grandad. You're going to have a great time.'

Arthur knew that Teddy was trying his best to calm his jitters, but he couldn't help but continue fretting over details in the various scenarios he had imagined.

'What about paying?' he had asked Teddy.

'You can split it if you want to or just see who offers. Don't be offended if they offer to pay. There's no rulebook.'

'What if I don't want to see one or both of them again?'

'Then you don't. Simple as that. Believe me, you'll both know if you can stand each other's company pretty fast. And don't forget, you might like him as a friend too.'

Arthur had briefly considered the possibility of this, but wasn't sure if it was something that he should even consider, especially when they had met on a dating website.

'You're going to be better at dating than I am, I guarantee it!' Teddy reassured him.

Their chat had been interrupted by Scarlett's arrival. Always excited to get her hands on a project, Scarlett quickly decided that Arthur's hair could do with a trim to make it look a 'bit more trendy'. She had insisting on taking care of it herself, using Patrick's as an example of how she knew exactly what she was doing. Once she had finished and triple-checked that he was happy with it, Arthur had unsuccessfully tried to choose an outfit. By the time he was finished trying on different shirts, he had to sit on the edge of the bed for several minutes to catch his breath.

'Going out like this at my age, it's absolute piffle. What do I know about dating?'

'Don't be so daft,' Madeleine said, hanging his last remaining shirt back up. 'We'll find you something. Now stop fretting, you remind me of Patrick as a toddler when he couldn't get his way.'

Which is how Arthur found himself shopping for shirts the day of his date. He had decided to avoid some of the bigger high street stores. Those shops weren't for him. He'd ventured into one once and felt like a lost pensioner when a fashionable young woman had taken to enunciating each word so loudly and clearly that he could only assume she thought he must be deaf. No, he was most definitely going to stick with Egerton's today. It was one of the longest-serving shops in town; Arthur could vividly remember being dragged inside by his mother for his first school uniform fitting. She had sobbed the whole way through it and was almost convulsing by the time she saw him in the whole outfit for the first time.

For a Saturday morning, the shop was quiet. Arthur didn't want to waste too much time browsing so went straight up the stairs to the menswear department. A sombre-looking young man jumped up from his chair behind the counter, clearly excited at the prospect of having someone to serve.

'Good morning, sir! Welcome to Egerton's, is there anything I can help you with today?' he said, gesturing dramatically at the different rails.

'No, thank you. I know what I'm looking for,' Arthur said.

'I'm here if you need any assistance.' The server's smile faded as he slowly returned to his chair. Arthur didn't recognize the young man. He'd known most of the Egerton family when he was younger, but over the years it became impossible to keep up with various grandsons and great-grandsons who would pop up to complete their stint in the family business. That was the Northbridge way after all. Family first. Arthur started at the rail closest to him, running his fingers along the different shirts which filled it.

Flowers.

Stripes.

More flowers.

More stripes.

Exasperated, Arthur sighed loudly.

'Are you sure you wouldn't like a hand?'

Arthur jumped. 'Jesus, lad, you nearly gave me a heart attack.'

'Sorry, sir, you just look like you're struggling a little. I assume you're looking for a shirt. What's the occasion?'

Arthur grimaced. 'A meeting.'

'Okay, so we want something professional.'

'Nothing too stuffy, though.'

The salesperson nodded as he looked around. 'You could definitely pull off something like this,' he said, lifting out a checked shirt. 'It has a nice autumnal vibe to it, don't you think?'

Arthur studied it. It wasn't awful. 'You don't think I'm a bit too old for something like this?'

'Absolutely not, a man of your age, what are we talking . . . late sixties? . . .could easily wear this.'

Arthur laughed. 'You're a born salesman. If you ever want to sell cars, let me know.'

The salesman introduced himself as Carl as he continued showing Arthur different shirts that he was confident would work.

'It's for a date,' Arthur admitted eventually, hoping it would help bring their quest to an end.

Carl clapped his hands together and hurried off, reappearing moments later with two more options.

'You really can't go wrong with either of these,' he said. 'This classic Oxford shirt or the gingham option. Both colours will go beautifully with your eyes.'

Arthur studied them both closely. It suddenly seemed impossible to make this decision for himself.

'I'll take both,' he said. 'Thank you very much for your help.'

Beaming, Carl packed both shirts into a bag as Arthur paid.

'Have a wonderful evening, sir. She's going to love whichever one you go with,' he said, handing over the bag.

Arthur gave Carl a curt nod, took the bag and hurried out of the shop.

*

'He also said you looked almost ten years younger!' Madeleine said, as Arthur told her about Carl's comment over lunch. 'The poor boy wasn't to know any better.'

'It's not just that. It's the assumption, isn't it? People will be staring at us; at me.'

'Since when did that bother you, Arthur Edwards? Let them stare. You're out for coffee and dinner with some friends. They don't know any better than the young man in Egerton's.'

'I suppose,' Arthur conceded. 'Do you really think I could pass for sixty-nine?'

'Of course, dear. And not a day more.' Madeleine laughed, taking a small bite of her sandwich to avoid having to elaborate.

After finally settling on the gingham shirt, Arthur was ready and waiting in Cora's just before 2 p.m. He was glad he had phoned ahead and asked Cora to keep him the table at the back which offered the most privacy.

'Is it the usual for you and Madeleine?' Cora asked him when he arrived.

'Oh, no, I'm meeting someone else, a friend.'

'No problem, my love, I'll come back to you when they're here.' Cora gave him an encouraging smile and went back behind the counter. The lunch rush was over, but Saturday afternoon shoppers were still coming and going. Every so often someone he recognized would appear, giving a small wave in his direction as they saw him sitting alone in the corner. There was no privacy at all. A wave of panic rushed through him. He couldn't do this. Meeting in Cora's of all places. It was a mistake. Arthur dabbed at his forehead with his napkin.

'Dad? Are you okay?'

Arthur opened his eyes. Elizabeth was staring down at him. She placed her hand on his shoulder.

'Oh, sorry, love. Is it me or is it just a little warm in here today? Cora must have been playing with the thermostat again.'

'Are you sure? You look a little pale. Are you with Mum?' Arthur suddenly wished he had asked Cora for a tea.

'No, um, she's not here. My frie . . . the person I'm meeting must be running a little late.' He shifted uncomfortably.

'Oh,' Elizabeth said quietly, her eyebrows rising as she realized what her father was actually doing in the café.

'You don't need to hang around if—'

'It's fine, I'm fine,' she insisted, her eyes darting around the café. 'I didn't know you were going on a, you know, so soon.'

'It's just a coffee, well it will be if he ever gets here.' Arthur glanced at the clock. Walter was already twenty-five minutes late.

'Do you want me to wait with you until he does? I can leave straight away.'

'You can, but I'm fine, I promise,' Arthur reassured her. 'I didn't even see you come in.'

'I was shopping with Eleanor. I just popped in to grab us some hot chocolates. She's in the car actually.'

'Don't leave the poor girl waiting then. I'm fine. Go on now.'

'Okay, just be careful please, Daddy. I'm not going to tell you how to live your life, but just look after yourself.' She gave him a quick peck on the cheek before going back to the counter.

Arthur watched as she ordered her drinks, gave him a small

151

wave and left the café. He sighed sadly as the clock struck half past. Almost eighty and he had been stood up. After all the nervous build-up, it had been for nothing. He felt like a complete fool sitting alone.

'Elizabeth said you might like a tea,' Cora said, setting the mug down. 'Your friend hasn't made it?'

'Thanks, Cora. No, I'm afraid I appear to have been stood up by my date.'

'Oh Arthur, you poor love. I didn't know it was a date.'

'I'm such a silly fool, Cora. I thought I could do it. He's done me a favour.' Arthur took a gulp of his tea. The heat of the mug felt soothing in his hands.

'We'll have none of that. You know this will always be a safe place for you, Arthur.'

He tried to smile at Cora's kind words, but he was in no hurry for a repeat of that afternoon, especially in front of people who knew him.

'Call Scarlett and tell her to cancel, I'm not going,' Arthur said as Madeleine drove him back home. 'I've never felt so stupid. Even Elizabeth looked at me like the silly old man I am.'

Madeleine sighed as they turned into the driveway.

'You can't cancel on Oscar, he didn't let you down this afternoon.'

'This was all a silly mistake. I don't know why I let myself get carried away.'

'Arthur Edwards, enough,' Madeleine said sternly as the car came to a halt. 'You are scared, I understand that better than anyone, but I am not going to let you throw away your second chance.'

'At love?'

'At life! At living, Arthur. At having friends who love you for exactly who you are.'

They both got out of the car and walked into the house. Arthur trudged off to the living room and threw himself down in his armchair.

'Will you please think about it? Oscar doesn't deserve to be let down now,' Madeleine said.

'I'm sorry, Madeleine. I thought I could do this, but I can't. I'm not going.'

CHAPTER SIXTEEN
Teddy

TEDDY DIDN'T KNOW how he made it from Lexie's flat to the office in time for work on Friday morning. He felt horrendous. He pinned his hopes on two paracetamol and several litres of water getting him through the day. Then he would have to deal with work. And Ben. The thought of facing Ben made his stomach squirm. Lexie had attempted to reassure him before he left, but nothing she said helped.

He could only hope that Ben was willing to talk to him. He didn't want to end things before they had even begun. He was going to come out. If Ben could trust him, he would feel even better doing it knowing he had the support.

'Morning,' Dylan said as Teddy plonked himself down on his chair with a groan. 'As rough as you sound, at least you made it in.'

Teddy spun round in his chair.

'Ben's not coming in today,' Dylan said, seeing the confused look on Teddy's face. 'He said he wasn't feeling great.'

'Oh right. Did he say anything else?'

'No. It's not ideal either, I had a couple of things for you both to do today, so you can take it up with him if you've got sore fingers by the time you leave.'

Teddy tried his best to focus on the various tasks Dylan gave him throughout the day. Every time his phone vibrated, he grabbed for it hopefully, desperate to see Ben's name flash up. He stayed at his desk during lunch, clinging to the idea that Ben might phone when he knew Dylan wouldn't be nearby. By 3 p.m. he couldn't wait any longer and sent a message saying hello. It had still had not been read by the time he left the office that evening, once Teddy had finally finished sorting through Dylan's messy receipts collection and expenses claim.

Teddy woke with a start on Saturday morning, momentarily forgetting that it was the weekend. His head felt fuzzy. He took a sip of the warm water from the glass beside his bed. If he'd had the energy he would have gone down and got a fresh glass, but not today. No. Today was a day to stay in bed with the curtains closed.

'I deserve it,' Teddy told himself as he fixed his pillows. He'd taken to turning one longways and almost cuddling it to help him sleep.

His phone pinged causing his heart to jump. Shakeel. He threw it down without opening the message, then immediately felt guilty for doing so and rummaged around on top of his quilt to find the phone. It wasn't Shakeel's fault if Ben wasn't responding. He read Shakeel's message. He wanted to know if they could talk.

'Hello,' Teddy said once Shakeel answered his call. 'Not like you to be up this early on a Saturday morning. What's going on?'

'I was just thinking about the other night and thought we could chat.'

Teddy sat upright in his bed. He knew when Shakeel said

chat that it was something he had been building himself up to saying.

'Oh right, I mean, if you want to, but I don't think—'

'Teddy, I don't trust him,' Shakeel blurted out. Teddy listened to Shakeel's heavy breathing on the end of the line.

'Are you serious, Shak? You don't even know him!'

'Do you? You've been on what, one date?'

'I've been working with him every day. I've a pretty good idea who he is.'

'Bullshit, Teddy. I've seen you around him, remember? Just because you fancy him doesn't mean you have to give him the job.'

Teddy took a deep breath. His nostrils flared.

'You've phoned me on a Saturday morning to lecture me about the first guy I might actually have feelings for?'

'Because I've been there, Teddy. I'm only saying this as your best mate. I know you don't want to listen, but just promise me you'll be careful. Please?'

'Fine, if that makes you feel better. If I haven't already messed it up, I'll be careful. Satisfied?'

Despite rolling his eyes numerous times throughout the remainder of their chat, Teddy felt the knot in the pit of his stomach tighten. Sure, he knew Ben wanted the job, probably even more than he did, but they'd surely get past that whatever the outcome. He would if Ben got the job.

His stomach groaned loudly. Food. He needed breakfast. It was as good a distraction from everything as any right now.

'Ah, I was just about to call you, Edward,' Elizabeth said as he entered the kitchen to the smell of freshly scrambled eggs.

'I thought I'd do your favourite breakfast. I've got some crispy bacon too.'

'What's all this in aid of?' Teddy looked around the kitchen, confused. There was no one else there.

'Can't I cook my son some breakfast?'

'Mum. Even you know it's been a while since you—'

'Fine, fine,' Elizabeth said, tipping the egg onto his plate. 'I just wanted to say how proud I am of you. We haven't had a chance to spend a lot of time together recently, but I know how hard you're working and I just want you to know how happy that makes me.'

Teddy's mouth was dry. It suddenly seemed impossible to form a sentence. Before he knew it, he could feel tears rolling down his cheeks.

'I'm sorry, I don't know what's wrong,' Teddy said, pulling out a stool to sit down. Elizabeth placed her hand on his back and rubbed it softly.

'Is everything all right? You know you can talk to me about absolutely anything, don't you? We've been through so much as a family together, Teddy, you know I'm always here for you.'

'Thanks, Mum. Don't worry, it's just a silly row with Shak and tiredness catching up with me. I'm fine, I promise.'

'Really?' Elizabeth frowned at him. 'I make you eggs and bacon and you start crying? Is my cooking that bad?'

Teddy laughed and wiped his eyes again.

'There's that smile, just like your dad's,' his mum said. 'I know there might be times when it feels like we don't get to spend a lot of time together, but I'll always be here for you, no matter what.'

His stomach churned. Food was the last thing on his mind. This was his moment. If he could just get the words right. If he could just find that extra bit of courage to force them out of his mouth.

'Mum,' he said, 'I need to, no, I want to tell you—'

The kitchen door flew open as Eleanor barged into the kitchen weighed down with shopping bags.

'Right, come on, Mum,' she whined. 'I've got to get these returns done. They've been sitting in my room for weeks.'

'And whose fault is that, Eleanor? Two minutes please, why don't you go on out to the car.'

'Is everything okay?' Eleanor said, her eyes lingering on Teddy's reddened eyes.

'Everything's fine, Eleanor. Just give us a minute.' They waited in silence until they heard the front door close. 'Sorry, I promised her we'd go shopping this morning. You were about to tell me something?'

Teddy smiled to himself. The tiny bit of courage he had plucked from somewhere just minutes before had drained away.

'I just wanted to say that I really appreciate you getting me in at *The Post*. I'm having a great time.'

'I can't tell you how happy that makes me, Edward,' Elizabeth said. 'No matter what, never forget how proud I am of you. Right, I better go before she starts honking the horn. Eat your breakfast while it's still hot.'

'Thanks, Mum,' Teddy said, as she leaned in and kissed him on the cheek. Images of Ben and Shakeel's disappointed faces flashed through his mind. After almost an hour of aimlessly moving the cold scrambled egg around his plate, he tipped it into the bin and retreated to his bedroom.

CHAPTER SEVENTEEN
Arthur

ARTHUR WOKE IN the armchair with a jump. A knock at the living-room door had startled him. He didn't even remember sinking into the chair and closing his eyes.

'Arthur? Hello? It's Scarlett, can I come in?' Her voice was higher than usual.

'Course, don't be daft, you don't need to knock.'

'Sorry, Madeleine said you had fallen asleep, but I just needed to apologize.'

Arthur waved his hand in the air and frowned.

'You didn't leave me sitting there.'

'But I pushed you—'

'You most certainly did not. We were going to do it with or without you, Scarlett, don't you be blaming yourself for someone else's rudeness.'

'Madeleine said you're not going to meet Oscar.'

Scarlett sat down on the sofa. Arthur knew she was going to try her best to change his mind as she played with the numerous rings on her fingers.

'Before you start trying—'

'Please, Arthur, let me just quickly say something.' Her eyes widened as she spoke, almost taken aback by own interruption. 'I've only known you for a couple of years, but do you remember what you told me the first time we met right here in this house? You told me you had never seen Patrick so happy. You told me I was going to be a part of your family.'

Arthur nodded. He remembered the afternoon vividly.

'I knew that meant taking the good with the bad, Arthur. Patrick had only been sober for six weeks, but I could see the man he was. That's a reflection of you. Every story he tells me about growing up is about you and how you supported and encouraged him. When he didn't want to take over the business, you made him realize that he could do it. He just had to believe in himself. Of course he was going to make mistakes, but he was going to learn from them. I think that's exactly what you would say to yourself today. Please don't let one person stop you. You'll regret not going more than anything. That's all I wanted to say, I'm sorry if you think I've spoken out of turn.'

Arthur stood up, setting the folded newspaper down on the coffee table. He glanced at the clock and took a deep breath.

'Well then, I suppose I better go and get ready. I don't want to keep Oscar waiting.'

It was impossible for him not to smile as Scarlett delightedly clapped her hands together.

Madeleine and Scarlett watched from the doorway as Arthur got into the back of the taxi which was taking him to the restaurant. He gave them a small wave before the car pulled out of the driveway onto the busy road into town.

'Lads' night, is it?' the taxi driver said as they waited at a red light. His voice sounded hoarse, possibly from his attempts at conversation with his various passengers.

'Just meeting a friend,' Arthur said, trying to avoid making eye contact with the driver who was watching him in the rear-view mirror.

'On your best behaviour when the missus is waiting up for you.' The driver laughed.

Arthur forced a smile in return before going back to looking out of the window. His legs were shaking. He tried placing both of his clammy palms on his knees to hold them steady. He knew that he was being silly. It was just dinner; a couple of hours and it would all be over.

He felt the taxi come to a halt. He looked out of the window; they had pulled up outside the restaurant, Catch 22.

'Have a good night, mate,' the driver said as Arthur climbed out of the car.

He suddenly felt very alone and exposed standing on the footpath outside of the restaurant. He was ten minutes early. Was there some kind of date etiquette in which this was frowned upon? Suddenly everything he hadn't thought about earlier that afternoon felt important. Should he go on in and be waiting at the table? What if Oscar was already inside? He might be sitting at the table watching him standing outside debating these very options. Arthur took a deep breath and pushed the door of the restaurant open.

'Good evening, sir, do you have a reservation?' A slim young woman dressed in black was holding an iPad just inside the entrance. Her long blonde hair was tied up in a neat, tight ponytail.

'Hello. It was for two. Oscar?'

'Ah yes, you're first to arrive, let me show you to your table.'

Arthur followed her through the restaurant as she strode between the tables of early evening diners. It wasn't as busy as he had feared it might be; mostly older couples occupying the tables, with a handful of small groups towards the back. They came to a halt at a small table. It was empty, as was the identically set table on the other side. Arthur thanked the hostess and sat down so that he could observe the front of the restaurant.

Several minutes passed. He watched as staff members floated between the tables. Every so often the door swung open and someone new arrived. His stomach gave a small jolt each time, a wave of disappointment spreading through him when he realized it wasn't Oscar. Then he saw him. The hostess was pointing towards Arthur. Oscar smiled and nodded and began walking towards him. Arthur took a deep breath and stood up.

Oscar was just a little shorter than he was. His tanned skin was aged, but each line looked like it had been purposely drawn, filled with memories of the life he had lived. A pair of glasses rested on his slightly crooked nose, but they didn't distract from his sparkling blue eyes.

'You must be Arthur,' he said, holding out his hand.

'Oscar, good to meet you.'

'Sorry I'm running a few minutes late. The traffic in this place doesn't get any easier, does it?'

'It gets worse by the day. Did you drive here?'

'I left my car at my friend's house. He lives just outside of town.'

They spent several minutes discussing Northbridge and

discovering that Arthur vaguely knew one of Oscar's friends – he'd bought a car from Arthur a number of years earlier. A waiter interrupted them to take their order before returning with a bottle of Pinot Gris.

'Cheers to a lovely evening,' Oscar said, holding up his glass to Arthur.

Arthur felt himself relaxing as they talked. It was like they had known each other for years. Very quickly he forgot his initial fears about topics of conversation or how it would feel to sit opposite a stranger in a potentially romantic setting. Arthur felt several people glance at them as they walked past to their own tables. Some of the faces he recognized, but couldn't quite put names to.

'So,' Oscar said. 'Your profile mentioned that you have two children. Tell me everything.'

'I do, Elizabeth and Patrick, both in their forties. Elizabeth has three children, my two granddaughters and grandson. Do you have any children?'

'No, just nieces and nephews. I presume you didn't come out until a little later in life then?'

Arthur set his glass down. 'Yes, just a few months ago, actually.'

Oscar's eyebrows almost hit the roof. 'Oh my, how brilliantly brave of you. How has it been?'

He sipped his wine as Arthur explained how he had come to the decision to finally tell his children and live as a gay man.

'It's wonderful that your wife is so supportive. She sounds like an absolute gem. I've heard lots of stories over the years, not all of them have happy endings.'

'I am a very lucky man,' Arthur said. 'We're making it

work. She actually convinced me to come tonight. I didn't think I should be dating at my age—'

'Stop right there,' Oscar said, raising his hand and smiling. 'None of this age business in front of me. I'll be eighty-three next year, but I'm not stopping until they've put me in the ground. There's still lots for me to do and a silly number isn't getting in the way.'

'Really?'

'Absolutely. Why would we stop? Because society thinks we should be tucked up in bed and watching *Call The Midwife*?'

'I guess you're right. I was worried about people judging me for being out tonight.'

'Why?'

'Well,' Arthur decided to admit the truth. 'You're actually the first person I've been out with since I . . .' His voice trailed off.

'I understand,' Oscar said, smiling. 'Well, I am absolutely honoured to be here with you. I think you're a very brave man for doing what you're doing.'

Arthur felt warmth spreading through him. Scarlett was right; he couldn't keep living in fear of these moments. He wasn't going to miss out anymore.

Arthur was blown away by Oscar's attitude to life. As they ate, he listened intently as Oscar told him about his experiences of being openly gay in some of the countries he had travelled to over the years. From being questioned by local police in a raided nightclub to all-night parties at Pride, he had stories from every corner of the globe.

'For my eighty-first birthday, a few of my friends chipped in and got me flying lessons,' he said, laughing. 'I've been doing them for just over a year now. It's one of the best things I've ever done in my whole life.'

'You're a braver man than me,' Arthur said.

'You've got it in you. You just need to remember that you can do anything you want. If you can be here having dinner with me, you can go and do karaoke with a drag queen, you can go to Pride and feel part of a community who love you no matter who you are.'

'And I could fly a plane.'

'And you could fly a plane! Well, not after two bottles of this.' Oscar laughed, giving the second empty bottle of wine a shake.

A man was waving his hand in the air, attempting to get the attention of the waiter who was standing at a nearby table. Arthur felt his heart beat faster. Eric Brown was sitting at the table with his wife Claudette.

Oscar asked, looking round in the direction Arthur was staring, 'Is that a friend?'

'He was,' Arthur said. 'Until I came out.'

Arthur explained what had happened with Eric and the Northbridge Foundation.

'Bigots, the lot of them,' Oscar said furiously. 'I'm so sorry you had to experience such horrible behaviour.'

'I don't blame them for being taken by surprise.'

'Don't excuse it, Arthur. I've a good mind to march over there now myself and put him right.'

'Oh no, no,' Arthur demurred. 'It's not worth it.'

'Well, I'll make sure he, or anybody else for that matter, never makes you feel that way again.'

Arthur realized what Oscar was saying. 'You want to keep in touch after tonight?'

Oscar grinned back at him. 'I don't know what it is you're looking for, Arthur, but I think we could be good friends, and right now, I think that's exactly what you need.'

Arthur nodded his head and sighed happily. He found himself lost for words at the kindness he was being shown by a relative stranger.

The waiter arrived with their bill a short while later. Arthur attempted to take it, but Oscar was quicker and insisted that he would pay.

'To the start of a great friendship,' he said, raising his glass one last time.

Arthur clinked glasses with him, feeling safe and content.

As he stood up, Arthur saw that Eric was staring across at their table. He didn't know if it was the alcohol or feeling inspired by Oscar's stories, but he found himself squeezing past the now full tables around them and making his way towards Eric and Claudette's table. As he approached them, he saw that they were with their teenage granddaughter, Sophie.

'Evening,' he said as he arrived beside them. 'Lovely to see you, Claudette and Sophie.'

'Hello, Arthur. No Madeleine tonight?' she asked, avoiding direct eye contact with him.

'No, she has her own plans tonight.'

'As do you, clearly,' Eric said, tilting his head towards Oscar who was now making his way over to them. Claudette finally looked up at Oscar, while Sophie kept her head down, her eyes focused on the plate of food in front of her. She had been much chattier when Arthur had met her on previous occasions. Arthur introduced Oscar, who held his hand out to shake Eric's.

'Pleasure to meet you,' he said, before turning to Arthur with a glint in his eye. 'Come on then, handsome, let's get going. You owe me dessert, remember?'

Barely concealing their laughter, they bid farewell to the Browns, whose mouths were practically resting on the floor by the time they reached the exit.

'I can't believe you said that.' Arthur laughed. 'Their faces!'

'See what I mean? Excuse my French, but fuck them, Arthur. You've got a chance to live for yourself, not them. Have fun, be brave and enjoy it; and if that means shutting up some homophobic cretins now and again, even better.'

They waited on the street outside for Oscar's taxi to arrive.

'Don't forget to tell Mrs Edwards how handsome I am,' Oscar said, as a car pulled in beside them. 'She doesn't need to be the only one out meeting attractive gentlemen.'

Arthur waved goodbye and watched as the car turned the corner and vanished from view.

He had done it. The evening had been a success. Romance hadn't even crossed his mind throughout the evening. Teddy had been right. Even without a romantic connection between them, he knew that he had found something even better in Oscar in just a few hours, something he hadn't realized he had been missing his whole life. A friend who truly understood him.

'Mr Edwards?'

Arthur looked around to see Eric's granddaughter, Sophie, behind him. Now that he could see her face he noticed just how tired the youngster looked.

'Is everything okay, Sophie?'

'Sorry to bother you, I just wanted to say that I think you're really brave.'

Arthur was slightly taken aback by the comment. 'Thank you, Sophie. That's very kind of you to say.'

'I'm sorry if my grandad said anything rude. He doesn't really—'

Arthur could see the colour in her cheeks rising, so raised his hand to stop her. 'You don't have to worry. I'm sure Eric will come round. After all, we've been friends for a long time. How are you getting on at college?'

'It's okay. I can't wait to move to the city,' Sophie said, her eyes lighting up at the prospect of leaving Northbridge behind.

'Everyone's always excited to get away from Northbridge,' Arthur said, smiling gently. 'I was once too, would you believe? Look at me now, almost eighty and still here.'

'Grandad Eric says the same thing. He says that even if I leave, I'll come back one day.'

Arthur had known Eric since they were knee-high. Eric had never had any interest in leaving Northbridge behind. In fact, he looked down on those who had spoken openly of their desire to move away. That felt so limiting to Arthur.

Even though his own children had built their lives here, Arthur hadn't ever discouraged them from the possibility of leaving.

'You'll know what feels right for you when the time comes, Sophie. Your grandad's bark is worse than his bite. He'll love you no matter what you choose to do.'

Arthur was glad to see the smile on her face as she said goodnight and went back into the restaurant to join her grandparents.

CHAPTER EIGHTEEN
Teddy

THE TWO SMALL ticks on Teddy's last message to Ben were now blue. His message had been read and ignored. That stung a little more than he wanted to admit to himself. Either way, he would finally see Ben tomorrow. Right now, all he wanted to focus on was his grandad and hearing about his night out with Oscar.

'Tell me everything then!' Teddy said, making himself comfortable on the sofa in the lounge.

Holding his cup and saucer, Arthur crossed his legs and sat back with a smile on his face.

'It was really lovely. Nothing like what I expected.'

'Him or the date? Did he look like his profile picture?'

'Both! Somehow he seemed even younger in person. There was a youthful energy to him that made me feel as old as the lines on my face.'

'As if. None of my friends can believe you're almost eighty!'

Teddy listened, amazed, as Arthur told him some of the stories Oscar had shared with him.

'Wow, that's a hell of a life he's had,' Teddy finally said. 'It's great he was able to come out and live that kind of life.'

'It takes an enormous amount of courage to do that, Teddy. Being who you are is hard. It doesn't matter where you're from or when you were born.'

Teddy got the sense that his grandad was talking as much about Teddy and himself as he was about Oscar and decided to change the subject.

'Are you going to see him again, Grandad?' He kept it vague, still not sure what his grandfather was really thinking.

'I think so,' Arthur said, before pausing briefly. 'He'll be a really lovely friend to have.'

Teddy tried to find any hint of disappointment in his grandfather's voice, but couldn't detect any. 'Just friends?' he tried.

'You were right, Teddy,' Arthur explained. 'I hadn't realized until I was there with him that I'm not looking for, you know, the other stuff. My time for the big love story has passed and I'm fine with that. Just having a friend and sharing some experiences is enough for me. Love can exist in so many forms, Teddy, especially friendship.'

'That does sound simpler, I guess.'

'Oh dear. I know that face. What's wrong?'

'Just the usual, I'm just getting frustrated with myself and taking it out on everyone else.'

'Has something happened?'

'No, not really, I think that's the problem. I'm afraid to let it because I'm still hiding who I am.'

'Ben will understand,' Arthur said. 'You don't need to put any more pressure on yourself.'

'You'd think, wouldn't you? I just don't want to start something with this secrecy hanging over me.'

'Do you know what it is that you want to say to Ben?'

That was a question he had been attempting to answer himself for a couple of days, especially with Shakeel's warning ringing in his ears. All Teddy knew was that what he had felt was real. He had wanted to kiss Ben, to feel his breath against his face, to hold him in his arms. He might not have felt it before, but he knew what it meant.

'Not really, maybe it doesn't matter anyway.'

'You're imagining the ending before it's even begun, Teddy.'

'I really did mess up, Grandad.'

'All of this worrying. I watched you and Ben at that car boot sale and I saw two young men who could have something special between them. You're letting your fears run your life for you, and that might feel easier sometimes, but one day you'll look back and regret it.'

That night Teddy thought a lot about what his grandad said. If he was to take things any further with Ben, he would have no choice but to come out to his family. Ben versus Mum; was that really what it was going to come down to in his head? What Shakeel was saying made sense. How could he risk everything for someone so new to his life? What if his mum kicked him out? Would he still have his job? Ben would need to understand that he needed more time. The thoughts replayed in his head all night long, even when he finally drifted off while lying on top of his duvet.

Neither Dylan nor Ben were at their desks when Teddy arrived early on Monday morning. He had stopped off and bought coffee and muffins, hoping the gesture might get things off to a good start. He set one of the cups and muffins down on Ben's desk. Just a couple of minutes later, his heart jumped as he saw Ben walking towards him carrying a cup from the café downstairs.

'Hello. Grabbed you a coffee and one of those muffins you like,' Teddy said, his voice sounding a little higher than he had anticipated.

Ben took off his jacket and sat down before responding.

'Thanks. I got one, so you might as well have it.'

Teddy watched in silence as Ben pushed the coffee he had bought him back onto his desk without another word.

'I know you're annoyed at me, but I hope we can talk about—' Teddy began.

'You know what, let's not right now. I want to focus on work today. I already fell behind after Friday.'

'You're not blaming me for that?'

'Come off it, they're probably already printing a full-time contract with your name on it now that I've given them the opportunity.'

'Point made,' Teddy said, stung by the dig. 'I'm not going to bother when you're like this.'

Teddy wanted to say something more, but he'd already made such a hash of things with Ben that he knew he couldn't push him further. He was grateful when Dylan started a conversation about his weekend, before going over what they had coming up for the week. Teddy and Ben locked eyes once during the morning, but Ben quickly turned away without a word. Teddy tried to hide his disappointment and got on with the story he was writing.

As lunch approached, Teddy tried to catch Ben's eye again in the hope of arranging to eat together so that they could finally talk properly.

'You coming up to the canteen?' he asked, taking the opportunity while Dylan was busy on the phone.

'No, I'm just gonna grab a sandwich and eat it here today,' Ben said, without removing his headphones.

Teddy knew that there was no point in pushing the issue so went to the canteen alone. He texted Lexie and Shakeel but both were in lunch meetings and could only promise to get in touch after work. He eventually gave up and made his way back down to his desk. It was only when Dylan had also returned and called their names that Ben finally looked away from his monitor.

'Sorry, guys, I hope neither of you has plans for tonight,' Dylan said. 'Martha was meant to be covering an event this evening, but apparently she's had to go home sick. No one else is available and . . . well, it could be a great opportunity to step up.'

'That sounds great. I can handle it alone if Teddy can't go,' Ben said quickly.

'I can actually. What is it, Dylan?'

'You know that waffly TV professor everyone loves, the space guy? His book launch is at the observatory. Pretty decent guestlist by the look of things too.'

'Professor Owen Armitage?' Ben asked. 'I'm a huge fan! Do we have any interview time?'

'Not yet, but I like your thinking, Ben. I'll forward you the email with all the details and you can get in touch with the publicist directly.'

'You know, you don't have to be so passive aggressive,' Teddy said once Dylan had turned away from them.

'I'm sorry; you thought that me literally saying I could manage without you was passive?'

'Whatever. We still have to work together tonight.'

'I'll make sure I have my questions for Professor Armitage ready for your approval.'

'No need, let's just hope you remember how to turn your Dictaphone on this time,' Teddy snapped. He couldn't help but feel a satisfied twinge when he heard Ben click his tongue.

Teddy spent the rest of the afternoon researching the various celebrities who had been confirmed to attend the launch. He made his wish list of people to speak to and scribbled down potential questions for them. The organizers of the event had arranged for a car to pick them up from the office and bring them directly to the observatory. Teddy and Ben made the half-hour drive in silence, only speaking when the driver had attempted to start a conversation about the event.

'Do you get photographs with the celebrities?' he asked when they told him who was meant to be there.

'I'm not sure,' Teddy said. He wasn't in the mood for making small talk.

'Here we are, gents,' the driver said as they drove through the large open gates into the grounds. The large dome which was home to the planetarium rose into view. They joined a queue of several cars which were dropping off guests.

'We'll jump out here,' Ben said, not waiting before opening his door. Teddy followed him up the path towards the entrance. They joined a line of smartly dressed guests who were waiting to enter the building.

'Good evening, can I see your invite please?' a woman said as they reached the front of the queue. She carefully checked the tickets and gave them a curt nod to go ahead.

They made their way past a crowd of photographers waiting

for the celebrity arrivals. Teddy pulled his notebook out of his pocket, opening it at the page of notes he had made about some of the people he wanted to find and interview.

'It's a great turnout, isn't it?' he said, forgetting that Ben wasn't talking to him. 'The Journey Through the Stars show is on every half-hour in the Planetarium, we should remember to check it out.'

'Yeah, sounds cool. I'm going to go and mingle,' Ben said distantly before walking off.

Teddy watched him go, walking into the crowd of people without looking back. Determined to make the most of the evening, Teddy took a glass of champagne from a waiter and headed in the opposite direction.

He was passing by a group of people when someone reached out and grabbed his wrist. He looked round to see Neena Anderson smiling back at him.

'Hello, I knew I recognized you and then it just clicked,' she said. 'Teddy, right?'

'I'm really impressed you remember!' Teddy grinned.

'I'm good with faces,' she said, 'and I was so excited when Stuart told me that Elizabeth Marsh's son was going to be doing that interview. I'm such a big fan.'

'You knew who I was?' Teddy said. Of course she did. Stuart hadn't mentioned it on the day he and Ben had interviewed Neena, but Dylan must have told him when he put him forward for it in the first place.

'Of course! I was on my best behaviour. Well, as much as I can ever be,' she said with a loud giggle.

Teddy had heard enough. 'Well, it's lovely to see you, Neena. Have a great night.'

He had been so proud of having helped rescue the interview and getting good quotes from Neena. Now he knew she'd been on her best behaviour with him because she happened to be a fan of his mum. It was only as he was walking away that he remembered that he was there for work and probably should have tried to get a quote from Neena. He looked round, tempted to double back, but she was already deep in conversation with another reporter whose Dictaphone was held high enough to record the conversation. He gulped down the rest of his glass and swiped another full one, then scanned the room for Ben.

He didn't want to talk to Ben, he just wanted to see what he was doing. But Ben was nowhere to be seen. If he didn't find him within the next fifteen minutes he was going to call it a night. 'Why wait?' he thought to himself with a shrug. He could slip off now and no one would even notice. He wasn't in the mood for talking to anyone now. After all, he'd only bothered coming so that he could try to fix things with Ben. He looked around to find the entrance he had come in and began walking towards it, impatiently pushing his way through the continuously growing crowd. Dylan would be pissed off but Teddy would find a believable excuse; he could simply say his Dictaphone had broken or that he had lost it. No one would fire him for that. Not Elizabeth Marsh's son.

He came to a sudden halt in the middle of a confused group of people; What the hell was he doing? Why was he giving in and walking away? He was becoming the person Ben accused him of being. He thought about his recent conversation with his mum. She had looked so genuinely happy when he had said that he was enjoying the job. Her beaming smile flashed in front of his eyes. The instant wave of guilt that flooded his body almost made him lose his footing. This was a job he liked, a job he knew he actually wanted. 'What's wrong with me?' Teddy said to himself. Here he was, lucky enough to find himself in a room filled with people he would have loved the opportunity to speak to just six months ago. Now he was risking proving people right by thinking he could get away with not trying. Even thinking it made him feel arrogant. He couldn't both resent the association and want to use it to protect himself when it suited. What Ben said was true. He had to stand on his own two feet; at home and at work.

Muttering his apologies, he turned on his heels and quickly made his way towards the stage which had been set up towards the back of the room. Professor Armitage still hadn't appeared to speak, so he was confident that Ben was still in the room. He wandered in the direction of the flashes from a photographer's camera. It wasn't until he was right up beside the photographer that he saw Ben, deep in conversation with a blonde woman he didn't recognize. Ben was talking animatedly. He couldn't help but smile as he watched him. He'd never seen Ben look so engrossed in what someone was saying. He really did love what he was doing. Teddy waited until he saw the conversation end as the woman answered a phone call.

'Hello,' Teddy said. 'You look like you're having a good time.'

Ben's lip curled. 'I was.'

Before Teddy could say anything, the woman turned back round to them after finishing her call.

'Lesley, this is my colleague, Teddy Marsh,' Ben said.

'Teddy, this is Lesley, the professor's publicist from his publishing house.'

'Lovely to meet you, Lesley. I'm a big fan of Professor Armitage's work.'

He could feel Ben's eyes burning into him as he said it. He knew he was lying.

'You'll love the book then. Make sure you pick up a gift bag, there's a signed copy in there. Put them there myself.'

'That's great,' Teddy said, fully aware that Ben was now looking around to see how he could make a quick escape. 'Sorry, do you mind if I drag Ben away for a few minutes?'

'No, not at all. I better go and make sure you-know-who is almost ready to give his speech.'

Ben was glaring at him, but Teddy didn't have time to care. He pulled him towards the side of the room where fewer people were standing.

'I cannot do this,' Teddy said.

'Do what? Tell the truth to people?'

'No, all of *this*. You. The attitude.'

'No one asked you to, Teddy. You said you wanted to come tonight, I wasn't going to stop you.'

'You know full well what I mean. You're not giving me a chance to explain.'

'I thought you made yourself perfectly clear the other night in front of your friends. You made me feel so small.'

Teddy felt the heat in his face rising.

'Are you actually serious right now? How did I end up the bad guy because I'm scared? There, I said it, I'm terrified. My mum isn't even speaking to my grandad right now. What will she do to *me* if I tell her? This is all new for me, Ben. How can you hold this against me?'

Ben shook his head and looked away.

'I'm sorry!' Teddy said desperately. 'I know it's not what you want to hear, but that's the situation.'

'It wasn't just that. Or the fact your best mate can't even hide that he doesn't like me.'

'Then what? What did I do to deserve the silent treatment?'

'Nothing, just leave it now.' Ben folded his arms and sighed. 'I'm sorry for how I've been. You're right, you . . .' he trailed off.

'Ben! Please tell me!'

Teddy watched as Ben frowned, struggling to find the right words.

'I panicked. I want to be there for you, but sometimes it feels like you're putting off coming out until the perfect moment and that doesn't exist. Believe me, I know.'

'What do you mean?'

'Life isn't perfect, Teddy. The sooner you accept that, the easier it will be for you.'

'You don't think I know that? You don't think that my dad dying turned my life upside down?' Teddy said. 'The fact my life isn't perfect is exactly why I need this moment to be as close to that as it can be. My mum has basically tried to cut my grandad out of our lives. How am I meant to deal with that? I'm well aware that there's no perfect moment, Ben, but the very least I need is to know that I could rely on someone who understands how important this is for me.'

Silence. The two stared at each other. Teddy's heart was racing.

'I understand now,' Ben said, breaking the silence. 'I want to be that person, Teddy.'

It was as if someone had hit mute on the entire room. The words echoed in Teddy's ears.

He cast his gaze around desperately, and saw a pair of closed doors. Grabbing Ben by the hand, he dragged him towards them; thankfully they opened. Teddy pulled Ben into the empty room beyond.

They were in the planetarium itself. The hemispheric domed ceiling was a dark blue. Teddy couldn't help but gasp when he realized where they were, standing under the twinkling stars high above. Ben fell silent, clearly as awed as Teddy. The projection wasn't moving, allowing the streaks of light splattered across the ceiling to sit above them, watching as the two men walked into the centre of the room, their eyes transfixed on the magical scene above them.

'I was going to kiss you,' Teddy blurted out without waiting for Ben to say anything. 'I was coming to find you because I needed to know you felt the same. That's the only reason I even went to the toilet the other night. After the office . . . Dylan's interruption . . . I couldn't stop thinking about you.'

Ben stopped staring at the stars and looked at Teddy. Teddy felt himself inching closer, their eyes locked on one another's. His heart was beating faster. It was as if time had abandoned them, joining the stars above, watching, waiting. Teddy felt Ben take his clammy hands in his, squeezing his fingers tight. He closed his eyes. He felt safe; an instant rush of warmth spread throughout his body. Their lips met. It was new, but familiar, like old lovers reunited after decades apart. Teddy felt Ben let go of his hand, but before he could panic, felt

Ben's warm palm slip around the back of his head. Their open mouths were pressed against each other as the projection above them burst into life, rotating slowly as a booming voice filled the nearly empty auditorium.

'Tonight, you will take a journey like no other,' the recording of Professor Armitage announced. 'Strap yourselves in as we journey through the stars to the moon and back!'

CHAPTER NINETEEN
Arthur

'EGGS BENEDICT FOR you, Madeleine, and just a coffee for Arthur,' Cora said, setting the tray down on the table. She clenched her left hand as she let go.

'What's wrong, Cora?' Madeleine asked.

'Just a busy few weeks catching up with me.'

'You need to watch that. My mother, God rest her, suffered with arthritis for over thirty years,' said Arthur.

'Thanks for that, Arthur,' Cora replied with her trademark hearty laugh. 'My uncle, must be only a few years older than you, has a touch of it so it's in the family. Something to look forward to, eh?'

She trotted off back towards the kitchen area, leaving Madeleine shaking her head and scowling at him.

'Don't give me that look, I was only making conversation.'

'She's only in her forties. She doesn't need to be fretting just yet.'

'If it's her joints she needs to be careful, that's all I was saying.'

'While we're on the subject, what did Doctor Thomas say when you spoke?'

Arthur glanced around but nobody at the tables closest was paying any attention to them. 'No, no, you're not getting out of telling me all about last night. How was it?'

Madeleine had spent most of the afternoon and early evening getting ready for her date with James, and hadn't arrived back home until after eleven. He had taken Madeleine to one of her favourite restaurants after she had dropped a subtle hint. Arthur knew all the tricks she had employed over the years and was more than impressed that James had recognized the hint so quickly and booked a table for their date.

'I'm not telling you his surname,' she insisted when pressed. 'You'll have Teddy on that phone of his finding out everything about him.'

Arthur tried to protest the notion, but he knew it was pointless; she wasn't wrong.

'It was a really lovely evening though,' Madeleine continued. 'He was the perfect gentleman, and we know those are few and far between these days, even at our age.'

'Oh Madeleine, that's so wonderful to hear. Did he ask much about our, erm, little set-up?'

'I explained it. He was very understanding. He said that he had had some gay friends over the years and we didn't really dwell on it much after that.'

'So have you made any plans to see him again?'

'I wanted to talk to you about that, actually,' she said, setting her knife and fork down on the plate. 'Are you sure you are okay with that? If I were to go out with James again?'

'I can't believe you're even asking,' Arthur said, laughing. 'Good Lord woman, nothing would make me happier than to see you out there enjoying yourself. I'm just relieved I didn't have to step in and stop Eric Brown hassling you for a date again.'

'Well, in that case,' she said, allowing her lips to curl into a small grin. 'James said he would like to take me out again this week.'

It was such a weight off Arthur's mind to know that Madeleine was excited to meet new people. Madeleine's support of him as they both moved forward was one thing, but he would never have felt comfortable believing that he was moving on and leaving her behind alone. The nights before announcing their engagement to their respective families had been spent trying to work out how their life together could work for both of them. Arthur had never expected to find himself married for fifty years with children, but happiness, something they had both craved, had come easily for them.

Harriet Parker gave a polite nod in their direction when she entered the café alone. She then engaged in a very hushed conversation with Cora before leaving without as much as another glance in their direction. They were now the only customers left in the café.

'That was a little odd,' Madeleine whispered as she watched Cora hurry back to the kitchen. 'Something must be wrong if Harriet doesn't have time to come over and offer another one of her pearls of wisdom.'

Cora reappeared a minute later, her face noticeably flushed. She kept her head bowed as she shuffled towards the door.

'I think Cora just locked the door,' Madeleine said, her neck craned. 'She did. She's turned the sign round. What on earth? Cora? Cora love, has something happened?'

Cora walked over, pulled a chair out from the table next to them and sat down.

'Terrible news,' she said, taking the tissue which Madeleine held out to her. She dabbed her eyes. 'Harriet called in; she'd just heard. I thought it was best to close up, but you finish up first.'

'Cora, what is it, what's happened?'

'Young Sophie Rice – popped in here every morning before college – she's taken her own life. They found her yesterday morning. Only just turned sixteen too.'

'How awful,' Madeleine said, clasping her hands to her chest. 'Are you okay, Arthur?'

He felt numb. His chest ached and he tried to remember to breathe. Both Madeleine and Cora were staring at him, their eyes wide with concern.

'Sophie Rice, Eric's granddaughter, I just spoke with her the other night,' he said softly, thinking back to their recent short conversation outside the restaurant. Sophie had briefly spoken about her desire to leave Northbridge, but she hadn't elaborated on why. Arthur felt a pang of regret at not having questioned her more about why she was so keen to do so. It wouldn't take long for news of Eric and Claudette Brown's granddaughter's death to spread around Northbridge and the neighbouring towns.

Arthur and Madeleine travelled back to the house in silence. The streets were still busy. Shops were still open, filled with customers carrying on, unaffected by the news. That was life. No one stopped for anyone. People would grieve, people would be sympathetic, but life would go on with no apologies.

'Do you think I should phone Eric?' he asked. He had been

185

debating the question in his head but wanted to know what Madeleine thought. She always knew what was right.

'I think it would be best to send something first to let them know you are thinking of them and then, if you're up to it, we can go to the house,' she said gently. 'Flowers and a card, perhaps.'

'Would you come with me?'

'Of course, Arthur. I know how difficult this is. I'll be there.'

Arthur didn't know what to do with himself for the rest of the day. Sitting still felt wrong, but he had nowhere to go. As he moped around the garden that evening, he heard Teddy arrive. He came straight out the back garden and hugged him.

'How are you doing, Grandad? It's too cold for you to be out here.'

'I'm fine, I'm fine. Poor Eric. The whole family, I can't stop thinking about them all.'

'I know. I couldn't believe it when I heard. I never knew.'

'Knew what?'

'Sophie. There were rumours about her sexuality. Evangelina was telling me before I got here. Apparently someone at college was threatening to out her and it all escalated.'

Arthur felt as if someone had punched him in the gut. His knees began to wobble. That must have been why Sophie wanted to move away. He could feel it in his bones. She knew the city would offer her the chance to live as who she was. And then someone had threatened to turn her life upside down, and she had seen no other way out of the situation.

'Come on, Grandad, let's get you back inside,' Teddy said, taking him by the arm and leading him towards the lounge. Once Arthur was settled, Teddy carried him in a cup of tea.

'Nan put two sugars in it,' he said. 'She thought you might need it.'

'Thanks, Teddy,' Arthur said gratefully. 'Sorry, today has been a tough one.'

'I understand. It hits hard, especially when it's someone you know.'

'That poor girl. She must have felt so alone. I can't bear to think of the suffering that she went through, to have had no one to turn to and to feel like that was the only option.'

Arthur stopped. He felt Teddy's eyes on him, waiting for him to continue.

'Not even your mother or Patrick know this, Teddy, but I'm only alive because of your grandmother. The months after Jack left were some of the worst of my life. I was living in fear. I didn't know who I could trust. Then I promised my parents I'd go to the appointments they had arranged. They said the doctor just wanted to talk and try to understand.'

'Are you saying what I think you're saying, Grandad?' Teddy said, sounding aghast.

'It started off as just talking. Then the pictures. The men and the women. It was the shoes,' he said slowly. 'The wires were connected to these rubber shoes I had to put on. They were going to cure me of this disease.'

'Oh my god.' Teddy breathed. 'That's conversion therapy. I can't believe you went through that. It's barbaric. There are people only now telling their stories because they haven't been able to talk about what they experienced, Grandad, so you're not alone. I still can't believe the things that went on. That still go on.'

'I've seen them talking about it on the news, people trying to act like it was meant to help. The apologies aren't worth the paper they're written on. Those monsters didn't care. It didn't stop until I tried to end it.'

'Grandad, are you saying . . . you tried to . . .?'

Teddy's eyes filled with tears as he processed what Arthur had just told him.

'Your grandmother found me almost unconscious,' Arthur said slowly. 'Poor woman. She bent me over the toilet until every last tablet was out of me. She never left my side that night. Nor any since.'

'I don't know what to say,' Teddy said, his eyes wet with tears. 'People are still suffering and I'm here worrying about telling people who I am.'

'You're allowed to worry. You'll get there, Teddy. Everyone's story is unique, I'm proof of that. I'm not just quoting that song you used to play all the time, but it's true that all of these things really do only make us stronger.'

'What if they don't, Grandad? What if Mum never talks to me again? What if I can't cope with everything? What if I don't have Nan to save me like she saved you?'

'You'll have me,' Arthur said. 'No matter what happens, you'll always have me.'

'Thanks, Grandad. I hope I can be half as strong as you have been throughout all of this.'

'I have no doubt about it. Now, let's talk about something else. Why don't you tell me what's going on with you and Ben?'

'Well, actually . . .' Teddy said slowly. 'We kissed!'

Arthur sat upright and slapped his hands on his knees.

'You waited until now to tell me some happy news? That's wonderful, Teddy.'

'Sorry, it didn't feel right to bring it up, but I've not been able to stop smiling since last night. Then I heard about Sophie at work and knew I had to come see you.'

'Did you talk to Ben about it?'

'Briefly. We were going to go for dinner tonight, but we'll do it in a few days instead. I told him I wanted to come straight home to check on you.'

'He's a good lad. Does this mean you are going to talk to your mum now?'

'That's the plan, but all of this . . . it feels like it changes things, doesn't it?'

'Does it?'

'I dunno, Grandad. I keep thinking about what I'd have done if someone had tried to out me when I was sixteen. Even now, look how I panicked I was when it felt like Ben was putting pressure on me. It scares me that I don't know what I'd have done if I was in Sophie's situation.'

'We never know how we'll react to situations until we're in them, Teddy. I never imagined any of this happening at seventy-nine after a lifetime of marriage and trying to live the life everyone expected of me. Don't do the same, even if you think it will make them happy.'

Arthur didn't sleep much that night. He tried reading, but found his eyes burning as he tried to focus on the words. Memories of waiting rooms and smiling doctors swirled around in his head.

Flashes of light lit up a small room.

A large projector.

A bottle of whiskey.

Tablets.

It was a relief to get out of bed when the early December sun began to rise in the sky.

The family arranged to attend the funeral together. Elizabeth wasn't going to join them due to having a meeting she couldn't rearrange. Patrick and Teddy arrived at the house early that morning. Both were smartly dressed in black suits.

'I didn't think it would still fit, to be honest with you,' Patrick said. 'Haven't worn it since—'

'Dad's funeral. I'm the same,' Teddy said.

'Are you sure your boss didn't mind you taking today off, Teddy?' Arthur asked.

'No, it wasn't a problem at all.'

'That's good. You make sure you work hard and catch up on what you miss.'

'Thanks, Grandad,' Teddy said with a smile. 'Ben said he would keep me updated.'

Arthur gave his shoulder a reassuring squeeze.

With Patrick driving, Madeleine sat in the front passenger seat, leaving Arthur and Teddy in the back.

Arthur knew what he was going to say. He'd thought about it numerous times while lying awake during the night. As much as he didn't want to say it, he couldn't bear to see his grandson risk a chance at happiness.

'I don't think you should tell your mum,' he said quickly.

'I'm sorry to say it, but I don't trust her to respond the way you need or deserve right now.'

Teddy's stomach flipped.

'What? What's making you say this?' he whispered.

'What if it's not the reaction you need, Teddy? I don't want to risk you being hurt by someone who doesn't understand you.'

'I see. Thanks, Grandad,' Teddy said, staring out the window as they passed by his old primary school.

They sat in silence the rest of the journey, pulling into the cemetery car park and joining the small queue of cars waiting to find a space.

'I've got tissues, so if anyone needs a packet, they're in my handbag,' Madeleine said once they were finally parked and out of the car. Patrick took her arm and led the way into the church.

'Ready, Grandad?' Teddy said, holding out his arm for Arthur to link as they walked inside together.

CHAPTER TWENTY
Teddy

THE SIGHT OF some of Sophie's belongings, including her drumsticks and a large teddy bear, on top of the coffin forcefully reminded Teddy of his own father's funeral, and he was soon asking Madeleine for her tissues. He could feel his legs trembling throughout the service, especially when one of Sophie's best friends spoke about her and her love of animals. They followed along quietly as they made their way from the church to the adjoining cemetery. Teddy saw Sophie's grandparents squeeze each other's hands as the coffin was lowered into the ground, with only the sound of sobbing filling the cold December air. Several times, Teddy saw people point out Arthur and Madeleine to the person they were with. He knew his grandparents' relationship was still a topic of town gossip, but he had hoped people would try to resist discussing it in honour of Sophie's memory. Apparently not.

As they filed out of the church, Teddy did a double-take, sure he had just seen his mum sitting in the second last pew. His eyes darted around trying to locate her, but whoever had caught his attention was now nowhere to be seen.

'So close to Christmas, poor loves,' Madeleine said as

they slowly made their way back to the car. Her shoes, she confessed, were hurting, so they had agreed to leave quickly.

'I can't go without seeing Eric,' Arthur said suddenly, closing the car door. 'I won't be long.'

Teddy looked at Madeleine and Patrick. He couldn't let his grandad go alone. He knew that Eric had been horribly rude to Arthur before, and it was impossible to know what state he'd be in today. It would hopefully be a little easier if Teddy was by his side.

'Thanks, Teddy,' Arthur whispered when he caught up.

Eric was now standing with his daughter Deborah, Sophie's mum. An elderly woman shook both of their hands before leaving them. Teddy followed behind as his grandad gingerly made his way towards his old friends.

'I wanted to pass on my sincerest condolences to you both,' Arthur began. 'It's such a terrible loss.'

'Thank you, Arthur, it's very kind of you to come,' Deborah said.

'Not at all, Deborah. It was a beautiful service for a special young woman.'

Eric was staring at the ground. Teddy watched him push a stone around with his foot.

'Eric, I want you to know that we're all here for you and your family,' Arthur said, holding out his hand.

Teddy could see it happening. It was like he was watching in slow-motion as Eric fell forward and hugged Arthur, then began sobbing loudly into his shoulder.

'Thank you for coming, Edward,' Deborah said, attempting a small smile. 'How are you enjoying your new job?'

'It's going well, thank you.'

'Your mum must be so proud of you. When your dear father passed away, I remember she did nothing but talk about you and how you were stepping up for her and your sisters.'

Teddy had no idea his mum had ever spoken about him like this to anyone, though after returning home from his grandparents', he had made a significant effort to take on more responsibilities around the house. His dad had always made sure he had watched him when doing various chores. He knew his mum and sisters didn't always need the opinions or help of their nineteen-year-old brother, but the sense of purpose gave him a reason to get out of bed in the morning.

'Thank you, Mrs Rice. If there's anything I can ever do to help, please do let me know.'

Teddy offered his condolences again and rejoined his grandad as they walked back down to the car.

'Poor man is broken,' Arthur said, his own voice hoarse. 'Apologized and everything. It's been such a shock for all of them.'

'Just goes to show that you never really know what's going on with the people closest to you,' Teddy said. He had been thinking about the language Sophie might have been exposed to since Arthur's coming out had become public knowledge. 'Imagine if she'd been listening to any of the stuff people said about you.'

'It doesn't even bear thinking about. I want you to promise me you'd never think suicide was your only option.'

'Is that why you think I shouldn't tell Mum? In case I couldn't handle her reaction?' Teddy gasped. Suddenly his grandfather's advice made sense.

'I know, I'm a silly old man, but I don't want you to have

to deal with the kind of things I've experienced since coming out. Northbridge is a small town and that isn't always a good thing. Maybe if you get away from here, you'll have chances I didn't. I missed my chance.'

Teddy spent the car ride home mulling over his grandad's words. Every time he felt like he was making progress towards finally having the conversation with Mum, something new filled him with doubt. Teddy didn't want to test Ben's support, but it was only becoming more and more difficult to imagine coming out and turning his world upside down. Hoping that setting himself a deadline would help, Teddy later told a surprised Ben that he was now aiming to do it before the end of the year, but with Christmas fast approaching, he was beginning to panic that Ben would only end up disappointed once again.

Elizabeth came to his room later that night.

'How are you doing after today?' she asked.

'It was tough, I'm glad I was there for Grandad.'

'It's just awful to think that someone so young couldn't see a future, that taking her own life felt like the easiest option.'

'It wasn't the easiest option, Mum. She must have thought it was her only one. She didn't think people would accept her for who she was and that can be terrifying,' Teddy said, sitting up on his bed. 'I don't think there's an age limit on that either.'

The corner of Elizabeth's mouth twitched.

'Just because Grandad is almost eighty doesn't mean he's not affected by things. He needs our love and support as much as Sophie needed her family's.'

'I know,' Elizabeth said softly. Teddy was slightly taken

aback to see that her eyes had filled with tears. He jumped off his bed and grabbed the box of tissues from his desk.

'Here you go,' he said, handing it to his mum. 'Look, I know it's going to take time, but we're a strong family who can get through anything. You taught us that. We've got Christmas coming up. Will you think about all of us spending it together, please?'

Elizabeth nodded her head as she dabbed her eyes with the tissue.

'Thank you, Mum,' Teddy said, feeling like there was some hope on the horizon for the first time in months.

'What was coming out like for you, Ben?'

Ben had surprised Teddy by taking him out for dinner at a small Greek restaurant after work. While wating for their main courses to arrive, Teddy realized that he had never properly asked Ben about his own experience. He watched as Ben digested the question.

'It could've gone better,' he said, taking a gulp of water from his glass.

'Sorry, we don't have to talk about—'

'Oh, no, it's fine. I knew I'd have to talk about it at some point.'

'I was a bit hesitant to ask,' Teddy admitted. 'You've mentioned your dad a couple of times, but never really said much about him or your mum.'

'The downside to being an only child is that when your parents basically reject you, you quickly find out how to get on with things yourself.'

'Shit, Ben, I'm so sorry you went through that.'

'Don't be. I'm not just saying that, Teddy, I mean it. Nothing was ever good enough for them. I wanted to be a journalist, not an accountant like my dad.'

'Did you always want to be a journalist?'

'Always! I told them they weren't going to change my mind when I went to uni. Nothing's changed now. Nothing and nobody is going to get in my way.'

Teddy reached across the table and took Ben's hand in his. He'd never done anything like that in public before, but it felt right. This was the life he wanted.

'I think you've inspired me to write something,' Teddy said. 'I was thinking about it after Sophie's death, about the experiences people have coming out. Do you think I should talk to Dylan about it?'

'Sure,' Ben said, not sounding entirely convinced. 'If it's something you think *The Post* would be interested in, go for it. They can only say no, I suppose.'

The following day, Teddy wasted no time in asking Dylan if they could have a quick chat about his pitch.

'I really love that you're coming up with ideas like this, but you need to make it a little clearer what the story is,' Dylan said after listening. 'There's something in there, you just need to really nail down the focus.'

'Thanks, Dylan, I'll have a think and come back to you. I need to talk to Sophie's mum to make sure she doesn't mind.'

Later that night, Teddy decided to run his new idea past Shakeel and Lexie.

'Sophie took her own life and she won't be the last. If her mum was to speak about this, it could be really important. It could save lives,' Teddy told them both on FaceTime.

'I think this is an amazing idea, Teddy,' Lexie said. 'I really hope Sophie's mum can help.'

'I know. Ben was a bit worried it might be too soon to ask her.'

'He is?' Shakeel said. 'I can't imagine why he's not keen on you working on a big piece.'

'He's been very supportive, Shak. He's not this bad guy who is trying to sabotage me or whatever you think he's doing. You've got him all wrong.'

'Sorry, ignore me. I've had a long day. Your idea sounds great.'

'Thanks, guys,' Teddy said. 'Right, I'm bloody knackered. I'm gonna head to bed.'

Shakeel's comment played on Teddy's mind as he lay awake. He had never seen his best friend be so openly negative about someone, never mind when he knew that Teddy and Ben were now dating. He needed to try and bring the two together, especially since Ben had already picked up on the animosity. He was going to need all of Lexie's help to do it.

Teddy saw Ben watching as he and Dylan returned to their desks after their follow-up chat the next day. Dylan was fully on board with his revised idea. Now all he had to do was talk to Mrs Rice.

'Seriously, Teddy. This is exactly the kind of stuff you guys should be coming up with,' Dylan said, slapping him on the back as he sat down at his desk. Despite his happiness, Teddy couldn't help but hear Shak's voice as he glanced across at Ben to gauge his reaction. He breathed a sigh of relief to see Ben beaming back at him.

'Proud of you, mate,' he whispered, discreetly placing his hand on Teddy's knee and giving it an affectionate rub. 'This is what it's all about. This is why we're here!'

'What a day. You're planning your big feature and I'm rounding up social media comments about the weather,' Ben said as they left the building a few hours later. Before Teddy could respond, he quickly came to a halt in the main entrance foyer of the building.

'Sorry, bit cranky. I didn't mean that to sound so bitchy.'

'Don't worry. You're always coming up with ideas! You're going to hit the right one soon, I just know it.' Teddy glanced around quickly to make sure that they were alone, before leaning across and giving him a kiss on the cheek.

'You know there's CCTV, right?'

'What? Are you ser—'

'Teddy, chill. I'm joking. Well, I'm not, but seriously, if someone in there thought that was exciting, they need to get out more.'

'Sorry, you just never know who knows who round here.'

'I know,' Ben sighed. 'The Christmas party is going to be fun when we're spending the evening dodging the mistletoe.'

'Don't be like that. We'll still have a good time.'

'I guess. It'd just be nice to enjoy it with you properly, rather than playing it straight for a few hours and then grabbing the train home again, you know?'

Teddy paused for a moment, an idea forming in his head.

'What if I was to stay the night?'

'What? Where?'

'With you, obviously.'

Ben looked at him, agog. 'I didn't even think to offer because I thought you'd shoot down the idea.'

'I'm getting a head start on my New Year's resolution to be brave here, do you mind?'

'Mind?' Ben laughed, his smile reaching from ear to ear. 'If I didn't think the security guard watching us would pass out, I'd reach over there and kiss you properly.'

'Behave! Come on, our reservation is for six.' Teddy laughed. In only eight days he would finally get to spend the night with Ben.

CHAPTER TWENTY-ONE
Arthur

'YOU'VE HARDLY SAID a word since I've been here, Arthur. I'm beginning to take it personally.'

'I'm sorry, Oscar. I'm not the best company right now.'

'I'll say. I could find more life in the cemetery.'

They both laughed. Several nearby ducks looked around at them. Despite the biting cold, they had wrapped up and gone for a walk around the local park. Sitting on the old wooden bench, staring out at the pond was a chance to breathe in the crisp air and relax and enjoy the morning.

'Do you have any regrets, Oscar?'

'Never heard of them.'

Arthur chuckled and let out an exasperated sigh.

'You're lucky.'

'Excuse me, there's nothing lucky about it. Life is in your hands. You might be late to the party, but it's still your party. It's up to you to make the most of it now. I don't know how many times I have to tell you this, Arthur. There's a big world out there.'

'Too big for the likes of me.'

'That's nonsense and you know it,' Oscar said, slapping his

hands down on his knees. 'Even if it were true, you can still enjoy life here. There's nothing stopping you. We'll both be in the ground soon enough without climbing in voluntarily.'

'I didn't imagine getting to eighty and feeling like I didn't know who I was anymore.'

'Well, we're going to change that!'

'I told you, I'm not going to dance class with you.' Arthur laughed. 'These two left feet have been the bane of my life.'

'More excuses. Poor Madeleine. I didn't realize she'd been suffering this for fifty years. Come on, up on those feet or you'll freeze to that bench.'

Spending time with Oscar was just what Arthur needed. Arthur knew Madeleine had been concerned about him after Sophie's death, but it was only when he heard her voice her concern to Oscar that he realized just how down he had been.

'What would make you happy, Arthur?' Oscar asked him, his tone was more serious than Arthur had ever heard him use in the short time that they had known each other. 'You strike me as a man who likes to be doing things, to feel like you're part of something.'

Arthur nodded slowly. He had always enjoyed being busy; it hadn't been easy adjusting to retired life and trying to find new ways to pass each day.

'Right, so what about these groups you're involved with, like that one with Eric?'

'What about it?'

'Well, what would you be doing? You do things for the community don't you?'

'Yes, but—'

'No buts! What would Arthur Edwards suggest you do if he was at the meeting?'

Arthur frowned as he tried to think of ideas as they walked back to Oscar's car.

'I hope that silence means you've got an answer,' Oscar said as they came to a halt.

'Fundraising?' Arthur said, trying to sound confident in his response.

'That sounded more like a question. Are you asking if I think that's a good idea?'

'Do you?'

'It depends. What for? What kind of event?'

'I could raise money for a charity that supports the LGBTQIA+ community or mental health.'

'Or both!' Oscar said. 'This will give you something to focus on. Come up with ideas.'

'We've done lots of different things, like coffee mornings and bake sales.'

Oscar shook his head at the suggestions. 'Think bigger, Arthur! This is your chance to do something, to shake things up. Next time I see you, I don't want to hear a word about bake sales, unless it's Madeleine offering me another basket of those glorious scones she's made.'

Oscar dropped Arthur right to the door. They weren't going to see each other until after Christmas, as Oscar was travelling up north to spend some time with his niece and her family.

'I'd tell you to behave yourself, but I know it would be pointless,' Arthur teased before waving him off.

'He's quite a man, isn't he?' Madeleine said, appearing in the doorway.

'He really is. I don't think I can keep up with him.'

'You can, I know you've still got that twinkle in your eye.'

'Madeleine,' he said suddenly, 'Elizabeth and Ralph are definitely coming for Christmas Day now, aren't they?'

'Yes, and the kids, and Patrick and Scarlett. It's going to be lovely to have everyone together again.'

'Excellent. I've decided I'm going to cook the dinner this year,' Arthur declared.

Northbridge was at its busiest on Christmas week. The shops were packed full of shoppers carrying bags full of presents. Arthur was queuing to collect the turkey from the butchers. He had insisted upon doing the shopping for dinner now that he was taking control of the meal. It had taken several hours to convince Madeleine that he was up for facing Northbridge on his own.

A couple of people wished him a merry Christmas as he visited the various shops, but to his delight, Arthur found that he was largely invisible to the other shoppers. As he climbed back into the car a short while later, he couldn't help but smile at the prospect that his personal life might finally be old news.

CHAPTER TWENTY-TWO
Teddy

TEDDY TOOK ONE last look at the document before attaching it to his email for Dylan. Everything had come together better than he had could ever have expected. Despite his initial concerns about doing so, Teddy had asked his mum for Deborah's number and explained his idea over the phone. Deborah was immediately open to the idea and arranged for him to come and visit once things had had some time. He wasn't sure how long he would be there, but in the end, he'd spent several hours at the Rice's home. Sophie had come out to her parents in a letter she wrote just hours before taking her life. He hadn't expected it, but he found himself alone sitting in tears as he read the letter after Deborah insisted that she would like him to do so.

'I'm so grateful that you want to tell Sophie's story,' Deborah had told him as he left their house. 'If just one life can be saved by people reading this, it'll be worth it, Edward. You can help stop one more family feeling this kind of pain.'

It felt surreal to be typing up words about someone who had lived just down the road from him. Even though he didn't really know Sophie personally, he thought about the various times they had acknowledged each other when passing in the street or had bumped into each other at the cinema or Cora's. Both of them trying to exist while hiding a secret behind their smiles. He tried to reassure himself that it wouldn't have made any difference to Sophie. There wasn't an unspoken code, a phrase he might have said that would have told her they shared a secret. They would simply have crossed paths and carried on, still hiding who they really were, dealing with their secrets in their own way.

'It's too good to waste on page thirty. I'm sure they're waiting for a quieter day to give it a good showing,' Ben said over lunch several days later as Teddy fretted about the lack of news on his piece. He appreciated Ben's sensible attitude, even if it was hard to believe.

Dylan was just finishing a phone call when they arrived back at their desks.

'You might want to grab a copy of the paper nice and early tomorrow, Teddy,' he said.

'Why do . . . wait, are you serious? It's going in the Saturday edition?'

'Sure is. They really loved it.'

'Holy shit. I don't know what to even say.'

'You handled the whole piece with so much sensitivity. It's great work.'

'Cheers, Dylan, and thank you for your help with editing it. I really learned a lot.'

There was a real buzz around the office that afternoon, with most people looking forward to the Christmas party the following night. While Teddy was excited about the party, he could happily have skipped it and gone straight to the part where he finally had the chance to have Ben all to himself. Every time he thought about it he had to stop himself jumping up and down on the spot.

With work quiet, Teddy and Ben took the opportunity to continue searching for Jack Johnson, hoping to find the man who had fled Northbridge over fifty years ago. Teddy had grown more and more frustrated with every dead end. It was proving impossible to narrow down their search. When Teddy finally suggested they just let it go and accept defeat, Ben passionately insisted that they shouldn't.

'Thank you for trying to help, but honestly, this doesn't feel right. Grandad didn't want me looking and I should never have involved you,' Teddy said. If Jack had purposely tried to remain hidden, he had done an excellent job of it.

'Are you feeling all right?' Teddy asked Ben as he returned from his second visit to the toilet in an hour. His face was looking paler than Teddy had ever seen him, while his forehead was glistening with sweat.

'I feel really awful,' he said, 'And the less said about that visit to the bathroom the better.'

'You look bloody awful. I think you need to go home.'

'I think I might, you know. I'm going to order a cab.'

Teddy walked Ben downstairs and made sure he got into his waiting car safely.

'Text me when you get to the flat,' he said. 'And drink plenty of water.'

He spent the rest of the afternoon finishing up several stories he was working on for the website. Ben let him know that he was going straight to bed to try and sleep. As the end of the shift approached, he found himself thinking about the following day's newspaper. Only a handful of people would know just how personal this feature was to him. He had the chance to publish something which could make a difference in the lives of others. He felt a slight pang of guilt, imagining what Deborah would say if she knew he was still in the closet. As close as he had come to telling her, it was just too close for comfort in Northbridge. He tried desperately to shake off the feeling as he left the office that evening. Ben didn't answer his call as he walked to the station to get the train home. Teddy hoped he was still sleeping and would wake up feeling better.

'Teddy! Teddy! Come down. I've got the paper.'

He jumped out of bed and dashed to the top of the stairs to see Evangelina waving the morning edition of *The Post* at him. He almost lost his footing halfway down the stairs, but somehow caught his balance and avoided toppling down onto his sister.

'Oh my God, take it easy, you absolute lunatic. It's only a newspaper,' she said.

'Excuse me, this is going to be my first solo byline and on a really important story.'

'Whoa,' she said, throwing her hands up and jumping back from him.

'What? What's wrong?'

'Your transformation into Mum is complete.'

Teddy scowled as he grabbed the paper and hurried into the kitchen leaving her cackling loudly in the hallway. He threw it down on the table and began hastily flicking through the pages to find the story.

'Holy shit!' he exclaimed, much louder than he had intended. 'It's a double page on six and seven. I can't believe it.'

His name, all in capital letters, made his heart jump. He'd done it.

'Nice one, Teddy, I'll read it later, but I'm sure it's great,' Evangelina said before disappearing out of the kitchen and back upstairs.

Teddy stood alone staring at the newspaper. His mum and Ralph were already out. He'd have to wait for them to get back to show them the feature. He stared at the pictures on the page. Sophie's smiling face stared back at him in several of the images Deborah had given him to use.

'Teddy! Your phone's ringing, are you deaf?'

'Huh?' he looked round. Eleanor was standing at the sink. He had been oblivious to her entering the kitchen.

'Sorry, I zoned out,' he said, his heart jumping as he glanced down at his phone. One new voicemail. He walked out of the kitchen holding the phone to his ear. Ben's voice was exactly the sound he needed to hear.

'Morning, Teddy. Hope you're really proud of the piece. I've not seen it yet, but I can't wait to. I'm really sorry, but I still feel awful and don't think I'm going to be able to go tonight. I'm really gutted. We'll rearrange soon though. Talk to you later.'

Teddy clenched his jaw as he hit replay on the message and absorbed Ben's words. He knew they would have plenty of opportunities, but right then, all he wanted to do was see him. His phone pinged again.

Hopeful that it might be a follow-up, Teddy opened it up to

find a short congratulations text from Shakeel. He had already been to the newsagent's and bought a copy of the paper. The text was quickly followed with a selfie of him beaming while proudly holding it up.

Overcome with a mixture of emotions, Teddy tried, but failed, to hold back his tears as he stared at the image.

CHAPTER TWENTY-THREE
Arthur

BEFORE ARTHUR KNEW it, Christmas Day had arrived. He hadn't felt this excited for years. Today felt like a chance to put the past few months behind him. Behind all of them. He would have his beloved family around the table again. That was what today was all about. Arthur couldn't hold back his small squeal of delight as he threw open his bedroom curtains to see a thick layer of snow had fallen overnight. Arthur loved snow. It awoke fond memories of snowball fights and sledging down the many hills that surrounded Northbridge. But it wasn't just about the fun. The snow brought a beauty to the town that he had always loved. The white blanket hid any ugliness that threatened to spoil the view. Today was going to be a perfect day, he just knew it.

Madeleine, true to style, had been unable to stop herself from lurking in the kitchen and keeping a watchful eye as Arthur began preparing the vegetables. Teddy arrived just after 9 a.m. and was quickly put to work peeling potatoes.

'Anything nice in the present haul this year?' Arthur asked.

'Some lovely bits and pieces. Mum and Ralph got me one of

those video calling devices, you know the one I was showing you recently?'

'I'll not pretend to have a clue about those things. What about . . .?' Arthur gave his head a little shake, resisting saying Ben's name out loud as if it might trigger a giant rainbow over the house for everyone to see.

'He bought me something online, but it hasn't arrived yet.'

'Just think, you could be spending Christmas together this time next year,' Arthur said as he watched Teddy progressing through the basin of potatoes. 'Be careful there, you're taking big lumps out of those. We have to feed the whole family!'

The turkey and ham were both making good progress, mouth-watering scents wafting through the house. Arthur felt his stomach groan. He'd been nibbling on bits as he cooked but was now beginning to wish he had eaten a big breakfast to carry him through the next couple of hours. It was too late to have something now, with lunch just over ninety minutes away.

'The pigs in blankets are ready and waiting to go in the oven, Grandad. I'm going to go and start setting the table.'

Teddy had only just left the kitchen when Madeleine slipped in to check on their progress.

'Don't worry, I'm not spying. I just wanted to make sure you're coping,' she whispered as Arthur looked up from the oven.

'Getting there. I don't know how you do it year in, year out. We'd be eating tomorrow if I didn't have Teddy's help.'

'He's a good boy. It's lovely seeing you both at work together like this.'

'I want today to be special for everyone.'

'Elizabeth and the girls should be here by midday. Apparently

Ralph will be a little behind. He's stopping by his aunt's on the way first, but the snow might slow him down a bit.'

Madeleine paused. 'I just want you to know that I'm really proud of you,' she finally said, her hands gripping the edge of the bench. 'Not just for everything this year, but for really making an effort like this. These are memories they'll all cherish.'

'That's enough of that,' Arthur said, looking up at the ceiling to hide the tears in his eyes. 'If I burn anything I'm putting the blame on you for distracting me.' He grinned as he waved his fork at her.

Before long, the sound of Elizabeth, Eleanor and Evangelina arriving filled the house.

'Hi, Grandad,' the girls called out. 'Merry Christmas!'

'Merry Christmas, Evangelina,' Arthur said, hugging his youngest grandchild tightly. 'Don't you look lovely. You're the absolute spit of your mother.' He laughed as she rolled her eyes; it wasn't the first time she had heard that. She shook the fresh snowflakes out of her thick brown hair.

'I'm not going to get in the way, but it smells really amazing. You could have some competition for best Christmas dinner here, Nan!' Evangelina said. She vanished as suddenly as she had appeared, carrying two glasses of red wine.

'I better go and say hello to your mum,' Arthur said, following Evangelina to the lounge.

Elizabeth was setting some presents under the large Christmas tree. He gave a small cough as he entered the room.

'Hi, Dad,' she said as she flattened out the wrinkles in her dress. 'Happy Christmas.' She gave him a light kiss on the cheek.

'Merry Christmas, Lizzie. You look lovely. Beautiful dress.'

'Thank you, it was a gift from Ralph. I'm sure the girls helped him pick it out.'

'They have their mother's eye for fashion.'

Elizabeth gave him a small smile. 'It smells really great in here. Everyone's good and hungry!'

'Excellent, Teddy and I are just putting the finishing touches to dinner. It shouldn't be much longer.'

Her eyes widened. 'Sorry, you and Edward? You're *both* cooking? I just assumed Teddy was coming over early to give *Mum* a hand.'

Arthur couldn't help but enjoy the surprise in her voice. He nodded proudly.

'Oh yes, a proper Christmas Day feast from the men of the house this year.'

'Well,' Elizabeth said hoarsely, still struggling to find her voice amid the shock. 'I'm going to need a drink if there are going to be any more surprises like this today!'

The house was full of life. Christmas music was playing throughout the downstairs. Outside, the snow continued to fall. It had been a full year since they had all been together in the family home and Madeleine was in her element fussing over her guests, ensuring that everyone had a drink. Evangelina was more than a little excited to finally accept a glass of champagne from her grandmother.

'It saves us having to pretend we didn't know she was sneaking them last year,' Madeleine said as she slipped back into the kitchen. 'Oh Arthur, it's all so lovely I could just cry with happiness.'

'You'll set us all off if you do,' he warned. 'Let's save the tears for when you taste these Brussels sprouts.'

Patrick was in a particularly cheerful mood, popping in and out of the kitchen asking for regular updates on when they would be serving up.

'Soon. I just want to make sure everything is perfect, that's all,' Arthur insisted.

'Go and sit down,' Teddy told Patrick impatiently on the fifth interruption. 'It's only going to be a couple more minutes.'

Arthur was last to leave the kitchen, carrying the turkey on a serving platter into the dining room. Everyone was seated, waiting for his arrival. Teddy and Evangelina clapped as he carefully set the tray down in the centre of the large rectangular table.

'This all looks incredible, Arthur,' Ralph said. 'You guys must be exhausted.'

'You can say that again. I'll eat and then sleep until New Year.'

'Are you going to carve, Arthur?' Madeleine asked.

'Actually, I was wondering if Ralph would like to do the honours.'

Elizabeth looked at him, her eyebrows arched.

'Are you sure, Arthur?' Ralph said. 'I don't want to step on any toes.'

'Not at all. You're a part of this family.' Arthur sat back and watched as Ralph pulled the turkey platter towards him, picked up the large carving knife and began slicing. He looked across at Elizabeth and met her gaze.

'Thank you,' she mouthed.

Once everyone had turkey on their plates, they began

passing the bowlfuls of food around the table. 'Be careful, that's hot,' Arthur warned Scarlett, passing the dish of roast potatoes.

'Excuse me, we need to do crackers,' Patrick said, standing up. 'I made special ones for everyone.'

Amused by the time Patrick had taken to make and decorate the box of special crackers, they each took the one he handed them.

'Everyone ready? On the count of three. One. Two . . .'

The chorus of small pops was met with laughter around the table as everyone checked the contents of their cracker.

'I can't find my present,' Scarlett said, shaking her cracker.

Patrick pushed his chair backwards and looked at the floor. 'There it is he said, I'll get it for you.'

Before they knew it, Patrick was on one knee, holding open a small red box in front of Scarlett.

'Scarlett Ruby Fletcher, I cannot even begin to explain how you have changed my life. You helped me find the light in the darkest period and every day your positivity helps me to be a better person. If you don't mind this crazy family, would you like to spend every Christmas with me?'

Arthur had to double-check Scarlett's answer it had been so muffled by the sobbing and subsequent cheers around the table.

'That was beautiful, son,' Arthur said, hugging Patrick. 'I'm so proud of you.'

Slowly everyone began to retake their seats around the table.

'Sorry, everyone. I hope your food isn't cold because of me,' Patrick said as they began to tuck in.

'If anyone needs it, there's hot gravy in the kitchen,' Teddy said. 'I can go and get it.'

'Just think,' Elizabeth said suddenly, 'this time next year, Ralph and I will be married, Patrick and Scarlett might be if they don't want to waste time and, if things keep going the right way, Eleanor could have a fiancé at the table, too.'

'Mum! Don't be so embarrassing.'

'Well Oliver isn't like most men, darling. Once he knows he's found the one, he's not going to let you go.'

Arthur glanced across the table at Teddy, who was watching the exchange between his mum and sister while he was eating.

'I'll still need a couple of years to plan a wedding,' Eleanor said with a laugh.

'You hear this, Mum?' Elizabeth said. 'These girls are going to keep me waiting for grandchildren.'

'There's always Teddy,' Scarlett said through a mouthful of her dinner.

'Well, if he cooked a young lady a dinner like this, he'd make her very happy,' Elizabeth said with a laugh as everyone looked towards Teddy.

'I actually do make someone happy,' Teddy said. His voice was soft, but strong. Arthur felt his muscles tense up as if his body knew what was about to happen. He couldn't do anything but watch as Teddy looked his mum directly in the eye.

'His name is Ben.'

CHAPTER TWENTY-FOUR
Teddy

IT WASN'T A dream. Teddy's eyes blurred as he tried to focus on the faces staring at him from around the table.

'*What did you just say?*'

His mum's voice shook him out of his momentary daze. He looked back at her; her eyes narrowed as she furrowed her brow.

There was no going back now. They'd all heard him; he might as well finish what he had started. He took a deep breath and allowed the words to finally leave his mouth.

'Mum, I'm gay.'

Relief swept through him. If he hadn't had his knees tucked under the table, he was convinced his body would have floated out of the chair and hit the ceiling. He felt his face muscles ache as his mouth broke into a smile. Unable to stop himself, he burst out laughing. He could feel the tears rolling down his face.

'Can someone please tell me what the hell is happening?' Elizabeth said, looking at the others as if they were going to confirm it was a prank of some sort.

'I think it's very clear, Elizabeth,' Madeleine said softly.

'Everyone, I think we should give Elizabeth and Teddy a few minutes alone.'

'We're eating here. Can't *they* go?' Evangelina whined, looking around at the half-eaten platefuls in front of them all.

'I'm sorry, everyone,' Elizabeth said, picking up her knife and fork again. 'Let's just carry on eating this lovely meal and we can talk about whatever this is afterwards.'

'For crying out loud, Elizabeth,' Madeleine said sternly. 'Go and talk with your son. The food will be there when you come back.'

Teddy held his breath as the table fell silent.

'Edward, let's go outside and talk then,' Elizabeth said softly, pushing her chair back and standing up. She straightened her dress and without waiting for a response, marched out of the room. Teddy looked across at Arthur, who gave him an encouraging smile. By the time he caught up with his mum, she was already by the back door of the utility room just off the kitchen.

Teddy followed her outside to the wooden bench which sat underneath the kitchen window. The snow had now stopped falling. He watched as she wiped a layer off the bench before sitting down. Teddy wished he had put his coat on.

'Okay,' she said, sitting down, crossing her legs. 'So, you've got something to say?'

'I think you heard what I had to say, Mum. Everyone else did.'

She glowered at him and pinched her mouth shut.

'So, when did you decide this?'

'There it is,' Teddy said, sighing.

'There's what?'

'The attitude. The Elizabeth Marsh response to something she doesn't like.'

'What's that supposed to mean?'

'*Decide*,' Teddy repeated. 'How and when did I *decide* to be gay? Well, now you mention it, Mum, I woke up yesterday morning and thought, "I wonder what would really piss Mum off at dinner on Christmas Day?" And here we are.'

She looked out at the garden without responding. Teddy rubbed his cold hands together.

'Are you annoyed because I dared to want to share a little bit of my happiness in that room?' Teddy asked, suddenly angry with her silence.

'So that's it?' his mother said. 'Your uncle proposes and you have to steal the limelight because you felt left out?'

'That's not what I'm saying. I'm just tired of having to sit there and not be myself. No, sorry, I might not be giving you any grandchildren, but is it so wrong of me to want you to know that without having to sit there and pretend? I spend every single day trying to live up to your expectations, to the expectations people put on me because I'm your son. This is me finally telling you that I can't always be that person. But I'm still your son and I want you to love me for who I am.'

'Why today though, Edward? You couldn't just let the family have a nice day together?'

'You don't think there have been hundreds of days I wanted to do this; to just blurt it out? But I haven't been able to. Because I can't hope you might not treat me like you've been treating Grandad.'

'Don't you dare sit there and use that situation against me, like I'm some sort of—'

'Homophobe? You're doing a pretty good job of it right now.'

Teddy didn't even have time to see her right hand flying towards his cheek. He contained a small whimper as the sting on his face made his eyes water.

'Edward, I'm so sorry!' She gasped, holding her hand to her mouth, her eyes widening with shock at what she had done.

'Save it. This is exactly what I expected,' Teddy said quietly. 'This is exactly why I've gone round in circles for years, trying to convince myself that coming out was a good idea, trying to believe that you might just step up for me and believe that I know what I'm doing for once.'

'I do,' she said, her voice cracking slightly. 'If you say you're gay, that's fine.'

'Fine? Gee, thanks, Mum. I'll be sure to put that on a T-shirt.'

'Don't I get a minute to process what you're saying?'

'This isn't about *you*, Mum! Sorry, I know that's difficult, but this is about *me* and who I am. I've just spent the last few months trying to hide who I am in case one of your pals at *The Post* might see something, being terrified that if it comes out that you'll be as awful to me as you've been to your own father. That's not how I want to live. I'm not doing it anymore.'

'Tell me what we're meant to do?' Elizabeth's voice suddenly sounded so lost.

'Just be supportive. Be my mum.'

'Fine,' she said, clasping her hands together. 'I'll tell everyone how proud I am of my gay dad and my gay son. The pair who seem determined to keep secrets and hide everything from me. What does it even matter what I think? It's clear neither of you need or even trust me.'

Teddy jumped up off the bench. His head was throbbing now.

'I'm going to give you some time. I can't do this right now.'

'Typical. You get to decide when you're going to drop this bombshell and then act like the hurt party because someone else might need a little time to come to terms with it.'

'Come to terms? Mum, do you ever just sit back and listen to yourself? All I've done is tell you that I like a boy called Ben. I suppose you think you know everything you need to know about him from Dylan. You don't need time. You just want to punish me. The same way you've just been punishing Grandad for months.'

'I'm not trying to punish anyone, Edward. You have no idea how it feels to be told that your whole life was based on a lie. How do you think it feels to look back on every memory and wonder what was real? Did he ever really love my mother? Did he resent us for existing and stopping him living his life?'

'You know Grandad would never think like that,' Teddy said.

'How do I know that? Maybe I'm overreacting, but I need to deal with this my way. This isn't a small lie to forgive and forget, this is my entire existence. Can't you understand that?'

'I understand,' Teddy said. 'Take all the time you need, but he doesn't deserve this. Neither of us do. We are still the same people.'

Teddy made his way back into the house and followed the noise of happy conversation back to the dining room. He was pleased to see that everyone had kept eating, and most of the plates were now empty. Evangelina and Eleanor were first to spot him slip back into the room.

'Is everything okay? Where's Mum?' Evangelina said.

He shrugged and took his seat.

'I just want to say that I think that was very brave,' Scarlett said. 'I'm not entirely surprised, but I always did have an excellent gaydar. In fact one of the boys I dated in college turned out to be gay.'

Teddy glanced across at Eleanor as she attempted to stifle a giggle.

'Yeah, thanks, Scarlett,' he said. 'Not everyone feels the same way.'

'Is *she* all right?' Patrick said with a nod towards the door. 'I'm sure she'll just need a little time.'

'Like she did with Grandad, yes, that has been established.' Teddy looked across at Arthur. He was struck by how sad his grandad looked.

'Grandad?'

'Everything's going to work itself out, Teddy. Don't worry.'

'I'm sorry I ruined dinner. I don't know where that came from and then suddenly, I was just saying it out loud.'

'I'm proud of you. We all are.' Arthur smiled warmly at Teddy.

'You're worried, I understand. Trust me, I'm fine. She said what she had to say. It's out there now and there's nothing I can do about it.'

It was only when he looked around the table that he noticed Ralph had left since he had come back. Teddy was glad that she wasn't still sitting outside alone.

'He took mum out her coat,' Evangelina explained, resting her chin in her hands. 'So, tell us about this Ben then. Is he fit?'

'He actually is,' her older sister interjected.

Evangelina spun to face Eleanor, who bit her lip as she realized her mistake.

'You knew?'

'It didn't exactly take a genius to figure it out, and then I met him at the car boot sale.'

'I cannot believe you didn't tell me. I'm the only reason you even went to that sale too,' Evangelina squeaked.

'Excuse me,' Teddy said, 'What's with the *actually*?'

'Nothing,' Eleanor grinned. 'He's obviously no Oliver, but you looked good together.'

Teddy rolled his eyes. 'Thanks, I'll be sure to let him know that.'

'Can we meet him?'

'You think I'm bringing him into this mad house any time soon? I actually like this guy.'

'Aww, couldn't he bring him here, Grandad?' Evangelina pleaded. 'He should come for New Year!'

'With the whole family? No chance. I don't want to scare him off.'

'Grandad, can't you make him?'

'I don't know what it is you want me to say, it's not up to me.' Arthur laughed. 'If and when they want to, Teddy knows that he and Ben are more than welcome here any time.'

'Are you sure?'

'Of course, whenever you want. Isn't that right, Madeleine?'

'Teddy knows he's always welcome here and so is Ben.'

'Is this what has been going on behind my back all along?'

Elizabeth said, reappearing in the doorway. 'Just cutting me out because I'm not organizing the Northbridge Pride parade?'

'Elizabeth, that's enough,' Madeleine said.

'Did you know, Mum?'

'No, Nan didn't,' Teddy interjected. 'And even if she did, what does it matter? I told Grandad after he came out, but I asked him not to tell anybody else until I was ready.'

'This just gets better,' Elizabeth said, her voice cracking. 'It makes total sense, because of course you would keep this secret, Dad. You're the professional around here.'

'Let's just take a moment,' Ralph said trying to rest his hand on Elizabeth's shoulder.

'No, Ralph, you heard them when we walked in, already planning their little get-togethers to sit and complain about me. I've given you kids everything I've got. Since your father died, I've tried to stay strong and keep this family together. Now I've found someone who makes me happy and helps me get through the days. Did I complain when Dad thought it was too soon to date Ralph? Did I throw a tantrum when Teddy spent the best part of a year living here as if I was some kind of monster? No. I got on with things, but I'll tell you what, if I'm so awful to be around, feel free to pack your bags. If you don't like the roof I put over your head, go ahead and find somewhere else to live.'

Teddy's mouth was dry. His mum wasn't looking at him, but every word hit him square in the chest. Nobody moved until Elizabeth spoke again.

'I'm afraid we won't be staying for dessert. Girls, get your things please.'

She was gone without another word.

'Bye, everyone. Thank you for dinner,' Ralph said with a small wave before hurrying after her.

'Are you coming?' Evangelina asked Teddy as she put on her coat.

'Not yet. You guys go on. I'll help clean up here and see you later.'

Teddy knew they were reluctant to leave, but it was for the best to try and keep the peace where possible, especially now that he had an idea to run by his grandparents.

'I know it puts you both in a slightly awkward position,' he said later, as he helped with the dishes, 'but would you mind if I was to stay here for a few nights?'

'You never have to ask,' Arthur said. 'That room is yours and always free for you.'

CHAPTER TWENTY-FIVE
Arthur

ARTHUR WALKED AROUND the garden, the snow crunching under his feet. The sound made him smile. He didn't have many memories of his father that he cherished, but the few he did all included snow. His father loved winter. Arthur remembered one morning when he could have been no more than nine years old, being woken up by the sound of snowballs hitting his bedroom window. He had thrown on several layers of clothes and rushed outside. They had played for hours, laughing freely as they held each other's hands and made snow angels. With his father's help, they had built the biggest snowman Arthur had ever seen. Children from across Northbridge had come by to look at it in awe for the three days it lasted. The snow would melt away, leaving no traces of the joy it had briefly brought to the Edwards household.

'I brought you a hot toddy, you must be freezing out here,' Madeleine said, handing over the steaming mug.

'Thanks, love, lost myself in the memories again.'

'It's been a few years since we had a snowfall like this. Do you remember?'

Arthur knew the one she was talking about. It had been

almost ten years ago now. He and Madeleine had been looking after Eleanor, Teddy and Evangelina while Harry whisked Elizabeth away for a surprise trip to Paris. The girls had had little interest in the snow, preferring to sit inside with their Nan drinking hot chocolate with marshmallows. Arthur and Teddy had taken a toboggan up the hill behind the house. Teddy had sat in front of Arthur as they slid down the hill, screaming with delight as the cold wind hit their faces.

'I know today wasn't the perfect day you wanted it to be,' Madeleine said.

'There are more important things. How is Teddy?'

'He's gone upstairs. Don't worry, Arthur. Things are going to be all right.'

Arthur sighed. He hadn't wanted this for Teddy. He didn't want him to have to endure this, hoping and waiting for other people to accept him.

'I couldn't live with myself if Teddy has to go through this because of me,' he said, prompting Madeleine to scowl at him.

'You are in no way to blame for any of this. Elizabeth just needs to process everything, but she is never going to turn her back on her son, on her family.'

Arthur sipped at his drink as Madeleine took a picture of the garden on her phone.

'I wanted to show you something actually,' she said, before tapping at her screen. 'I saw this in a box the other day and took a photo of it.'

She handed the phone over to Arthur who stared down at it.

His young face was staring back at him. He was wearing the black overalls he spent most of his days in while working in the garage. Madeleine was standing beside him.

'Well, that's a blast from the past,' Arthur said. 'The day we decided to get married. I'm sorry it wasn't more romantic.'

'I didn't need anything else, Arthur. We saved ourselves that day.'

'It feels like yesterday. The two kids in that picture wouldn't believe how far we've come.'

'We're not done yet, Arthur.'

They were walking in a loop around the garden.

'I spoke to Doctor Thomas again. The results of the PSA test concerned him.'

'Arthur! Why didn't you tell me?'

'I was going to wait until Christmas was over, but he thinks it might be back.'

Madeleine's eyes filled with tears.

'We knew there was always a chance, Madeleine. Half the battle is finding it early.'

'We can't do it alone this time, Arthur. You need as much support as possible.'

'If it comes to that, we'll talk about it. Until then, let's leave them be.'

Arthur knew Madeleine wanted to keep discussing it. He knew he had expected a lot of her to keep his cancer secret, but they had got through it together at the time. Now, he couldn't expect that of her, not when she was embarking on a new life. He had freed her from any obligations, but for today, he didn't want to think about what might lie ahead.

Suddenly he smiled to himself. An idea had just popped into his head.

'Madeleine, can you go inside and get Patrick and Scarlett then meet me out the front? Make sure you all wrap up.'

As she set off back inside, Arthur went to the garage and began rummaging around. He knew they had to be in here somewhere. After several minutes of searching, he finally found the two wooden sledges which had been carefully stored away.

'Dad, what are you up to?' Patrick said, eyeing up the toboggans Arthur was pulling behind him. 'It's going to be dark soon.'

'We're going to make some memories!' Arthur said. 'Scarlett, have you ever been sledging?'

She shook her head nervously.

'There's a first time for everything then. Come on, gang, we're going up the hill!'

They chatted and laughed as they trudged up the hill, fighting against the wind and falling snow. Arthur's nose was bright red by the time they reached the top.

'I've not been up here for years,' Patrick said, looking across the hills as the sun began to set. 'We used to play up here all the time. I remember taking my first girlfriend for a picnic – but we probably don't need to talk about that.' He stopped talking as Scarlett playfully scooped up a handful of snow and began shaping it into a ball.

'Come on, we can race!' Arthur said, sitting himself on one of the sledges. His heart was racing. 'Madeleine, climb on!'

Arthur laughed as Madeleine positioned herself between his legs and Patrick and Scarlett copied them.

'On your marks,' Arthur shouted. 'Get set. Go!'

The sound of screams and laughter filled the air as the two sledges raced down the hill. Arthur gripped the rope as Madeleine held tightly on to his legs.

The sledges were side by side as they flew towards the

bottom. Scarlett was clinging on to Patrick for dear life as they took the lead.

'That was AMAZING!' Scarlett shouted as she jumped up once they had come to a halt. 'If I had the energy I'd climb back to the top and do it all again!'

'Let me help you up,' Arthur said to Madeleine, holding out his hand. They had both slipped off their sledge, landing in the snow on top of each other. As he took hold of it, he pulled her back down into the snow. Laughing, they lay beside each other, staring up at the sky.

'Patrick! Scarlett! We're going to make snow angels.'

Arthur kept hold of Madeleine's hand as they moved their outstretched arms and legs in unison.

'I could stay here forever,' he said happily as fresh flakes of snow landed on his face.

CHAPTER TWENTY-SIX
Teddy

WITH THE PLATES stacked away into the dishwasher, Teddy slipped upstairs to the room he usually stayed in. He saw Arthur walking around the garden from his bedroom window and felt guilty for his revelation spoiling what his grandad had so wanted to be a perfect day.

His bedroom wasn't particularly large, but it held a small double bed and some old furniture. His whole body felt exhausted. Just looking at the bed made his already strained eyes burn. Just five minutes lying down would help, then he would go back downstairs for dessert. His nan's Christmas pudding was worth the effort. The last thing he remembered was his head hitting the pillow.

Knock.

Knock.

Knock.

The room was engulfed in darkness, with only the moonlight allowing him to see where he had left his phone. He groaned as he stretched for it.

Knock.

Knock.

'Teddy? Are you awake?'

He recognized the voice immediately and sat up. 'Shakeel?'

The door opened with a creak. Shakeel peered round it; his face broke into a smile. 'Hello, sleepyhead. Merry Christmas.'

'What the hell are you doing here? Is everything okay?'

'Eleanor phoned me – she told me what happened, so I jumped in the car and came straight over.'

The memory of events at lunch flooded through Teddy. He'd really done it.

'Oh God,' he groaned as he put his head in his hands. 'I feel like I'm hungover and I haven't even had a drink. Is everyone still downstairs?'

'Yeah, it was a bit weird, your grandparents, uncle and his girlfriend were walking up the driveway covered in snow.'

Shakeel sat down on the bed beside him. 'I thought Eleanor was joking at first, you know.'

'Really?'

'Totally. Of all the days, of course you blurted it out at dinner on Christmas Day. I'm so proud of you, Teddy.'

'Don't. I still can't believe it. It all just happened so fast.'

'Talk me through it then. What did everyone else say?'

Teddy tried not to grimace as he recalled his uncle's proposal and the conversation which had prompted him to grab the moment so unexpectedly.

'Do you think your mum will come round?' Shak asked gently.

'Who knows?' Teddy said wearily. 'All these years of building this moment up in my head and within a few minutes it's over. I don't really know what to think right now.'

'Did you tell people about you and Ben?'

'Yeah, that part was really funny. Evangelina is dying to meet him.'

'Where is he today, anyway?'

'He's at his uncle's,' Teddy said. He hadn't broken Ben's confidence and told Shakeel or Lexie about his relationship with his parents. 'He's got four nieces so it's nice and fun on Christmas Day. What about your fella?'

'Working.' Shakeel averted his eyes from Teddy's gaze and scanned the bedroom.

'You're too nice, Shak.' Teddy reached out and placed his hand on his friend's knee. 'You deserve someone who can give you the time of day, take you out to dinner, go to the cinema and do all the things you love.'

'We do get time together,' Shak said, his voice a little distant.

'I'm not saying you don't, mate,' Teddy said, shaking his head. Why was Shak so defensive about his mysterious boyfriend? 'You know I just want you to have someone who deserves you. You're the smartest, kindest, most loving—'

It all happened so fast; he was still sitting frozen when Shakeel took his lips from Teddy's. It had lasted mere seconds, but felt like a lifetime. The two stared at each other for a long moment, their eyes wide.

'Shakeel—'

'Oh my God, I'm so sorry, I don't know why I just did that.' Shakeel's voice cracked as he gasped for air.

'You . . . you kissed me?'

'I have to go, I'm so sorry. Please, just forget that happened.'

'No, stop—'

'I'm going, Teddy. I'm sorry! Please forget this ever happened.'

He threw open the bedroom door and ran from the room.

Teddy couldn't follow him. His feet were glued to the floor. One wrong move and he was sure that he would topple over. He placed his index finger on his bottom lip. His mind was racing. What the hell had just happened?

CHAPTER TWENTY-SEVEN
Arthur

ARTHUR DIDN'T WANT to hassle him, but it was obvious that Teddy wasn't himself. He had tried to talk to him, but his grandson insisted that there was nothing to worry about.

'Do you regret what you did?'

'Not at all, it's nothing to do with that. Honestly, it's work stuff, that's all,' Teddy insisted. Arthur decided to leave it alone. If Teddy was going to be staying with them indefinitely, he wanted him to feel like he had the privacy to live his own life.

'Elizabeth checked in on him again this morning,' Madeleine said as she poured her tea. 'That's every day for two weeks now.'

'She is still his mother, no matter what's going on between them. She should message him directly.'

'She probably thinks he could do the same thing.' She sighed, taking a sip from the china cup. 'They're both so stubborn and we know where they get that from.'

Arthur had just completed his crossword when Oscar pulled up into the driveway. He had accepted an invite to come over for dinner now that he had returned from his trip. Madeleine had initially planned to go out with James again, but Oscar had insisted that Arthur tell her to join them.

Arthur jumped up from the chair as he remembered that he had forgotten to get out the photo albums he had brought down from the attic during their clear-out. He had promised Oscar that he would show them to him. They were waiting for him in the bottom drawer of the chest in Teddy's room. He spotted the bundle of letters he had brought down with him that same day. Arthur hadn't been able to bring himself to read them and instead had thrown them into the drawer alongside the albums. He lifted the small bundle out and sat down on the bed.

It had been decades since he had last looked inside the collection of envelopes, but Arthur still knew the contents of each letter. He could still smell the blue ink with which they had been written. Jack's poor handwriting was indecipherable to most, but he had always been able to read his well-chosen words with ease. He'd kept his notes short and vague, never wanting to draw attention to his true meaning if the letter was to fall into the wrong hands. Arthur opened the envelope at the top of the pile. He knew what he was looking for; it had been safely stored between the letter's pages since the day he had received it. Arthur pulled out the letter and unfolded the piece of yellowed paper.

A small black and white image fell out onto the bed. Arthur lifted it up and turned it over.

Jack Johnson's thin face was as handsome and full of warmth as he remembered. His square jaw was usually hidden under a neatly trimmed beard, but for some reason, he had been clean-shaven the day the image was taken. He liked growing the beard to hide the small scar on his chin; the permanent reminder of an accident when he was younger. His lips were curled into a tight grin. Arthur knew that mischievous grin well; it wouldn't last long before breaking into a wide smile that showed off his teeth. Jack was leaning against a car in the image. Arthur didn't know if it was his or how he had come to have his photograph taken with it; Jack had not gone into detail in the accompanying note. Jack's eyes were staring back at him. Even in black and white, they were filled with the kindness Arthur remembered so vividly.

'Arthur? Arthur, are you upstairs?'

'Coming now. I'm just grabbing the albums.'

He carefully set the photograph of Jack down on the page, which he folded over before slotting it back into the envelope. No one, not even Madeleine, had seen or read these.

Madeleine was waiting for him in the kitchen where she had a tray set up with her finest guest china.

'You don't need to go to so much trouble for Oscar.' Arthur laughed. 'Some tea and scones and the man will be as happy as Larry.'

'Nonsense, a well-travelled man like Oscar deserves a proper meal. Did you find the albums?'

Arthur set them down on the counter. 'All here. It's been a while since we saw some of these. I'm sure he'll have a good chuckle at our expense.'

Oscar wasted no time in grabbing hold of the albums once he was settled at the dining table. He was so eager to dive into the collection that he cut short his own New Year's Eve story to do so.

'Oh, it was nothing that exciting.' He laughed when

Madeleine's inquisitiveness got the better of her after half an hour. 'Lots of potential drama, but it all fizzled out without a pop. Although, it doesn't sound like that was the case *here* on Christmas Day!'

'The less said about that the better.' Madeleine sighed, her cheeks reddening at the memory.

'Now, dear lady, what's life without a little bit of drama; a proposal and a coming out? You had the best seat in the house.'

'Well, that's one way to look at it, I suppose.' She laughed. 'Did Arthur tell you he and Teddy cooked the whole dinner?'

'No, he did not. Arthur! You kept that quiet, you sly dog.'

'It was mostly Teddy, I was just there to guide him along. And Madeleine did the pudding.'

Oscar rolled his eyes playfully before turning to Madeleine: 'Was he always this modest?'

'The stories I could tell you!'

'Next time, Madeleine, we're keeping the china in the dresser and getting out the champagne glasses.'

'Do I get invited to this?' Arthur said.

Oscar and Madeleine both shrugged as their laughter filled the room.

'Now, dear Madeleine, Arthur tells me you've been out protesting. I knew you weren't one to be messed with.'

'Don't get me started, Oscar,' Madeleine said with a sigh. Arthur smiled to himself. He knew Madeleine was more than happy to get started on the topic when she had a willing pair of fresh ears. The latest injustice was threats to close the accident and emergency department of the local hospital. Never one to sit back, she had been among the first to mobilise the community into taking action and protesting against the cuts.

Teddy arrived home not long after they had finished eating Madeleine's homemade lasagne.

'Hello, sorry, I forgot you had company this evening,' he said, popping his head round the dining-room door.

'Not to worry, come on in. Teddy, this is Oscar.'

Oscar stood up and met Teddy's handshake.

'A pleasure to meet you. I've heard absolutely wonderful things about you, young man. A credit to both of your grandparents.'

'That's very kind of you to say. Good to meet you too, Oscar.'

'Teddy, why don't you join us,' Madeleine said, standing. 'There's still some food in the oven, I'll go and grab it for you.'

'No, no, Nan, don't worry, I'll get it and come back. Just give me a couple of minutes to go and get changed.'

'He is the absolute double of you, Arthur. Looks just like you in some of those pictures,' Oscar said as Teddy closed the door behind him. 'And you've met the boyfriend?'

Arthur nodded. 'Lovely lad; came along and helped us at the car boot sale. I'm not actually sure if he's calling him his boyfriend yet, though.'

'And his mum, she's having a tough time with it all?' Oscar glanced at the door to make sure they were still talking privately.

'I don't think it's him being gay that bothers her. She's hurt that he couldn't talk to her, which coming so soon after me . . . well, it all blew up, as you can imagine.'

'He's lucky to have grandparents like you to turn to. Imagine that in our day. The gossip alone would have sent them to an early grave, God rest their souls.'

Once Teddy had returned to the dining room and eaten his dinner, Oscar wasted no time in turning his attention back to him.

'Young ones these days, I can't keep up with all the new words I keep hearing, you'll have to give me a lesson,' he said, sipping at the cup of tea Madeleine had just poured.

'I'm not sure I'm the best person for that really.'

'You should invite Shakeel round next time Oscar is here, they'd get on like a house on fire.'

'Yeah, maybe.' Teddy quickly averted his eyes and began scrunching up the napkin in his hand.

'What's wrong?'

'Nothing, he's just very busy at work at the minute, it's been hard to pin him down since Christmas.'

'And a hard worker?' Oscar laughed. 'Sounds like you've bagged yourself a good one.'

'Oh no, I'm not dat . . . Shak's just a friend.'

'Shakeel is Teddy's best friend,' Arthur explained. 'Ben's the boyfr . . . the other friend I was telling you about.'

'I do beg your pardon. As much as I try to stop it, age gets the better of me sometimes.'

'It's fine, like Grandad said, Ben is . . . Ben.'

'And how is young love since coming out?'

Arthur watched closely to see how Teddy would react. He hadn't been able to get much out of him during their recent chats. Despite Teddy's reassurances that everything was fine, he wanted to see how he handled the questioning from someone else.

'It's been strange since coming out. I didn't really think about how I would feel after it. You forget that it's not just one moment. It's a moment you have with every single person after that too.'

'I know exactly what you mean and I'm sure your grand-father does too.'

'Yeah, so it was a little awkward going into work and trying to find the balance of what I'm comfortable with, if that makes sense.'

'Ah,' Oscar said, his right eyebrow rising. 'Ben's ready for a more public relationship?'

'Pretty much. He thought that me coming out to Mum would be the end of it, but I'm still me, I'm not someone who wants the whole office to know who I'm dating. It's none of their business.'

'It takes time. He's probably just proud to have a handsome young man like you to show off to all of his friends. The key is in the communication; you have to discuss all of these things.'

'He's not wrong there,' Arthur said. 'Ben's understanding. These things don't just change overnight. He knows the office is a difficult situation, given the relationship between you and your mum.'

'I hope so. Even though she knows, I don't want her hear-ing second-hand gossip about my relationship. Honestly, it wouldn't be any different if I was straight.'

'You've got your head screwed on right, just like your grandfather here. You can help me find him someone.'

'I didn't know he was even looking!'

'He's not,' Arthur said, scoffing at the pair.

'Oh, go on, Arthur. You came to meet me!'

'And I've suffered enough for that, thank you very much.'

'Well, I'll consider myself honoured. Young man, we have a job on our hands making sure this one has some fun.'

'Actually, while Madeleine's at the toilet, I suppose I could run this little idea past you,' Arthur whispered, leaning in towards them.

Arthur had spent several weeks trying to think of a fund-raising idea he could present to the Northbridge Foundation. Everything felt too simple. He was determined to follow Oscar's advice and come up with something different. He didn't want to just raise a few hundred pounds and then move on. This had to be special.

'You're keeping us in suspense,' Oscar said, resting his arms on the table. 'I'm dying to hear what you've come up with.'

'I remembered you mentioned flying lessons, Oscar.'

'Your nan's going to have me strung up,' Oscar said turning towards a grinning Teddy.

'Hang on, you're not actually going to learn how to fly, are you?' Teddy said, his eyes wide with surprise. 'You hate flying!'

'I'm not planning to be inside the plane,' Arthur said, enjoying watching their puzzled expressions. 'I'm going to do a wing walk.'

'Excuse me? Did I hear you right?' Oscar said, genuinely surprised. 'Teddy, did I actually hear what I think I just heard come out of your grandfather's mouth?'

Teddy was staring at him, utterly perplexed.

'Are you sure you know what that is, Grandad? You don't mean something else?'

'I do. And that is exactly why I've decided to do it. It's the last thing anybody will expect.'

'Are you even allowed to go wing walking at your age?' Teddy asked, sounding hopeful that he might have stumbled across the thing which would put an end to the idea.

'I can use the computer too, thank you. I've watched the videos. There was a woman of eighty-three who did one last year. Oldest in the country to do it.'

'I don't know what to say,' Oscar said. 'It's an amazing idea!'

'What?' Teddy shrieked at Oscar's sudden change of heart.

'Don't be like that, Teddy. I need you on board.'

'Do you want me to write something about it?' Teddy said slowly.

'There is that,' Arthur said, before glancing up at the ceiling. 'But I also need you there to back me up when I tell your nan.'

CHAPTER TWENTY-EIGHT
Teddy

'HOLD UP A second, did you just say that your seventy-nine-year-old grandfather is going to go wing walking for charity?'

Ben was looking at Teddy like he had just sprouted a second head. They were lying beside each other on the bed in Ben's apartment. It was Teddy's third time there. The studio felt like it was becoming smaller each time he visited, but Ben didn't seem to mind. It was his space, his sanctuary. Teddy knew how important that was to have.

'I sure did. I wish you had been there to see Nan's face; it was bloody priceless. Part of me thinks that she still hopes he's winding her up.'

'That's incredible. Your family is completely ridiculous; I love it.'

Ben turned on his side, closing the laptop they had been bingeing a new TV series on. He placed his hand on Teddy's chest.

'Has your grandad ever done anything like this before?'

'You mean has he ever been strapped onto the top wing of a plane and flown up to 700 feet in the air? No, not that I know off.'

'He's braver than I am, that's for sure. I hope I can come and see this for myself.'

'Of course you can!' Teddy said. 'Grandad will want a crowd there cheering him on.'

'Do you think your mum will go?'

'I hadn't even thought about that, to be honest. Why?'

'Just thinking how nice it would be if she was there to support him. Then I can finally meet her.'

Teddy shifted on the bed to face him. Ben's hand slipped off his chest as he did.

'I wouldn't expect her to roll out the red carpet for you, even if you do meet. She's not that kind of person, but you know that already.'

Teddy wasn't in the mood to talk about his mum again. If she wanted to be there to support his grandad, he would be delighted. Arthur's idea had helped him to push his own worries to the back of his mind. It had been nice to have a new topic of conversation with Ben, one which didn't involve his mind drifting back to Shakeel. None of it made sense to him. Why had Shakeel kissed him? They'd always been close, but he didn't think Shakeel thought of him as anything more than his best friend. Now, even as he lay beside Ben on the bed, Teddy couldn't allow himself to enjoy the moment.

'You seem a bit off,' Ben said, 'Sorry, I probably shouldn't have mentioned your mum.'

'It's fine. Sorry, Ben. I just don't really want to think about all of it right now. I'd just love to switch off for the night and—'

'Say no more,' Ben said, pushing himself closer and sliding his arm under Teddy. 'We can just lie here and chill.'

Teddy allowed his body to relax into Ben's arms as they

wrapped around him. He didn't remember falling asleep, but Shakeel's panicked face stared back at him once he'd finally allowed his eyes to close.

Several days later, Ben pulled several printouts out of the folder on his desk, eager to present them to Teddy.

'I know you've been busy with other stuff, but I was digging around in some more records and found some death certificates that might match Jack Johnson.' He paused, looking up to make sure that he had Teddy's full attention. 'I get that you're not keen on the idea, but do you not think you could ask Arthur for some more information?'

'We've been over this, Ben.' Teddy sighed. 'I specifically asked you not to carry on. Grandad didn't want me looking into Jack and I should have respected that. Let's just leave it.'

'You want to know as much as I do, though.'

'I did. But it's not our business. Promise me you'll let it go this time, please. Forget I ever told you about Jack.'

He knew Ben wasn't happy with his request not to carry on searching, but right now, it was the last thing he needed to worry about.

'Are we still going out for dinner tonight?' Ben asked several minutes later, his voice strained as he attempted to break the silence that had fallen between them.

'Yeah, why has something come up?'

'No, not with me, I was just checking with you just in case . . .'

'In case what?'

'You've cancelled on me twice this week, Teddy. I think I'm entitled to ask.'

'I'm sorry, but you know I've been totally snowed under with work. I'm damned if I do and damned if I don't.' Teddy knew he was being overly defensive, but he couldn't help it.

'I just want to be sure that you're not too busy for me.' Teddy didn't respond as he watched the lines on Ben's forehead form. 'Look, maybe I'm ahead of you in the whole out and proud thing, but yeah, I can't wait to tell people about us. But I want to be with someone who is proud to be my boyfriend, Teddy.'

'I'm sorry, you're right. Let me make it up to you, okay?'

'Really? Because if you don't want to do this—'

'I do! I'm really looking forward to dinner tonight.'

Teddy knew he had been distant, even when they were together. Every time he looked at Ben he felt guilty for not telling him the truth about Shakeel kissing him. It didn't help matters that Shakeel had refused to speak to him since Christmas Day. Every text and call had gone unanswered. He needed to talk to Shak, to find out what was going on with him. Shakeel's silence was now becoming worrying. Teddy knew that he couldn't let things go on much longer.

Dylan arrived back from lunch, dropping several bags down on the floor. Teddy remembered that he wanted to mention his grandad's charity event to him.

'Damn, rather him than me,' Dylan said after hearing about the plan. He pulled his phone from his pocket. 'When's this happening?'

'Start of March. Do you think we could run something? It would be cool if we could raise awareness and maybe link to his donation page. He's hoping to raise as much money as he can for charities that help young people who are struggling with their sexuality.'

'Can't see it being a problem. Actually, let me run it past my other half too and come back to you.'

'Dude,' Ben hissed at him. 'You know his girlfriend is a producer on *Good Morning Live*, right? If she's interested . . . well, this could be huge.'

Ben wasn't wrong. Within an hour, Dylan was telling them that his girlfriend, Maya, wanted to hear more about Arthur's wing walk.

'I'll send you her email and you can get in touch directly.' Dylan smiled at him.

'This is incredible,' Teddy said, still shocked at the speed with which things were moving. 'Thanks, Dylan. Grandad will be over the moon.'

His mum had been right about one thing. Having Dylan in his corner had been one of her better ideas.

'You won't hear me say this too often, but you two make a really good team,' Dylan said to Teddy and Ben. 'Keep the ideas coming. You can talk to Leo on the features desk about what kind of stories he likes.'

Teddy's cheeks ached as he smiled. As exciting as the day's events were, as much as he wanted to be excited about dinner with Ben, he was too distracted by Shakeel. He wondered how he was spending his week off work. He desperately needed to talk to his friend, it couldn't wait any longer.

'Dylan, I've just remembered I said I'd meet a publicist for coffee. It's on the other side of town, so I might not be back before the end of the day, but I'll be on email.'

Teddy felt Ben's eyes on him.

'I'll go straight to the restaurant and see you there,' he said, standing before Ben had a chance to say anything.

Teddy didn't pay attention to where he was going as he made his way through the busy office, squeezed into the lift and ran through the noisy reception area onto the main road. There was a taxi stopped at the red light just across the street. Without looking, he ran across and rapped on the window.

'Could you take me to sixty-five Union Row please, as fast as possible?'

Teddy was already fastening his seat belt in the back of the cab before the driver had found the address on his sat nav. His head was spinning. What was he going to say? What did he want to hear from Shakeel? Why was he doing this now?

'We're here mate.' The driver's voice shook him out of his daze. He looked out of the window at the apartment building they had pulled up outside and took a deep breath.

Teddy slipped through the open door as a harassed-looking woman pushing a buggy exited the building. He stood alone in the lift, his heart thumping. He still hadn't figured out what he was going to say as he walked between the beige walls of the seventh floor, the narrow corridor threatening to close in on him if he didn't find the door he was looking for. Seventy-four. He closed his eyes and felt his knuckles hit the wood three times.

Shakeel opened the door and stared blankly at him.

'Hi,' Teddy said. 'I'm glad you're here, I didn't know if you would be.'

'That's why you don't just drop by unannounced, Teddy.' Shak sounded distant, cold.

'I wouldn't have to if you would answer a text or talk to me at all, Shak. You think this is what I want?'

Shakeel scoffed and looked out into the hallway to make

sure they were alone. 'What *do* you want, Teddy? Why are you here?'

'I wanted to make sure you were all right. You kissed me and then disappeared. What the hell am I meant to think?'

'I'm sorry, you're right, that was unfair of me. I was embarrassed and didn't know how to tell you—'

'Tell me what?'

'That it was all a stupid bloody mistake. I was confused and lonely and made a mistake.'

'Really?' Teddy said.

'The stupidest. I've regretted it ever since and I'm sorry I was too embarrassed to just say that to you and move on. I didn't know if you could understand and forgive me.'

'I want you to be able to talk to me, Shak, to tell me how you're feeling.'

'I've told you. It was a mistake. You have Ben and I have . . . I have Simon.'

'Simon? That's the boyfriend's name, is it?' Teddy said. 'Did you tell him you kissed me?'

'Can you please just go. He's coming over and I really can't do this now.'

'All these weeks you've just blanked me and now you're telling me it was a silly mistake and I don't get a proper explanation?'

'Please, Teddy, just forget about it. Goodbye.'

He closed the door. Teddy stood motionless staring at it, lost in the heavy silence that had once again filled the unwelcoming corridor. A stupid mistake; that was what Shakeel had called it. He didn't have time to debate if he was telling the truth or not now. The light above him flickered as he glanced down at

251

his watch. Ben would be leaving the office soon. Teddy would still be on time to meet him at the restaurant if the rush-hour traffic wasn't too bad.

Ben gave Teddy a small wave as he entered the Italian restaurant. The journey had been nothing more than a blur. His mind was racing, but as he walked across the room, he used every ounce of energy he had left to force a smile. Ben stood up as Teddy approached the table.

'What a gent,' Teddy said, forcing himself to sound cheerful.

'Only the finest for Mr Marsh. I have to admit, I thought you were going to be later.'

'Tell me about it. Luckily the driver knew a few shortcuts.'

'So, how was coffee?' Ben poured two glasses of water from the jug which had been left on the table. 'Who was it you were meeting again?'

'Just Lauren, she looks after a few celebrities, TV presenters, that type.'

'Sounds good. Does she have much coming up?'

'A few bits, but she said she'd email all the details. Anyway, no work talk, you said!'

'Cheers to that,' Ben said raising his glass. 'I love spending time with you, Teddy.'

'Same, and I just wanted to say that I'm sorry. You were right that I've been a bit off since Christmas. I think the whole thing caught up with me.'

Teddy took a deep breath. 'Obviously I'm glad I've come out, but I've really had to process everything that comes with it. Suddenly I was out and that was it. It wasn't the big cure to all my worries; it just brought more. I don't know what I was expecting, but it all just felt a bit overwhelming.'

'I understand, and I'm sorry if I've been putting pressure on you to rush into things.'

'Thank you, it's not your fault. I just need to take this at my own pace. That's not because of the office or my mum, it's just who I am. I really like you and I don't want to ruin whatever this is or could become.'

'I'm really glad you can talk to me about it,' Ben said, reaching across and taking both of Teddy's hands in his. 'This isn't about anyone but you and me. Forget about Dylan and everyone else in that place. We're still just getting to know each other and if that means taking things slow, then that's fine with me.'

Teddy knew that he was hungry, but it didn't mask the weight in the pit of his stomach. He felt Ben release his clammy hands as their smiling waitress approached carrying drinks.

'I ordered when I knew you were on your way,' Ben said, as she set the two Negroni Sbagliatos down. 'With prosecco,' he said, passing one of the glasses across the table.

'My favourite,' Teddy grinned, taking a large sip.

It was the first of a few drinks he planned on having that evening.

Teddy threw himself down on his bed once he had returned home later that night. Before going to sleep, he sent Maya a detailed email about his grandad's fundraiser. He explained how Arthur had come out as gay and the reaction it had been met with in Northbridge, but how his grandad had now been inspired to step up and do something after Sophie Rice's death. Now he was going to do a charity wing walk, scheduled for his eightieth birthday on the first of March. Maya had replied within minutes, thanking him for the all the information and eager to talk on the phone the following morning.

The next evening Teddy burst through the door to tell his grandad all about his conversation with the producer. 'Nan, come into the room, you should hear this too,' he shouted as Madeleine made her way from the kitchen to join them.

'So, I have a little news about your fundraiser,' Teddy said as his grandparents stared at him. 'A producer at *Good Morning Live* thinks it sounds really incredible and loved your story. They want to do a whole segment about it.'

'They want to come and film me?' Arthur asked, his eyes widening as he sat forward on the edge of the sofa.

'Better! They want you to come to the studio and talk about it beforehand, and then they'll come and film the whole thing!'

'Teddy, this is amazing news,' Madeleine said, grabbing hold of Arthur's arm.

'They want to interview me about why I'm doing this?'

'That's right, what inspired you and why it's so important to you. Is that all right?'

'I suppose,' Arthur said as his grey brows furrowed deeper. 'I never imagined talking about all of this on the television. Do you think this is okay, Madeleine?'

'Of course it is, but it's up to you. You're doing something incredibly brave to raise money and now you can share your story to inspire other people.'

'Well then,' Arthur said, getting up off the sofa. 'We better start looking for what I'm going to wear!'

CHAPTER TWENTY-NINE
Arthur

BEFORE ARTHUR KNEW it he was sitting in a fancy hotel room staring across the river at the lights of the city. He'd spent lots of time coming in and out of the capital over the years, but there was something different about being an overnight guest for the first time. He watched the sun set behind the tall buildings which filled the skyline, their shadows creeping up the winding river and eventually fading into the darkness. In order to avoid travelling in early, Teddy and Oscar had surprised Arthur by booking a hotel for the night before. Delighted, Arthur had initially suggested that he and Madeleine book a second night, but her plans changed when James invited her away for a long weekend by the coast. Arthur insisted that she shouldn't turn him down; seeing Madeleine's beaming smile whenever she returned from spending time with James made him so happy. He was thrilled to see that she had so quickly found someone she enjoyed spending time with.

'Grandad, anything you want to go over before tomorrow?' Teddy said, sitting down at the desk in the corner of the room and going over their plans for the following day. 'The car is picking us up at 10 a.m., so we have a good amount of time when we get to the studio to get settled, eat something and meet Maya. She says we should be done by midday.'

'That all sounds straightforward,' Arthur said. 'What do we do afterwards?'

'You'll find that out tomorrow!' Teddy teased as he walked into the bathroom, closing the door behind him.

Trying to guess what Teddy's surprise was served as a nice distraction as Arthur got changed and climbed into one of the double beds. He yawned as he pulled the quilt up over himself. He missed his firmer pillows as he lay looking up at the finely detailed decorative ceiling panels above him. It didn't take long before the sound of his muffled snores filled the room.

The next morning, Teddy had him ready and waiting in the hotel foyer with five minutes to spare. After a text from the driver, they were soon in the back of a car on their way to the studio.

Teddy showed Arthur the fundraising page on his phone. They had already reached nearly £1,000. Arthur stared at it in disbelief, his eyes filling up as he looked through the messages people had left with their donations.

'We could even double that today,' Teddy said. 'There are going to be lots of people watching you.'

Arthur put his head back and closed his eyes. It wasn't that he was nervous about sitting in front of the television cameras and talking about his life; it was making sure that he did enough to make people want to donate.

'We're here, Grandad.' Teddy tilted his head and looked out at the large glass building they had stopped outside of. The driver had already left the car and was now holding the door open for them. After thanking him profusely, Arthur joined Teddy in walking into the brightly lit reception area. They waited several minutes before a young man arrived to collect them and take them upstairs. The walls of the narrow corridor were filled with framed pictures of various TV hosts and celebrities.

'You'll be on with Alex and Vanessa today,' the runner told them as they walked past portraits of the pair. 'They're both really lovely, you're in safe hands.'

He ushered them into a room to wait for Maya.

'This is a bit surreal, isn't it?' Teddy said, taking a bottle of water from the well-stocked fridge.

'I still can't believe we're here. Me on television. What would my old man say now?'

'You don't need to think about that today, Grandad. I'm sure he'd be proud of you in his own way for doing what you're doing.'

'I hope so,' Arthur said. He didn't believe it, but it was a nice thought to have. He was saved from dwelling on how his parents would react to him going on national television to discuss his sexuality by Maya's arrival. She beamed with delight as she shook Arthur's hand before sitting down beside him.

'It's so lovely to meet you, Arthur. We just fell in love with your story as soon as we heard it,' she said. 'I'm sure you'll be feeling a little nervous about going into the studio, but I want to reassure you that Alex and Vanessa are both lovely and really looking forward to meeting you.'

'That's very kind, thank you. They know everything already?'

'They have all the information about your story and what

you're doing for charity. If there's anything else you want me to pass on, we'll make sure everyone is up to speed. We just want you to be happy and comfortable.'

'That all sounds good to me. Teddy?' Arthur looked up at his grandson in case there was anything he wanted to add or ask.

'Oh, yes, all good. They'll be able to show the donation page too, won't they?'

'They will mention it and we'll link to it on the website and on our social media channels, so there will be lots of eyes on it today.'

Before leaving, Maya let them know that someone was going to bring some food while they were waiting. 'There will be some other guests in and out throughout the morning. There's a TV there so you can watch the show,' she said. 'One of the lovely runners will be back to get you when we're ready. If there's anything you need, just ask one of the team.'

Arthur felt himself nod off on the large leather sofa after eating some toast. It felt like he had only just closed his eyes when one of the runners let them know that it was almost time for them to come through to the studio. While he was waiting outside, a small woman appeared out of nowhere and began to rub a soft make-up brush across his face.

'Makes you look extra handsome under the lights,' she told him with a wink.

'Okay, Arthur, come on,' Maya said, holding out her arm and leading him into the studio.

Arthur's mouth fell open. His eyes, no matter how big they got, couldn't take it all in.

The set he knew so well from watching the programme was

right in front of him, the presenters were sitting waiting for him on the familiar blue sofas. The intense heat of the bright studio lights hit him as he stepped under them. He dabbed his forehead with his handkerchief.

'It gets pretty hot under these,' the grey-haired man said, pointing up at the ceiling as he stepped forward to shake Arthur's hand. 'Lovely to meet you, Arthur. I'm Alex and this is Vanessa.' He gestured to the smiling tall woman who mimicked her co-host's movement and held out her hand.

'Take a seat here, Arthur. We're going to do a quick link and competition when we come back from the break, and then you'll be on. Who is here with you today?'

'That's my grandson, Teddy,' Arthur said pointing over at Teddy who was standing behind one of the cameramen to watch.

Arthur sat quietly as the show hosts looked down their cameras and read their lines. His heart was pounding, but before he knew it, he heard his own name and sat up straight.

'Joining us now is a man with a remarkable story. At seventy-nine, Arthur Edwards bravely decided to come out as gay,' Alex said, before Vanessa picked up the next part of the introduction.

'Now, Arthur is here to tell us why he's celebrating his eightieth birthday by doing a daredevil stunt for charity. Arthur, it's so lovely to have you with us this morning.'

'Thank you for having me, I never thought I'd be sitting here.'

'Well, here you are and it's a hell of a story. Take us back to the beginning. Why at seventy-nine did you make this massive decision to come out?'

'There were lots of reasons, but I just knew in my heart that I couldn't go on as I was. Every day felt like it was a waste and I had to make a big decision about how I wanted to spend the years I have left. My wife, Madeleine, she's away at the minute but she'll be watching, was so supportive and helped me tell our two children.'

'That must have been quite a shock for them.'

'It was. It's not been easy at all, but I never wanted to hurt or embarrass them.'

'Your daughter Elizabeth Marsh is a writer well known for giving her opinions. How has she dealt with all of this?'

Arthur frowned. No one had mentioned going into detail about his children on national television.

'I'm the proudest father in the world. Elizabeth has given me three wonderful grandchildren and so much love and support. She's getting married in a few months and we can't wait to celebrate that together.'

He glanced across at Teddy, who gave him a thumbs up.

'Was it tough when people started to find out? Did anyone treat you differently?'

'Of course, I suppose it took people by surprise, and some-times they reacted less positively than I might have hoped. That's never nice, but I'm proud of who I am and where I'm from. People will always have questions and opinions. That's why I'm doing what I'm doing and hoping to raise money for charities that can make a difference.'

'Tell us a little more about what you have planned, and how it all came about,' Vanessa said, tilting her head and looking sombre in anticipation of his response.

'Well, very sadly a good friend of mine, Eric, his

granddaughter Sophie took her own life at the end of last year. Very few people knew that she was struggling to come to terms with her sexuality, but she was being put under pressure to come out by some nasty people. It's heartbreaking to think she felt she had nowhere to turn.'

'Now you want to raise money for charities which help people like Sophie and yourself.'

'That's right. It doesn't matter if you're sixteen or seventy-nine, age is just a silly number that holds us back. People should be able to live as who they are. Like my wonderful grandson Teddy, who is with me today, and his boyfriend.'

'Teddy, come on over here,' Alex instructed, waving him across the studio floor. 'Sit yourself down there beside your grandfather.'

'Sorry,' Arthur said as Teddy walked onto the set and sat down beside him.

'Don't worry,' Teddy murmured. Then more loudly, 'I'm really proud of Grandad, just like he's been saying, it's all about raising money and awareness.'

'So, who came out first?'

'That would actually be Grandad. He's been very inspiring and hugely supportive, not just now but throughout my whole life.'

'What's it been like having a gay grandfather? That must be quite a conversation-starter?'

'Um, not really. Grandad's always been popular with my friends simply for being who he is. It doesn't suddenly make him any more interesting or cooler to people, in the same way it doesn't make me any different either.'

'Has Arthur given you any tips for finding love?' Vanessa

said with a wink. 'He mentioned you have a boyfriend of your own.'

'That's a bit nosy,' Arthur said as the lines across his forehead deepened. 'I've only ever told Teddy to do what feels right and to make sure he's safe and happy, the exact same advice I'd give to anyone. I've lived a good life, that's all I want for everyone else.'

'That's so lovely, Arthur,' Vanessa said, dramatically wiping a tear from her cheek. 'You've set me off! Tell us about your big adventure; you're taking to the skies to do a wing walk?'

'That's right. I wanted to do something that pushed my boundaries. I'm not the greatest fan of heights you see, so this felt like a big enough challenge which could raise money. We set up a page for donations and people have been so generous. All the money is going to charities that help young people who struggle like Sophie.'

'You're a braver man than me, Arthur! We've got the details on screen now and we'll put them all on the website so that people know how they can show their support. Thanks so much for being here with us today, Arthur. We're going to be with Arthur as he takes to the skies, so look out for that in a couple of weeks' time. We'll be right back after the break.'

A member of the production team took some pictures of them with Alex and Vanessa before they left the studio.

'You were brilliant!' Teddy said as they sat back down in the green room.

'Didn't think much of some of those questions.'

'I know, but you handled them really well, like a total professional.'

'I'm sorry I involved you, I was just so proud to be able to talk about you and next thing I knew I—'

'Stop worrying, Grandad,' Teddy reassured him. 'I'm out now! And you didn't mention Ben by name, so it's not like everyone at work will know about us.'

'Guys, thank you so much for coming. Everything good?' Maya asked as she walked across the room to them.

'All great, thank you so much for all your help,' Arthur said.

'Are you sure you don't need a car to take you back to the hotel?'

'Thanks, Maya, we're all sorted,' Teddy said, glancing at Arthur.

'We are?'

'It's part of your surprise!'

After saying their goodbyes, Arthur followed Teddy down into the reception area. Teddy was grinning at his phone as he tapped on the screen.

'It must be a proper celebrity in that thing,' Arthur said pointing at a black limo that was parked outside.

'It might be. Do you want to meet them?' Teddy walked over to the car window and knocked.

As Arthur peered into the now open window, a loud roar of 'Surprise!' greeted him.

He couldn't believe his eyes as he looked inside the limo to find Oscar, Ben, Lexie and Shakeel waiting for him.

'Surprise, Grandad!' Teddy said, a gigantic grin spread across his face. 'You're going to have a day of being treated like a proper A-lister!'

Arthur climbed into the limo, his eyes dancing as he took in his surroundings.

'I could only get the baby limo at short notice, but look, we can still throw a party,' Oscar explained as he hit a switch and turned on a strip of neon blue lighting.

'We watched the interview, Arthur. It was brilliant,' Shakeel said as Lexie and Ben nodded in agreement.

'You really killed it, Arthur. And it was so cute when you talked about Teddy.'

'Oh God, how did my hair look, Lex? I did not expect that at all.' Teddy ran his hand through his thick hair.

'Give over,' Ben said, creating space for Teddy to sit down beside him. 'You looked handsome. And I guess you're out to the whole nation now!' He kissed Teddy on the cheek.

People walking past were glancing at the limo, intrigued by the vehicle and who might be travelling in it. Arthur gave a little wave to two women who had stopped to stare.

'They can't see in, Arthur.' Oscar grinned. 'Let them think they're waving at some Hollywood hunk.'

Everyone laughed and waved back. The two women must have been able to see the movement inside as they began to shriek enthusiastically.

'Where are we going?' Arthur said, leaning across to Teddy as the car began to move.

'Wait and see; Oscar's got a big day planned for us!'

CHAPTER THIRTY
Teddy

SHAKEEL WAS DEEP in conversation with Oscar and Arthur. Teddy strained to try and make out what they were talking about, but Lexie and Ben were on either side of him engaged in a heated discussion about reality television.

'Sorry, guys, I just want to have a word with Grandad,' he said as he clambered over Ben's legs and squeezed himself in next to Shakeel.

'Thank you for coming today,' Teddy said quietly.

'It's all right. You know I love Arthur like he's family.'

'How are you doing?'

'I've been better, but it doesn't matter today.'

'I get you,' Teddy said. 'It's been nice having all of this going on.'

'You must hardly have time for . . . other stuff.' Teddy saw Shak glance towards Ben, who was now showing Lexie something on his phone.

'It's all good,' Teddy said, not wanting Shakeel to focus on Ben for too long. 'I hope we can hang out properly soon. I'm missing our after-work drinks.'

'Me too, we'll arrange something soon.'

'What's this?' Ben said, his eyes wide as he turned away from Lexie mid-conversation.

'Nothing, Shak and I were just talking about after-work drinks.'

'Lovely, I'm always up for that,' Ben said before turning his attention to Shakeel. 'Maybe you can bring your fella along too, Shakeel. No one has met him yet, have they?'

Teddy felt Shakeel's body tense up beside him, but breathed a sigh of relief when Oscar interrupted him before he could respond.

'Doesn't it make you miss being young, Arthur?' Oscar said fondly.

'Not for a single second. I'm quite content with my lot; let the kids have their fun.'

'You wouldn't like to go back and do it differently, Arthur?' Lexie turned round, suddenly taking the conversation much more seriously.

'I don't think so. Experiences make us who we are. Of course, there are things I wish had happened differently, but then I wouldn't be sitting here in a limousine with all of you, would I?'

'Did you ever have a boyfriend?' Ben asked, clearly trying to make the question he already knew the answer to sound as casual as possible. Teddy glared at him but Ben refused to meet his gaze. He could feel Shakeel's eyes on him and quickly hid the flash of annoyance which had spread across his face.

'I suppose you could say I did, yes,' Arthur said softly. 'His name was Jack.'

The car fell completely silent as they listened intently to Arthur's story. Teddy watched the reactions of the others as they heard how Arthur and Jack's secret relationship had come to an end all those years ago.

'It's like a movie,' Lexie said, wiping her damp eyes on her sleeve. 'And he wrote to you?'

'For a little while anyway. Then I assume he went off and lived his life.'

'I can't believe you've never tracked him down.' Lexie blew her nose into the tissue Shakeel had pulled from his pocket. 'He's just out there somewhere.'

'It was for the best,' Arthur said. 'I want the life that Jack lived to be the one in my head. That's the happy ending he deserved.'

'But Arthur,' Ben said. 'What if he was still alive and out there? What if he saw you on television today?'

'No point in getting carried away,' Arthur said, waving his hand in the air. 'I'm not digging up old memories when he might not want that. Anyway, that's enough of reminiscing. Today was meant to be about celebrating.'

'I could help you look—'

'Arthur said thanks but no thanks, Ben, didn't you hear him?' Shakeel interrupted. Teddy looked around quickly at Shakeel, who was now glowering in Ben's direction.

'I did, thanks, Shakeel. I'm just being polite.' Ben sounded offended. Teddy was completely thrown by how well Ben was pretending to know nothing about the situation.

'Anyway,' Shakeel said. 'We're here to celebrate, like Arthur said.'

'Quite right!' Oscar clapped his hands together before pressing another button on the control panel beside him to turn on the sound system.

'I know he's your friend, but I could do without goody two shoes Shakeel biting my head off,' Ben whispered into Teddy's ear.

'I specifically asked you to drop it about Jack, so don't turn this on Shak now,' Teddy whispered back. 'He's known Grandad for years; he's just protective of him.'

'And I can't be?'

'I'm not saying that. It's not a competition, but how could you sit there pretending to know nothing and then act offended?'

'Sorry, would you rather I'd told your grandad that you went behind his back and told me all about his private life? No. I didn't think so, Teddy.'

Teddy's stomach tightened. He'd only ever involved Ben when he wanted to give them something to work on together. 'Come on,' he said, trying to shake off the feeling he had just been threatened. 'Let's just try and enjoy the rest of today.'

But Ben and Shakeel seemed intent on making digs at each other. Being caught between them was not how Teddy wanted to spend the day. Even as he glanced at them both, he couldn't begin to understand his feelings.

He had never ever thought of Shakeel as anything other than his best friend. They'd shared every major experience in their lives, from his dad dying to Shakeel's coming out. Now he could see something different in the way Shakeel looked at him. He wasn't the type of person to pick fights, but here he was taking on Ben at every opportunity he got. Teddy couldn't deny it, he liked seeing this side of Shak. It didn't matter though. Shak had insisted they move on. Did he really want that? If he did, why was he still acting like this? Why did Teddy keep catching him watching him?

Teddy closed his eyes. They'd always flirted and teased each other in a playful way. Shakeel becoming anything more than his best friend would be risking years of friendship. Was it really worth taking that chance when he was just getting to know Ben? His head was spinning. He groaned as he felt the sinking feeling in his stomach. The last thing he ever expected or wanted was to find himself in a situation where there was a chance of him losing either Shakeel or Ben from his life.

How had it come to this? Just weeks after one of the biggest moments of his life, he found himself wishing he could turn back the clock and start again.

After a sight-seeing tour of the city, Oscar had arranged for the group to have afternoon tea at a hotel where he knew one of the managers.

'This is absolutely ridiculous,' Lexie said, looking around the lavish dining room. 'I couldn't even afford a glass of water in here.'

'I'm not keen on places like this,' Shakeel said. 'I always feel like everyone is staring at me.'

Teddy was ready to agree with him when Ben grabbed his hand and led him to a seat on the far side of a large round table.

'Well, I love it,' Ben announced, pointedly. 'We should come back here for dinner.' Teddy gave a small nod in agreement. This was the last place he would want to come on a date and Ben knew it.

'Oscar, I can't believe you've gone to so much effort,' Arthur said as he surveyed the selection of delicious foods as it was laid out for them.

'Nonsense, you're about to go wing walking. Of course,

269

this is all part of your birthday present, so don't be expecting another gift.'

The waiter placed two stands filled with finger sandwiches, scones and cakes on the table. Teddy watched, amused, as Oscar and Arthur animatedly disagreed on whether the cream or jam should be put on the scones first. Before long, Lexie was sipping a glass of champagne and doing her best impression of Vanessa during Arthur and Teddy's interview.

It seemed only minutes had passed before Oscar was looking at his watch and trying to round them up to move on to their next stop. Teddy doubled over laughing when he caught Shakeel wrapping up several remaining pastries in his napkin to take with him.

'What? I might need a snack wherever we end up next!' Shak protested. 'You won't be laughing when you're reaching into my pocket to grab one.'

Teddy raised an eyebrow.

'Behave!' Shakeel said. But the nervous grin on his face made Teddy's heart leap.

Once they were on their way again, Oscar revealed the next part of his plan for the day.

'I hope nobody is afraid of water,' he said seriously. 'Because we are going wine tasting on the river!'

'Oscar, this is all incredible. I can't believe you're doing all of this for Grandad.'

'It's my pleasure. Your grandad reminded me how fortunate I've been in my life, and getting to know all of you has been so lovely. It's like I've found the family I never had.'

'You've been such a fantastic friend to him these past few months. I've never seen him so happy and alive.'

'Stop, stop, I'm not going to cry at someone else's party,' Oscar said, reaching for the tissue in his pocket. The smile on his face never faded as he dabbed his eyes.

Teddy did his best to hover between the two groups which formed as they enjoyed the wine tasting. With Lexie, Shakeel and Oscar keeping each other well entertained, he stayed close to Arthur and Ben.

'I just wanted to apologize about earlier, Arthur. I didn't mean to sound like I was pushing you about Jack,' Ben said as they made their way through the various wines on offer. Teddy stayed silent.

'Not at all. I understand your questions, I've asked them myself many times.'

'I just can't imagine if in fifty years I had the chance to find out what Teddy was doing and turning that down,' Ben said, sounding a little melancholy.

'That's the difference though, young man. You have the chance to live your life and not need to look back and wonder, what if? You don't need to read old letters or stare at an old photograph for that.'

'You have a photograph, Grandad?' Teddy spun round on the spot, shocked to learn that Arthur had not mentioned having a photo of Jack before.

'Just the one. He sent it in the last letter he wrote to me.'

'That reminds me,' Ben said reaching for his phone. 'Let's take some pictures of us together.'

Teddy felt Shakeel's eyes on him as they posed and Ben encouraged him and Arthur to pull funny faces. He was sure his cheeks were burning bright by the time Ben lowered his phone and turned to the others.

'Maybe Shakeel could take a proper one of the three of us. Shakeel? Do you mind?'

Teddy groaned as he watched Shakeel set his latest empty glass down and take the phone from Ben, who proceeded to place himself in the middle of himself and Arthur, throwing his arms around their shoulders.

Teddy had seen Shakeel pretending not to be drunk in front of his parents many times. He now recognized the slightly vacant expression on his face as he wobbled on the spot. Shakeel stared at the screen as he took photos. Teddy was sure he saw his eyes narrow at one point, but he quickly handed the phone back to Ben.

Ben flicked through the images.

'You're not exactly Annie Leibovitz, are you Shakeel?' Ben laughed.

Teddy managed to grab Shakeel by the arm just in time to stop him tumbling over. 'Lexie, can you just give me a hand please?'

'What's going on?' Lexie said, looking around confused as she took Shakeel's other arm.

'No more alcohol for you, mister. Can we get off this boat already?'

They sat Shakeel down on an empty chair. Within seconds he was lightly snoring.

'Come on, Shak,' Lexie said. 'You promised me you weren't going to do this today.'

It suddenly dawned on Teddy. 'He told you, didn't he? About the kiss?'

He didn't need to wait for an answer as Lexie bit her bottom lip nervously.

'Holy fuck, Lex. You could have said you knew!'

'I'm sorry, seriously, Teddy, I was desperate to, but I promised him. He's been so down about it and I couldn't go behind his back.'

'I don't know what's going on, Lex. He won't talk to me about how he's feeling.'

'He's frightened, Teddy. He risked your friendship and is trying to move on so you won't hate him for it.' Lexie frowned. 'You've got Ben. Let Shak get over his feelings however he needs to.'

'Hang on. He really thinks I would push him away?'

Shakeel made a mumbling sound. 'Mum boy. Mummy boy.'

Teddy's mouth fell open. 'Is he . . . is he calling me a mummy's boy in his sleep?'

'I don't know what's going on in that thick head of his, Teddy,' Lexie said, ignoring Shakeel's mumbles. 'I just know he needs to get over whatever this is, with or without your help.'

She turned her attention back to Shakeel as he began to stir again.

Ben was still showing the photographs to Arthur and Oscar when Teddy rejoined them.

'I don't think I fancy any more wine,' he said, turning down the glass from Ben, who happily prevented it from going to waste.

'What?' He grinned. 'At least I'm not as wasted as Shak.'

He didn't give Teddy the chance to respond before holding out another refilled glass to Arthur.

'No, I think I've had enough too. It's been lovely, but I'm not—' Arthur began.

'You're not bailing on me yet, Arthur Edwards.' Oscar threw his arms up in the air. 'We have one more stop to make.'

'Is it in the hotel?'

'Very droll.' Oscar laughed. 'We are taking you to your first gay bar!'

Teddy had only ever been to a gay bar when visiting Shakeel at university. Even the ones in the city had felt too close to home when he still wasn't out publicly. He didn't have that excuse now. The club was busier than he had anticipated, but Arthur and Oscar didn't seem to mind as they made their way in. Teddy happily let Oscar take the lead and focus on showing Arthur around. 'Shall we get some drinks for everyone?' he asked.

'I'll come with you,' Ben said, grabbing hold of Teddy's hand and leading him across to the bar.

'You doing all right?' Teddy said as they waited for the barman to finish with another customer.

'All good, might make this my last though and then head home.'

'Maybe you should have a water and then grab a taxi? I could come with you if you want.'

Ben shook his head. 'It's fine, I've an early start tomorrow anyway. You should stay with Arthur.'

'OK, let's get these drinks and then you can say goodbye to everyone.'

Ben didn't hang around long after helping carry the drinks back to the table Oscar and Arthur were now sitting at. He said his goodbyes and disappeared back through the crowd towards the exit.

'Where'd Ben go?' Lexie asked, leaving Shakeel dancing with a group of people he didn't know.

'He's got an early start. I think he'd had enough to drink.'

'I noticed. I don't think Shak will be too upset that he's gone,' she said.

'Don't, Lex, please,' he said, pre-empting her next question. 'I know what you're going to say.'

'Do you actually want to be with Ben, Teddy?'

'I think so. Yes. Sometimes?'

'I think we've found our problem.' She sighed, taking a gulp from her bottle of water.

'It's on me, Lex. I keep pushing him away and finding reasons to stop us moving any faster. He's just—'

'Listen to yourself, Teddy. You're making endless excuses for him. If you think there's even the slightest possibility that you feel the same way Shak does, he deserves to know. Sort your shit out, before somebody gets hurt.'

'I can't do it.'

'Bullshit. You *can*. You're just afraid, the same way you were afraid of taking the job because your mum got it for you and the same way you were afraid to come out. Now look at you. Stop waiting for someone else to tell you what and who you really want.'

She looked around, quickly realizing she couldn't find who she was searching for. 'Oh god, where did Shak go? I left him right there.'

'I'll go and look for him.' Teddy put his drink down and pushed his way through the groups of people who now filled the small space. The smell of alcohol and sweat grew stronger as he reached the centre of the dance floor. Once he was sure that Shakeel wasn't there, he headed towards the toilets. He tried not to panic about where he would look next if Shak wasn't in there.

'Oi! Watch where you're going,' a voice yelled at him as Teddy tripped over a foot.

'Sorry, mate, I didn't—'

He stopped. His eyes were still adjusting to the light in the small narrow corridor which led to the dingy toilets, but it was clear what he was seeing.

'Shak? What the fuck are you doing? Get off him!'

He reached out and pulled whoever it was that had draped themselves over Shakeel off him. 'I'm guessing this isn't Simon?' Teddy said as he let go of the stranger who swore angrily at him.

Before Teddy could stop him, Shakeel had chugged the remainder of his drink, pushed past him and dashed back out towards the bar.

'Shakeel, stop!' Teddy called, chasing after him. 'Where the hell are you going?'

He finally caught up to him down the street from the main entrance.

'What? Go on, Teddy, say your bit,' Shakeel said, shaking his head and refusing to look directly at him. 'So what? I kissed someone. Aren't you just glad it wasn't you?'

But Teddy's mind was blank. There was so much he had thought about saying but now, staring back at his best friend, it was all gone. His heart pounded in his chest. He hated seeing Shakeel like this.

'That's just great, Teddy. You're the one who has been desperate to talk, but now you don't know what to say to me?'

'What's that supposed to mean? Is there something you want me to say?'

'I . . . no.' Shak suddenly looked tired. 'None of this was meant to happen.' He put his head in his hands.

'Talk to me, please! You're the one who kissed me, Shakeel, remember? Call me a mummy's boy to my face.'

Shakeel leaned back against the wall and stared up at the clear night sky. The shrieking of a nearby car alarm broke the silence.

'Wha . . . how do you—'

'When you were drunk earlier. So, that's what you think of me is it?'

'How can you even ask me that? That wasn't me talking. It was—'

'Don't even bother saying it was the drink, Shak. At least own it.'

They stood in silence again as a police car drove past them.

'I shouldn't have kissed you on Christmas Day,' Shakeel said softly, the moonlight reflecting in his eyes. 'It wasn't meant to happen like that. Not after all this time.'

'You mean—'

'And I don't want to spoil Arthur's big day either, but I thought you'd hate me for ruining our friendship. You probably should!' He lowered his head and stared at the ground.

'You didn't even wait to find out how I felt about it, Shak. You won't talk to me so I have no way of understanding what's going on with you.'

'This isn't right, Teddy. There's nothing left to say – you've got a boyfriend. Let's just forget it ever happened and try to get back to normal.'

'We need to sort this out.'

'You're the one who won't let it go, Teddy.'

'Because you're my best friend! I care about you and want to make sure you're okay.'

Shakeel made to move, but Teddy reached out to grab his arm.

'Get off!' Shak hissed using his full force to push Teddy backwards. Stumbling, Teddy fell back onto the pavement with a thud. His whole body ached.

'What the fuck did you do that for?' Teddy gasped.

'Why can't you ever just let anything go?' Shakeel shouted, his eyes filled with tears.

Before Teddy could respond, he was walking down the street without looking back.

'Fuck,' Teddy mumbled to himself as he climbed to his feet. The graze on his hand was bleeding. Several people were staring at him, a few laughing at the scene they had just witnessed. Ignoring them, he hurried back inside. His grandad and Oscar were in the karaoke room. Teddy threw himself down on the chair beside a dozing Arthur who looked around startled.

'Is he *still* singing?' Arthur said with a grin as he sat himself upright.

'You're awake! Just in time, I need a Sonny for my Cher.'

Teddy couldn't help but laugh as Oscar grabbed Arthur's hand and pulled him off the chair, before handing him a spare microphone.

'I don't know what you're laughing at,' Arthur said as the music began to play. 'It's your turn next.'

CHAPTER THIRTY-ONE
Arthur

NOTHING COULD HAVE prepared Arthur for what followed his appearance on *Good Morning Live*. From tripling his fundraising target to being stopped in the street for pictures, Northbridge had turned into Arthur's very own fan club.

'Mum let slip that several people mentioned the interview to her at work,' Teddy told Arthur. 'I think she's still a bit surprised by the positive reaction and how interesting people find you coming out at your age to be, Grandad.'

'They should see me when I'm just trying to get the vegetables for dinner and people start appearing out of nowhere and asking for pictures,' Arthur said with a sigh. Despite his attempts at making it sound like a hassle, Arthur knew that the glint in his eye gave him away.

'You love it really, Grandad,' Teddy said with a knowing grin. 'Enjoy every second of it!'

'I have to go the pharmacy now, so if I'm not back in half an hour, you can come and rescue me from all of my fans.'

Northbridge was busy as ever. Cars that couldn't find a space in the several car parks scattered around the town lined the streets, daring the lurking traffic warden to pounce on his easy prey. Arthur felt a pang of guilt as he drove past the pharmacy. He hated lying to Teddy about where he was going but for now, it was still on a need-to-know basis only. He couldn't believe his luck when he spotted the empty space right outside the entrance to the hospital. He was just in time for his appointment with the oncologist.

Almost as if she knew that he could talk, Madeleine's name flashed up on his phone.

'I'm just about to go inside now,' he said. 'I'll see you when I get home.'

He took a deep breath and stepped out of the car.

'Excuse me, you're the man doing the charity event, aren't you?'

Arthur turned to see a woman, who he guessed was in her late fifties, staring back him. Her hair was neatly tied into a bun at the nape of her neck.

'Hello, that's me, Arthur Edwards,' he said, holding his hand out to her. She grabbed hold of it and shook it enthusiastically.

'I knew I recognized that friendly face,' she said. 'I saw you on the television. I donated and posted the link for my friends to do the same.'

'Thank you so much, that's very kind of you,' Arthur said. He could feel his eyes beginning to well up as a wave of emotion rushed over him. 'I'm so sorry, I have an appointment to get to.'

'Not at all, I just want to wish you good luck,' she said, releasing his hand.

Arthur hurried along, keeping his head down until he was safely inside the building. He walked through the corridors until he arrived in the empty waiting room. As he waited for his appointment, Arthur suddenly found himself regretting his insistence that Madeleine didn't need to accompany him.

'Mr Edwards?' a woman said softly, placing her hand on his shoulder. 'Hello. We're ready for you.'

Arthur felt his legs shaking as he stood up from the chair and followed her through the double doors.

'Grandad? Is that you back?' Teddy shouted after hearing the front door close.

'Yes, yes, I'll be down in a minute. Just popping upstairs.'

Arthur closed the bedroom door behind him and sat down on the edge of his bed. He knew Madeleine was waiting to talk to him, but he needed a minute to himself.

Inevitably, Madeleine knocked on the door several minutes later. Before she could even ask him anything, Arthur burst into tears.

'I can't do it, Madeleine,' he said as she sat down on the edge of the bed beside him. 'I have to cancel the wing walk. I've made a terrible mistake.'

'Stop right there, Arthur Edwards.'

He twisted around so that he could see her face.

'I wondered how long it would take before this happened. We've been here before, Arthur.'

He scratched his neck. He didn't understand what Madeleine was talking about.

'Oh Arthur,' she said softly, patting his arm. 'The night before you came out, remember? What did you want to do?'

'I wanted to cancel dinner,' Arthur said, remembering how he had come so close to phoning Elizabeth and Patrick to tell them they didn't need to come over.

'Are you glad I stopped you doing that?'

He nodded his head.

'Good. Now tell me what happened with the consultant to prompt this.'

Madeleine listened as Arthur carefully explained what he had been told earlier that afternoon.

'You studied the statistics around prostate cancer last time, Arthur. They wouldn't recommend surgery if they didn't think it would work.'

'I thought that last time, Madeleine. Now here I am again.'

'You can do this.'

Arthur shook his head.

'What? You're giving up already? That's not the Arthur Edwards I know. That's not the man I married and it certainly isn't the man who people saw on television talking about standing on a plane in the sky!'

He laughed softly as Madeleine squeezed his hand.

'I'm not out there saving the A & E department from closure, am I? You rallied the community and made a real difference.'

'It's not saved just yet,' Madeleine said. 'But look at you, you've always been the bravest, most determined man I know. When people ask, do you know what I tell them about you?'

As Arthur shook his head, Madeleine smiled at him.

'That you're my best friend. It doesn't matter about the rings on our fingers or whatever people consider normal these days.

We are our own little family and we always have been. You'll be there for me and I'll be there for you, even if it does mean putting up with daredevil stunts!'

'Thank you, love,' Arthur said. 'Even when I'm hundreds of feet in the air on Saturday afternoon, it's only your smile I'll be looking for.'

CHAPTER THIRTY-TWO
Teddy

TEDDY HADN'T SEEN or heard from Shakeel since their argument outside the club.

Not that it mattered; he hadn't a clue what he would say even if he had got in touch. Shakeel was his best friend. Ben was his boyfriend. Why couldn't he just let what had happened go? What further explanation did he want to hear from Shakeel? He had found himself lying in bed every night since running over endless questions, confused about what was going on between them.

'How did the rest of the night go? Did Arthur enjoy himself?' Ben asked Teddy.

'Pretty uneventful. We eventually got Grandad and Oscar to put down the microphones.'

Teddy's stomach ached as he watched Ben laugh.

'Damn, I wish I had been able to stay and join in. I was shattered.'

'It was a long day,' Teddy agreed. 'I know it wasn't the easiest day either.'

His voice trailed off, but it didn't matter. The look on Ben's face told Teddy that he understood what he meant.

'I really want to make this work, Teddy,' Ben said quietly. 'But every time I think we're getting somewhere . . . I don't know, it's like you don't want it.'

'Sorry . . . I don't really know what else to say.'

'Yeah, I had a feeling you'd say that,' Ben said. 'That's half the problem. It's like you're still not ready to be whoever you are. Even on our first day at work together I knew it. You couldn't decide if you were embarrassed by your surname or not. Then it was the same about being gay. Now it feels like it's my turn. Am I your boyfriend or some big secret?'

'You're not a secret, Ben. I'm just not like you.'

'Like me? I didn't wake up like this, Teddy. You think being kicked out by my dad or not having any contact with my mum or having to fight for a job that pays enough for me to live in a tiny box was my big life dream?'

'I didn't mean—'

'Nah, Teddy, you never do. You woke up in the big house with the mum who could help you achieve your dream even after you fucked about for a few years.'

Teddy felt the blood rush to his face.

'Fucked about? My dad was dead. I didn't want to get out of bed in the morning. Nothing mattered; not Mum, Grandad, my friends, certainly not any of these opportunities Mum thought would suddenly fix me. I never got to tell my dad that I was gay. I never got to know if he loved me for who I am. All I wanted was to make him proud of me and I'll never get to do that.'

The garden area outside the building was empty. Ben got up off the bench they were sitting on.

'Of course he would be proud of you,' Ben said. 'How could he not be?'

'I've made plenty of mistakes, Ben. During those dark times, I was horrible to the people I love most. Finally doing this placement was my way of starting to make it up to Mum. I don't want people to think of me as a failure who had to be handed a job, especially you.'

Ben sat back down on the bench beside him.

'Look, it's up to you, but do you want me to come to Arthur's event or not?'

It was a yes or no question. Teddy could give Ben the chance he deserved. Or he could end it now. He felt Ben's hand on his shoulder. He took a deep breath and looked up straight into his dark brown eyes.

CHAPTER THIRTY-THREE
Arthur

PATRICK AND SCARLETT stopped by to check on Arthur the night before the event. Scarlett hugged him so hard he almost considered asking for help to remove her.

'There's a good chance of Scarlett squeezing the life out of me before I even get up in the air!' Arthur laughed as he sat back down.

'I still can't believe you're actually doing this, Arthur!' Scarlett said with a loud squee. Patrick was helping Madeleine serve the tea.

Arthur smiled at his daughter-in-law to be as she absent-mindedly twirled the ruby engagement ring on her finger.

'Have you started planning yet?'

'No, there's no rush. We don't want anything over the top.'

'Don't waste time,' Arthur said. 'Remember the quote, "Don't put off until tomorrow what you can do today". Live your lives.'

'Thanks, Arthur. We won't. I can't wait to be part of this family.'

'Really? We don't embarrass you?'

'Why would you ask that? Did it look like something offended me? Oh my gosh, because—'

'No, no, I'm sorry, that was a silly question. I just know that there are still people out there who don't exactly approve of what I've done.'

'That's their loss,' Scarlett said sternly, frowning. 'Your family is the kindest, most loving family I've ever met. The way you supported Patrick showed me that. Now I see how Madeleine and you stick together, and how you both are with Teddy. Why would anyone be ashamed of that?'

'You always see the good, Scarlett. It's a very special quality.'

'I try,' she said with a smile. 'Life can be tough. I learned that the hard way, but then I realized I could smile and try to spread positivity. Some people don't like that and that's fine, but it's who I am.'

'Good. I'm glad you're here to do that for all of us.'

'Any time.'

'You two gossiping about me?' Patrick asked as he sat down next to his fiancée.

'Yes actually, Scarlett tells me you want to do the wing walk with me and I think that's a brilliant idea!'

'What?' He gasped, choking on a mouthful of hot tea as they both laughed.

Arthur took himself off to bed early that night. Madeleine had covered his pillows in some of her lavender spray, insistent that it would help him sleep. He didn't need to be at the airfield until 2 p.m. the next day, but he wanted to be as well rested as possible. He felt even better about going through with the wing walk after his talk with Scarlett. He thought about the kind woman he had met outside the hospital. She had taken the time to donate and encourage others to do the same. That was what it was all about. He smiled to himself. He had made it through his seventies and was entering a whole new chapter of his life. His eyelids felt heavy and began to droop. Arthur knew he was about to have the best night's sleep he had had in months.

'Happy Birthday, Grandad!' Teddy said, hugging Arthur as he arrived at the house the following morning. Madeleine had prepared him a special birthday breakfast.

'I know you probably haven't heard of it, Grandad, but a journalist from a magazine called *Gay Life* got in touch with me,' Teddy said as he and Arthur sat down at the table in the dining room. Teddy didn't miss the look of recognition on his face. 'Oh, maybe you do know it then, well that's even better.'

'I am vaguely familiar,' Arthur said with a small grin. 'Are they offering you a job?'

'Ha, I wish. No, they're after you of course. They want to do an interview. Would you be up for it?'

Arthur thought back to standing in the newsagents several months ago. Even just staring at the cover of the magazine had made him feel nervous.

'I guess it couldn't hurt,' Arthur said. 'Would you mind sorting it out for me?'

'Of course, I'll let you know what's happening,' Teddy said. 'Oh, and Oscar is going to be here just before one o'clock.'

'Thank you, Teddy, that's the third time you've told me this morning.'

Arthur felt as ready as he could be. There was nothing more he could do to prepare himself. No diagnosis was going to get in his way now. He hummed along to the song on the radio as everyone else scurried around the house. They'd tried to make a fuss of it being his birthday, but he'd warned them that all of that could wait until afterwards. He didn't need the distraction until his feet were firmly back on the ground.

'I told James not to make too much fuss, but he insisted on bringing a picnic,' Madeleine complained to herself as she wiped down the bench. 'Like I could sit, calmly eating sandwiches while Arthur is doing *that* in the air above us.' She waved her arms dramatically.

'I hope I'm not doing *that*!' Arthur laughed, mimicking her. 'You and James will have a lovely afternoon. It's really very kind of him to come along with you.'

'You don't mind, do you?'

'Madeleine, we're not having this conversation again. You just focus on keeping Oscar away or *he'll* be the one enjoying your picnic.'

Ben arrived in Northbridge just after 11 a.m. He and Teddy were planning to leave just after midday so that they could go and collect Shakeel and Lexie from the station before driving to the location. Arthur just happened to catch the end of a conversation as he entered the room.

'With any luck maybe Shakeel will decide he can't come at the last minute,' Ben said glumly.

'I hope not, he's part of the family,' Arthur said. 'Try to talk to him today for me please. Clear the air between you.'

The tips of Ben's ears went red as he realized that he had been overheard.

'Sorry, Arthur, I will of course.'

'Any word on your mum, Teddy?' Arthur asked.

'Nothing. Sorry, Grandad. I really thought she might visit this morning.'

'Don't worry. We carry on!' Arthur tried to mask his disappointment as best he could. He'd told himself over and over not to get his hopes up that Elizabeth might take the opportunity to visit. She had spoken to Teddy on the phone a couple of times. While he was pleased that they were talking at all, Arthur had still hoped she might come over. Every knock on the door had given him a moment of pause, only resulting in a sinking disappointment when it wasn't her.

Before long it was only Arthur left in the house waiting for Oscar's arrival. He'd said a brief hello to James when he arrived to pick Madeleine up.

'Are you sure you're all right?' Madeleine had said, looking at him closely before she stepped out of the front door.

'I've never been better. Now go, please, have fun and I'll see you both there in a while.'

Oscar was running late. Arthur knew it was likely to happen, so had allowed a little leeway in his timings. He heard the grandfather clock in the dining room chime; now they were into genuinely late territory. He paced around the lounge, watching out of the window which overlooked the driveway. Almost forty-five minutes later than arranged, Oscar finally pulled up.

'I'm so sorry, Arthur. There was an accident and I stupidly left my phone at home. Absolute nightmare.' He continued apologizing profusely as he gulped down a glass of water. He wiped at his damp forehead with a tissue.

'You're here now, we better get on the road again or we'll never make it there on time.'

'It's going to take an hour to get there, and that's without running into traffic,' Arthur said.

'We'll take the back roads. I've already got it in the satnav.'

The winding narrow roads weren't suitable for large vehicles. Arthur usually avoided them at all costs. The overgrown trees and bushes invaded the little space the road offered with no mercy. Meeting an oncoming car would result in a battle of wills until either frustrated driver gave in and tried to reverse back to a point at which the other could manoeuvre themselves past. His eyes were focused on the clock on the dashboard. Every minute felt like ten.

'Oh dear,' Oscar said, his grip tightening on the vibrating steering wheel as the car began to judder.

'What's wrong?'

'It must be the engine.'

'Look, there's a lay-by. Pull in.'

They both jumped out of the car as soon as it came to a halt. Oscar pressed down on the bonnet and allowed it to rise into the air. Black smoke came billowing out, engulfing them both. Arthur's stomach twisted uncomfortably.

'I think we might have a little problem.' Oscar coughed as he jumped back from the groaning vehicle.

CHAPTER THIRTY-FOUR
Teddy

'THANK YOU FOR being here today, Ben,' Teddy said quietly. He contemplated resting his hand on Ben's knee, but pulled back at the last second. 'I really appreciate you coming.'

The main road was busier than usual. Teddy was glad that they had been able to leave early to get to the station in the centre of town. Lexie and Shakeel had noticed the congestion and walked down from the station to meet them at a quieter junction, and the four were now in the car, driving to the airfield. No matter how hard he had tried to change the plan, Ben had insisted on picking the other two up.

'I can't believe Arthur is really eighty today,' Lexie said, breaking the silence.

'I know,' Shakeel agreed. 'It's crazy how little he's changed over the years.'

Teddy glanced in the mirror, but Shakeel was gazing out the window.

'How's work, Shak?' Lexie asked as they crossed the bridge out of town.

'Busy, but no dramas, so I won't jinx it.' Shakeel spoke so quietly Teddy had to strain to hear him over the radio. 'I'm looking forward to booking a couple of weeks away at some point. It'll be nice to escape.'

Teddy admired Lexie's efforts at keeping conversation flowing. They'd spoken the night before, during which she had promised to do her best to keep things simple. He hated things being weird with Shakeel, so if normal conversation was what he wanted, he was going to do his best to do just that.

'What about you, Ben? Any plans for a holiday?'

'Nope,' Ben answered quickly. 'I don't know if I'll even have a job this time next month, so I can't really plan that far ahead yet.'

Teddy glanced across at him, surprised that he was bringing up the job situation. With everything going on, Teddy had pushed the possibility of one of them leaving *The Post* to the back of his mind. From the corner of his eye he could see Shakeel continue to stare out at the passing fields.

They were among the first to arrive at the airfield. Even the TV crew hadn't arrived yet.

'Would you ever do anything like this?' Ben asked him.

'I'm not brave enough. I don't think I could even sit in a plane that small. What about you?'

'Maybe. I think I'd rather do something like a skydive.'

'You're on your own there too, I'm afraid.' Teddy laughed.

'I'd do a skydive.' Shakeel's interjection took them all by surprise.

'As if. You hate heights.' Lexie scoffed, as Teddy turned in his seat to face his two friends.

'Yeah well, that's part of the challenge isn't it? Doing something different, something nobody would expect, like Arthur.'

Teddy didn't know if he was meant to laugh or not. Shakeel finally stared him straight in the eye as if daring him to even crack the smallest smile.

'I think I'll stick to sitting in planes that are taking me to a sunny beach far away,' Lexie said.

Teddy shifted in his seat. He needed to escape the car and quickly.

'I'm gonna go into the office and let them know we've arrived,' he said, pushing the car door open. 'I need to find Wi-Fi. The 4G is bloody useless out here.'

'I'll come with you,' Ben said, following Teddy out of the car and strolling alongside him. He had been uncharacteristically quiet all morning.

Once inside the small terminal building, Teddy found someone who suggested that he set up his laptop in the back office. Teddy rang Dylan to confirm that he was going to upload the story with images as soon as possible.

'While I have you,' Dylan said, 'You didn't hear anything from me, but there's a job coming up. I can't say much more right now, I just wanted you both to be aware that they'll probably interview you guys and some other trainees.'

'Oh wow, okay, thanks, Dylan. I'll let Ben know.'

'Are you with him now?'

'Yes, is something wrong?'

'Leo was complaining that he hadn't filed something. I'm not sure what he was working on, but tell him not to keep him waiting much longer.'

'Oh, I didn't know he was working on anything. I'll make sure he knows. Do you know what it's about?'

'Haven't a clue. Leo didn't say. Right, better go, I hope today goes well.'

Ben was watching him as he hung up. 'What's that?'

'There's a job coming up. We're going to hear about interviews this week.'

'Oh right,' Ben said. 'Well, we both knew it was going to happen sooner or later.'

'I guess so. He doesn't know when exactly yet, but wanted to give us a heads up. He also said that Leo was waiting for your story. I didn't know you were working on something for him. Why didn't you mention it?'

'He must be confused,' Ben said, his forehead furrowed. 'I was talking about one for next week. I just mentioned an idea in passing and he liked it. I'll just go and call him now.'

Teddy watched as he left the office and walked back outside with the phone to his ear. He chewed his lip as he wondered what Ben could be working on for the following week, as there was nothing he was aware of in their shared diary.

'Knock, knock. Can I come in?'

'Hey, Lex. Where's Shak?'

'He's with your grandmother and her fella. By the way, how utterly adorable are they together?' She clasped her hands over her heart and sighed. 'I want that.'

'I know. They're cute together. Suppose it must be a bit odd for him coming along today.'

'I know! Imagine going to an event with your girlfriend to watch her gay husband wing walk! I love your family so much.'

Teddy couldn't help but laugh. Lexie's ability to succinctly describe the absurdity of their experiences was unrivalled. It was a gift she had always had.

'How are things with you?' Lexie sat opposite him, her effortless switch from stand-up to talk-show host being made in record time. 'I sensed a little tension in the car.'

'It's nothing. Ben's been . . . understanding.'

Lexie played with the ball of Blu Tack on the desk. 'Shak nearly didn't come today.'

'Really? How did you change his mind?'

'I didn't,' she said. 'One minute he wasn't coming, the next he was up and dressed. I think he was nervous about seeing you after . . . you know.'

'He shoved me to the ground? Yeah, I know. He knows I'm here for him if he wants to talk now; what else am I meant to do? He's the one who kissed me out of nowhere.'

'Wake up, Teddy,' Lexie said. 'He's spent the last six months stomping around, frowning every time you mentioned Ben's name. He would do anything for you and your family. How can you not see how he really feels for you?'

Teddy couldn't believe it. It had been more than just a kiss. He'd really been that oblivious to Shakeel's true feelings all this time.

'Why didn't he tell me?'

'Oh, sweetie. I love you, but you really are hopeless some-times. Look, I'm not saying anything else. Talk to Ben. Talk to Shakeel. Talk to whoever can sort this!'

'Argh!' Teddy put his head down on the desk. 'This is such a mess. I'm such a mess.'

'Don't freak out right now. You have to focus on your grandad and getting this story done.'

'You're right, I do,' he said, glancing at his watch. 'Actually,

Grandad should really be here by now. I should go check what's going on.'

Teddy walked outside and looked for Arthur and Oscar. He spotted only his grandmother, looking worried. 'Nan, is there no sign yet?'

'Nothing and his phone isn't ringing either,' she said, her voice cracking. 'I hope they're okay.'

'Apparently there's been an accident and it's causing delays in and around Northbridge,' Shakeel said, looking up from his phone. 'It doesn't give any details but maybe they're caught in traffic.'

Teddy saw the sudden panic in his grandmother's wide eyes.

'I'm sure they're just delayed, Nan. Why don't you go and sit back down? They'll be sitting in traffic and Grandad probably just forgot to charge his phone.'

He watched as James held Madeleine's hand and walked her to a small picnic table. It felt like time had come to a standstill as they all waited together, staring at the entrance to the car park. Ben had gone back inside to use the toilet.

'Anything?' Shakeel said when he saw Teddy glance at his phone again.

'Nothing. What if something's wrong, Shak?' He hadn't let himself dare to think anything might have happened until that moment. 'What if—'

'Stop it. Don't panic. They're going to be here, okay? Any minute now.' Teddy's heart jumped as he felt Shakeel put his arm around his shoulder. He gave him a small smile. Shakeel was his best friend. Why did this feel different? Lexie was right. Shakeel would do anything for him. And he would do anything for Shakeel.

CHAPTER THIRTY-FIVE
Arthur

ARTHUR SCRAMBLED IN his pocket for his phone. Someone would surely be able to come and pick them up. Things were going to be fine.

'There's no bloody signal. Nothing at all out here,' he said, holding the phone up to the sky. 'We're bloody buggered.'

Arthur started pacing up and down. He thought of the people sitting at the airfield, waiting for him. The *Good Morning Live* crew set up, ready to film. Everyone who had donated money. His stomach churned.

'Come and sit down, Arthur,' Oscar pleaded. 'Everything's going to be fine.'

Arthur could only laugh. Not even Oscar's optimism was going to save this disaster.

'What's the point, Oscar? It's not happening.'

'Arthur—'

'They'll think I'm a coward and haven't turned up.'

'Look, Arthur, there's—' Oscar's voice was getting higher with every word.

'I can't show my face now. No one will ever believe that we—'

'Dad?'

Arthur's heart leapt as he spun around to see Elizabeth staring at him from the open window of her car. He had been so engrossed in his worry that he had completely failed to notice her pulling up beside them. 'Aren't you meant to be at the airfield now?'

'I'm so glad to see you. We've broken down!'

'I guess you better both get in then. Come on, quickly!' Oscar and Arthur leapt in.

'What are you doing out here?' Arthur asked.

'Traffic. There's an accident and . . . well, I needed to get to the airfield on time.'

Arthur felt his throat tighten. 'You . . . you're coming?'

'Dad, I'm so sorry. I left it so late and then I was too embarrassed to come over to the house this morning. Ralph had already gone with the girls and I was just sitting there on my own.'

'It doesn't matter. None of it matters. You're here now,' he said, squeezing her hand.

'I've been awful, Dad. I don't know how you can even look at me.'

'How many times did I tell you, Lizzie? I knew you needed time and space. I was never going anywhere.'

'You were so lovely on the show. I felt like such a bitch afterwards when people were telling me how lucky I was and how proud I should be, and all this time I've treated you so terribly.'

'Every word I spoke was true,' Arthur said. 'I couldn't be prouder to call you my daughter. We all love you so much.'

'I don't think Edward would agree with you.'

'You're too alike. But you're both still adjusting to relying on each other without Harry in between. Teddy just needs to know you're there for him, ready to accept him for who he is.'

'I've done this all so wrong. What if he can't forgive me?'

'He will, trust me. As soon as he sees you today, he'll know that it's taken a lot.'

Once he had reception back on his phone, Arthur let Madeleine know that they were on their way again. At worst, he thought they might end up being only fifteen minutes late.

'We're not far away now,' Oscar piped up from the back seat. Arthur had never seen him sit as quietly as he did during the journey. Every so often the sound of a gentle sob reminded them that he was there.

'It's all just so lovely, like one of those family reunion documentaries. I'm going to need some champagne,' Oscar said, taking a third tissue from the box next to him.

'There will be none of that until we're back at the house afterwards.'

'Am I allowed back in after the last time?' Elizabeth said quietly. Arthur saw the same uncertain expression on her face that she had had since she was a small child.

'We're going to celebrate together as a family.'

The airfield finally came into view. A wave of excitement spread through Arthur's body. They pulled into the busy car park and Oscar jumped out of the car, ready to let them know that they had arrived.

'Dad,' Elizabeth said, grabbing hold of his arm, 'I just want to say that I'm really proud of you and that I love you.'

Her eyes were filled with tears. Arthur leaned forward and

hugged her. Her arms wrapped around him and squeezed him tight.

'Happy birthday, Daddy,' she said, her voice breaking as her tears fell onto Arthur's shoulder.

CHAPTER THIRTY-SIX
Teddy

THOSE WHO HAD arrived were spread out in various groups across the field in front of the building. The silence among them was eventually broken by Madeleine.

'They're on their way!' she called out, her voice filled with relief. 'Your grandad just texted. Everything's absolutely fine.'

'Thank God for that,' Teddy said as he felt Shakeel's other arm wrap around him. It felt like they had been hugging for several minutes, oblivious to everyone else around them.

'What a relief,' Ben said, walking across to them from Madeleine.

Teddy pulled himself away from Shakeel, the tips of his ears burning as he fixed his jacket. He hadn't even noticed that Ben had come back.

'Yeah, I was really starting to freak out.'

'Come on,' Ben said. 'Let's go grab a tea from the van before they get here.'

'Sure, that sounds good. Shak, you coming?'

'Oh, erm, no, I'll just . . . I'm gonna go talk to Lexie.'

'I'm glad he said no,' Ben said as they walked in the direction of the tea van.

'Excuse me?'

'Why would you ask him? I asked you alone purposely.'

'I can't tell if this is a joke or not, Ben. What would be wrong with him coming to get a drink with us?'

'Did all that hugging make him thirsty?'

Teddy stopped walking and glared at Ben.

'There it is. If you have a point to make, go ahead and say it.'

'Come on, like I'm not the only one thinking it. You two are always snapping away at each other like an old married couple. I'm just the tag-along trying to get my boyfriend's attention while he's clearly totally distracted by someone else.'

He stormed on ahead of Teddy, his fists clenched.

'Ben! Please don't walk away from me, let me explain.'

He came to a sudden halt and rounded on Teddy, his eyes bulging with fury. 'Answer me one question, Teddy, because I don't know why I'm actually here,' he said. 'Do you want to be my boyfriend?'

'I'm trying to figure everything out, Ben. I . . . I really . . .' His voice trailed off.

'Thanks, Teddy, that says it all. You can go hang out with Shakeel, I need some space.'

After watching Ben storm off, Teddy dragged himself back across the field towards the car park. He wished he had just done it there and then and told Ben the truth. He was still deep in thought when he caught sight of a flustered-looking Oscar running towards him.

'Teddy! Your grandad's here!'

He forgot all about his fight with Ben and ran towards Lexie and into the car park. 'Grandad!' He threw his arms around

Arthur so forcefully he almost knocked him off his feet. 'Jesus, don't do that to us again. Poor Nan is going to need a drink.'

'I'm so sorry, we tried to bypass the traffic and then we broke down, but then your mum found us.'

'Mum?' Teddy shook his head in disbelief. 'I don't understand.'

'She was coming to watch. We had a good talk in the car, Teddy. She's really here.'

His head was filled with questions, but he didn't have time to organize his thoughts before they began spilling out to an amused Arthur.

'Did she apologize?'

'Not that I needed to hear it, but she did. We can talk about everything later, but just let her try today. Give her that chance. For me?'

Teddy closed his eyes and nodded. Arthur gave his shoulder a squeeze.

'Come on, Arthur,' Oscar shouted, waving his arm in the air. 'You're still doing this if you can get a bloody move on!'

He watched as his grandad hurried across the grass as fast as his feet would carry him. Teddy followed slowly behind him. Lexie was sitting on a bench nearby.

'You're giving me that look, Lex. What's wrong?' Teddy asked sitting down beside her.

'That wasn't the quietest conversation you and Ben have ever had. Sorry, I didn't mean to eavesdrop, but I was kind of right there.'

'I don't want us fighting to spoil today. I'll try and smooth things over back at the house,' Teddy said miserably. 'He knows something is off with me and Shak, I couldn't tell him the truth.'

'Look at your grandad, Teddy,' she said. 'He's eighty years old and he's not only come out but he's also about to stand on top of a tiny plane.'

'Get to the point, Lex, please.'

'Be braver!' she shouted. 'I think, deep down, you know why you're so focused on Shakeel. You need to admit how you feel to yourself and then do something about it.'

Before Teddy had a chance to say anything, Lexie jumped off the bench. 'Speaking of being brave . . . your Mum's coming right for us,' she added quietly.

Teddy's heart skipped a beat as he looked up and saw his mum striding across the field.

'Hi, Mrs Marsh, lovely to see you.'

'Hello, Lexie. How's work?.'

'Busy, but I'm enjoying it a lot. I'll leave you two to . . .'

Teddy watched as Lexie skipped off across the field and joined the group waiting in the viewing area.

'Hello,' Elizabeth said sitting down beside him. 'This is all a little crazy, isn't it?'

'Yeah. I can't believe it's finally happening after all the weeks of planning.'

'You've done amazing work, Edward. You should be very proud of helping your grandfather raise so much money.'

'Thanks, Mum,' he said, staring out across the airfield. 'It's been a lot of fun too.'

'That's good. The house has been quiet without you around.'

'I'm sure it hasn't. I thought you might have moved the wedding planner into my room by now.'

Elizabeth tried to frown but couldn't help but smile.

'How are the plans coming along?'

His mum's eyes lit up as she began to talk about the wedding. It was now just over three months away.

'Just wait until you see the venue, Teddy. The estate is so beautiful,' she gushed. 'Anyway, I want you to know that your room is still there whenever you want it. Your sisters would love to have you home, too. We all miss you so much.'

'Thanks, Mum,' Teddy said. 'That would be nice. I might take a few more nights just to sort a few things out.'

'Okay, that's fair. If there's anything I can do, you know you can ask me for help, don't you?'

She beamed back at him as he nodded. That reassurance that he would turn to her was all she wanted.

'Thank you for doing what you did for Grandad today,' Teddy said. 'It meant the world to him and means a lot to me too. You being here makes today worth it for him.'

'And you?'

'It's a good place to start, Mum. I'm glad you're here.'

Teddy couldn't help but smile as he felt his mum reach across and take his hand in hers. Her eyes were filled with tears, but she was smiling back at him.

'I'm sorry for slapping you, Edward. I've been disgusted with myself for how I handled what you told me. You needed me and I let you down because I was angry and scared when I had no right to be.'

'I understand, Mum. I know it's been a lot for you to process, but me being gay—'

'You being gay is not a problem. I love you for who you are. You'll always be my son. After your dad died we drifted apart and all of this just reminded me that you felt like you couldn't talk to me. I failed you, failed as a mother.'

The tears in her eyes finally gave way and began rolling down her cheeks.

'You didn't,' Teddy said. 'Please don't ever think that, Mum. I didn't know who I was for so long after Dad died. How was I meant to keep going without such a big part of my life? I gave up on everything, but you kept pushing me. That's why I'm here today.'

'But you should have been able to talk to me. What if you had ended up like poor Sophie? How could I have lived with myself? Watching Deborah at the funeral. What if that had been me?'

'Wait,' Teddy said. 'At the funeral? You were there?'

Elizabeth nodded. 'I didn't want to get in the way so I went alone.'

'You sat at the back, didn't you? I knew I saw you that day.'

'Even then you were afraid of telling me. Scared that I couldn't love you for who you are.'

'I convinced myself that I couldn't tell you. It was nothing you did, Mum. Then after Grandad—'

'I made such a mess of all of this when you both needed my support,' she said, gently dabbing at her eyes with the tissue she had pulled from her handbag.

'Forget that. You're here now, that's the most important thing.'

They both looked around as a small cheer went up from the group as Arthur emerged from the building in his flying gear.

'Come on, let's go watch Grandad,' Teddy said, giving her hand another reassuring squeeze. 'Uncle Patrick bet me a tenner that he'll take a nap when he's up there.'

CHAPTER THIRTY-SEVEN
Arthur

ARTHUR WAS STRAPPED to the top wing of the Boeing Stearman. He lifted his arm and waved to the watching crowd. He couldn't make everyone out, but he could see Madeleine front and centre with Elizabeth by her side. Both were waving enthusiastically at him. Just knowing they were there together made his heart want to burst with happiness. The sun had finally broken through the clouds and was beating down on the countryside which surrounded them. He hadn't managed to catch her name, but the woman who had checked his harness had told him that the conditions were perfect. He took a deep breath as the engine roared to life.

The breeze against his face began to pick up speed as they taxied across the field. The adrenaline rushed through his body as he felt the small plane finally lift off the ground. Fully exposed to the elements, he felt the sting of the air on his face, but it was worth it as he looked out across the sky and the patchwork fields below him. He was flying! It was like nothing he had ever experienced. He felt more alive than he had done in years as the plane circled the fields below. Arthur could just about lift his arms to wave at everyone as the plane dipped close by the viewing enclosure.

'I'm flying!' he yelled to the clear blue sky above him, his heart pounding. Arthur felt his body shift as the pilot took them back up, accelerating before twisting and turning high in the sky. Before Arthur knew it, they were beginning their descent and back on the ground, the plane coming to a halt back where it had started.

'Careful now, you're going to be a bit wobbly,' the woman said as she took his hand and helped him down. With both feet on the ground, he looked back up at the yellow aircraft and beamed. He'd done it. He threw his fist into the air and let out a cheer. Another roar of applause filled the air as he began walking towards his friends and family.

Everyone was at the house waiting for them. Arthur knew that Elizabeth had purposely driven slowly to allow everyone to get home before them, but he was still buzzing. He had talked the whole way back, recalling every second of the experience to his daughter in great detail. If at any point she was growing bored by it, she didn't show it.

'Do you think you'd ever want to do anything like that again, Dad?'

'Once is more than enough.' He laughed. 'That's that ticked off my bucket list.'

'You have a bucket list? What else is on there?'

'Oh, just a few silly things,' Arthur said, regretting his choice of words. He didn't want to think about that now. He looked up at the clear blue sky above them. No, today was a day for celebration. He was going to cherish every single moment he had.

Arthur led the way into the house, throwing his arms up in the air in mock surprise as a cheer erupted as he entered the kitchen. He beamed with pride as he looked around at the faces smiling back at him.

'We're so proud of you, Grandad!' Eleanor exclaimed as she wrapped her arms around him. 'I thought I was going to puke when the plane was swooping towards the ground!'

'You looked so small up there. Like a dot in the sky,' Scarlett said, holding her finger and thumb close together to emphasise just how tiny she meant.

'I felt tiny, too. My whole body . . . it was like I was floating, I felt completely weightless.'

'That sounds amazing.' Scarlett's eyes lit up. 'Careful, Arthur, you'll convince me to have a go next!'

Arthur pulled Teddy aside once he had a moment to himself.

'I just wanted to thank you, Teddy,' he said, sitting down on the stool in the corner of the kitchen. 'For all of this. I couldn't have done this without your help and support. You've reminded me to live. I don't have to be like other people my age, I can still go out there and have all kinds of experiences.'

'You could never be like any other eighty-year-old, Grandad,' Teddy declared. 'You're the one inspiring all of us.'

'I am so proud of the young man you've become, Teddy. I just want to make sure you know that.'

Arthur wobbled on the stool as Teddy, without saying a word, threw both of his arms around him and hugged him tightly.

Eric and Claudette Brown stopped by to congratulate Arthur that evening.

'I'm so sorry we weren't able to come along, but we saw some videos online,' Claudette explained. 'Your hearts must have been in your mouths watching him up there!'

'I won't pretend to be jealous of you, Arthur, but that looks like an incredible experience. You're one of a kind, Arthur Edwards,' Eric said, clapping his hand on Arthur's back.

'We really can't thank you enough for doing this in honour of Sophie. All that money raised, we can't even begin to say how much it means to us all that you did this,' Claudette added, her eyes welling up. 'Especially after, well, how we behaved towards you.'

'That is all in the past,' Arthur insisted, reaching out to shake Eric's hand.

'This town is damn lucky to have you,' Eric said. 'And you too, Madeleine. I hear we might still have an emergency department thanks to you.'

'I was just telling Eric on the way over that that MP of ours was finally doing his bit to help save the department,' Claudette explained. 'You must be exhausted dealing with these people, Madeleine.'

'It's been quite the palaver, but Mr Mitchell said he would be in touch this week, so we might finally be able to stand down!'

They didn't stay long, but Arthur appreciated the effort that they had made in coming round at all. Both were still keeping a low profile in town, Madeleine informed him, and Claudette had stepped down from chairing one of their local community groups.

'Poor loves, grief is a terrible thing,' she said. 'Remind me to call round at some point this week, Arthur. I'll do some baking and take a few things over.'

Teddy rushed in carrying his laptop.

'Look,' he exclaimed, showing Arthur a website. 'I filed my story right away and it's already gone live! They've managed to include pictures and the bit of footage I sent over too,' he said, setting the laptop down for Arthur to read.

'Daredevil Grandad? Is that what you're calling me now?' He laughed.

'I can't take the credit for that one, it was Dylan. Still, not too many can say that their eighty-year-old grandad just flew through the air on top of a plane!'

'He's going to be insufferable.' Madeleine laughed, playfully rolling her eyes as Arthur lingered on another image of himself. 'That's a brilliant picture though, who took that?'

'Me!' Shakeel said, pushing closer so that he could look at the screen. 'Whoa, I didn't think they'd use it.'

'Do you think we would be able to get a copy, Shakeel?'

'Sure, Mrs Edwards,' he said. 'I'll sort that out for you as soon as I can.'

Arthur squinted at the screen. A headline further down the page had caught his eye.

'Teddy, what's that? It says my name on it.'

'It's probably just a pop-up, Grandad. Let me have a look.'

Teddy turned the laptop towards himself to check. Without another word, he closed it down and lifted it off the table.

'Yep, that's the internet for you,' he said. 'Pop-ups.'

'Horrible things, they know far too much about us.'

'I'm surprised the paparazzi aren't camped outside already.'

Oscar laughed, pretending to take pictures of them with an invisible camera.

'Only if you've tipped them off!'

Madeleine appeared carrying a large sponge cake, decorated with lit candles in the shape of an 80. Arthur couldn't help but groan. This was the part he had always hated the most. But he stood up as she walked across the room leading the group in a loud rendition of 'Happy Birthday', and found a lump forming in his throat as he looked around at the smiling, singing faces. Each one full of joy, there to share that moment with him. Madeleine sat the cake down on the table.

'Hip hip, hooray!'

'Hip hip, hooray!'

'Hip hip, hooray!'

'Thank you, all. I really don't know what I did to deserve to have all of you here with me, but this has been a birthday I will never ever forget.'

Arthur threw his arms around Madeleine. 'Thank *you* for everything.'

'Nonsense,' she said. 'No one deserves this more than you do, Arthur.'

'Where did Teddy go? Did he miss the cake?'

'He must have, he left with the laptop,' Oscar said. 'I saw Ben arrive a few minutes ago, so we shouldn't be interrupting them if you catch my drift.'

'No more wine for Oscar,' Lexie said, grabbing the bottle from the table and pretending to hide it from him.

Arthur didn't even remember climbing into bed when he woke the following morning. He rubbed his eyes as he sat up. The day before felt like a complete blur. It took a few seconds before the memory of flying through the air washed over him. He grinned to himself as he stared up at the ceiling. The thought of doing it all over again suddenly didn't seem so bad. Maybe he wouldn't mention that, though, not today at least.

He carried out his morning routine, throwing freezing cold water over his face after thoroughly scrubbing his teeth. Looking in the mirror, he carefully applied the expensive moisturiser Madeleine had bought him for Christmas under his eyes. Feeling fresher, he pulled on his corduroy trousers, buttoned up his shirt and put on his trusty crew-neck jumper. Just because he was eighty didn't mean everything had to change.

He arrived at the bottom of the stairs just in time to see the newspaper delivery boy push the new edition of *The Post* through the letterbox. He heard the sound of the young lad's bicycle tyres crossing the gravel as he bent down and picked it up. What he saw stopped him dead in his tracks.

Arthur stood motionless, staring at the front page. His own eyes were staring back him. He slowly walked to the lounge and sat down, taking as deep a breath as his lungs would allow. He felt his insides squirm as he lifted the paper up again.

EXCLUSIVE: GAY DAREDEVIL GRANDAD'S SECRET LOVE SHAME

By Benjamin King

ARTHUR EDWARDS *has affectionately become known to millions as the daredevil grandad who is raising tens of thousands of pounds for charity. Today,* The Post *can reveal the secret heartache that the Northbridge pensioner has kept*

hidden from his family and friends for over fifty years. Turn
to pages eight and nine to read the full story.

Every word he read felt like another punch to the stomach. It was all there in black and white. Every detail from how he had first met Jack Johnson to how his father had run Jack out of town under the threat of death. Arthur didn't know when he had started to cry; it was only when the tears fell from his face onto the paper that he realized. He looked at the images which filled the pages.

Arthur, Madeleine and their children.

Arthur and Teddy.

Arthur on top of the plane.

And finally, a photo of Jack Johnson.

His stomach flipped as his eyes fell on the picture of Jack. It was the photo he had sent Arthur in that last letter. The photo he had cherished for over five decades, now there for everyone to see. He couldn't read any more of it. He threw it aside and hurried out of the room.

The fresh air was what he needed. He lost track of time as he sat alone on the bench under the kitchen window, oblivious to everything going on around him as he stared out into the garden. He didn't want to think now. Thinking meant acknowledging that any of what was happening was real, that this was not a nightmare he was going to wake up from any minute. Thinking meant knowing that Elizabeth and Patrick would read about their own grandfather's actions; that they would know their father had loved someone with all his heart before Madeleine. There was nothing he could do but let the tears roll down his cheeks.

CHAPTER THIRTY-EIGHT
Teddy

TEDDY HAD SLIPPED out of the room unnoticed, the laptop under his arm. His hands were shaking and his heart was thumping as he ran up the stairs, taking two at a time. He reached his bedroom, closed the door behind him and threw the laptop down on his bed. Perhaps he had read it wrong. Maybe it wasn't what he thought it was. He opened it up and waited for the website to appear on the screen again. His stomach dropped as he read the snippet before clicking on the headline, written entirely in capital letters. An image of his grandfather's smiling face filled the page. His twinkling eyes stared back at him.

Teddy's eyes widened as he read Ben's name underneath the image. Of course. It could only have been him.

Knock. Knock.

'Teddy? You here?'

Ben walked into the room, his face lighting up as he found who he had been searching for.

'I was looking for you! Look, I know we haven't had a chance to clear the air, but today is about your grandad, so can we put it aside?' Ben said. He frowned when Teddy didn't respond. 'Why are you hiding away up here? What have I missed?'

'Nothing, Ben. You've obviously missed nothing.'

'What's that supposed to mean?' Ben sat down on the edge of the bed and stared at him. 'Seriously, Teddy, what's going on?'

'Drop the pretence, *Benjamin*. Why don't we start from the beginning; like, I dunno, how about when you decided to write a story about my grandfather's personal life when I told you to drop it?'

Ben's entire body went tense. 'Okay, Teddy, let me explain,' he said cautiously. 'I know this looks bad.' He tried to reach out and close the laptop, but Teddy quickly pulled it away from him.

'Whoa, you do?' Teddy's voice cracked as he tried to remain composed.

'I panicked. I needed something. You don't understand—'

'You're going to sit in his home and try to justify this? Do you even hear yourself?'

'I'm not making excuses. I know what I did, but it's what anyone in my position would have done if they wanted this job as much as I do.' He held his hands out to Teddy, as though begging him to understand. 'Listen to me, Teddy. It's a great story. This is what we do. You had this story just sitting there and you weren't going to even consider it.'

Ben got up off the bed and tried to take hold of Teddy's hand.

'Don't touch me,' Teddy said, swatting Ben away. 'Don't you dare talk about using my grandad's pain so casually, as a headline to try and make a name for yourself. Was all this just to get one over on me? Is that all you wanted? I knew you wanted the job, but I didn't realize that meant screwing us all over.'

'What now then?' Ben said quietly, tears welling in his eyes.

'I'm going to try and get this down off the website.'

'It's going in the paper, Teddy.'

'What? How do you know?'

'One of the guys texted to let me know. It's . . . it's on the front page.'

Teddy's entire body was shaking.

'You need to go,' he said as calmly as he could. 'Get out of this house right now.'

'Please, we need to talk. I'll speak to Arthur, I promise. I'll explain everything to him.'

'No, you won't. You'll never see my grandad again. He trusted you. I should never have got you involved in anything to do with this. I *asked* you to let it go when you kept going on and on about Jack. Is that what this is all about? Is that why you're with me? Were you just trying to get your big scoop?'

'I just knew it would be an amazing story!' Ben protested. 'I did it for Arthur, too. Wouldn't it be amazing if we could find Jack for him?'

'Do you even hear yourself right now, Ben?' Teddy glared at him. 'He practically begged you not to get involved. He told you he didn't want to know anything, not just for his sake, but for Jack's. If he's even alive. Did you stop to think what it might do to Grandad if he finds out that Jack is dead? No, of course not, because it's *just a story* to you. Just a *job*.'

The colour had all but drained from Ben's face. He lurched forward again attempting to grab Teddy's hand.

'I'm not saying it again,' Teddy said, jumping up off the bed. 'I want you to get out of this house now without a fuss. Don't say goodbye to anybody, just go. Let Grandad enjoy his birthday and I'll pick up the pieces of what you've done.'

'Fine, I'll go, but please just promise me that you'll listen and let me explain when you've calmed down.'

Ben stood up slowly and walked across the room. He opened the door and stepped out into the hallway. Teddy could hear 'Happy Birthday' being sung loudly downstairs.

'Great, I've missed that now,' Teddy said furiously. 'Anything else you'd like to ruin while you're here?'

Ben bowed his head and silently made his way down the stairs, only stopping to take one last look back up at Teddy before he left, gently shutting the front door behind him.

Everyone was having fun downstairs. Teddy considered going straight to bed, but he knew his absence would only attract attention. He was determined to see Arthur enjoy his celebration.

It was 1.am. when he finally returned to his room. He had tried to clear up as much of the mess as possible once his grandparents had gone to bed. The rest could wait until the morning. Washing the dishes had given him time to think of a plan. It would be impossible to stop his grandfather from seeing the newspaper, but he could at least get to the copy that would be delivered in the morning before him. That would buy him a little time to sit down and explain things. He felt a lump in his throat at the thought of having to break it to Arthur, to tell him that the person he had invited into his home was responsible for such a terrible betrayal.

By 3 a.m. Teddy had given up hope of falling asleep. He

tossed and turned, replaying his conversation with Ben over and over in his head. His eyes stung with tiredness, but it felt impossible to sleep while the anger raged inside him.

Sunlight was peeking through the narrow gap between Teddy's hastily pulled curtains. Somehow, he had finally nodded off. His body ached. He searched around for his phone, which had somehow travelled down the bed from under his pillow. It was eight thirty. His heart sank as he climbed out of bed. The newspaper delivery boy would have been by now.

Down the hallway, his grandfather's bedroom door was open; his bed had been made perfectly as it was every morning. He stopped at the door to his nan's bedroom and peered through the small gap. She was still sleeping. Teddy knew it would be a while before she woke up after seeing her and his mum finish several bottles of wine at the party. He dashed to the bottom of the stairs; the newspaper wasn't on the floor. Perhaps Arthur had picked it up but not looked at it yet. He might still have a chance. His head was already throbbing with pain.

'Grandad? Grandad, where are you?'

Only the sound of heating pipes groaning throughout the house answered his call. He checked every room downstairs before heading towards the back door. It was unlocked. He opened it and finally breathed a sigh of relief. Arthur was sitting on the bench, gazing out at the garden.

'There you are, Grandad. Are you okay?'

'Morning, Teddy. Did you sleep okay?'

'No, but right now there's something I need to do and then I need to talk to you.'

'The newspaper already arrived, Teddy.'

Teddy felt the colour drain from his face. It felt as though someone had hit pause on everything around them.

'You've got it? Where is it?'

'It's in the living room. I read as much as I could.' Arthur turned to look at him. His usually sparkling eyes were now filled with sadness. Teddy's chest ached as he stared into them.

'Grandad, I'm so sorry. I can't believe he did this. Don't worry though, he's gone and he won't be coming back.'

Arthur frowned as he shook his head.

'Who? Who won't be coming back, Teddy?'

'Ben. He wrote the story. It was all him.'

Teddy held Arthur's hand as they sat in silence. Only the chirping of the birds as they searched the damp grass for their breakfast threatened to interrupt them.

'I didn't want to spoil your party when I found out last night,' Teddy finally said. 'I thought I might have time to try and get it taken down, but then . . . well, I knew I couldn't hide it for ever. I thought I might get to the paper first, maybe buy some time to prepare you. I'm so sorry, this is all my fault. I told him about Jack in the first place. I had hoped we could find out more about Jack's life for you.'

The guilt had been eating away at him from the moment he saw the headline. He had set Ben down this path. It didn't matter how angry he was at him, he was the one who'd betrayed his grandad's trust in the first place.

'There's no need to apologize, Teddy. I told him my story too. It's all there, he didn't make any of it up after all.'

'It doesn't matter, Grandad. You asked him not to look into it. I even showed him the photos. I caused this. But

I didn't know about the story. I asked him to stop, I promise you I did.'

Arthur waved his hand to try and silence him.

'No, no, stop. None of that. It's too late now. There's no point in getting all worked up.'

'Grandad, it's your life splashed all over the—'

'Exactly, Teddy, my life,' Arthur said softly. 'I'm not ashamed of it. Did I ever imagine sharing it? No. Am I embarrassed because everyone might know I once loved a man who made me feel happy and safe, who made me laugh like nobody else? No. I have to be strong for your nan now.'

The sound of the shrill doorbell rang throughout the house and out the back door.

'I swear to God, if he has had the nerve to come back here already, I won't be responsible for my actions,' Teddy said.

'Be kind, Teddy. Mistakes are to be learned from, remember that.'

Teddy stood up and made his way back inside towards the hallway as Arthur followed behind, trying to keep up.

Teddy unlocked the door, taking a deep breath as he pulled the door open.

'Cora? Sorry, is everything okay?' He stared at the woman smiling back at him.

Cora was carrying a box containing coffee cups and a bag of pastries.

'I thought I might bring these round,' she said, holding up the tray. 'It's been a bit of a long night and morning, and I didn't want to come empty-handed. Good morning, Arthur.'

Arthur stepped forward and stood beside Teddy. He looked as perplexed as his grandson.

'Morning, Cora. You're not doing deliveries now, are you?'

'No, I'm afraid not, Arthur. This is a bit of a special one you see. I saw the story on the paper's website last night and, well, my poor heart was in my mouth.'

Cora was practically dancing on the spot as she spoke; each word seemed to fill her with more excitement. Teddy was convinced she was going to burst.

'We were rather taken by surprise by the story, truthfully,' Arthur said, not quite sure why it should be of interest to her. Outside of their visits to the café, Teddy wasn't aware of his grandparents being particularly close to Cora.

'I was too. I jumped in the car straight away. Couple of hours there and back, but I just had to when I saw it last night.'

Nothing she was saying made sense to Teddy. But then the passenger door of the car opened. A man, almost as tall as Teddy, got out and walked towards them, stopping beside Cora. He looked tired, but his eyes were filled with a sparkling, youthful energy.

'Arthur,' Cora said softly, before turning back to them. 'I think you know my Uncle Jack.'

CHAPTER THIRTY-NINE
Arthur

ARTHUR STARED AT the man standing at his front door. Jack was just as handsome as he remembered. His thick head of silver hair glistened in the weak sunshine.

Cora was beaming, her eyes darting from Jack to Arthur.

'Grandad? Are you all right?'

Arthur pulled his arm away as Teddy reached out to steady him. He didn't need Teddy to support him. He stepped forward and out of the doorway. Jack didn't move as Arthur walked up to him.

He was slightly smaller than Jack; he always had been.

Jack didn't speak as Arthur placed his two hands on either side of his face. Arthur's heart beat faster as the palm of his hands connected with Jack's warm cheeks. His faintly wrinkled skin was still as soft as he remembered. Arthur's whole body tingled as he ran his finger over the small scar on Jack's chin. It felt like a volcano of emotions, dormant for more than fifty years, might erupt from within him at any second.

'You've got old, Jack Johnson,' Arthur whispered.

Jack's lips twitched as his mouth broke into the wide smile Arthur knew so well.

'I call it maturing with style. You should try it, Artie Edwards.'

No one else had ever called him Artie. It felt like his heart could burst out of his chest. Jack's voice had aged, but it was still the voice Arthur had never forgotten. Even when he hadn't thought about him for a long period of time, he could still hear his gravelly calm tone and the loud, joy-filled laugh which would make him smile when he was at his lowest. Arthur couldn't wait another second. He opened his arms, took one final step forward and grasped Jack's body. He felt Jack's arms do the same, squeezing him tightly for the first time in over five decades.

'I'm going to need something stronger than a coffee,' Cora sobbed, the hot drinks spilling from their cups as her whole body shook.

Once inside, Teddy and Cora insisted on leaving Jack and Arthur alone in the lounge to catch up.

'I'm going to wake Nan up, Grandad,' Teddy said, closing the door behind him.

'Teddy is my grandson. He's a good lad, but he's a bit of a worrier,' Arthur explained.

'He sounds like someone I know, or maybe I should say, used to know,' Jack said, smiling.

Arthur couldn't refute that. Everything had been a worry back then. Jack would always listen to his concerns and come up with solutions, reassuring him when he needed it most. It hadn't always been unjustified. Jack had had his own fears about life in Northbridge and hiding their secrets, but he refused to ever put them on Arthur. It was a fault that was discussed by them many times; one of their only sources of tension as they tried to live their secret life under the noses of those closest to them.

'I like to think I've got better at worrying less and at being spontaneous,' Arthur said.

'Is this the man who was standing on top of a plane twenty-four hours ago?' Jack said, laughing.

'How do you . . . oh, the newspaper.'

Arthur had momentarily forgotten how Jack had come to be here, sitting on the sofa in his lounge.

'Cora told me you were on the television, but I was in France at the time, so it completely bypassed me. I hope you have a recording for me to watch.'

'It was the first thing Madeleine made sure we had,' Arthur said. 'I just want to say I'm sorry if the article upset you. It's come as a bit of a shock to me this morning.'

Jack clasped his hands together and shook his head.

'Upset?' He laughed. 'I was over the damn moon when Cora phoned. There you were in all those wonderful pictures. I was so happy to just see your face. I couldn't believe it when I read it.'

'It's been a hell of a year, I can tell you that.'

'What happened, Arthur? I know you didn't wake up one morning and decide to come out.'

'No, it was a bit of a journey, but the pieces all came together in the end.' Arthur straightened himself up and cleared his throat. He took a deep breath as he prepared to finally admit what had led to him deciding to come out.

'Only Madeleine knows,' he began, 'but near the best part of three years ago, I wasn't well. Up and down to the toilet all day and night. I just took it as getting old. Madeleine, bless her, insisted on dragging me to the doctor. Of course, she was right. They told me I had prostate cancer.' A wave of relief rushed through his entire body as he said it out loud.

'Arthur, I'm so sorry.' Jack placed his left hand on Arthur's right knee.

'They got it good and early, but I didn't want any fuss or everyone getting worried.'

'So you had treatment?'

'I can't remember what it's called now, but it did the job.'

'External beam radiotherapy?'

'That's it,' Arthur said, raising his eyebrows. 'How did you know that?'

'My brother. You remember I told you about my older brother Richard? They tried radiotherapy, but it was spreading too fast, God rest his soul.'

'Oh, Jack. I'm sorry to hear that. Bastard disease. There's not a week goes by that cancer doesn't take someone round here.'

'Cora is Richard's daughter,' Jack explained. 'I live near the rest of his family now. Running after all the little ones keeps me fit and healthy.'

'Did you ever settle down?'

Arthur didn't know what made him ask it so directly. He wanted the ground to swallow him up as soon as the words had left his mouth. He felt like the young man who had first tried to figure out this newcomer, all those years ago.

'I did. Lovely woman, seven children would you believe?'

Jack couldn't even finish the sentence before his serious expression faded and a large grin spread across his entire face.

'No, Arthur. I never did. I tried, but . . .' He shrugged. 'Life had other plans for me.'

'Tell me about it. I want to hear all about your adventures.'

'Ireland was tough, but I thought it would be the safest place after I left Northbridge. I was still hiding who I was, but I kept my head down and got on with things. I stayed there almost fifteen years, travelling around different counties. Spent a few years in Fermanagh in the north,' he added. 'I came back when Richard opened a garage and offered me a job. He knew I was gay at this point. I think keeping me close was a way to keep an eye on me. You know what it was like then in the Eighties. They didn't want me . . . well, you know.'

'You did stay out of trouble though, didn't you?'

'Surprisingly, yes. Richard and Catherine never judged me. They talked openly around the children, and being gay was never an issue, it was just who I was. I was very fortunate to have some family who accepted me for who I was, even when everything around them was designed to frighten them about people like me. They got me through the dark times.'

'I'm so glad you had that support network, I worried about you out there in the world,' Arthur said. 'I still can't believe Cora is your niece though; all this time in the same town.'

There had been a connection to Jack right there under his nose all along.

'She didn't know everything,' Jack said, sipping his tea. 'When she was younger, I'd told her all about this funny little town, the happy memories and how I had fallen in love. I told her that man had left a long time ago. Cora being Cora went for a nosy and fell in love with the place. She spent a few years coming to Northbridge for little holidays here and there. I'll never forget the day she came back full of ideas for the building that was for sale. Next thing we knew she was packing up and moving here.'

'Why did you never visit? You could have come after all these years.'

Jack shook his head.

'I made a promise to you,' he said sternly. 'You asked me to let you move on, to make things work with Madeleine. I loved you too much to risk your life, Arthur. You needed to be free of me.'

'I'm sorry,' Arthur said, hanging his head.

'For what? None of this is your fault.'

'Me, my father, my whole family. None of it would have happened if you hadn't met any of us. Those brutes left you for dead. How could I have lived with myself if you hadn't got out of here?'

Jack let out a soft whistle.

'You didn't do any of that. It almost killed me leaving you here, not knowing if you were safe or what they might do to you. I could only sleep at night once I knew you had Madeleine. You did what you had to do to stay alive and you found happiness.'

'I wish you had too.'

'I did, Arthur. I really did! I worked and I had fun, I went on holidays and watched the family grow up. I've been well loved. I loved others as well as I could.'

'What do you mean?' Arthur asked, his heart in his mouth. He watched as Jack leaned forward and set his cup down on the table.

'No one was Arthur Edwards,' Jack said wistfully. 'There

330

were lovely men, great men, men who made me laugh and cry, but I always knew they weren't you. I fell in love in this town and left my heart here. Now look at us, two lives lived, looking for our next adventure.'

'You sound like someone I've got to know recently. He's become a really good friend.'

'Oh really?'

'Yes, you and Oscar will get along like a house on fire.'

'You're already planning to introduce me to your friends? Am I being invited to stick around?'

'If you would, I would love you to. I'm not ready to say goodbye again so soon.'

Madeleine was already crying when she walked into the lounge. Jack stood up as she did. Before she said anything, she threw both arms around him.

'Don't mind her, she's always emotional the morning after she's had a drink,' Arthur said with a chuckle.

They had only met a handful of times before Jack left Northbridge, but over the first few years of her relationship with Arthur, Madeleine had come to learn more about the man who had kept his promise and disappeared from her new husband's life.

'I can't believe you're actually here. All of this is really happening and look at me, stood here in my dressing gown,' she said, holding her hands up to her face.

'You look as radiant as the first time I saw you over fifty years ago,' Jack said, prompting Madeleine to roll her eyes at him. 'I hear you tried to convince him to look for me.'

'He told you that? I thought he might be too proud to admit

that he wouldn't. No, he refused. He said you would have moved on and he didn't want to disrupt your life.'

'Imagine that, and then I go and land on your doorstep on a Sunday morning.'

Arthur sat back and let them carry on. Madeleine was right, it was happening, it was happening right there in front of him. He watched Jack as he talked animatedly, his hands gesticulating as his laughter filled the room.

'I also hear we have you and your young man to thank for making this happen,' Jack said, pausing beside Teddy in the kitchen. Cora had gone to the café for a few hours, promising to return with more pastries later that afternoon.

'I don't think I can really take credit for this one actually, Mr Johnson, but I am really glad you're here,' Teddy said. 'My . . . erm, my colleague Ben wrote and published it without our permission.'

'Teddy didn't know about the article about us,' Arthur explained. 'He's torn over being angry that it happened but now perhaps a little pleased that it was published. Is that a fair assessment, Teddy?' Arthur grinned at him.

'That might be the case,' Teddy said. 'But Ben still did what he did behind our backs.'

'Your grandfather always was the most forgiving man, almost to a fault, Teddy. It's a quality that others – and I have been guilty of this myself – find hard to understand and tolerate at times, but really it's the part we should all try to emulate the most.'

'I told you he was the smart one, didn't I?' Arthur said, tapping Teddy on the arm.

'Smart was staying alive and being happy, Arthur. You're the smartest man I've ever met.'

'His head is going to get way too big if you're staying around, Mr Johnson.' Teddy laughed.

Arthur's insides tightened at the mere thought of Jack staying. He didn't want to put a time frame on their reunion, to know that he was counting down the hours to watching Jack wave goodbye. At least they might actually have a proper goodbye this time.

'Do you have any idea how long you might stay?' he asked tentatively.

'I don't know,' Jack said. 'I don't want to overstay my welcome, but I'm sure I'll be here in town for a few days to reacquaint myself with Northbridge and the locals.'

Arthur tried to quell the disappointment in his gut and force his mouth into a smile. He didn't want to spoil things by dwelling on Jack's impending departure already. He had a life to get back to. It couldn't be easy for him being back in Northbridge after all this time either.

That afternoon Arthur took Jack to see the car showroom. The building stood on the site of the old garage where they had first met.

'You've created something incredible here, Arthur,' Jack said in awe as he walked around the forecourt, shaking his head in amazement.

'It's been a bit of a journey from the old garage and a couple of cars out front.' Arthur chuckled.

'I knew you would do great things. Your whole family must be so proud of you.'

'I don't know about that,' Arthur said. 'Patrick's running it now. He got engaged to a lovely woman at Christmas. I'm sure you'll meet them both while you're here.'

'I'd love that. Being here and having the chance to meet your family is something I never ever expected, Arthur, but I'm really glad I'm here with you.'

Arthur tried to focus on Jack's smile, but each one felt like it was one less for him to enjoy before Jack would leave him all over again.

From the garage, they walked the path which followed the river back into town. It was a path that they had walked side by side many times before, over fifty years earlier. Amazingly, it was more or less unchanged.

'That's never the old bench, is it?' Jack asked, squinting as it came into view. 'The nights we would just sit here and gaze at the stars.'

They sat down beside each other. Two young men were making their way up the river in a rowing boat.

'You weren't paying attention to the stars,' Arthur said, chuckling. 'I know you were just humouring me.'

Jack grinned and held his hands up. 'Still, you knew that and you kept bringing me back here.'

'I loved this spot. Hidden away, only the sound of the river and the stars watching over us. I always felt safe here with you, Jack.'

Their knees were pressed against each other's.

'Oscar wants to take us both for lunch this week if you don't mind,' Arthur said, suddenly remembering the message that Madeleine had passed on to him.

'That will be lovely, I'm looking forward to meeting him.'

'Is there anything else you'd like to do while you're here?'

Jack turned to look at him. He lifted Arthur's hand off his knee and held it in his warm one.

'I want to kiss you, Arthur Edwards.'

They moved their heads towards each other. Arthur felt his heart thumping as he closed his eyes. It felt like fireworks exploding throughout his body as their lips met.

CHAPTER FORTY
Teddy

ON MONDAY MORNING Teddy glanced around at the empty desks which filled the office. The seats would soon be occupied by people tapping away at their keyboards. His head was still spinning from the weekend, having run through every possible conversation he could have with Ben in advance of seeing him again. He dropped down into his chair. The photograph of himself, Shakeel and Lexie, which he had pinned up at his desk during his first week, stared back at him. Other than that and the fact his diary lay open by his keyboard, no one would know that he had sat there day in, day out for the last six months. Ben, on the other hand, had gone to great lengths to decorate his desk with pictures and items he had collected throughout the months. Teddy tipped the contents of an abandoned bottle of water into a wilted pot plant on his desk.

'Hi.' It was Ben. He smiled sheepishly as Teddy looked up at him.

'Hello. I thought we could talk before Dylan gets here.'

'Yes, I'd like that. I'm glad you texted,' Ben said as he pulled out his chair and sat down beside Teddy.

'You wanted to explain things, so . . . I'm listening.'

'First of all, I am sorry,' Ben said, and Teddy heard a ring of truth in his voice. 'I know you feel like I went behind your back and did this terrible thing . . .' He continued to stare at the floor.

'Which you did. No, sorry, go on.'

'You don't understand the pressure I've been under,' Ben said as Teddy bit his lip to stop himself interrupting. 'I needed to do something. This job, this whole opportunity, I could feel it slipping away every day.'

Ben looked up at him; the heavy bags under his eyes were darker than Teddy had ever seen. 'You're good at what you do, but is your heart really in it?' he said. 'You never seem happy to be here and yet you make it all look effortless. I can feel myself scrambling just to keep up with you. Dylan tries to pretend, but I know he doesn't think my ideas are ever as good.'

Teddy didn't speak as Ben paused for breath.

'I wanted to talk to you about the story; wanted to try to talk you into pursuing it, but we've not really been in the greatest place recently. Then your grandad told us more about Jack and I could feel myself outlining the article in my head. I promise you, I wasn't going to write it, but then Leo asked me if I had any feature ideas and I knew if I said no that I would never have a chance at getting this job. The next thing I knew I was telling him. We could see how people reacted to Arthur after his interview on *Good Morning Live*. It was too good an opportunity to pass up.'

He leaned forward in his chair, his head bowed.

'You could have though, couldn't you?' Teddy said, shaking his head. 'You didn't need to do this to try and prove yourself.'

'Do you remember our first day here?' Ben said.

'Not really. We didn't do much, did we?'

'When I arrived there wasn't even a record of me at reception. You don't know what it's like to get your dream opportunity and then find out they've forgotten to tell anyone, even Dylan, that I was starting. Then I found out who you were and I knew I would have to fight for anyone to take even the slightest bit of notice of me.'

They both looked around at the sound of the lift door opening. A man Teddy vaguely recognized from the politics team walked to his desk without as much as acknowledging their presence.

'I understand all that and I get feeling under pressure to deliver,' Teddy said, returning his attention to Ben. 'I can get my head around not knowing how to talk to me about the whole thing and I know a lot of that is my fault. What I can't forgive is you being in my grandfather's house and going through his belongings. He showed me where he kept the letters and I was stupid enough to trust you with that information. You weren't under pressure to give anyone that picture of Jack. You know that the story would have worked without it. You violated his privacy.'

'Is Arthur okay? Is he angry?' Ben asked.

'He is, but you know what he's like by now. He doesn't think there's any point sitting around dewy-eyed. He's already making excuses for you and telling me that I need to forgive you.'

'Can you?'

In every scenario Teddy had imagined this was where he had struggled with what he would say next. It was only now as he sat in front of Ben that he realized the answer he needed to give.

'Yes, I can forgive you.'

Ben's eyes lit up. He moved to stand, but stopped suddenly as Teddy held his hands up.

'I forgive you, but we're done with whatever this is, Ben.' Teddy felt a lump form in his throat. 'You said it yourself at the wing walk. You and me, it doesn't work. Maybe we could still be friends if we are going to be working together. But nothing more.'

Ben stood and began to pace.

'You could have done this weeks ago,' Ben said, his voice cracking. 'You made me feel guilty, like I was pressuring you when you weren't ready to come out, but you're the one who has been stringing me along this whole time.'

'That's completely unfair! I've been trying to figure my life out,' Teddy said. 'And that doesn't change what you did, Ben. How do I know you weren't just keeping me close so that you could get your big story?'

Ben stopped in front of Teddy, his eyes narrowed as though he was finally completing an elaborate puzzle.

'Oh my God,' he sneered. 'It's Shakeel, isn't it? I knew something was going on. I could feel it in my stomach at the weekend.'

'I'm not doing this, Ben. You don't get to turn this around on me.'

'There you go again, not denying it. Connor was right. The way Shakeel looks at you, the way he talks to me. That night in the pub, I should have thumped Shakeel when he spoke to me like shit.'

Teddy got to his feet. 'That's enough, Ben. This isn't about Shakeel. This is about you going behind my back, behind my family's backs.'

339

'I did what I had to do and I'd do it again too,' Ben spat at him. 'I was right about you on day one. I'm done working the hardest I possibly can only to be second best to Elizabeth Marsh's entitled brat of a son. A mummy's boy who can't make a decision for himself.'

Teddy held up his hand as he remembered something. Shak hadn't been drunkenly calling him a mummy's boy on the boat during the wine tasting; he had simply repeated Ben's words. How could he have even thought that Shak would think of him like that?

'Mummy's boy,' he repeated, laughing to himself. 'Well, you've made your point loud and clear.' Teddy grabbed his coat off the back of the chair as Ben looked on wide-eyed.

'Where are you going?'

'You know what, Ben, it's none of your damn business.'

CHAPTER FORTY-ONE
Arthur

ARTHUR AND ELIZABETH were deep in conversation, while Madeleine was showing Jack and Ralph photographs from one of the family albums.

'Eleanor really is the double of you,' Ralph said, grinning at a picture of teenage Elizabeth holding hands with her college boyfriend. 'Will your hair be as big as this at the wedding?'

'Of all the photographs, Mother, did you really need to keep that one?' Elizabeth said, realizing what image had prompted the outburst of laughter. 'If you think that's impressive, you should have seen it when it was crimped.'

Arthur looked around the table. They'd been in Cora's café for over an hour. Cora had insisted on bringing them a second pot of tea after they'd finished their lunch.

'Eric called when you were out earlier,' Arthur said, leaning across the table to talk to Madeleine. 'Invited me back to the Foundation. I told him I'd think about it.'

Madeleine frowned at him.

'Don't give me that look. The town didn't fall apart because I wasn't there. Maybe it's time for the young ones to start making the decisions. If Northbridge wants to survive, those are the voices we need to be listening to.'

'And I can't think of a better person than you to make sure that happens,' Madeleine said. 'You're the one who can make sure this town is a place that is safe and happy for everyone.'

'I'll go back if you run for town council. Mayor Madeleine Edwards has a nice ring to it.'

'You're right. I'll think about it just for you.' She laughed before lowering her voice to no more than a whisper. 'Cicely let me know that your magazine is in, by the way. I'll pop by and pick it up when we're done here.'

Arthur shook his head. 'You stay, keep chatting. Let me get this one.'

After excusing himself from the table, Arthur stepped out into the street. It was only a short walk up the high street towards the newsagent's. He pulled his woollen scarf tighter; there was still an unwelcome chill in the air.

Arthur let the two schoolchildren leave the shop before he pushed the door open and stepped into the warmth.

'Afternoon, Arthur,' Cicely said cheerily from behind the counter. 'On your own?'

'Just popping in to collect my magazine. Madeleine said it was in?'

Cicely's face lit up as she reached down below the counter to retrieve the new edition of *Gay Life*.

'I've got it right here. I couldn't stop smiling when I saw it!'

Slightly bemused, Arthur reached out and took the magazine from her.

'Good Lord,' he gasped, his jaw almost hitting the floor.

No one had told him that he was going to feature on the front cover of the magazine.

'It's amazing,' Cicely said. 'I'm going to buy a copy for you to sign!'

Arthur continued to stare at the cover, his own face smiling back at him. He'd expected to have to rifle through to find a small article.

'Are you okay? Do you need to sit down?'

'Oh no, I've never been better. I'm just a bit speechless is all.'

Cicely laughed as she placed a second copy of the magazine on the counter and set a black marker on top of it.

'I thought you were joking.' Arthur laughed, looking from Cicely to the pen.

'Someone from Northbridge on the cover of a magazine? This must be like history or something!'

Arthur's face ached from grinning so much as he carefully signed the cover.

'You need to get that home and get it framed, Arthur!'

'Thank you, Cicely. I might just do that.'

Arthur walked back to Cora's café in something of a daze. Every so often he heard a passer-by greet him, no doubt thinking his large smile was for their benefit.

'Daddy?' Elizabeth said, looking up as Arthur sat back down at the table. They had all refilled their cups, prompted by Cora's arrival with a plateful of leftover desserts.

'I think I might treat myself to a caramel square,' Arthur said, reaching for the plate. 'Just to celebrate.'

They all looked at him quizzically.

'What are you celebrating?' Jack asked.

'Just being on the cover of *Gay Life* magazine!' Arthur held the magazine up proudly for them all to see. Tears filled his eyes as a chorus of cheers and applause erupted around the table.

'It's just wonderful, Daddy.' Elizabeth beamed, taking the magazine and beginning to flick through it.

'Aren't you the man who couldn't even look at this magazine in the shop last year?' Madeleine said, gazing at him with a wry smile. 'You've come so far.'

Arthur's heart swelled as he watched Jack read the feature. It didn't matter what might lie ahead; right now, he wanted to enjoy every single moment.

CHAPTER FORTY-TWO
Teddy

HOURS PASSED AS Teddy walked aimlessly around the city. His head was spinning. There was only one person he wanted to see right now. His feet, trapped within the confines of his work shoes, were aching. He breathed a sigh of relief as he eventually found a park bench to sit down on. He had ignored a phone call from Dylan while picturing Ben telling him how he had stormed out. Reluctantly, he finally listened to the voicemail. Dylan confirmed that their job interviews were going to take place in several days' time.

He felt another pang of sadness. He would finally go up against Ben for a full-time position at *The Post*. This was what it had all been for. Even when he didn't want to admit it, this was what he had wanted long before he had ever laid eyes on Ben.

He frowned at his phone as it began vibrating again in his hand. It wasn't a number he recognized. Intrigued, he answered the call.

'Hello?'

'Hi, is that Teddy? It's Maya from *Good Morning Live*.' Teddy smiled as he recognized the friendly voice on the other end of the line.

'Yes, hi Maya, how are you?'

'Great, thanks. I tried your office number, but they said you were out. Listen, I wanted to run something by you if you have a moment?'

'Sure, is this about Grandad?'

'Actually, this is about you,' she said. 'We were so impressed with you and how you brought the whole event for Arthur together. But as well as that, your work with *The Post* has been great. Dylan has been singing your praises for months now.'

'He has?' Teddy said. Dylan wasn't one for throwing compliments around, so he never quite knew what he thought of their work. 'So, what is it I can do for you?'

'Well, we're looking for a junior news producer to work on the show and I thought it might be something you would be interested in. If you are, you could come in for a proper chat and we could go from there.'

Teddy was sure he had misheard her.

'You want to talk to *me*?'

'Absolutely, lots of the team have started out in press working on newspapers and online. You need to have a good nose for a story and it's pretty obvious you have that.'

'I don't know what to say, Maya . . . um—'

'Look, come in for a chat with me on Wednesday. You don't have to say yes or no right away.'

Teddy kept on walking, not stopping to process his conversation with Maya. That could wait. His phone battery was drained, but it didn't matter. He didn't need an app; his feet were taking him to exactly where he wanted to be.

He came to a halt and looked up at the building in front of him. The door flew open as a man hurried out. Teddy grabbed the door before it shut. There was nobody else around as he made his way inside and to the lift.

He knew no one would answer, but he still knocked on number seventy-four. His knuckles were red from the cold and they stung as they collided with the wooden door. No response. He was happy to wait. After all, he had nowhere else to be.

He put his back to the door and slid down onto the floor.

Teddy lost track of time as he waited. Replaying the conversation with Maya in his head again, he didn't notice Shakeel stepping out of the lift and walking towards him looking confused.

'Teddy? Why are you here?' he asked. 'Here, gimme your hand.'

Teddy grabbed hold of Shakeel and pulled himself up off the ground.

'I had to see you. It's over with Ben.'

'You better come in then,' Shakeel said as he unlocked the door. Once inside, Teddy sat down on the sofa, suddenly unsure of how to explain everything that had happened. He watched in silence as Shakeel made two mugs of tea.

'Why aren't you at work?' Shakeel asked him as he handed over the hot drink.

'Yeah, I kind of didn't bother with work today. I spent the day walking.'

'Walking?'

'Until I got here. I had to see you.'

Shakeel surveyed him, his forehead furrowed.

'I've been in a bit of a daze for weeks, maybe even months, trying to figure out what was going on with you. I didn't realize *why* I was dwelling on it. Then everything happened over the weekend . . . it was like it all suddenly made sense. You and me.'

Shakeel seemed to be holding his breath.

'Ben can do one,' Teddy said. 'None of this would ever have happened if I'd listened to you, Shak. You were right about not trusting him.'

Shakeel stared back at him, but Teddy held his hand up before he had a chance to respond.

'Before you say anything, I just want you to know that I didn't come here to put you in an awkward position. I don't expect anything from you, but I have to be honest with you.' Teddy sat his mug down on the coffee table. 'It's taken me so long to accept why I cared that you kissed me. You're the person who I turn to for everything. But how can I sit here and tell you that I think I have feelings for you when I don't want to ruin whatever you and Simon have?'

Shakeel put his head in his hands.

'There is no Simon,' he said, finally lifting his hands off his face. 'There's no boyfriend.'

A wave of relief flooded Teddy's entire body. They stared at each other. Then, unexpectedly, they both burst out laughing.

'Oh my God, Teddy, I can't believe I'm admitting this. I've been lying because I was jealous. I was jealous of Ben.'

'You could have talked to me, Shak. You never said anything!'

'When would I have? When is ever the right time to tell your best friend that you want more? That you can't stop thinking about him. That when you're with him, you just want to reach out and hold his hand.' His eyes filled with tears as he spoke.

'You've always been my person, Shak. When Dad died, you were there for me like nobody else.'

'I'm there for you because I want to be, because I want to be that person for you through all of these things, but I also want to be the person you come home to at the end of the day. Loving you has broken my heart so many times, but I keep coming back because I can't step away and know you're out there somewhere and not with me.'

'I want to be with you,' Teddy said, his hands reaching forward to take Shakeel's. 'You've been right here in front of me for so long and I didn't see it. I didn't realize what an important part of my life you are. Why am I always the last to figure everything out?'

Shakeel fidgeted with the sleeve of his jumper. He began to shake his head.

'Why now though, Teddy? I'm sorry to ask, but I just want to make sure we're on the same page before we risk our friendship again.'

Teddy shut his eyes.

'The last few months,' he said, 'I was so distracted, so caught up in trying to understand why something had changed for you that I didn't grasp that it had for me too. I was lost, trying to juggle Ben and work. Everything that's happened put things into perspective. It's like this fog lifted. That's why I'm here, Shakeel. I'm going to do everything I can to prove to you that it's you I want. Mummy's boy is making a decision.'

Shakeel looked at him, confused.

'He called me that today. Why didn't you tell me when you heard it on the boat?'

'I didn't hear it,' Shakeel admitted. 'I was taking photos on his phone and a message from that guy Connor popped up. He called you that.'

'You should have told me, Shak. I would have confronted him about it.'

Shakeel was shaking his head. 'Come off it. Would you really have believed me if I'd said it then? I was pissed. I wasn't even sure if I'd made it up when I thought about it.'

'None of that really matters anyway. We're here now.'

Shakeel smiled back at him. He took his hand, pulling Teddy closer to him until their noses were touching. Teddy felt Shakeel's breath on his face, closing his eyes just as he felt their lips collide. Shakeel's hand rested on his chest, before he pushed him back until he was flat on the sofa. Their mouths didn't separate as Shakeel moved forward, lying his entire body on him as if they were stacking blocks.

'Ouch!' Teddy yelped.

'What's wrong?'

Shakeel pulled his mouth away to look round. 'Your knee. Kind of want to keep those . . .' He pointed downwards.

'Sorry, let me make it up to you.'

Teddy felt a flutter in his chest as Shakeel started undoing the buttons of his shirt, pulling it open. He stopped to undo and remove his own, before throwing it behind him. It hit the lamp on the table, causing it to wobble and crash to the floor.

'I hated that lamp anyway,' Shakeel said, pulling Teddy closer to him. They'd seen each other shirtless before, but Teddy couldn't help but stare at Shakeel's chest as if it was the first time. He put his hands on his broad shoulders and began to rub them. His fingers moved across Shakeel's smooth skin with ease. Shakeel kissed him again, moaning softly as their tongues met. Teddy felt his entire body quiver as their bare chests pressed against each other for the first time.

He saw the phone screen light up before he heard it vibrate against the wooden table.

'Shak. Shak, your phone.'

'Ignore it.'

Shakeel's hot lips were pressed against his neck.

'It's still going, Shak.'

'Fine.' He sighed, pulling himself up off Teddy and reaching for the phone.

Teddy watched as he answered, clambering to sit upright as the smile on Shakeel's face disappeared.

'Yes, he's with me. Why, what's wrong?'

He felt his body begin to shake. He couldn't speak as Shakeel hung up and grabbed both of his hands.

'We need to go; it's your grandad.'

CHAPTER FORTY-THREE
Arthur

IT HAD ONLY been three hours and Arthur was already desperate to get out of the bed and back home. He shook his head, annoyed at having ended up in hospital in the first place. He'd insisted that Oscar didn't phone for an ambulance when he started feeling unwell following their walk that afternoon, but Oscar had taken one look at Arthur's pale face and decided to ignore him. Now Arthur found himself in an impossible situation. He couldn't avoid the truth any longer. Reluctantly, he had agreed that Madeleine should tell the family.

'Please, no fussing,' he insisted. 'They'll hear I'm having surgery and panic.'

The room wasn't fancy but at least it was private. He'd spent more than enough time in these rooms over the last three years. His specialist had explained that there were various options available to him, including a radical prostatectomy which would remove the prostate gland and tissues surrounding it. After a sleepless night, he had agreed to go ahead with it. There would be no secrets this time, no hiding the truth from those who loved him. He was fighting this for all of them. For Jack.

As he had expected, Elizabeth and Teddy were first through

the door. Elizabeth didn't speak before rushing to the side of his bed and wrapping her arms around him.

'I'll pay for you to go private, Daddy. We're not taking any chances,' she insisted a short while later. She kept Arthur's hand in a tight grip. 'I'll book an appointment as soon as possible.'

Arthur didn't bother arguing. Elizabeth needed to feel like she could do something to help him. After recent events, he was just glad she was by his side.

'You have to take things easier though,' she continued. 'You might just have been feeling a little weak and tired today, but we can't risk that happening again.'

Madeleine brought Oscar in next. Oscar gave him a small smile. Arthur could see that his eyes were red from crying; he couldn't stay mad at him. He knew he'd done the right thing in phoning the ambulance.

'I'm going to head back to the house to sort some things out. Teddy, do you want a lift?' Madeleine asked, pulling on her coat.

'Yes please,' Teddy said. 'Please try and get some rest, Grandad. I'll see you tomorrow morning.'

Oscar and Elizabeth were talking when Arthur woke from a short nap. His eyes strained against the fluorescent lighting.

'You two not got homes to go to?'

'Oh, he's awake and ready to complain again.' Oscar laughed. 'How are you feeling? Do you need a nurse?'

'No, no, I'm fine,' he insisted. 'It's just all of this . . . It's a reminder, isn't it, how fragile everything is. One minute we're here, the next we're gone. It's like life keeps trying to tell me this.'

'What do you think you need to do?'

'I don't know. I came out. That was supposed to be the biggest change in my life. But now I've done a wing walk, turned eighty . . . Jack's come back . . . it wasn't part of the plan.'

'There's a plan? You could have let me know about that.'

Arthur scowled but then couldn't help but smile as Oscar grinned back at him.

'I always just thought I'd be happy finally saying it out loud; I'm a gay man. Having Madeleine and the children accept and love me. Teddy and the girls could be proud of their silly old grandad. Then you came along and I could see that there was so much more to life even when you're old.'

'I do have that effect on people,' Oscar said smugly.

'And Jack wasn't part of the equation. He was a memory, a painful but happy one. I could live out the rest of my days just hoping he might be proud of me for finally being who I am.'

'Is he going to come and see you? I thought he'd be here.'

'No.' Arthur sighed. 'I asked Madeleine to tell Cora not to worry him. I'll see him when I'm out of this place. Another reason for me not to be wasting time here.'

'I still can't believe he's here, Arthur.'

'I know. It's the best thing that could ever have happened, but having him here in Northbridge, it's like I'm twenty-five again, waiting for it all to go wrong.' Arthur felt restless. He tried to push himself up in the bed.

'So, what are you saying, Arthur?'

'I can't let Jack go. Not again.'

'Can he stay?'

'I don't know. I haven't asked.'

'What are you waiting for? Why are you sitting here telling me?'

'I—'

'Talk to him!' Oscar said, sitting up. 'Come on, Arthur. At our age we know how this works. Life isn't filled with happy endings, but if you have a chance, even the smallest chance at one, you have to grab it. Stop waiting for other people to make it happen for you.'

Arthur stared back at his friend.

Oscar sighed. 'I've only had the pleasure of knowing you for a few months, Arthur Edwards, but even I can see that you put yourself last. You're so apologetic for wanting to live your life that you make sure everyone else is happy before you even think to consider yourself. Jack was out there all along, but you wouldn't take the risk of looking for him. Even after all these years, you didn't think you deserved that. Now he's here and you're still that frightened young man determined to put everyone else's happiness above his own. Well, not on my watch. If I could get you out of that bed, I'd drive you to him myself.'

'That won't be necessary,' Elizabeth said, her eyes lighting up.

'I wasn't really going to—'

'Dad, you need to rest tonight but I'll take you to Jack. First thing tomorrow. As soon as we leave here.'

'You don't have to do that, Lizzy.'

'No arguments, Daddy. You're going to go and tell the man you love that you don't want to lose him again.'

*

They were waiting at a red light, now just minutes away from Cora's house where Jack was staying. Elizabeth tapped the steering wheel impatiently, muttering to herself as she craned her neck to stare at the light.

'This is ridiculous, it shouldn't take this long.' She sighed.

'It's okay, love, there's no rush.'

'I know, it's just so frustrating.'

'Are you sure about this, Elizabeth? Last night, I meant it when I said—'

'Dad, you don't have to ask that,' she said, finally turning her eyes away from the lights. 'You deserve this. It's only been a few days and I can already see the difference it's made to you to have Jack here.'

'And if he were here all the time?'

'That would be amazing, but please don't get your hopes up, Dad. I don't want you to get hurt if he can't stay.'

'We've said goodbye once before. It could never hurt as much as that did.'

'Dad, if I had known, even just a little bit, about what you went through back then—'

'It's water under the bridge.'

'It's not, though, Dad. It's your life. It's Jack's life. The pain you both endured. I didn't stop to think about any of that. Now you have this chance, Jack has this chance, why would any of us get in the way of that?'

Arthur pulled a tissue from his pocket and handed it to her.

'Thanks, Dad,' she said as she dabbed her eyes. 'I got a second chance with Ralph and it was the last thing I expected after Harry died.'

'I owe you an apology for how I handled your relationship

with Ralph, Elizabeth. It wouldn't be fair of me to pretend I wasn't shocked or worried about you bringing someone new into the children's lives, but you knew what was best for you. I'm sorry I put my own concerns above your happiness.'

'Thank you, Daddy, I really appreciate that. You've welcomed Ralph into your heart and I can do the same for Jack.'

The waiting car behind them honked loudly; the light had turned green.

They pulled up outside Cora's house several minutes later. Thick green ivy covered the building. Arthur took a deep breath. He hadn't practised what he was going to say.

'Don't worry, you'll know what you need to say when you're with him,' Elizabeth said. She leaned forward in her seat and kissed Arthur on the cheek, then wiped the smudge of red lipstick off it.

'Now go, I'll be right here waiting. Good luck, Dad.'

A smiling Cora opened the front door to Arthur.

'I'm so glad you're okay, Arthur,' she said, hugging him tightly. 'I told him you weren't feeling too well yesterday evening, so he doesn't know anything.' She walked him to the small living room where Jack was watching an afternoon quiz show.

'I'm going to pop out and chat with Elizabeth,' she said. 'Just shout if either of you need anything.'

Jack was waiting for Arthur as he walked in.

'I thought I heard your voice. How are you feeling?' he asked, his voice filled with concern.

'I'm fine. Sorry I had to cancel yesterday. No, no, please don't be getting up.'

He sat down on the sofa beside Jack. He knew from the café that Cora loved flowers, but he had never imagined it was possible to fit so many different types of flower patterns into one small room.

'I'm sorry to come by unannounced, I should have phoned Cora and checked first.'

'Is something wrong?'

'Yes actually, that's why I'm here.'

He felt the weight of Jack's eyes on him waiting for him to continue. He knew he had to come out with it now or he might never say it.

'I don't want you to leave Northbridge again.' Arthur couldn't bring himself to look up at Jack. He didn't want to see the look in his eyes, or to watch him trying to find the words to explain that he had no choice but to return home.

'Arthur—'

'I know,' Arthur said quickly. 'I'm sorry to just blurt that out.'

'Arthur, that's all I needed to hear.'

Arthur looked up. A smile was spreading across Jack's face.

'You mean—'

'Of course I want to stay. I wanted to stay fifty years ago. I wanted to visit you every day, after every story I heard from Cora. You and this town have been part of my life even when I haven't been here.'

'You're really going to stay?'

'If you want me to, I wouldn't want to be anywhere else. I just needed to be sure that you felt the same way, that I wasn't imposing myself on the life you've built.'

'You wouldn't be at all. You should be here with me.'

'I've already talked to Cora about moving in here.'

'Oh, well that's a good idea.'

'Did you have another suggestion?' Jack asked, seeing Arthur's smile fade.

'I was just going to say that if you wanted to, and it's completely up to you, that you could always stay with me.'

'Are you asking me to move in with you, Arthur Edwards?'

'If you promise not to make me watch daytime TV, yes.'

Jack smiled and placed his hand on the side of Arthur's face. 'I won't need any distractions when I'm with you.'

CHAPTER FORTY-FOUR
Teddy

'I CANNOT BELIEVE you two are finally doing this!'

Lexie beamed at Teddy and Shakeel. They had gathered around a small table on the balcony of a bar close to Lexie's office.

'I can't believe it took me so long . . . I was so distracted.'

'We know,' Lexie teased as Shak grinned at him.

'Anyway, I have a couple of days off so I can prepare for this bloody interview without having to face *him*.'

'Do you still want to work at the paper?'

'I just need to see what Maya says and then try to figure things out.'

Teddy was still clueless as to what he really wanted. Just thinking about it made his head throb. He'd never considered the idea of television, but he had loved visiting the studio with Arthur. The buzz of being in that environment every day was an exciting prospect. As much as he had enjoyed working at *The Post*, it would always be a job his mother had got him. This . . . this could be something new.

'I think you know what you want. I saw it in your face when

you told me about Maya,' Shakeel said. 'You never have that sparkle in your eye when it comes to the paper.'

'Don't let my mum hear you saying things like that.'

'Speaking of which, how is your mum with the proposed new arrangements?' Lexie asked, taking her eyes off the dessert menu.

'You mean Grandad and Jack?'

'I can't believe they'll be living together after all these years. It's so romantic!'

'Honestly, it's like living with a different person. It's like she woke up one morning and everything made sense in her head. I wouldn't be surprised if she's the one dragging them to Pride this year.'

They all laughed as the server set three cups of coffee down on the table.

'There better be a spare room for me when you two move in together.'

'We're taking things slow for now,' Teddy said, looking to Shakeel for confirmation. He nodded, slapping his hand down on Teddy's leg.

'I never got to properly thank you, Lex,' Shakeel said. 'Even when I was crying on the phone to you in the middle of the night, you never told me to piss off.'

'What can I say?' Lexie grinned. 'I'm a romantic! You two are perfect for each other. I knew it the first time I met Teddy and saw you together.'

'Gee, thanks, you could've given us a heads-up!'

'It wouldn't have mattered anyway. There's no rushing these things,' Teddy said. 'Look at Grandad and Jack. They found their way back to each other after all these years.'

'Uhm, hang on there.' Shakeel smirked at him, holding his hand up to silence Teddy. 'I know we agreed to go slow, but I'm not waiting fifty years for you.'

Teddy sat back in his chair. He wanted to enjoy these moments with Shakeel and Lexie. He had almost let his fears get in the way of something good once again, but despite everything, he had found himself where he wanted to be. He couldn't but grin. There was nothing left to fear now.

Maya was waiting for Teddy in reception. She strode across to shake his hand as soon as he'd pushed his way through the revolving doors.

'Thanks so much for coming, Teddy,' she said. 'Let's grab a coffee and I can tell you everything.'

They walked up the flight of stairs to a small canteen where a barista took their order. Drinks in hand, they sat down at an empty table. Teddy listened as she explained the general details of the job.

'Everyone was really impressed by you and the coverage you got your grandfather. You made all of that happen. Not many people can say that they've organized a charity fundraiser that raised over £100,000, especially at your age.'

Teddy felt his cheeks redden as he accepted the praise. 'Thanks. I don't think any of us contemplated how big the whole thing was going to become when Grandad had the initial idea. It all kind of spiralled from the one little story I wrote for the website.'

'That's what it's all about though, Teddy,' Maya said, excitement filling her eyes. 'You had the eye for the story and that's what we want. This job means being on the ball to spot great stories and understanding what our viewers will be interested in, but I think you've got that.'

'That's really nice of you to say,' Teddy said. 'It does sound like an incredible opportunity and I love working in the city.'

'Oh, I thought I mentioned that, did I not? Sorry, Teddy, this role is based with the team in the northern office.'

'Sorry? The northern one?'

'Yes, we're really expanding the team up there. You'd be working with some great people.'

His heart sank as disappointment flooded his body. It had all been too good to be true. How could he even consider a job that would take him away from his family, from Shakeel?

'I'm sorry, I thought I'd said that to you.'

'No, you probably did and I missed it.' He didn't want to make things more awkward. He knew his face had dropped on hearing what she had said.

'I know that sounds a little scary and it would be a big change, but you're young and have your whole career ahead of you. Please give it some careful thought. This is an incredible opportunity and not one that comes along every day.'

'I understand, I really appreciate you even thinking of me.'

'Fabulous. You would fit in really well with the team up there. I've been singing your praises to the guys. There might be a formal chat or two, but honestly, if you want this, you just have to say the word and we'll get things moving. We'll get you moving!'

Teddy forced as enthusiastic a laugh as he possibly could.

'Give me a call as soon as possible,' Maya said before making her way back upstairs.

His body felt as though it were glued to the chair, like it

was holding him hostage until he made his decision there and then. Everything had sounded perfect. He had felt the excitement bubbling inside of him when Maya told him about the job. If she hadn't dropped that bombshell on him, he would almost have considered accepting it there and then. But now his stomach twisted as he realized he needed to get home and finish prepping for the interview at *The Post* tomorrow. It might be his only option.

As much as Teddy tried to focus on the interview, he couldn't stop himself from mulling over the TV job. He tried to shake off the anxious feeling in the pit of his stomach. He shouldn't even be considering it. How could he possibly consider leaving Northbridge now? How could he tell Shakeel he had even thought about it? No. *The Post* was where he needed to be. Everyone was sure it was his job for the taking, after all.

'Tell me everything then, when do you start?' Shakeel's face popped up on his screen later than evening when he called after work.

'She's lovely and the job sounds great, but I don't know if it's for me yet. I need to think about it.'

'But you said it was a huge opportunity? You're not doubting yourself, are you?'

'I dunno. Look, I'm just going to focus on tomorrow and do my best for that.'

Teddy's chest tightened as Shakeel frowned at the despondency in his voice.

'Do you want to practise any questions tonight?'

'Nah, I'm good. I'm better off getting a good kip.'

There was no point in explaining about the other job yet.

He didn't want to have that conversation. Shakeel might never need to know why he was turning it down. But even as he shut down his laptop and climbed into bed, he knew it was going to be a long and restless night.

Teddy hadn't been to the 15th floor of the building before. He looked around as he stepped out of the lift. It was laid out exactly how the 13th was, except for the large meeting rooms which took up the right-hand side of the floor. He bumped into Dylan coming out of one of them.

'How are you feeling?' Dylan asked.

'I'm good, thanks. I've done as much as I could to prepare.'

'Don't worry, they're not looking to catch you out. Anyway, these guys aren't stupid, they're not going to miss out on hiring Elizabeth Marsh's son.'

'Oh right.' The familiar feeling of dread hit him square in the chest. The interview wasn't about him. It was about his mother.

'Bet they're already drawing up the contract. I better go, late again, catch up with you later.'

Teddy mulled over Dylan's words. The job was his? Dylan was so confident in what he had said. Had he heard something or was he just making assumptions because of who Teddy was? Either option made him want to rush to the bathroom and scrub himself down. He didn't want the job like this. He'd spent months trying to prove himself, to step out of his mum's shadow and show that he deserved the job on his own merit.

'Edward? We're ready for you.'

Teddy's legs shook as he made his way into the conference

room. He didn't recognize either of the people waiting for him behind the desk.

'Thanks for coming, Edward,' the man said as he sat down. 'We've heard a lot of really great things about your work.'

'Thank you. It's been a great opportunity to really get stuck in and learn from Dylan.'

'Has anything about the day-to-day work surprised you?'

'I suppose it's been the freedom to work across various departments and learn from everyone. I've really enjoyed being able to—'

Teddy stared at them. His mind was blank. He didn't know how to finish the sentence. He thought back over his experiences from the last few months. Ben had always been excited by every opportunity the job offered him, whether it was writing stories for the website or interviewing a celebrity he loved. Teddy knew what he needed to do.

'Edward?' The man's face was filled with confusion.

'Sorry. I'm just wondering, why do you want to hire me?'

'Excuse me?' The woman spoke for the first time; her voice filled the small office.

'Why me? You've looked at what I've done since I've been here. I want to make sure this is a real interview, and not a formality.'

'We're not really here to—'

'Is it because of my mum? Is that why? I'm grateful if it is, I know she loves this paper, but I don't want that to be the reason I get the job.'

Their mouths were hanging open. Teddy's heart was thumping. He couldn't quite believe what he was saying.

'If we carry on with the interview, we'll get to your work,' the woman said.

'I don't think we need to.'

They stared blankly at him. Teddy knew what his heart was telling him to do.

'I know there are other trainees, but you should give this job to Benjamin King,' he declared. 'He loves this place. Almost as much as my mum does. This job means the world to him and he's good at it. Like, really good at it.'

'You don't want the job that you're here interviewing for right now?' The two interviewers looked at each other in complete astonishment.

'Sorry, I didn't mean to waste your time. I didn't expect to do this, but sitting here, I'm realizing that even if I'm good at it, my heart just isn't in it. I shouldn't take that from someone who wants it. And Ben really does want it. I know that more than anyone.'

'I don't know what to say, Edward. No one has ever quit midway through an interview before,' the woman said, dropping her pen onto the notebook in front of her.

'I guess I should go then. Thank you for having me and for the whole opportunity, I really do appreciate it.'

Teddy stood up and walked out, closing the door behind him. His body was shaking. He put his head in his hands. It felt like a massive weight had been lifted off his shoulders. The shock of what he had done was beginning to hit him.

'Hi.'

He lifted his hands off his face to see Ben staring back at him.

'Hello,' he said.

'Are you finished in there already?'

'Yeah, it wasn't too bad. They were nice.'

'Oh right, that's good. I nearly didn't come today. I'm a bit nervous.' Ben stared at the floor, as if he was ashamed of admitting his nerves out loud to his rival.

'Don't be,' Teddy told him. 'Remember you're really good at this and they would be lucky to have you. You want this job, don't you?'

Ben watched him closely, appearing both confused and cautious. 'I don't know anymore. I'm not proud of what I did. I don't really know if this is where I belong. I think my parents were right, you know.'

'No, they weren't. You want this. Learn from your mistakes and be the great journalist I know you can be.'

'Why are you being so nice to me?'

'Thanks.' Teddy laughed. 'You came into my life at the right time and helped push me in the right direction, Ben. I'll never forget that.'

'Thanks, Teddy. I know that's more than I deserve after everything.'

'Maybe, but your article brought Grandad and Jack together again,' Teddy said as two women squeezed past them to enter the lift. 'If he isn't upset, how can I be? You did what you felt you needed to for the job. Do I agree with it? No. But I don't hate you for it.'

'Benjamin?' The interviewer's head appeared from behind the door. He nodded at Teddy before disappearing again.

'I better go,' Ben said, rubbing his hands together.

'Good luck, whatever you decide. Remember, they'll be really lucky to have you, Ben, not the other way around. Don't let them take you for granted.'

Ben gave him one last quizzical look before heading into

the office. Teddy didn't bother hanging around. He couldn't wait to get out of there.

Elizabeth folded her arms across her chest. Teddy knew the stance well. It was how she took a moment to compose herself after hearing something shocking. She threw her head back and looked at the ceiling of the kitchen before sighing loudly.

'I don't know what we are going to do with you, Edward.'

'So, you're not mad?'

She lowered her eyes to look at him, tilting her head as she did.

'What's the point in being mad? You know yourself better than I do. You made your decision. I know that there's only so far I can push you before you have to take matters into your own hands. I'm proud of you for doing that, at least.'

Teddy almost wanted to pinch himself to make sure he was hearing her correctly. He had honestly expected her to yell at him, even kick him out of the house again.

'Honestly, Mum, I thought you were going to be fuming.'

'You're almost twenty-two, Edward. I can't hold your hand through your whole life, as much as I'd like to. I want you to be happy and content, to love whatever you do as much as I do. Never, ever forget that you make me and your dad so proud.'

'Thanks, Mum. That means a lot to me. What do you think I should do about Maya?'

'That's a decision only you can make. I'm here to support you either way, but if it's an opportunity you really don't want to pass up on, you owe it to yourself to grab it with both hands.'

'But what about—'

'I know,' Elizabeth said softly. 'Talk to Shakeel. Explain the situation. I've always known you were meant for bigger and better things than Northbridge, Edward. Maybe it's time for you to spread your wings.'

Teddy had plenty to think about as he made his way into the city that evening. His mind was still racing as he knocked on the door of number seventy-four.

'You're early! I was surprised when you buzzed,' Shakeel said.

'I don't want to get a reputation like Uncle Patrick.' Teddy laughed, shutting the door behind him. 'He'll be late to his own funeral.'

'I only ordered a few minutes ago, so I hope you're not too hungry,' Shak said.

'I'm good. It actually gives us time to talk first.'

'Yikes, there's something you never want to hear,' Shakeel said, fixing the cushion on the armchair before he sat down.

'I turned down the job at *The Post*,' Teddy blurted out. 'Before you ask why, I need to tell you about Maya and the job that's on offer at *Good Morning Live*.'

Shakeel listened as Teddy explained everything about Maya's offer and how he had decided mid-interview to turn down *The Post*.

'When are you leaving, then?'

Teddy almost laughed at the abruptness with which Shakeel asked the question.

'Very funny.'

'You're not turning this down, Teddy.'

'But—'

'Don't you dare. Don't sit there and use me as an excuse not to take that job.'

'It's not an excuse, Shak.'

'Yes, it is,' Shakeel said, the frustration in his voice growing. 'Come on, we don't even know what this is yet. You can't risk an opportunity like that for something that might never work anyway.'

'But shouldn't we at least try?'

'Shouldn't you at least try the job?'

Teddy pressed the cushion against his face and let out a frustrated scream. 'I hate this,' he shouted. 'Why couldn't it just be here? Why couldn't things just be simple for once?'

'That's life, Teddy. Maybe this is for the best.'

'What do you mean? How can it be?'

'Look at it this way; maybe this job came along to save us from ruining our friendship. Maybe none of any of this was meant to work out, but now we get to stay in each other's lives.'

'How can you be so chill about all of this, Shak?'

'I've had to be, remember? Every time I thought my heart was breaking over you, I told myself that this was just the path I was on and that it was happening for a reason. Everything has to happen for a reason, right? Good and bad. As long as we're in each other's lives . . .'

'I don't know what I'll do without you,' Teddy said, as he felt his eyes begin to burn.

'Without me? Did you not just hear me? I'll come to visit. You'll be back here whenever you can. We'll still talk all the time. This is just another chapter.'

Teddy felt Shakeel take his hand and pull him up off the

sofa. He wrapped both of his arms around him and held him. They stood like that in silence for several minutes.

'You know Lexie is going to want to visit you up there every weekend, right?'

'Oh I know. She'll probably be planning her own move up there next.'

The idea hit Teddy as soon as he said it. He grabbed Shakeel's hand excitedly.

'Move!' he said.

'What?'

'Come with me, move with me.'

Shakeel was staring blankly at him. Teddy's hands were shaking.

'I understand everything you're saying, but I can't do any of this without you.'

'Teddy, hang on—'

'Please, come with me,' he said. 'I can't do this without you. I love you, Shakeel.'

CHAPTER FORTY-FIVE

Three months later

'COME ON, GRANDAD! Hurry up!'

Teddy sighed as he paced the hallway, checking his watch every thirty seconds. He stopped to look in the mirror and fix his tie. His mum would never tolerate a messy tie, especially on her wedding day. His stomach churned. Weeks and months of planning had come down to this. Teddy stared at the newly hung framed cover of *Gay Life*. It had been given pride of place in the hallway.

'Is he *still* not down yet?' Oscar asked exasperatedly, coming in from outside to check for the third time. 'I thought dear Madeleine was joking about his skincare regime.'

'Sorry, Oscar, I didn't think we'd keep your friend waiting this long.'

'Don't worry. I know you've enough to be dealing with today,' Oscar said.

'It's not every day you get the opportunity to do something like this.'

'Any regrets?'

'About the job? None. Moving up north just wasn't for me.

But Mum was right, I did need to spread my wings, I just didn't think that would mean going so far.'

'We're all really proud of you, young man.' Oscar beamed back at him. He had become something of a surrogate grandfather over the last few months as he assisted Teddy with the wedding preparations while Arthur recovered from his surgery.

'Thanks Oscar, it means a lot,' he said. 'Now, I just need to get grandad out of here on time.'

'Do I hear my only grandson complaining?'

Arthur was halfway down the stairs, grinning at them.

'Yes, you bloody well do and I'll not be the only one if we're even a second late.'

Teddy stepped back as Arthur stood in front of the mirror in the hallway to look at his suit.

'You'll be the most handsome man there,' Oscar said, holding his hand to his chest.

'Don't let Ralph hear you say that.'

'Or Jack!' Arthur said with a laugh, before turning to stare at them both.

'Before we go, I just want to say thank you to both of you. You got me here. Organising all of this. I couldn't have got through the last couple of months after the operation without . . . well, you know. Getting the all-clear and being able to look forward to today and now it's finally here.'

'Don't set me off already,' Oscar said, dabbing his eye. 'Look at you now, about to marry the man you love!'

'We've actually got one more surprise for you, Grandad.'

'What is it? Nothing fancy I hope.' He held his finger up to Teddy. 'I warned you.'

'Don't worry. Just let me take your jacket, you don't need it.'

'Why not? Your mother won't like—'

'She won't even see it. Here, take this.'

Teddy opened the suit bag that was hanging off the living-room doorframe. Arthur's eyes lit up as he saw the old leather jacket that they had found while cleaning out the attic.

'I thought I told you to keep that?'

'I did, I kept it safe and now I want you to wear it while you're on your way.'

Arthur pushed his arms through the sleeves of the jacket and fixed it over his waistcoat.

'Not quite perfect, but it'll do,' he said as he looked in the mirror. 'It's a bit warm for the car though, isn't it?'

'You're not going in the car, Grandad.'

Arthur drew a breath to question him, but Teddy was already opening the front door and ushering him outside. 'It took a while, but Oscar's friend managed to track one down,' he said, gleefully.

'Track what down?'

Arthur's jaw dropped as his eyes fell upon the Norton Commando motorcycle which was waiting for him. A man was astride it, already helmeted up, and holding a second helmet out to Arthur.

'I remembered you mentioned your Uncle Frank's bike and well . . . here we are!'

Arthur grabbed Teddy into a tight hug before he even finished the sentence.

'I don't know what to say. This is . . . it's just . . .'

'You don't have to say anything. Come on. Seamus is going to take you there and Oscar and I will be right behind.'

Teddy watched as his grandad fastened his helmet and climbed onto the back of the bike.

'Have fun!' Oscar shouted as Seamus kicked the engine into life. Arthur gave them a wave as they pulled out of the driveway. Teddy breathed a huge sigh of relief at having pulled off the surprise.

'Right, young man,' Oscar said, jangling his keys. 'We've got a wedding to get to!'

The large vintage-style gazebo had been set up in the grounds of the old country manor. It looked every bit as magical as his mum had described. They drove around the large fountain and up the short road towards the impressive property. The small car park was already full.

'I see the girls, so I'll just jump out here, thanks, Oscar.'

Eleanor and Evangelina waved at Teddy as they saw him approaching. 'Everything good to go?'

'All good,' Teddy reassured them. 'Grandad will be here any second now. Seamus was taking him around the grounds on the bike first. Is Mum all set?'

'She's with Nan,' Evangelina said. 'I just have to text when Grandad gets here and she'll come out to you. Are you nervous?'

'I thought I would be, but I think I'm just excited to do it. How's Jack?'

'Good. I only saw him briefly, but he's in there now waiting. His family are so lovely.'

They heard the roar of the engine before they saw the motorbike coming up the road towards them. Arthur was beaming as he pulled off the helmet and profusely thanked Seamus for the experience.

'You look so cool, Grandad! I can't believe you used to ride one of those,' Evangelina said, hugging Arthur. 'Mum would never let me go on one.'

'You should ask your mum about her first boyfriend, Stevie, see if she remembers his bike.'

'Mum's coming!' Eleanor said, as Elizabeth and Madeleine made their way out of the house and over towards them.

'You look beautiful, Mum,' Teddy said, kissing her on the cheek. Madeleine was already handing out small packets of tissues to Eleanor and Evangelina.

Arthur stood back and held his arms out. 'My little girl. I'm so proud of you.'

'Don't set me off, Daddy,' Elizabeth said, taking hold of his hand. 'Shall we get this show on the road before I start crying and ruin my make-up *again*?'

With everyone seated, Teddy waited at the entrance to the marquee. Madeleine hovered beside him as Elizabeth and Arthur spoke outside.

'How are you feeling, Nan?'

'I'm okay, Teddy,' she said softly. 'It's all happy tears today!'

'We're all in awe of you, you know that, don't you?'

'Not as much as I am of you, young man,' Madeleine said.

'I'm not the one who stopped them closing A & E. You know, I think Grandad is right, you really should consider running for mayor. Like you told him, age is no excuse to stop you doing these things.'

'You're very kind, lovely, but I think I've earned a good rest.

Anyway, you've better things to be focusing on, like jetting off and having experiences most of us could only dream of.'

'Never say never, Nan. I'll take you anywhere you want to go if you could do one thing for me please.'

'What's that?'

'Will you teach me how to bake when I'm back?'

'Really?' Madeleine said, her voice filled with surprise. 'I would love nothing more, Teddy.'

She looked around as Elizabeth and Arthur made their way in to join them. Arthur and Madeleine hugged before Madeleine went to sit down next to James.

'I'm so proud to have you give me away today, Edward,' Elizabeth said as she stood beside him. 'Thank you for doing this. I want you to know that your father would be so proud of the man you have become; not just today, but every single day.'

'Thanks, Mum. I can't say this is something I ever expected to do, but here we are.'

He looked around. 'Grandad? Ready?'

With Teddy in the middle, Elizabeth linked onto his right arm, while Arthur did the same to his left. Teddy heard those gathered noisily get to their feet as the violinist began to play.

'Let's go,' he said, as the three of them made their way up the aisle.

Teddy kept focused on the altar as they walked, not wanting to look round at the faces staring back at them. They came to a stop in front of the smiling registrar.

'I love you, Mum,' Teddy whispered as Ralph held his hand out for Elizabeth.

He turned to Arthur. 'I'm so proud to do this for you, Grandad. Jack, look after him please.'

Jack took Arthur's hand and kissed him on the cheek.

Teddy took his seat beside his sisters and nan as the registrar began to speak.

'We are gathered here today to celebrate love. Love comes in many forms; in all shapes, sizes and colours. Today is a first for me, but it is my honour to be here to celebrate the love between Elizabeth and Ralph and Arthur and Jack.'

Teddy pulled a tissue out of his pocket and handed it to his sobbing nan as James held her hand. 'She shouldn't have given away all of her tissues,' Evangelina whispered to him with a cheeky grin on her face.

The sun was beating down on the grounds. Teddy had taken a short walk around the gardens following the ceremony. He could finally breathe after throwing himself into organizing his grandad's wedding. Now that it was over . . . well, it was all that had been keeping him here.

After turning down Maya's offer, he realized that he not only wanted to get out of Northbridge, but the whole country. Travelling hadn't been something he had even considered until his mum had suggested it in passing. After exploring his options, he discovered that teaching English was the opportunity he had been looking for. His original plan had been to leave as soon as possible after declining the job up north. However, when his grandad and Jack took everyone by surprise and announced that they wanted to get married, he had happily postponed his plans so that he could stay and arrange the event. It was to all of their surprise that Elizabeth had then come up with the idea of a double wedding. With everyone in agreement, and much to Ralph's amusement, the big day became even bigger.

'How does it feel to have given away your mum and grandad on the same day?' Lexie grabbed hold of his arm and walked alongside him. 'Don't worry, I'm not asking you to do the same for me.'

'I can't believe it's all done,' Teddy said, running his hand along the top of the perfectly manicured hedges. 'After all that, they're now married.'

'I know, now you actually have to start thinking about packing.'

'Don't, Lex,' he said, prompting her to laugh. 'I've so much to sort out.'

'So you're all flying out together?'

'Yep. Grandad and Jack are going to stay for a week before going on to Singapore.'

'Arthur in Singapore. I wish I could be there to see it! Are you nervous?'

'About them or myself?' He laughed. 'They'll have an amazing time. I don't know what I'm going to do without them for so long though. Every day has been so ridiculous, they're such a double act it's hard to believe that they were ever apart.'

'Speaking of being apart,' Lexie said sheepishly. 'You should go and talk to Shakeel.'

'I will, don't worry. I'm glad he still came today.'

'He wouldn't have missed it. He's just giving you some space after everything.'

'We've spoken, Lex, don't worry. We're good. I understand his reasons. Escaping here is going to be good for me – for him. I need to see new things, meet new people.'

'And when you get back?'

'Who knows? He'll always be my best friend.'

'And me?'

'Well, that depends; just don't go replacing me with one of those younger, fancier gays.'

People were starting to take their seats around the tables for the wedding breakfast. Teddy smiled to himself as he recognized a voice in the crowd as he walked past.

'Hey, Dylan!' he said, tapping his former colleague on the shoulder.

'Teddy, I was hoping to run into you today. How is everything? I hear you're off travelling soon.'

'Yeah, I can't wait. It'll be an experience.'

'I'm jealous,' Dylan said wistfully. 'I wish I'd taken the chance at your age. Listen, if you ever want to do some travel writing while you're off on your adventures, just drop me an email. You know there's always room for a Marsh at *The Post*.'

'Thanks, Dylan.' Teddy laughed, rolling his eyes. 'How's Ben getting on?'

'What? Didn't you hear? He took a job at *The Globe*. Friend of mine over there says he's settled in well.'

'Oh wow,' Teddy said. 'That's good to hear. Anyway, I better go, it was good to see you, Dylan.'

'Enjoy the travelling. Don't be getting yourself into any trouble,' he said, as he gripped and shook Teddy's hand before returning to his conversation.

Teddy was exhausted by the time the meal was finished. Word of his upcoming travels seemed to have spread quickly around the extended family, with everyone keen to find out more and wish him good luck. He couldn't wait to get home and relax before he had to face sorting out his luggage.

Ralph's older brother kicked off the speeches as the sun set over the estate.

'I'd just like to say a couple of words,' Arthur said when he finally took the microphone. 'Today is obviously a very special day for many reasons. My little girl found happiness after our family experienced a terrible loss. Ralph put that gorgeous smile back on her face. Thank you, Ralph, for looking after my Lizzie and my three amazing grandchildren. Madeleine, I want to take a minute to thank you for being my guardian angel. You've been there for me at my lowest, you showed me what love could be and you've given me years of happy memories. James, keep making this incredible woman smile and laugh. I also want to say thank you and good luck to my grandson, Teddy, who is about to set off on an incredible adventure of a lifetime. We couldn't be prouder of you and the man you have become. My Patrick, to say we are proud of you is an understatement. I know you are going to make an incredible husband to the lovely Scarlett and I can't wait for your happy day next year. Thank you all for making today so special for all of us, especially my new husband. That's a sentence I never thought I would say out loud, never mind while standing here in front of you all at eighty years of age. But I wouldn't change a thing about this. Life has given us a second chance and now we get to have an adventure of our own, together. I'd like everyone to raise a glass to second chances and not being afraid of grabbing them.'

Teddy joined the chorus. Arthur beamed back at him, tipping his glass in his direction.

'How many chances do we have?' The familiar voice made Teddy's heart skip a beat. He looked around to see Shakeel leaning on the back of his chair.

'There you are!' Teddy jumped up from his chair and looked Shakeel up and down as he stood in front of him in his navy blue suit. 'You look so handsome.'

'As do you. Reminds me of the suit you wore to the formal. You looked . . .' His voice trailed off as he lost himself in the memory. 'Sorry, I didn't come over sooner, I was giving you—'

'Don't say space. I'm out of here in a few days and the last thing I need from anyone, especially you, is space.'

'Sorry. Bad habit. How are you feeling?'

Teddy tried to maintain eye contact as he answered him. 'Excited. Nervous. To be honest, I've been so busy with all of this' – he waved his hands at the wedding – 'that I kind of haven't had a lot of time to think about it.'

'It'll be amazing, Teddy. You deserve this, I'm really proud of you.'

Just hearing that Shakeel was proud of him made Teddy's throat tighten.

'A little more adventurous than up north,' he said after taking a gulp of water.

Even though Shakeel laughed, his eyes were still filled with sadness.

'I'm sorry I couldn't go with you,' he said, his voice lowered. 'I thought you were just panicking about us and . . . that was your opportunity, not mine.'

'I get it, Shak. I shouldn't have put that on you and expected you to just drop everything for me.'

'Listen to you, you've grown up before you've even left.'

'That's what happens when you spend every day with Arthur and Jack.'

'You love it, really. You'll be just like them one day.'

'I hope we both will be. Look at them, happier than any of us.'

They grinned at each other as they watched Jack feed a forkful of cake to a laughing Arthur.

The dance floor filled up quickly as the band took to the stage. Elizabeth had booked a band she and Ralph had seen on one of their first dates. Teddy watched as Arthur and Madeleine danced together, before they each paired off with Elizabeth and Ralph.

'Come on, two left feet or not, you're not sitting here,' Shakeel said, grabbing Teddy by the arm and dragging him out of his seat. 'I want a dance before you leave me.'

'I can't, Shak. You know I can't dance, I'll embarrass both of us.'

'Is my grandson refusing to show off his moves?' Arthur said, appearing behind them. 'What's that saying again?'

Teddy stared blankly at him.

'We're fools whether or not we dance, so we might as well dance.'

Shakeel grinned and held out his hand for Teddy to take. Arthur slapped him on the back before making his way back to Jack.

Teddy and Shakeel held on to each other as the couples swayed around them.

'What are you going to do?' Teddy asked him as they danced.

'I dunno. Keep working, I suppose. And someone has to look after Lex.'

'It's true, she can be quite a handful.'

'I wish your job offer was now,' Shakeel said suddenly.

'Why?'

'Because I'd say yes. I'd leave with you tonight.'

CHAPTER FORTY-SIX

One week later

'HOW ON EARTH do you sleep in when you know you've got a flight? Honestly, Edward!'

Teddy groaned as he threw his case into the boot and slammed it shut.

'I don't need a lecture now, Mum,' he said. 'We just need to get to the airport. Jack says they're already queuing to go through security.'

He tried to relax as they travelled, weaving in and out of traffic. He wasn't sure if it was the nerves or his mum's driving that made his stomach feel queasier.

'You've packed everything you need?'

'Yes, Mum.'

'All your creams and insect repellents?'

'Yes, Mum.'

'You'll call and text, won't you?'

'Of course,' he said, turning his head towards her. Her eyes were already filling with tears.

'I'll write every day and call you as often as I can, I promise. You're not getting rid of me that easily.'

'Look after each other, I don't want any accidents. You hear terrible things on the news all the time these days.'

'Please stop worrying. And Grandad and Jack will be home in a couple of weeks.'

'I'm so proud of you, Teddy.'

'Thanks, Mum,' he said, his eyes widening in shock. 'I think that's the first time you've ever called me Teddy!'

'Don't get too used to it.' Elizabeth laughed. 'You'll always be my little Edward.'

After hugging his mum goodbye, Teddy dashed into the airport and dropped off his luggage. His heart was thumping. Despite fearing the worst when he saw the long queue, he made it through security with relative ease, before running to his gate.

'Cutting it fine, Mr Marsh,' the man checking his ticket growled at him. He wiped his sweating forehead as he made his way down the gangway.

As he stepped onto the plane, Teddy saw Arthur's hand waving dramatically above the head of the passenger in front of him. He'd made it. After pushing his way up through the crowded aisle, Teddy finally dropped down into the seat beside his grandad. Jack was looking out of the small window, watching their luggage being loaded into the belly of the plane.

'You cut it fine,' Arthur said as Teddy clicked his seat belt together.

'Tell me about it. I'm exhausted already. Mum sends her love, by the way.'

Teddy turned to look across the aisle. 'Mum also said to send her love to you, but I told her you were all sorted.'

'Because you love me so much?' Shakeel grinned back at him.

'Exactly.'

'I gotta admit,' Shak whispered, leaning forward so that only Teddy could hear him. 'I thought you were about to send me to Vietnam alone with your grandad and Jack.'

'It would serve you right. That's what happens when you keep me up all night panic-booking what we should have done a week ago.'

'You've made your point. I'm here, aren't I?'

Shakeel held his hand out across the aisle. Teddy took hold of it and squeezed it gently.

'I can't believe we're doing this. We're actually doing this!'

Just seeing Shakeel grinning like a Cheshire cat made Teddy's heart want to burst.

'I know. Some smart-arse told me that everything happens for a reason. I think he might have had a good point, you know.'

Shakeel leaned forward and picked something up off the floor. 'Check it out, someone must have dropped this. It might keep you entertained during the flight.'

Teddy took the Rubik's cube from Shak and grinned. 'Yeah, I'm good, thanks. I hate these things.'

ACKNOWLEDGEMENTS

Writing has been my constant companion through the good, bad and downright awful times. The thing I could turn to when I was at my happiest and saddest, whether it was writing a letter the night I attempted suicide or writing an email coming out to my parents. It's only now when I look back that I can understand how lucky I was to have so much love for something that I took for granted. Thankfully, Mum and Dad were always there to remind me.

Sharing these experiences and having you both by my side means the absolute world to me. You both inspire me beyond words every day. Doing you proud every day makes all those experiences along the way worthwhile. Thank you for being my heroes. I love you both so much.

Where would I be without younger siblings to keep me right and bring me back down to Earth every now and again? Clara, Tess, Jack and Páidí, you guys are the best brothers and sisters anyone could ask for. Characters I love are filled with the very best of each of you, all shining bright in your own brilliant ways. I'm the proudest big brother in the world.

Is it okay to thank my dogs here? Well, I'm going to. Bailey and Buddy, my best boys. You kept me sane and brought a smile back to my face when I didn't think it was possible. When I was writing late into the night, you were both there watching me until I finally shut my laptop and dragged myself up to bed. I miss you so much, Bailey, but you'll always have a special place in my heart and right here now too.

Mikey Abegunde, your endless words of love, support and encouragement will never be forgotten. One of the best friends a person could ever ask for. Adeel Amini, it's been a hell of a journey so far. The Yang to my Grey. Thank you for being my person all these years. Richard Dawson, you're one of a kind. Knowing you has made me a better person. I can't imagine every day without you putting a smile on my face.

Megan Carver, I don't know whether to call you a guardian angel or a fairy godmother, but thank you for not only believing in me, but for always pushing me to believe in myself.

To Team HQ, every single one of you who has been a part of this, allowing me to become part of your lives and learn so much on every step of this journey. To Lisa Milton and my incredible editor Cicely Aspinall, from our first emails to today, thank you doesn't seem nearly enough. You've made my dreams come true and I couldn't have asked for better, more brilliant, talented people to share it with. I can't wait to do this all again with you!

Meg Davis and The Ki Agency, for taking a chance on me and making me part of your family. Anne Perry, you are a true friend for life. I knew from our very first Zoom chat that you were special and every day since it has been an absolute pleasure to get to know and learn from you.

I'm going to wrap this up because I can already hear the

Oscars music playing, trying to get me off stage. Finally, the Twitter writing community is a special place. A lot can be said about social media, but there are little communities that remind you just how brilliant, kind and supportive people can be. Find those people if you can, they make every day of this surreal experience just that little bit more special.

ONE PLACE. MANY STORIES

Bold, innovative and
empowering publishing.

FOLLOW US ON:

@HQStories